M000104773

The Girls from Hangar B

The Girls from Hangar ß

KRISTIN CAMPBELL NAIL

*Uncle Ron &
Aunt Verdine
Thanks for being here
at my big moment: Alove
you folks
Kist Campbell Nail*

GOODFELLOW PRESS

Goodfellow Press

8522 10th Ave. NW
Seattle, WA 98117
206-782-2799 / 206-706-2367 fax

Copyright © 2001
All rights reserved. This book, or parts thereof, may not be reproduced in any form without permission from the publisher.

ISBN:
Library of Congress:
Edited by Pamela R. Goodfellow
Jacket design by Rohani Design, Edmonds, WA
Cover illustration by Larry Parkhurst
Book design by Brandon Massey
Authors photo by Curtis McClary
Thanks to the Museum of Flight, Seattle, Washington for use of the B-29 in author photo.

This is a work of fiction. The events described are imaginary; the characters are fictitious and are not intended to represent actual living persons.

The text is set in 14 point New Century Schoolbook with 146point leading.

For more information please visit us at:

www.goodfellowpress.com

For Mom and Dad, who gave me wings;

For Orv, who taught me to fly.

<u>Acknowledgments</u>

Thanks to Sara Jewett, Janis Wildy and Tim Arnold—Fourth Avenue Writers—who prevented me from jumping many times.

Shelly, Scott and Matt for always believing.

Angie Yarger and Linda Kriss for their never ending good cheer and support.

Pamela Goodfellow for her vision and courage.

Prologue

Coos Bay Herald --April 2, 1943

HELP WANTED - WOMEN

Do Your Part for the War Effort!

20 Positions Open
Union Scale
War Production - Seattle
No Experience Necessary
Room Sharing Available

Annie gripped the sides of the battered grade school desk until her knuckles showed white. Her legs tingled and her back had a permanent indentation from the metal pipe holding the seat and the backrest together. She would probably have to wear this child's combination chair and writing table home because there was no way she could get her tall frame extricated from it without a battle. She was definitely going to be embarrassed in front of this group of job seekers who shared the classroom with her.

But none of that mattered. Not one bit. She was going to Seattle. She was going to work in an airplane factory. And she was going to make more money in an hour than she'd ever made in a day.

That is, if she'd heard this man correctly. Her voice went up a couple of notches as she asked the question. "You mean me? Annie Tosh?"

He'd called several names and those people had gone forward to get papers from him. Somehow though, she hadn't expected to hear her own name.

"I can have the job? Just like that?"

She could hear a titter from the others in the room. The recruiter pulled the cigar stub from between his teeth and smiled for the first time since they'd entered the classroom. He echoed her words. "Yep. Just like that."

Annie rose and the desk took care of itself by clanging to the linoleum. She could hear more laughter. When the noise subsided she grinned at the wintry-faced fellow. And then couldn't stop grinning.

When it looked as if the conventional future she'd prescribed for herself was permanent, a detour had appeared. And that excited her more than anything had in a very long time.

CHAPTER ONE

Light filtered through the amber colored lampshade and dusted the living room with faint stripes of yellow. Gerald Tosh put down the dented pocket watch he was repairing, raised the jewelers loupe connected to his glasses and gazed at his daughter Annie. The lamp glow created a halo around her scarlet hair as she sat with legs curled under and a book placed precariously on the arm of the worn horsehair sofa. If he squinted just right, he could almost see his mother sitting there, same curly mop of hair, same strong build, same quiet intensity.

With a smile, he watched Annie's head slip forward. She was fighting sleep. She never gave up easily, this child of his. Or woman if he were to be accurate. Six-foot-two and twenty-eight years old, she certainly didn't fit the description of a child.

An image slid unwanted through his mind. The future, only two days away, this house, quiet and empty when she went north. His shoulders drooped and he fought the familiar hollow feeling that had started when his boys enlisted. Somehow he'd always thought he would grow old with his children and grandchildren close by. This damned war.

Sighing, he focused on pleasant memories. He saw a six-year old Annie, red braids flying as she raced to catch her brothers. The scene was so clear he could almost hear their laughter. He stared at the dented gold faceplate and sighed. Picking up the watch, he moved the loupe back in place then paused again, looking at his daughter. He hoped this job she'd taken in Seattle would help her shake free of the tight web of obligation and predictability that had surrounded her for the last year. He would give anything to see that tall child running hell bent for leather across the fields one more time.

When her head jerked up, he grinned. Stretching her arms, she spread her fingers in a long cat stretch then she placed her sock-clad feet onto the faded Aubusson carpet. The tightness in his shoulders eased at the sight. Her hands, covered with freckles, were a female version of his own, right down to the last short, squared off thumb. And the height. Straight from his mother, to him and now all his children. He'd expected it in his sons but not in her. The only thing she'd inherited from her mother's side of the family was brown eyes.

"I think I'm going to bed, Dad. I can't keep my eyes open. Do you want anything before I go?"

She stood waiting as he finished the adjustment. The talk he wanted to have with her would have been so much easier if she were one of her brothers. And if he didn't have to worry what her mother would say. Annie's near miss marriage, now engagement meant different things to each of her parents. He was stalling, searching for just the right words. After a few moments he shrugged, giving up.

"No, thanks anyway, girl. I've just got a couple of these to finish and then I'm off myself. Could you check to make sure the drapes are pulled tight on your way? I don't need Mrs. Johnson yelling at me again."

A grin started at the side of her mouth. "I know, the tiniest bit of light showing through the blackout curtains and she'll be nattering on at you. And then you'll yell back. Then she can complain, about what a mean person you are, to Mom."

He grunted. "Not to mention the hoard of Japanese who will see the light and drop bombs on us."

"Right. Not to mention them." Her head was thrown back and a wide smile stretched clear across her face. A little tug at his heart reminded him how much he treasured her rare smile. Its appearance generally caused a chain reaction of similar smiling with anyone in the vicinity.

But the mention of their neighbor had the opposite effect on him. His jaw muscles tightened up like a bridge span. His throat felt raspy when he spoke. "If that woman doesn't leave me alone I'll . . . I'll . . . I'll scalp her."

Gladys Johnson still dumbfounded him. He was positive that the dratted woman spent every waking moment thinking of ways to annoy him. After he'd built the long anticipated rose arbor for Annie's mother, Mrs. Johnson had her handyman construct one that ran the entire length of the driveway, making his tiny structure look sick. Since the bombing of Pearl Harbor, they had moved the arena of their feud to war strategy. If he brought up a point of interest at their discussion group, she always found some part to argue. When he'd refute her argument, point by point, she merely waved a hand and started on another point, as if he'd never spoken.

The colored map of the world hanging on the wall next to the gray chesterfield was the field of their own personal war zone. A month ago he'd reported to the group that he thought Montgomery's victory at El Alamein in November of 1942 and then Tripoli in January of this year would be a turning point in the war. He said Rommel was on the run now and his stranglehold on Africa ended. Of course, Gladys Johnson had insisted that Rommel had more tanks hidden away, just like the reserves of gasoline the Allies found in the dunes, and that he would be coming back, stronger than ever. She seemed determined to defend this point although the evidence spoke strongly to the contrary. Even the relentless addition of the white pins marking Allied positions in Algeria and removal of the black Axis pins made no dent in her reasoning. He wondered if she did it just to get his goat. When he thought about that for a moment, he had to chuckle. It was working beautifully.

Annie was yawning. She closed her book, placing a piece of string between the pages to hold her place. She'd taken only a few steps toward the bedroom when Gerald realized this might be the last time he would get to speak with her alone. She would be leaving within two days.

"So, have you made peace with your mother?"

Annie turned back to him, a line appearing on her forehead. She stepped back and sat down slowly on the sofa she'd just vacated. Her gaze was level with his when she spoke. "You know Mom is dead set against my going up north."

"Is that so important?"

Her head jerked up and a frown reached her eyes. "What do you mean? I don't know how much more she can take."

Gerald nodded and tapped a finger on the pine surface of the desk. With both of their sons in the middle of the action, Myrtle Tosh spent a great portion of her day worrying. He knew the uncomfortable, slightly off feeling in his stomach was definitely guilt. He was about to go against everything he'd learned from his wife about women. Women were to be protected. Women needed to care for the home and family. Women didn't go to cities far away and work for a living either. And they certainly didn't leave a perfectly good chance for marriage and a ready-made family to try their hand at building airplanes.

He studied his daughter's face, her eyebrows now elevated waiting for his response. The sight of her physical size and set chin confirmed what he already knew. She was not like 'other' women. He would simply try again to convince Myrtle that their daughter would have to make her own way. What the heck, Myrtle could only kill him once.

"And what about Howard?"

The line on her forehead deepened and she sat back against the sofa cushions. The quiet crackle of the fireplace was the only sound as he waited for her reply.

"You mean would I be marrying Howard if it weren't for Mom?"

"Yes."

She was still for several moments, thoughts scattered across her expressive face like ripples on water. When she spoke, her voice had a defensive edge.

"Dad, I don't understand why you feel this way about Howard. I've told you how grateful I am that he has asked me to marry him." She reached up and flipped back an errant curl that had fallen forward. "He's a wonderful guy and we're great pals. If his call-up had been two days later, we'd be married already. His children need a mother too." She ended with a note of finality as if that answered the whole question.

Annie rested her head on the tatted throw that covered the worn spots on the sofa. He remembered when Myrtle had made that piece. He realized with a jolt that it must have been at least twenty years ago.

He shook his head. The crooked set of her mouth declared she wasn't sure of her decision, but would die before she admitted it. He would never understand where she got this narrow view of married life. His marriage to her mother may seem tame and uninteresting to Annie but it had always been filled with much love. He just couldn't quite figure how to tell her that. Certainly the frontal approach never worked with her.

"And . . ."

"And what?"

"And why else are you marrying him? Seems to me that's not a list for a husband. I could be wrong though. I quite often am. Just ask your mother." They both chuckled. Myrtle was strong in so many ways. Sometimes it drove them all crazy, but it was a good thing as well. With his dicey heart she'd stepped in more than once in the last couple of years at the store and at home.

He stared at the fingers of his hands now splayed out on the desk and thought of the things he'd had to give up doing.

"Okay, I don't know if I'd be marrying Howard if it weren't for Mom, but it doesn't matter. He's a good, honest man with a lot of heart and certainly doesn't deserve to be jilted because I don't happen to have the stars-in-your-eyes, little-girl-giddy kind of love you seem to think is so important." She looked straight at him and finished with a flat, cold statement. "Anyway, there isn't exactly a long line of men rushing to marry me."

"Annie." He held up a hand to stop her. He'd guessed she felt that way but had never heard her say it straight-out before. And he knew where the idea had come from. His wife was tiny and graceful, a bit like a small, bright bird. Between her desire for their only daughter to be like her and later, Annie's own class-mates' awe at her size, their daughter had built up this strange idea that she was too big to be appealing to the opposite sex.

She rose and walked over to his worktable, her long wool robe rustling as she moved. He couldn't believe any woman who looked like she did, even in an old robe, could have doubts like this. The fire cast flat, dark shadows and it appeared she was walking through a late evening forest. He struggled to find the right words to tell her that she was appealing, that the idiots in Coos Bay were just blind.

"It's all right, Dad, I really don't mind. And I might never have a chance for children or a regular marriage if I don't take this one. Maybe it's not a fairy tale, but I don't know a lot of peo-ple who get that anyway."

She rested her hand on his worktable then turned and paced slowly back to the couch. The only light in the room was from his work lamp and the burning logs. When she turned back, her face was shadowed.

"You know I don't always do what Mom wants but there are times when what she suggests makes a lot of sense. I feel as if I'll be letting her or you or the family or sometimes even the whole town down if I don't marry Howard."

Silence filled the room as he chewed on his bottom lip and stared into the dark hallway. The wall fixtures and pine floors were the only items visible in the gloom. He took a deep breath.

"Annie, I'm sorry. It seems to be so damned important to her that you follow in her footsteps. She gave up on the boys and me long ago, but you're different. Being the only girl, I think she feels that she's the one who knows the most about what should make you happy. Unfortunately, I think her best intentions tend to make you miserable." He had to laugh at that. "Now that sounds like the darndest, most confusing thing I've ever said."

Annie sighed. "The worst part is that she really does want me to be happy. It's just that her ideas and mine are so differ-ent. If I go, maybe she and I can be happy at the same time. And it's time I did something important for the war effort."

Gerald shook his head. "Well, I can't say as how I'm crazy about the logic, but I guess it works. Since you're not going to marry Howard before the end of the war anyway, it might work out for the best after all. Howard's a fine fella, I think maybe fine for anybody but you." Removing his glasses from the bridge of his nose, he pulled an ironed white handkerchief from his pocket. He huffed on the lenses then cleaned them slowly and deliberately. He felt exhausted, he wasn't used to working so hard to say the right thing.

"With Phillip and Roger both in the middle of it, I feel sort of useless here. Men are dying and I'm rolling bandages with the ladies. You said it yourself, Dad, this war isn't for sitting and waiting, it's for doing. It's a matter of survival. And look at me, I'm certainly built to do more than distribute coupon books."

He stopped his rubbing for a moment and lifted his head, looking directly at her. She was right but it made him sigh. He was secretly delighted that at least one of his children wasn't in an active war zone. "I know, Annie. I guess I'm as bad as your mom, wanting you and your brothers to be more than just passersby in life. But no matter, I think you should do what you feel is the best. And quit thinking. That's one of your problems, girl, thinking things to death. Sometimes it's a predicament for a woman to be as smart as you are."

Annie's head jerked up and he rushed to stave off her anger. "Okay, maybe not a predicament but sometimes certainly more trouble. Quit worrying girl." He grinned.

She strode over to his desk. "Dad, I'm long past being a girl. But I do love you."

She looked as if she might lean over and hug him but stopped. Their family had never been very much for hugging or any kind of touching for that matter. He supposed it might be because his grandmother thought all that contact was somehow in bad taste, showing a lack of breeding. There was certainly never a lack of love. He sometimes thought it was a shame. Annie placed her hand lightly on his arm then gave him a little wave and, wrapping her robe more tightly around her, started upstairs. For the first time in a long time, she seemed to move more freely, almost as if she were feeling lighter now that the decision had been made.

The metal sides of the silver trailer caught the midday Seattle sunlight and reflected the glare back into Annie's eyes. She sat in the cab and stared at its fat, bullet-shaped outline repeated forty times on this street of the park. It was only May of this difficult year, 1943, and dust was already rising from the dry ruts left by the heavy rains of winter. The raw wood picnic tables beside each mobile gave the park an unfinished, temporary look. Her mouth was dry and she felt stuck fast, as if moving would start a downhill slide she wasn't sure she could stop.

"Lady? You gonna get out here?" The taxi driver's voice startled her and she struggled to climb out of the car, bumping her head on the doorframe when she forgot to duck. Rubbing the tender spot, she scrunched down and eased out. She'd picked this cab from the short row at the Seattle bus station because she'd felt sorry for the driver. His shirt had been neatly pinned up above the elbow and he dragged his left leg. The man had that raw, half angry look she'd seen on a few other severely injured vets. It was as if their bodies' injuries were healing but the wounds were still fresh in their minds. And he was one of the lucky ones, he was still alive. The muscles in her jaw tightened and she swallowed hard. This was why she was here, for however long it took to end this war.

With a start, she realized the driver was standing at the trunk, her suitcase half lifted out. She rushed over and grabbed the leather handle of her worn bag on one end, lifting it out over the lip of the trunk. Instead of letting go of his side, he continued to grip the other handle. The powerful heave on her end dragged him forward and they both stumbled, finally dropping the case with a soft whomp on the ground. He grunted then straightened up with a stiff, awkward thrust of his leg and shoulder. Annie started to help him then stopped herself. She saw his mouth turn down on the sides. Gulping, she tried to think of something to say but figured she'd probably insulted him enough already.

Fumbling with her change purse, she jammed one dollar into his hand, twenty-five cents more than the meter read. He started to hand her back the extra quarter and she shook her head, mumbling that he should keep it. He looked at her again, his expression still flat and hard. He turned and settled into the driver's seat and started the car.

She'd been intrigued when she'd seen him start the car before they'd left the bus terminal. With one arm, he shouldn't have been able to drive but he used a combination of a necker knob on the steering wheel, gear shift on the column, and the top of his leg to work the shifting process. Annie had never seen anything quite like it but they had arrived safely and she guessed that was about as much as you could expect.

She watched the taxi drive off, its license plate hanging loose on one side and rattling against the bumper. She squashed the urge to wave at the retreating vehicle. A hollow feeling in her chest reminded her that she was over four hundred miles from home and, so far, she hadn't made any friends.

She swallowed hard. Best get going here. Men and boys were dying thousands of miles from home, in much worse places than this, and all she could do was whine. She reminded herself that this might be her only chance to help bring them home and she'd better get on with it. She took a shaky breath and caught the scent of new-mown grass. Glancing around, she saw that several of the trailer residents had planted the seeds for a lawn. Yellow-green shoots were appearing between dusty patches.

A loud crash followed by shouting came from inside the trailer and she moved toward the temporary steps placed outside the front door. She stopped for a moment debating if she should wait until the noise level subsided. The hesitation saved her a bash in the face as the door was flung open with such force that it bounced against the wall and nearly closed itself again. A slight form backed out of the entrance.

The figure turned, Annie blinked then shook her head. The apparition did not change. The figure materialized into a woman of no more than five feet in height but nine feet in sexual impact. Her light cotton blouse and pants were tight and short and revealed more skin, cleavage and midriff than Annie had seen anywhere.

White-blond hair sat atop a face smoothed and accentuated by thick makeup. A slash of red adorned her lips and kohl liner made huge brown eyes startling. Annie supposed that it allowed anyone who managed to get past the sight of so much flesh to take a second look at her face. Annie tried to look away but was drawn back by a glimpse of darkish blue on the skin of the woman's left breast. She couldn't tell if it was a bruise or a tattoo but thought probably the latter. For some reason, instead of shocking her, the sight of it made her want to laugh.

"So, what you starin' at?" The voice was brash and taunting. The woman stood with her hands on her hips and waited as Annie took a step backward and stuttered her response.

"I . . . um . . . I . . . um. Oh, I'm sorry. My name is Annie Tosh and I'm looking for nineteen Plum Lane. I must be lost. The number on the next trailer is eighteen so the cab driver and I thought that this must be the place." She stopped then and took a short, jerky breath. This woman was nearly as tiny as her mother and she suddenly had a picture of what she looked like standing next to her; a big, awkward countrywoman with no polish. A flash of heat crawled from her neck to her cheeks.

"This is it. You must be number four."

"Number four?" Annie echoed the other woman's words and tried to pull her eyes from what she had determined was definitely a tattoo. She couldn't make out the design, maybe a snake, maybe a flower. A shiver ran down her back as she thought about what it would feel like to get a tattoo.

"Yeah. Number four. You're here for the house sharing through Boeing, right?"

Annie nodded and the woman continued, one hand resting on her hip, the other holding the metal doorframe. "They think four of us can share this teakettle of a place and not kill each other. When they said there wasn't much housing in this damn town they weren't kidding. We'll see. I'm Sparkle Melody."

Annie felt as if the world had started moving at twice its normal speed. It had been like this since she left home. She couldn't quite catch her breath before something would spin her around again. Two days ago she'd been in Coos Bay, Oregon, sitting on the front porch glider in the late afternoon shadows and listening to her mother tell her how dangerous it was in the big city. Just because there was a war on didn't mean she had to go all the way to Seattle to work in the airplane factory, for heaven's sake. Annie had hardly been able to sit still with the anticipation of traveling to Washington, meeting her roommates and moving into the 'compact and efficient' living quarters. Somehow, she had the idea that most of the women working in the factory would be a bit like her, big or at least strong. She wondered how this tiny woman would fare building airplanes. And she'd never imagined the living quarters to be quite so small.

A car started up next door with a pop and a grind and she turned to see a cloud of black smoke coming from the back of a rusty pickup. Only the legs and round behind of the person working on the motor were showing. When she looked back, Sparkle was staring at her.

"You're sure a big'un, aren't you? Goddamn, this place keeps getting smaller."

Annie felt her cheeks grow warm again as the arrow of hurt hit its mark in her chest. She drew herself to her full height then stopped and sighed. Most people laughed at her behind her back. At least this Sparkle was honest. She should certainly be used to being a tall woman by now.

"It's okay, we can use some of that muscle. C'mon." Sparkle waved her hand for Annie to follow and entered the doorway of the trailer. As she walked, the blonde's high, sling-back heels made clicking sounds on the wood steps and her rear swayed dangerously from side to side. Annie shook her head. She wondered how old Sparkle might be, maybe twenty-five? Her outrageous appearance made it hard to tell.

She turned and pulled at her suitcase, hesitated, then left it propped up against the steps leading into the trailer. She'd never been less sure of anything than whether to follow that swaying rear end into the interior. She bit her lip then reminded herself that here she was and here she was going to stay until the war was over. Taking a deep breath, she ducked her head and entered the relative gloom of nineteen Plum Lane.

As her eyes adjusted to the light, her first impression was of clothes. Clothes and clutter. Dresses, coats, blouses and skirts were suspended from every available hook and surface. A closet door hung open toward the front, revealing wisps of lace and silk dresses and lingerie attached to hangers. The trailer was smaller than her Grandma Hazel's cottage. There was some sort of table and green bench seats taking up the front. The middle was a narrow tunnel of space, twenty feet long. The first half was taken up by the tiniest white stove Annie had ever seen on the left side and a matching miniature refrigerator on the right. Past the kitchen was a storage area on the right and what looked like the bathroom on the left. The curved ceiling on both sides made it impossible for her to stand up straight anywhere but dead center. She wasn't sure she could fit.

"Can't you get the cot out?" Sparkle's rough voice held a challenge as she yelled at the two women standing in what appeared to be the only bedroom. They had moved the small bed in question about a quarter of the way through the door.

"No." The response from the women was in unison.

Sparkle pushed Annie and muttered in her ear. "You might as well meet all the girls in the band now."

As they moved forward the tangy scent of lemon and roses assaulted Annie, sort of like catching a bouquet at a wedding. She stopped and glanced back at Sparkle.

"What's that smell?"

"Goddamit. That's what's left of a five-dollar bottle of perfume. Looks like our roomies aren't so careful with other people's expensive things."

Light from the small bulb fitted cleverly into the round part of the ceiling fell on what remained of a thick glass perfume bottle. Annie looked at the person holding it and her first thought was brown and round.

The woman's face was round, her body was round, round wire framed glasses made her eyes look round, even her hair, frizzed out from her head, made a perfect circle. She wasn't much taller than Sparkle, only five-foot-two at most but seemed shorter because of her width. She smiled and the white of her teeth contrasted sharply against the chocolate color of her skin. She was perhaps, in her mid-twenties and was wearing a flowered housedress hanging a good two inches longer in the back than the front. Annie blinked and swallowed hard. This was the first colored person she had been close to and she didn't have a clue how to act or what she should say. Thank goodness the woman spoke first. Her words were slow and for a moment, Annie thought she was speaking in a foreign language.

"Lo there. Ah'm Birdie, nice ta meet 'cha." She turned to Sparkle and lowered her voice. "Yo' sure got a passel of stuff here. It 'peers as tho' there ain't enuff room for half of it."

Sparkle's face turned a cherry red color and she nearly snarled when she spoke. "Why the hell are you pawing through my stuff? Don't you know enough to keep your hands off other people's things, nigger?"

Annie felt her breath catch in her throat. She was wondering what kind of a group she'd gotten herself into when Birdie stepped forward and planted her index finger in Sparkle's chest. Her chin was set in a determined line.

"Who you callin' niggah?" Annie gasped and raised a hand to see if she could stop the fight. Neither of the women paid her any attention. The third person, a girl of seventeen or so who hadn't said anything yet, looked as startled as Annie felt. The dimples on Birdie's face had disappeared. "And who are you to be yellin' that way? Gloria here is trying her darndest to share this bedroom with you while all your junk is spread out every which way. We're trying to make some room for her stuff too."

Annie's instinct was to protect someone. She just wasn't sure which person needed protecting. She had an odd, wobbly feeling when she realized that this was the first time she'd ever tried to mediate between two women. Her expertise had been keeping Phillip and Roger from killing each other.

Sparkle leaned into Birdie's finger and glared. "I told you before. I'll be damned if I'll share a room with anyone. Particularly someone with enough stuff to start a department store. I'd rather eat bugs. What if I should have a gentleman caller?"

Birdie made a suggestion from between clenched teeth. "If he's trying to share a room in here, he ain't no gentleman. We'd probably better move you somewhere else if you're gonna' have a problem with that. I think you should take the front bed." Annie continued to stand, one hand in the air. As she lowered it, she tried to picture Sparkle's 'gentleman.' She felt a little as if she'd been punched in the stomach, out of air and out of ideas.

Sparkle stood back and shifted her weight from one foot to the other, reminding Annie of a prizefighter. "You mean out there in front of God and everybody? Are you crazy? All we need to do is get this cot out of here and set it up in that little area next to the door." Sparkle's voice trailed off when she found the three other women staring at her. Her white blond hair seemed to stick out from her head with the energy of her righteousness as she pulled herself up squarely. "What are you all staring at? There's plenty of room."

Three heads swiveled to take in the small space tentatively designated as the portion of the trailer with 'room.' Right now it was stacked with boxes and suitcases. There wasn't enough room for a matchstick, much less a bed.

Annie's scalp prickled with a claustrophobic itch and she wanted to back out of the overcrowded trailer. Taking a deep breath, she steadied herself. Maybe she'd just try to ease her way through this. She asked the obvious question. "Why would you want to move the bed out here?"

The answer from Birdie was quick and caustic. "'Cause little Missy Queen of the See-Through Nighties here thinks we'all should have our own little area. You know, her area is the onliest bedroom in this place, our areas are the teeny inches beside the other beds. It's not gonna work. I 'spect we're going to have to put two of us in that bedroom. If she don' want to be one of 'um, that's okay by me."

For the first time the young woman next to Birdie spoke. "Now I am sure that is not what she meant. I think she just wanted us to give everyone a little privacy. She did not mean . . . ."

"What the hell, did I just lose my voice?" Sparkle stood with both feet apart, hands on hips and chin jutting forward. Her words were directed at the girl who had finally spoken. This must be the fourth roommate and she was what Annie's mother called bandbox perfect. Even in the middle of pushing beds around, she looked like she'd just been shined up and presented for a recital.

The familiar wrenching feeling in her stomach reminded Annie that she wasn't that far from the jealous teenager who would have given the world to be small and cute. Occasionally, being big had it advantages, reaching things up high and being able to hold her own on building projects with her dad and brothers. But there were times, like now, that she'd give it all up for one day of being tiny and cute.

Gloria's smooth brown hair fell in a perfect line from forehead to chin, swinging gently with each movement. She stood about five-foot-six. Pencil thin brows, a shade darker than her hair, framed her blue eyes. A beige colored jacket hung lightly over a simple shift dress of the same fabric but a slightly darker shade. A hesitant smile touched her lips and she flushed at Sparkle's question. The movement of her mouth showed a flash of slightly buckteeth. The overall effect was of a very well turned out schoolgirl or maybe a dressed-up mouse.

Annie grinned at the sheer clean freshness of the girl and
the jealousy returned obediently to the locked place she'd built
for it years before. Stepping back, something gently brushed her
face and she turned to find a midnight blue nightgown now
drifting back against the wall. The slight breeze from the open
door had been enough to move the light material. The smooth
fabric slipped over her skin like cool water and she thought
about her own nightwear, a serviceable long cotton gown. She
wondered what it would be like to sleep in something that light.

Gloria spoke with a faint lisp. "I am sorry, I am being very
rude. My name is Gloria Westfall. Sparkle's been here the
longest, about a week, I arrived three days ago and Birdie came
in just this morning. It's amazing how fast this place fills up."
She looked at Sparkle but got no response. She raised a hand
and smoothed her hair. She turned back to Annie. "Well, you
must be Miss Tosh. We're very pleased to have you here."

Gloria put her hand forward and Annie shook it gingerly,
thinking of bird bones. She felt lightheaded, as if she couldn't
quite catch up in a race. Instead of roommates much like herself, these women were so different it was comical. The more she
thought about it, the more inclined she was to laugh. At least
the next few months wouldn't be boring.

The girl was speaking again. "I am sorry we're in such a
mess here. We thought we could have this done by the time you
arrived. Unfortunately, we can't move this bed out and now it
doesn't look as if we've got enough room out there anyway."
When she talked, Gloria bent her head forward a little, as if
apologizing, words running over each other. "I never realized
that it might be so hard to get moved in. Someone else has
always done it for me, well, I mean, well you know. The advertisement said sleeps four comfortably."

The four women were quiet for a moment, gazing collective-
ly down the short length of the trailer, where every surface was
covered with boxes, clothing, bottles or shoes.

Finally, Birdie laughed. "Must'a been a man said that."

They all laughed and Annie felt a ripple of relief run through her. She looked past Birdie and saw another bed in the small bedroom at the back of the trailer. She shrugged then looked at her three roommates.

"So how shall we set this up? I can move that cot thingy back into the bedroom and two of us can sleep in there. Did you say the front table made into a bed?"

Gloria gazed at her for a moment. She had a faint lisp that made each sentence sound like a question.

"Yes. It's quite ingenious, actually. And look at this." As she spoke, she reached up and pulled on a handle.

Annie was startled to see a bed drop down noiselessly, attached by long, metal hinges. She shook her head in amazement. She'd never actually seen the inside of a trailer. Compact was an understatement. But she had to agree, someone had certainly taken the time to make this as efficient as possible for the amount of space available.

Birdie spoke from behind her. "Gloria, you're pretty much the youngest and mos' bendy o' the bunch. Why don' you figger on takin' that one. An' Sparkle since you don' want to share a room with nobody, how about you take the bed up front." She turned to Annie and looked at her squarely, no hint of a smile this time. "How about you an' me sharin' this little room? You take the bed and I'll take the cot. The bed's longer."

Annie felt her face flush. She gulped then took a step closer to the bedroom and looked inside. When she turned back she saw that Birdie hadn't changed expression. "Will we fit?"

The merest flash of a dimple and then a wide smile appeared, curving up the sides of her round cheeks. "You bet gal. It's bigger'n it looks. Let's get all this stuff put away. I think it'll work jes fine. C'mon, let's push this cot back in."

Annie turned to help Birdie. She saw that Sparkle stood very close with a strange, mutinous look on her face. "How did you get in with us anyway, Birdie?"

Birdie shrugged. "Ah didn't tel'um ah's colored."

Sparkle pulled herself up to her full height and stared at Annie and Gloria. Annie hesitated but couldn't think what to add. This wasn't the South so she was pretty sure it wasn't illegal to share a room with Birdie.

Sparkle looked hard at Annie and spoke again in a deliberately flat tone. "So, you don't mind sharing a room with her?"

Annie turned to Birdie, now feeling embarrassed. Maybe there was some reason she wasn't supposed to sleep in the same room with the colored women. But Birdie's smile held no uncertainty. Deciding to cast her vote for the one she felt most comfortable with, she shrugged, then turned back to Sparkle and shook her head. The blond sniffed, then swayed toward the front of the trailer.

Her voice trailed behind. "Well, at least that gets me a little more room. I don't have to be cheek by jowl with all you."

Annie raised an eyebrow. Ten feet away didn't seem that far, but it appeared to be important that Sparkle have the last word. She started to push on the bed, now half in and half out of her new bedroom. With Gloria and Birdie guiding, it slipped back into the room easily. When it was positioned, she could see that it did look as if she just might fit after all.

Annie stretched her arms over her head and tried to work the kinks out of her muscles. The late afternoon sun warmed her shoulders. The bed was bigger than Birdie's cot but it wasn't made for someone her size. She'd been in Seattle nearly twenty-four hours and it still felt just about as strange as when she'd stepped out of the cab. They'd managed to reach an uneasy truce as far as the sleeping arrangements were concerned. The matter of the extra clothes had been solved for the moment by stuffing bags under the dinette and over the bunk but she knew that battle wasn't over. She couldn't believe the sheer volume of clothing from both Gloria and Sparkle. She and Birdie had given half of the small closet in their bedroom to the other two.

Annie had never needed many clothes, much to her mother's dismay. She found the plain skirts and shirts she wore to work at the jewelry store, her overalls for rough work and her two good dresses to be plenty. She hated making decisions every morning about what she would wear.

The four roommates sat at the picnic table outside their new home and ate silently. The sound of children's laughter floated by. When she looked up, she could see several neighbors occupying tables beside their own trailers and enjoying the early spring warmth. She glanced down at her plate. On it were beans floating like shipwrecked rum barrels in a thin red sauce. She'd placed the pale bun wrapped around a modest sausage on the high side of the plate to keep it out of the red goo but it seemed to like it there and kept sliding back. The beans had a strange sour taste and the sausage didn't seem to come from any identifiable meat source.

While pushing the beans from one side to the other, she looked at Sparkle, the designated cook and tried to keep her voice even. "These are interesting beans, what did you put in them?"

"What's wrong? You don't like plain cooking? Do you want to cook tomorrow night?"

Annie gulped. She hated cooking. She'd have to be careful.

Sparkle continued when Annie didn't speak. "If you really want to know, I put vinegar and that new ketchup stuff in 'em. Gives 'um zip."

"Oh." Annie sat back on the bench, careful of slivers from the new wood, and wondered if Sparkle always attacked first or was it just certain subjects she was touchy about. If Annie had to defend herself constantly, it would get tiresome quickly. Sparkle seemed to be the kind of person you watched blow up and then you discussed whatever you wanted to after she cooled down. Annie reminded herself that she was here to help build planes and win a war, not get in arguments.

Pushing the plate aside, she scratched the mosquito bite on her elbow and gazed at the rows of identical silver trailers surrounding them. Hard packed dirt and struggling grass was the overall effect but some green weeds had started showing in spots between the tiny homes.

She wondered as she studied her new roommates, if there were ever four women less alike in appearance and background. Annie was seated on the same side of the table as Birdie and she had to make a deliberate effort not to ease away from her. She knew her parents would be aghast to find she was living with a Negro. It wasn't that they would treat Birdie rudely. It was just that they had a firm belief that all 'those' people should stay in 'their' place. Gazing sidelong at Birdie, she realized she'd always accepted her parents' view of other races. Startled and a little uneasy, she focused on the group again, then placed her elbows on the table and asked the question she'd been curious about since she arrived.

"So, what brings you three here?"

Sparkle looked at her, squinting into the sun. A drop of bean juice had settled on her white blouse near where the light material just barely covered her tattoo. "You first, lady. Why'd you come from that place in Oregon?"

Annie blinked. She was having trouble looking Sparkle in the eye when they spoke. Her own gaze kept returning to the design on the woman's chest. She pondered the phenomenon a moment, but decided she'd better steer clear of the subject. She was also having trouble with Sparkle throwing every question back in her face. If she were honest, she was lousy at any kind of verbal dispute. She was always sputtering to find the right words or worse, she remained mute. She had to admire Sparkle's ability to snarl out loud.

"Coos Bay. That's the place in Oregon I come from. Coos Bay. My dad found the advertisement in our local paper for anyone with experience with tools. I ran the jewelry store for him, mostly taking care of the books and keeping up with orders, that kind of thing. And every once in a while, I'd help him repair watches and clocks. Funny, when I told the recruiter that part, he said they'd give me a try." She paused, knowing she should mention Howard now, but he just didn't seem to fit here.

Sparkle snorted. "Wow. You probably scared him so bad he gave you the job. How tall are you, six five?"

Annie laughed. "No, not nearly that tall, only six two."

Sparkle squinted one eye at her. "Okay. You're a tiny six two and look like you could pick up this picnic table and toss it around. Also sounds like you might be pretty smart. Has a man ever asked you out?"

That was it. Annie started to rise. She didn't need to listen to this. Her heart was thudding loudly in her ears. As she rose, quick lines of pain grabbed her at the back of her knees and thighs as they caught on the seat and the tabletop of the picnic bench. She was stuck fast.

"Don't be getting your panties in a bundle. I'm just making an observation."

Annie settled back down on the seat with a rueful smile. Not five minutes before, she'd decided not to react to Sparkle, but let her blow off steam first. Here she was about to blow up herself. This might take some practice.

"And watch repair? Boy, they're sure stretchin' since they've upped the order for so many more planes. When I started six months ago, you had to have machine shop experience before they'd even train you. I had a hell of a time convincing 'um that the month I spent working in Sid's garage was enough."

Birdie's voice was low and musical, interrupting the one-way conversation. "Did y'all really work in a garage? I never heard of a woman workin' in a place like that before."

Annie enjoyed the soft, southern cadence of the words. The evening sun had begun its slide behind the clouds and long, blue shadows played across the table, making crosshatches with the lines of the wood.

The sides of Sparkle's mouth rose into a crooked, knowing smile. "Well, I didn't really work there, I mean I didn't do mechanical work or anything."

Annie's head jerked up. The look on Sparkle's face didn't make her think she was kidding.

"What kind of job did you do then?" It was the first time Gloria had spoken during the meal. Annie glanced at the girl and a tight sensation squeezed her chest. Gloria's pale blue blouse and dark wool skirt were simple and plain, but somehow, she looked cleaner, thinner and just better tended than the rest of them. Annie looked down at her own wrinkled plaid shirt and blue trousers and sighed. Even the few times she'd really tried, she'd never looked that perfect.

"Just odds and ends." Sparkle's voice was sharp. Her stark blond hair seemed to bristle when she was annoyed, which was most of the time so far. She thrust her chest forward and pulled her blouse down so even more of the tattoo showed, then deliberately pulled a cigarette from the package next to her plate and lit it. She blew smoky rings above her head.

Annie wanted to laugh. She kept thinking that Sparkle was exactly what her mother would describe as a 'lady of the evening.' Annie was unsure how to carry on a conversation with a person of that profession or even if it were safe to live with her. She knew what her mom would have said. She had to chuckle a bit. Perhaps both she and Sparkle were changing careers. It was interesting being around this woman. She was feisty but shot about as straight as anyone Annie'd ever met.

With thoughts of her mother came a quick stir of pleasure. Finally, at the ripe old age of twenty-eight, she didn't have to hear her mother's opinion on every single thing. She hadn't expected to be quite so happy about that.

Annie glanced over at Birdie, still valiantly trying to eat a sausage. She'd taken it out of the bun and cut it into several pieces but that did not make it palatable. Birdie squirmed from one round hip to the other on the picnic bench, obviously finding it uncomfortable.

"Well, I didn't just work on watches, I helped my dad add an extra room on the house and my brothers and I built a barn just before the war started. I really like doing things like that. It's nice to step back and admire something you've built."

Birdie and Gloria nodded but it didn't appear that Sparkle had even heard.

"You come from somewhere in the South, don't you?" Annie was having almost as much trouble talking with this friendly woman as she was with Sparkle. It was her first real conversation with a Negro person and it was difficult to act naturally. In Coos Bay, everyone not a Swede or Norwegian was considered strange. When she tried to act naturally, it came out sort of stiff. She'd have to think before she spoke. She'd be embarrassed if she came out with her parents' opinion.

Birdie raised her head and gave her a lopsided grin. "Y'all c'n pro'bly tell from my accent hunh?"

"Well, that's a part of it."

Birdie laid down her fork and pulled her iced tea closer. "Y'r right. I come from a little town in Georgia. Place called Sweetwillow. No mor'n fifty people all together. Awful pretty tho'."

"What did you do in Sweetwillow?" Sparkle's tone was odd and it made Annie look at her sharply. The woman's brow was clear and she rested the elbow of her right arm on the table, taking a long drag from her cigarette.

Birdie pushed her glasses up with a finger and proceeded to answer as if she hadn't noticed the tone. "Not much to do there. I used to go five miles down the road everyday to the widow Wolcott's home. Her man been dead for twenty years. I been cookin' and cleaning for her since I was twelve."

"Good grief, 'um . . . how old are you now?" Annie was more startled by her working at twelve than curious about her age but she'd started talking and needed to say something.

"Twenty-nine. She been pretty good to me. Took me in when my mom got sick. She's the reason I married my Beauregard. He was working on her place. Doing the heavy work in the yard and in the field."

"You're married?"

"Oh yeah. Been fourteen years now. Sure do miss him."

"Fourteen years?" Annie could hear the faint sound of disbelief in Gloria's voice. "That means you were married at fifteen?"

"That's right."

Sparkle interrupted. "And where is your husband, um . . . your Beauregard now?" Again, her question sounded simple but didn't feel like it. Annie flinched but Birdie continued on as if she hadn't heard the sarcasm.

"Ah think he's some place in Africa or somewhere. Anyway, last letter I got said he was seeing an awful lot of people just like him. Pretty sure that's got to be Africa. And that's about all I could get between the censor's black marks and cut-out places. They sure do mess up a letter."

Annie nodded in agreement. The last two letters she'd received, one from Phillip and one from Roger, had so many black lines through them it was like trying to finish a jigsaw puzzle with half the pieces missing. But the sight of those letters generated huge relief. At least, her brothers were alive.

As Annie watched, Sparkle took a long assessing look at Birdie, one eyebrow raised.

"So why'd you come up here? Seems to me like you're a long way from your own people."

"My kids."

"You got kids?"

"Yeah. Four."

"My God, four kids. So what the hell you doing here?"

"Supportin' 'um. Takes a heap a money to keep 'um eatin'. Had to leave home to get a decent wage. Lot' sa places still won't hire us. Specially me bein' a woman an all. My Beauregard's mama is watchin' my kids now." Birdie hitched herself forward on the picnic bench and placed her elbows on the table. "I sure do miss my kids. Beauregard too. If the war is over quick, I'll jez' go home. If it lasts a while and I can save some money, I'll bring 'em up here. Then when Beuregard gets out we can figger where we want to be. Would be kinda nice to have a choice."

"So, what sort of mechanical work have you been doing?"

"Well, y'all probably won't think much of it." Birdie looked at Sparkle and her easy drawl became clipped. "But I's always been good at fixin' things. Mostly even better than my Beau. Ah tol' em I was good with tools and stuff. Just didn't tell them that the tools was mosly a 'tato masher and a frying pan. I'm sure hopin' I c'n do the work."

Annie realized she'd been anxious about her own lack of skill. Now it appeared that Birdie's skills were less than hers. It must have taken incredible courage to leave her children and the home and come all the way to Seattle.

She recalled the chain-smoking man who had interviewed her. He'd been so eager to fill the position that he hadn't been very specific about job skills. In fact, he'd stressed the fact that there was a month's training school and that being so big and strong she wouldn't have any trouble. It appeared that others were even more untrained than she.

"Well I'm glad someone else doesn't know much about what they will be doing. How much training will we be getting?"

Sparkle snorted. "Just about enough to teach you one end of the rivet gun from the other." Annie exchanged a glance of apprehension with Gloria and Birdie. Sparkle let out a sound that was close to a laugh. "Ah, it's not that tough. There's enough of us doing the same thing. Someone can always tell you what to do."

It was quiet for a moment around the table and the women relaxed. Annie could hear crickets in the woods behind the park.

Gloria ended the silence. The odd, lisping sound in her voice, made it seem as if the words had trouble getting past her teeth. "I would imagine it is like a vacation for you."

Birdie sighed. "Oh you mean being away from the kids an all? Kinda thought so myself at first leavin' all them noisy folks but it ain't much fun really. The minute you leave 'um you get to worryin'. Guess I won't feel right till I get 'um up here."

Gloria ran her fingers through her hair. The effect was like water momentarily diverted from its course, then falling back into place again. She put her fingers gently on the side of her plate then slid it forward out of her way.

"My mother used to say it was the happiest day of the whole year when my brother and I went off to camp for the summer. Said she could finally get something done."

Annie gasped then tried to cover it with a cough. She was surprised that anyone who looked as polished as Gloria would have a parent who sounded so heartless. She remembered her own summers. She and her brothers would spend hours outdoors, only stopping long enough to eat the huge meals her mother would prepare for them. The summer she'd broken her leg, her mother had helped her put together endless puzzles and trekked back and forth to the library twice a week to bring home armloads of books. Myrtle Tosh insisted that her children were a whole lot more fun than the ironing and darning that would pile up during the summer. The thought of Gloria's summer made her feel hollow inside.

"You went away for the whole summer?" Birdie stared.

"Yes. It was actually nice after the first couple of years. I made friends and we did quite a few fun things. They had horses and a lake and everything."

"How old were you?"

"Oh, I was five my first year. I went every summer until I entered college. I rather miss it now."

Birdie shook her head. "How come yer mother didn't watch you? She must 'a had some kind of 'portant job."

Gloria's forehead wrinkled in concentration. "Well no, my mother didn't work. But she has many social engagements. She has been the head of almost every charity group in Portland. Our nanny, Lucille, took care of us most of the time." She lowered her voice and looked quickly over her shoulder. "Mother is quite high-strung, you understand."

Annie tried to picture someone high-strung. Gloria spoke as though things like nannies and summer camps were familiar to them all.

Sparkle looked directly at Annie and rolled her eyes. Looking away, Annie felt another uneasy prickle between her shoulders. It was hard to tell if Sparkle were really offering to be friends with her or just making fun of Gloria. If she had to guess, she would lean toward the latter. The good-natured needling her family had engaged in never seemed to have the nasty edge

Sparkle's did. It made her uncomfortable even trying to figure it out.

Birdie interrupted her thinking. "Sounds to me like yer family don' need no money. What the heck you doin' workin', girl? And, lawdy mercy, livin' here?" Birdie cocked her head to the side as she asked the question.

Gloria's answer came out in a rush, as if she had been waiting for someone to ask. "Well, that's true, I certainly do not need the money. But, you see, I was in a sociology class one day and our speaker talked about how badly the war was going and I just thought that I was not doing any good sitting in that old classroom so I decided to get a job and help out, get the men home sooner and all. And I did not want to live anywhere nice, I think it builds moral fiber if you are just one of the workers." Gloria took a deep breath and looked at the others, a worried expression transforming her face. "But, you know, they neglected to tell me I needed any special skills. I have never worked on a machine in my life."

"My God, I don't believe it." Sparkle pulled herself from her seat on the picnic bench and walked dramatically around the table, one hand on her forehead. She finally stopped at one end and pointed at Annie. "You looked like the best of the three, like maybe you could at least throw around some heavy stuff if we had to. Instead you been workin' on teeny watches, probably start you out sortin' rivets or something."

Annie felt her face go hot.

"No, don't be gettin' mad, I'm just trying to get this straight."

Next she pointed at Birdie. "And you been cleaning some white lady's house and takin' care of a bunch of kids. You're gonna be as much help as my old cat, Stupid. But, I'll give you credit, at least you lied about being able to work with tools and about what goddamn color you are. Can't think of any other reason we never heard anything about our roommate being a nigger. I guess you might be useful for something."

She sighed and stretched an arm out, gazing off into the distance as if for more information about the future. Annie looked at Birdie and saw that the woman was looking fixedly in the other direction, a quiet, bemused smile on her face. With a jolt, Annie realized Sparkle was right, the woman from the South had lied. She exchanged looks with Gloria and saw her own feelings of confusion mirrored in the girl's face.

Sparkle finally shook her head and turned back to her three roommates. "And you . . ." She pointed at Gloria, her finger reminding Annie of a water witch's divining rod bending toward the source. "You're telling us that this place sure ain't as nice as your daddy's but since there's a war on you'll make the big sacrifice and stay with the poor folks. You're a kid with no experience doin' anything, so they'll probably have you running the whole show in a few months. Probably make you top cheese with the union too." Sparkle threw up both hands in a theatrical movement.

A rush of hot anger pushed through her. The woman either hadn't listened or wanted to ignore Annie's construction experience. Then, just as quickly as the anger came, she felt a laugh begin to bubble up. Hard as it was to admit, the blond firecracker was right. Here they were, three eager, patriotic women who knew absolutely nothing about building anything, about to begin working on some of the largest, most complicated and vital machines ever built. She pictured the world holding out its hand for saving and the three of them running along with watchmakers tools, a frying pan and school books earnestly trying to do just that. It was ridiculous. She didn't know if she should cry or laugh, so she found herself doing both. Soon her sides began to hurt and tears flowed as she struggled for control.

At first Birdie looked at her as if she'd grown another head, then her eyes got a glitter of amusement and she joined in. Gloria soon added her short, breathless giggles. Their laughter floated through the rows of trailers. Sparkle watched them with her head cocked to one side and a half sneer on her face, but as they continued, the sneer turned to a real smile and she joined in. Her laugh was short and raspy, as if she didn't use it much.

CHAPTER TWO

The slick cheesy smell of starch rose from Annie's shirt and her nose wrinkled as she tried to stifle a sneeze. When she thought of Gloria, Birdie and herself carefully ironing their clothes the night before, she sighed. All that starch and energy and now they were covered by so much dust and grime it was impossible to tell them from the planes they were passing. The heat, dust and noise created by the enormous machine behind her made her skin prickle.

Things were not going well. Certainly not anything like she'd expected for her first day of training. She'd thought it would be an orderly, first day of school type thing where you learned what you needed for the rest of the year. So far the three of them had been yelled at by a man whom none of them could understand and Annie had whacked her head so hard on a low beam she'd seen stars. All fifteen trainees, eleven women, two teenage boys and one man who looked to be about eighty, had been gathered unceremoniously into a herd, moved through the huge plant and barked at by a machine gun speaking instructor, Miss Weintaub. Annie wondered if she would feel this out of place if she were being shot at on the front lines.

And, as usual, the worst part was that she stood out like a cow at a pig party. She was a good head taller than anyone else in the crowd and her red hair attracted startled glances. Her broad shoulders had presented a problem every time she'd had to pass between the tightly packed machinery and plane parts. None of the others seemed to be having trouble.

But as uncomfortable as it was, it couldn't dim the memory of her first sight of the airplanes. They'd walked past the rollout area where ten enormous B-17's, or Flying Fortresses as their instructor called them, were waiting for their first flight test. She knew she would never forget the goose bumps that had risen on her arms. The planes were simply magnificent and soon she would be building these monsters. Before that moment, the whole journey to Seattle, her introduction to her roommates and their tiny living quarters had seemed like a long, strange dream. Standing on the hard cement, breathing fumes from planes taking off and being nearly deafened by the sound of motors, she knew for sure that she was where she was meant to be.

During the last two bleak years, the traitorous, sick feeling that the United States might lose the war skulked like dirty fog just out of conscious thought. No matter how many times she listened to President Roosevelt speak on the radio, she was frightened, and then angry. Phillip and Roger were in danger of dying every second because of a madman who wanted to dominate the world. She didn't understand why, but this was her country and she wouldn't let it go without a hell of a fight. Up to now, she hadn't thought that anything she was doing was much help. Looking over the line of bombers, Annie felt a surge of hope rush through her chest. Her country did have a chance. And a good part of that chance was lined up in front of her.

As many times as they'd been told not to touch anything, Annie felt the urge to run her hands over the sleek aluminum skin and rivet bumps she knew she would soon be learning to master. The very act of taking the plain metal pieces and making them fit and form together and finally grow into something strong and useful filled her with an absurd sense of wonder. She'd always felt guilty about that. She had never known another woman who enjoyed building. Her mother and friends seemed content to confine their creations to sewing and knitting, both pursuits destined to drive her mad. The only traditional woman's art she'd ever been interested in was weaving and that was mainly because she enjoyed combining colors and the mathematical process of setting up the loom.

With a start, she realized that she hadn't been listening for some time and if she didn't listen carefully, she couldn't understand her instructor. Someone had told her Edna Weintaub had a New York accent. She was surprised that anyone from the States could sound so foreign. She decided to concentrate on watching intently as her teacher's lips moved.

Annie felt a stiffening in the women packed close around her. She saw a tall, thin man with a pronounced limp approach from the maze of clanking machines.

Her interest quickened at the sight of a person taller than she. From her vantage point in the crowd, it appeared that he was at least six-foot-four. A cruel slash running from mustache to chin accentuated the painful thinness of the man. She wondered what had caused the scar and the limp, then chided herself. She was a respectfully engaged woman for heaven's sake. She was not like some women, just looking for a man, any man.

"Ladies!" The short barked command was loud. As Annie watched, Miss Weintaub's spray of hair jabbed angrily at the air as she tried to gain back the attention of the group. The action made her look like a startled rooster. Her large, rawboned body fit awkwardly in tight gray slacks and ruffled red blouse.

"This is Cain Adamson. He is your trainer and a union steward too, in case any of you have any problems. And I'm the union secretary." She made her position sound just slightly less important than God. "Mr. Adamson is going to tell you all there is to know about a rivet gun and bucking bar. Pay attention!"

Miss Weintaub's voice was slower and softer when she spoke of him and there was a strange puckering of her lips as she rested her hand possessively on his shoulder. A slight shrug of his arm dislodged her hold as the man put distance between the two of them. Annie was surprised at Edna's flirtatious movement but intrigued by the ease with which he'd shrugged her off. She wished she had the ease to handle such a situation as quietly and efficiently as he had.

His voice was low and difficult to hear over the din. As one, the group of trainees moved forward pulling Annie with them as if she were in the same school of fish. She knew they all wanted to learn as quickly as possible, but she wished they didn't all need to be quite so close together. Cain coughed then started again, louder this time.

"Have any of you ever used a tool like this?" He raised the metal apparatus then looked over the gathering of women. He was greeted by silence.

"Have any of you ever used mechanical equipment at all?" His voice seemed to hold little hope for a positive response. Again, the room was still. Almost as if by itself Annie's arm rose in the air. Her heart started pounding faster. The man looked at her, his head cocked slightly to one side.

"What kind of equipment have you used?" His voice was kind and he seemed to be actually interested in what she might have to say. She gulped and tried to swallow around her suddenly very dry throat.

"Well . . .." She'd raised her hand because she'd wanted very much to lessen the look of disappointment on his face when he saw the lack of experience in the group. She knew that she wouldn't have a problem with that gun, she'd certainly used similar drills at home. The room was so quiet she could hear her heart beating and knew all eyes were glued on her. Even the clattering machinery seemed to have quieted for a moment. She was sweating in earnest now and it felt as if her brain had been unexpectedly sent out for repair.

"No . . . uh . . . I mean yes, I have used tools." Her voice was much higher than her normal tone. She cleared her throat, and searched the group of women surrounding her.

A dark brown face in the crowd stood out from the rest. The sight of Birdie's round smiling visage calmed Annie. And although it was meant to be encouraging, Birdie's smile made her realize why she'd hesitated speaking. Remembering the conversation at the picnic table the day before, she was sure most of the other women didn't have anywhere near her experience. Pointing that out right now would be a slap in the face of the rest of them.

"Yes, I've worked with tools. I've worked for seven years in a watch repair shop. I can use all the small equipment that one normally finds in such a shop."

Her words slowed at the end of her sentence. Ridiculous. The contrast between the heavy, unwieldy equipment he held in his hand and the tiny precision tools she was describing was laughable. She looked reluctantly at Cain Adamson's face.

His expression was flat and unreadable. "Well, that's not quite the same is it?" There seemed to be no sarcasm in his words, just an overriding weariness.

Annie's temples were beginning to pound. She looked down at her big square hands, then at her absurd size twelve feet made huge-looking by her work boots. She knew she could handle the rivet gun and the drill. What she couldn't handle was her own idiotic failure to say what she meant to in a crowd. Pressing her lips together, she angrily blinked away the sudden tingling in her eyes. The crowd near her let out a collective sigh, all apparently relieved that they had not responded.

The next week was a blur of training, safety sessions and flag waving. Her dreams began to include the instructors standing behind her and watching her every move. Annie learned that many workers called the airplanes ships. She could wake from a dead sleep and spout the sales line to "Buy War Bonds!" With all the different levels of talent, the first few training sessions were a bit like grade school but as the days progressed, they were pushed hard to learn as fast as possible. The position she was forced to assume to do the job inside the plane left her wondering if she'd ever be able to straighten up again. To her relief after only a couple of hours, they'd decided that Annie was just too big to be inside the plane bucking so she was taught how to handle the rivet gun.

The process was simple. Annie would take a rivet from her apron, being careful to select the correct size. She would place the rivet in the gun, then put it over the pre-drilled hole and pull the trigger.

Depending on the kind of rivet required, another person, called the bucker, stood on the other side of the plate and held a bucking bar to spread the rivets as they entered. She learned about explosive rivets and flush riveting on the wings of the fuselage which cut down on the drag of the plane. Most importantly, Annie learned not to hold the rivets in her mouth. They were soaked in grease to keep them from corroding.

She was used to hard work and this task was actually easier for her than the precision task of helping her father fix watches. Within three days she was helping the others in the class. A strange excitement spread through her. It seemed, after all, that she was truly suited for the work.

The class was held at Boeing's Plant 2 on Spokane Street. Gloria kept calling it Plant B because the sign outside was so faded she was said it looked like a B, not a 2. After two weeks, twenty of them were working on a real ship for the first time. Edna was making sure they did everything up to standard while Cain was giving lessons at the welding school

Annie wiped the sweat from her neck and stood with feet apart. The unseasonably warm May made the factory unbearably hot. The flat roof absorbed heat and blasted it to the interior.

She was focused on making sure the line of rivets was straight and clean when Edna's shrill voice cut through her concentration like a saw through sheet metal. She ignored the sound until she heard 'Tosh' included in the string of words. Turning, she found the instructor yelling at her, pointing a bony finger and making little jabbing motions. Annie sighed and knocked four times on the side of the aluminum skin of the fuselage they were working on to let Gloria know she was stopping. It seemed that Edna was never more satisfied than when she found someone doing something wrong, particularly Annie. The better Annie did, the more the trainer tried to find fault. A hard knot formed in her stomach and she could feel the blood begin to pound in her ears. She hated the belittling tone Edna used to correct anyone. Annie turned back slowly, not anxious to hear what had gone wrong this time. The woman's face had taken on a slightly purple hue and she spluttered when she spoke.

"Miss Tosh how can you keep hammering away when you have no idea what's happening on the other side of the plate? Look at those rivets. Every one will have to be redone."

Annie stepped through the opening in the plane and saw Gloria, stretched out nearly horizontal, her arm flung forward in an attempt to hold the bucking bar against the incoming rivet. She had obviously been behind for a spell. Instead of the rivets being squashed even with the interior, the row they'd been working on resembled a severe case of acne. Gloria's face twisted up in a frightened scowl. The girl tired easily and needed more time than most of the trainees. Annie had forgotten and started going too fast again. She knew Gloria was embarrassed about it.

Annie turned to find Miss Weintaub less than two inches away, her finger pointing upward toward Annie's nose. She noticed that the woman's eyes were a peculiar, flat blue color. When she spoke, fine droplets of spit sprayed Annie's face.

"She needs to go home. She isn't going to make it. And I don't know about you. How many times to I have to tell you about safety? If you don't know what's going on around you, you could cause an injury to yourself or someone else."

Annie stepped back two paces. "She's not that slow. I just forgot and went too fast. It's my fault."

Edna stared at her for several seconds. "Okay, but you're responsible. You have to learn how to lead and she has to learn to keep up." Edna's voice clicked on some words and Annie realized the sound was from badly fitting false teeth. Watching the retreating back, Annie sighed. She'd be delighted when she was put on a regular crew and away from this cranky woman.

"I am so sorry I got you in trouble." Gloria's voice fluttered through the sentence like a timid moth. There were tears shining in her eyes and her mouth was trembling. Annie leaned over and put a hand on her arm.

"It's all right. I just keep forgetting to let you catch up." She worked to make her voice calm, knowing that right now, encouragement was the only thing that would steady the girl. Annie certainly wasn't about to tell her that she had serious doubts that Gloria would ever be able to handle this. "Just remember to give three raps on the metal if you need me to slow down."

Her efforts didn't help and the tears spilled over and down the pale cheeks. "She is going to fire me." Gloria raised her arm and held it over her eyes. At nineteen, Annie might have done the same. She waited and when the flood was over and Gloria took her arm away, she smiled at the shaken girl.

"No she's not. You're just nervous. All this takes is a little practice. Listen, one of the guys from swing said he'd come over here as soon as Edna leaves and give us a hand. He'll shoot while you and I will work together on the bucking. We'll fix the bad rivets and get started on a new line. It's only a half-hour until she has to leave. You'll make it." Annie could see a slight relaxation of Gloria's jaw muscles.

"Birdie needs some help too. Between the three of us, I'm sure we can figure out how to turn you into a pretty good bucker. And maybe we'll have you sell a thousand dollars of those bonds, that should make her sit up and take notice."

Gloria sniffed. "Oh, I do want to learn. And I do not want to go home and tell my dad he was right. I will try harder, Annie, I really will."

Annie felt the warmth of affection tug at her heart. It didn't seem possible that this girl could be so exasperating and endearing at the same time. With a shrug, she indicated that they should get back to work. They still had a half-hour of Edna's rule before they could relax.

The transition from training to work was about ten hours. One day they were being watched every second, the next they were supposed to know everything and get the job done. Annie felt a kink in the back of her neck and the prickle of sweat under her arms. Three hours into her first shift of real work and she was wondering how she was going to make it the rest of the day. She'd been delighted to be put on day shifts to start. She, Gloria and Birdie worked from seven in the morning until four thirty in the afternoon. She'd heard that at any given moment they could be moved to swing shift, which started at four in the afternoon and lasted until eleven thirty at night. Or even worse, graveyard, which meant arriving at work at eleven at night and working until seven in the morning. She wasn't sure if she could say awake on that shift.

Shaking her head, she pushed the little nibbles of worry away. She was where she wanted to be and she'd make it, no matter what shift she drew. Unfortunately, she'd been assigned to bucking despite her training with the rivet gun. She stood braced with her hands gripping the outside edge of the rivet bar and tried to ignore the laughter of the two women working only about five feet away. Blind bucking meant standing firm on the cramped interior of the plane and holding the metal piece that stopped and spread the rivets that were being shot home from the outside. The problem was, every time they'd make a turn, she'd forget which way the riveter was supposed to be going next. She had to think about it when it should have been automatic. It seemed that every time she thought she was good at this, something would happen and she'd look like a fool.

She, Birdie and Gloria had gotten so they could at least keep up with one another. The job called for coordination and something like clairvoyance between two people. She'd been assigned to a riveter, Jonathan Makepeace, who had simply scoffed when she said she hadn't trained as a bucker. He waved a skinny hand in the air and told her to get inside. The two of them were stuck in the chaos method of work so far, him yelling and swearing and her sweating and guessing wrong over and over. To make it worse, Edna Weintaub was working on the outside of the plane. Apparently she filled in on the regular shifts when she wasn't

instructing. Annie was sure Edna had heard all the yelling that
Jonathan had been directing at her.

She shifted her feet trying to get more leverage to lean into
the small plate instead of having to hold the bar steady with her
hands. She hadn't figured yet how to use any shoulder or leg
muscle and her hand and arm muscles burned. The continuous
laughter and noise from the other team working close by was
distracting. They made it appear so easy she wanted to slug
them. She wished she had been put on the same team as Gloria
or Birdie. The smell of grease and dust and hot drills was so
strong she hated to breath very deeply.

Jonathan, who came up to just about midshoulder on Annie,
appeared wrinkled enough to be a hundred years old and, so far,
was in a constant bad mood. He was supremely capable and
appeared to have no tiring point, just put the rivet in, slam it
home, then go to the next. Annie could still hear Edna 's instructions in her head. 'Bucking spreads the rivets entering the hole,
forcing them in straight and true. A good riveter gets the rivets
to nearly melt into the aluminum skin.' Shaking her head, she
decided she sure wasn't there yet. She was still stumbling
around like a drunk on the internal skeleton while Jonathan,
the steel grasshopper, walked around on the relatively smooth
surface of the scaffolding outside.

The fuselage of the huge warplane balanced twenty feet
from the ground, supported by the wood and metal scaffolding
holding the frame steady as they worked. The bright overhead
lights made shadows along the interior of the hull and it was
getting harder to see all the time.

She blinked as sweat dribbled into her eyes and tried to wipe
her forehead with the back of her sleeve while simultaneously
moving to the next space. At the start of the shift, she'd been
determined to show the man that she was not only good, but
would probably be one of the best. This reminded her horribly of
the first day of training when she'd raised her hand and Cain
Adamson had called on her. She knew she could do this job. She
just needed a little time. But time didn't seem to be something

anyone had. Now, she just wanted to finish the shift without hurting herself by tripping on a stringer or catching a rivet with her finger instead of the bar.

Gritting her teeth, she pushed the bar against the tube and leaned forward as the metal slammed into her arms again. She felt herself backing up and tried to push forward, only to have the slick metal turn in her hand and slide toward the floor. She tried grabbing it, but it was too late, the heavy piece clanged on the metal surface and bounced. Each successive bang made her wince. When the clamor finally subsided she felt sweat cool on her back and arms.

Turning her head, she saw that the other set of riveters, Lulu and Joan, had stopped what they were doing and swung around to see what had caused the noise. Their faces were sympathetic. As if on cue, Jonathan appeared in the opening of the Fort, his face screwed up like an apple doll and a greasy cap pushed back on his head.

"Whatcha doin' in here dearie, takin' tea? Doin' yer nails?" It sounded as if he were using a microphone in the suddenly quiet interior of the airplane shell. The fact that he was almost stone deaf made it hard for him to judge how loudly he was speaking, and right now, it didn't seem that he cared. "Doncha know there's a war on, lady?"

Annie's mouth was dry. "I'm sorry." She could tell from the blank look on his face that he couldn't hear her. She repeated her words, flinching at the volume of her own voice. She felt like an idiot, screaming her apology to a man half her size and not ten feet away.

He grunted, then spat a stream of tobacco expertly out the opening. "Nobody on the front line's going to care if you're sorry, lady. Jesus, just give me one good man and I'd have this thing done in a jiffy. I'm goin up to the office for a minute."

Jonathan pivoted on his heel and left the opening in the plane as quickly as he had come. She felt her face flame with heat and she wondered if he were going to tell them she couldn't do the job.

Joan shook her head. "Don't worry about him. He just about never gets up on the right side of the bed. And he doesn't think anybody can do the job as good as he does." She smiled, turned back to her work and put the bucking bar deftly to the hole. Annie could hear Jonathan's feet thudding on the wooden boards, then the rattling of metal as he made his way down the tall flights of steps to the floor of the plant. She sighed and leaned back, propping one foot on a rib and listening to the sound of the others working on the plane, relieved that he was gone even for a few minutes.

She looked around and felt a goose bumpy kind of thrill. She was really doing something that made a difference. She gazed at two women drilling holes for the Clecos on the outside of the fuselage. The small tubes were used to hold the drill holes in line until the rivets were shot home.

A thin man, almost as tall as she, checked the accuracy of the drilled holes. A third fellow, Jerome, was near the front putting in metal clips to hold some of the many miles of electrical wire. It was amazing that everyone could work in such a tight area and still get the job done. She knew in her bones that she could be very good at this job.

Annie straightened her back and heard vertebrae pop. Relieved to be upright again, the tension in her muscles subsided. She was trying to find somewhere to sit when she heard a stifled scream from outside the structure. She turned in that direction and stood for a moment, then moved forward when she heard the sound again. She stumbled twice as she made her way toward the opening, the boards set to keep people from walking on the base were not made for running and dangling wires caught her as she tried to move quickly. When she slammed her arm into one of the sharp metal pieces, she had to slow down. She finally got one foot on the scaffolding outside and peered through the opening.

The sight confused her. Edna seemed to be on the outside of the scaffolding, her body sliding and hands grasping frantically for a hold. Annie felt air leave her lungs in a woosh, then a flood of relief as she saw one of the woman's large hands grab the rail to stop her fall. Every ounce of Annie's energy propelled her toward the woman frantically trying to get two hands on the metal.

She tried to run along the planks even as she could see Edna's hand slipping and her face turning chalky white. Terror twisted Edna's face and her hair stood straight up in that awful topknot. Her mouth was open and a scream of horror filled the air. Annie launched herself forward, falling and skidding along the wood on her stomach. Edna made a desperate attempt to grab at the railing with her other hand. Annie finally reached her and felt the slight brush of Edna's fingers, then nothing.

The next sound was softer than she would have imagined, just a quiet thud and then there was nothing. A shudder ran down Annie's back and her breath seemed to stop in her mouth. She pulled herself up on one knee and looked over the side in dread, hoping for a miracle.

The large, rawboned woman lay curled like a child, one arm covering her head as if to protect it from the unforgiving concrete. No movement was evident in her body and people began to gather around her, their faces registering horror at the spectacle. Dark blood was seeping onto the concrete under Edna's head.

Annie looked back to where she had fallen. Edna must have stepped back in just the right place, where the scaffolding was loose. She thought of the woman's insistence on safety at all times. She had assumed it was only the new people who had to be careful. Looking at Edna now, she realized something that Edna's words had never driven home. These ships came at a price and this was a very dangerous place to work.

The days after Edna's death were distressing. Annie found that workplace fatalities like this one were not uncommon. The men generally thought she or probably all females weren't tough enough when it came to this kind of thing. She'd asked several union men what they were doing about safety. Her questions met with blank looks and shuffling feet. They seemed more interested in finding another secretary for their meetings. And somehow, the fact that Edna was abrasive and had few friends cast a shadow of apathy on the whole thing. It was almost as if her cranky personality made it permissible to quit being concerned.

A week later the investigation was over. Edna's funeral was held in a dim little chapel with a heavy oak door hung with rusty hinges. Unfortunately, the door had screeched very few times, the pews were empty save for the first couple of rows. The minister was short and bald, his robes dusty on the bottom edges. Although kind of face, he seemed distracted, as if he had better things to do than bury Edna on this fine spring day. As she followed Birdie and Gloria out the wide doors, her feet seemed too heavy to lift. When she'd stepped down the last step to the sidewalk, she stopped and breathed in deeply.

She'd learned that the inviolate set of rules she'd been taught at home didn't necessarily apply here. The speed with which those magnificent planes rolled out came at a high price.

Gloria tried getting her legs into a more comfortable position in the bed. First she lay on one side, then the other, but nothing seemed to help very much. Before working at the plant, she'd never believed any part of her body could hurt like this. She finally flopped over onto her stomach and put her head on her arms. The small sleeping cot she had been assigned was cramped but comfortable if she didn't try to raise her head up too far. The scent of the cotton pillowcase was of the outdoors. It had finally stopped raining these last few days of May and they had been able to hang their laundry on the line outside. One of the things she found the hardest to accept here was the constant onslaught of unpleasant odors. She thought longingly of her bed at home. The maids had laundered her sheets in lavender water and she'd gone to sleep for years with that heavenly aroma filling her nose. Working at the plant made her finally appreciate being surrounded by lovely scents. Everything at work seemed marinated in the unpleasant odor of grease.

Her roommates were seated in the dinette area at the front of the trailer. Birdie and Annie were reading. The occasional slap of a card and snort of pleasure told her that Sparkle had won at solitaire again. She seemed extraordinarily lucky at cards and Gloria wondered if she cheated, like her brother Fred. She sighed and rolled over on her back, thinking that he was certainly the one she missed the most. He could always make her feel better when her father would yell and scream. Fred didn't seem to mind as much as she. He told her that if you just turned off your brain and thought about horses or airplanes or automobiles, it wasn't so bad. She'd had to translate that to chiffon dresses and a new haircut to make it work but it finally had. The thought of him brought an ache and she pressed both palms on her chest, trying to make the pain go away.

At eighteen her brother was the perfect age to be drafted. Her father had spent several hundreds of dollars in placing Fred in a position with the local rationing board where he would be exempt. As usual, her dad had been very clear about what he had done. Particularly, how hard it had been and how much he had to pay to get the position secured. Fred had worked there for several months, counting out the various coupons and dealing with the complaints. Most people were patriotic enough to feel that rationing was simply another aspect of winning the war. But there were always a few who were unhappy about the mandatory limits. After a time, Fred had become quiet and withdrawn. He seldom joined them for dinner, always with a plausible excuse but Gloria had begun to worry about him.

And then one night, Fred had come to her room and awakened her with a gentle shake of her shoulder. A few whispered words and then he was gone. He'd joined the Marines and was leaving for boot camp that night. He wasn't telling anyone in the family but her, since he knew their father would protest. Fred told her he wouldn't write for several months. He wanted to be sure that their father couldn't find him and pull him out of the action.

When he'd said 'action' his eyes had taken on such an expectant blaze that she'd been immediately terrified. How would her gentle, quiet brother do in a world with much death and killing? She'd thought for a moment that she would wake her father so he could stop him. Then her brother had given her his long, slow smile, hugged her and she'd not had the heart to spoil his dream. When he'd closed the door of her peach-colored bedroom, she'd been more alone than she could ever remember.

A wave of longing for Fred swept over her, so strong she felt tears fill her eyes. She did not know what to do. She had a problem she couldn't solve alone. Her supervisor, Ed Bartell, was a tall, emaciated middle-aged man with a huge red nose pocked with holes the size of peas. He made Gloria think of a not very well-preserved cadaver. He had an unending store of nasty jokes that he delighted in telling when she was around to hear. The sight of him made her shudder and when he got close she thought she might faint. He smelled like chewing tobacco and sweat. She had hoped that his odd interest in her was just because she was new. But as the week progressed, she found him hovering over her much more than he did with anyone else on the crew. She wiped tears away with the lace handkerchief she kept tucked beneath her pillow.

She was troubled that she might be doing something to encourage him. Her father always said that a certain kind of woman just invited trouble. He'd never specified what that type of woman might act like, so she was unsure if she might be doing something wrong. She bit her lip, rubbed at her eyes and tried to concentrate on what was happening right now instead of at work.

At least for the moment everything was quiet in their little home. She heard the slap of cards on the table and then Sparkle declaring victory.

"I did it again. Nobody's as good as me."

Sparkle spread the cards out on the table and rose from the dinette. In doing so, she turned too quickly and knocked down three of Gloria's blouses hanging from the cord stretched between the kitchen cabinet and the seating area.

"Well shit." Sparkle's voice was muffled as she turned to look at the scattered shirts. "Wish to hell we didn't have so damned many clothes in here."

Birdie murmured something and Gloria could see Sparkle stiffen. "Not all of us have twenty blouses that have to be washed by hand every week."

Gloria could see the tension rise in the little group at the table. She grabbed the handle on the side of the bed and slid out. When she'd shuffled her way to the front of the trailer, Annie was already picking up the shirts.

"Don't get excited Sparkle, they're just hanging out too far. Let's push them back a bit and they won't be in the way." Annie spoke softly and hung the blouses on the hangers, trying to brush off the dust picked up from the floor. Gloria wondered what advice Fred would have right now.

The volume of clothes she'd brought caused a problem. Now it seemed that the problem continued. She couldn't get anything right. She'd never had to take care of her own clothes before and she thought she was doing great to wash and hang them by herself. She'd been proud that she kept herself so clean in this really dirty world. She realized now that she should have thought about the other women in the trailer and how much room it took to hang everything. Tears started welling up in her eyes. She opened her mouth to apologize and simply burst out crying. A backward step and a twist of her mouth showed that Sparkle thought she was being a baby. She turned quickly to escape back to the rear of the trailer, and her own little bed, when she felt a hand on her shoulder.

"It's all right, Gloria, Sparkle's just tired. We all are. Come on back and sit down with us." Annie's voice was calm with no hint of anger or pity. Gloria looked up through the stream of tears and snuffled, then let herself be led to the table. She took the

large blue handkerchief Annie had handed her and wiped her
eyes, then blew her nose.

"I'm sorry. I didn't think it would be in the way. I'm sorry
about . . ." Gloria stopped unable to remember why she was
sorry.

"No need to be sorry, girl. This woman's jez' got a hair trigger temper. Don' pay her no mind." Birdie had put her book
down and was watching Gloria with one eyebrow raised. "Is
there something bothering you?"

The concern in Birdie's voice brought on a fresh onslaught of
tears. When she'd gulped herself quiet again, Gloria tried to
articulate carefully. It seemed hours before she was finally able
to speak coherently.

"It's Mr. Bartell. He won't . . . he won't . . . he won't . . ." Each
word seemed to bring about another spate of tears. She eventually had to talk right through them.

"He won't leave me alone. He keeps standing so close I can
smell his awful breath and he keeps rubbing up against me
when he thinks no one is looking." She gulped and sat back on
the bench seat. "I told him I wished he would stop and he just
laughed." When she had finally gotten out the words the group
was quiet for a moment and Gloria's stomach began to ache
even more. "I am sure I did not do anything to make him think
I was a girl like that. But I know he is my boss and I have to be
respectful."

Sparkle let out a snort. The three roommates exchanged a
look that involved a lot of head nodding and hm'ming, none of
which Gloria could understand. Birdie reached across the table
and put her warm brown hand on Gloria's arm. She felt some of
the strain across her shoulders ease.

"Darlin' we don't think YOU did anything wrong. It's that
piece of horse dung that's your boss. How come you didn't tell us
sooner?"

She swallowed hard and tried to talk slowly. "On Friday he
was awful. Every time I turned around there he was right next
to me. What should I do?"

Sparkle leaned over and pulled her purse from under the table. She opened it carefully and pulled a long, silver knife from between the wallet, makeup and hairbrush stored there. When she pressed a button, a thin blade shot out with a barely audible snicking sound. "Here, carry this with you. The sucker gets too close again you just pull it out and let him see it. He won't be nearly so excited about being that close again, I guarantee it."

Gloria could feel her eyes widen in horror at the sight of the instrument.

Birdie chuckled beside her. "Ah'm thinking Gloria may not be quite the person for that sort of thing. Looks like we just need some ideas for how to have her handle this problem. Without weapons would be best."

Birdie had not released her arm and Gloria felt oddly comforted. This must be what it was like to have a regular mother.

"Or we get her off that crew." Annie was staring at the deadly blade as well, her mouth set in a thin line and eyes narrowed. Gloria stared at her tall roommate and felt a light sense of relief slip through her. It was almost like having Fred here to help. Annie was almost better than Fred. This woman had thought of something that would get Gloria out of the situation entirely instead of just living with it. She pushed that thought aside as disloyal to Fred.

"Think it would easier to stick him."

"Where in the world did you get that thing, Sparkle?"

"Don't matter to you."

Birdie finally stopped all the suggestions with a hand. "We got to be thinking about what she's gonna do on Monday. And I agree with Annie. Don't think Gloria's the kind gonna' stick somebody. How 'bout we talk to the other women on the crew? Maybe get them to help out. Maybe even try to get some of the fellas. Don't know anybody that likes Bartell too much."

Sparkle folded up the blade and no one spoke until she had placed it back in her purse. "I still think she needs the knife. But

I do know some guys on the crew. Maybe I could talk to them. See if they could do something."

The look on Sparkle's face made her uneasy. Gloria could never decide if Sparkle were being kind or making fun of her. She shook her head and felt the pain in her chest begin to ease. She thought maybe things weren't going to be quite so bad. Her roommates seemed to be taking on the situation with no hesitation.

Annie carefully picked up the cards Sparkle had spread on the table and returned them to the cardboard holder. "And if that doesn't work, I'll see if I can figure out who we could talk to at the union. We can figure this out somehow. It will be all right, Gloria. We'll back you up."

Gloria sighed and sat back. Suddenly the wrinkles and the dust on her blouses were no longer important.

Annie worried about Gloria for the next few days but there didn't seem to be much they could do except work with her crew to keep another woman around her as much as possible. It certainly wasn't the best solution but it did solve the problem for the moment. Annie continued to ponder a more permanent solution. The job was becoming more absorbing and life in the little trailer was always interesting, if not exactly restful. There seemed to be an underlying edge of tension with the four women that never really went away. When she had time to reflect, she was amazed that they managed as well as they did. She couldn't imagine four more different women living together. In Coos Bay she could have told you, with a great deal of accuracy, what most of her family and friends would be doing on any given day. In this place, nothing was predictable. She was beginning to enjoy it. She'd been putting in double shifts the last two days, working from seven in the morning to one thirty in the morning. And now, even walking home at two o'clock, she had no idea who would be home.

Natives of Washington kept insisting that this hot weather in June was freakish. Instead of the normal temperatures in the sixties, the thermometer had registered eighty during the day. Annie wondered if the war and all the bombs had anything to do with it, like she'd heard on the radio. Sometimes it seemed to her that people blamed everything on the war; two headed cows, stillborn children, the breakup of thirty-year marriages. She supposed that in some ways it was responsible for lots of things, but surely not for a week of hot weather in Seattle. The war had taken on a new reality since she'd been working. Not quite so gloriously patriotic but more like a plain hard job. That thought made her smile. Somehow it seemed easier to think of it as a job rather than being responsible for bringing peace to the world all on her own.

She bent down and tied her shoelace. She sure didn't need any light for the job. The moon was so bright you could drive rivets in a black plane without looking twice. She was half way home and the air was still and warm. She could hear crickets in the woods lining the sidewalk and smell sweet, dry summer grass from the lot next door. She liked this quiet part of the evening, walking the four blocks from the bus stop with no one to talk to, no one to listen to, certainly no one complaining. She'd decided that it was just natural that when you put a whole bunch of people together, somebody ended up complaining about something. Over all, she preferred swing shift to day shift since it was one of the few times she had time to think. So much had happened in the last few weeks that she hadn't had five minutes to sort out her feelings.

Yesterday she'd received two letters, one from Howard, and she'd had to think again. Think about him somewhere on a dusty battlefield in Africa. Think about him struggling everyday just to stay alive. He'd written about how he was looking forward to coming home and seeing his two children, seeing his mother, seeing his hunting dogs and, as a last minute addition, seeing Annie. The letter had the rather pedantic tone that their relationship had taken from the beginning with no escalation of feeling since. It was, of course, exactly as they had agreed during their initial discussions of marriage. It was just that it seemed the longer they were apart, the more she felt their friendly arrangement wasn't as appealing as it had been when they'd first agreed. Apprehension edged her consciousness. She couldn't believe how easy it was becoming to forget him.

With the extra shifts at Boeing and the constant job of living with three other women, she often thought of little else. After living with brothers all those years, she was finding living with three women quite an adjustment. Not bad really, just strange how they seemed to get under her skin more than the boys ever had. She supposed it was because they never let her get away with simply saying she didn't feel like talking. That just raised a red flag for them and they needled her until she said something. They were determined to hear all about her life.

Howard's letters were infrequent. He'd promised to write once or twice a month and she always sat down and wrote him right back, but the time in between began to stretch out into a life without him.

The second letter she'd received was from her father. He'd been terribly excited. He'd received a letter from her brother, Roger. They knew he was assigned to the U.S. 7th Army. As always, the letter had been heavily blacked out, so much so it was almost impossible to find a complete sentence. From what her father could determine, Roger had been promoted in the field. Apparently, most of the rest of his platoon was sick and Roger, showing no signs of the malady, was to lead the most able bodied of the group ashore. Her father had deciphered this from Roger having written 'It was worse than the night he, Annie and Phillip had taken the Aunt Lena out for a sail.'

Her father had deduced from these snippets of information that Roger had been part of the action in North Africa. There were troop landings and they'd heard the weather had been harrowing. A north wind, foul weather, short heavy swells had rendered over half the men seasick. As far as she knew, the battle was still going on. She hoped her brother still possessed his uncanny knack of staying one step ahead of disaster.

She rounded the corner of the trailer park and saw that someone had left the tiny light outside of the trailer turned on. With a smile, she climbed the steps, reaching up to rub the back of her neck. It would be wonderful to lie down and rest.

Opening the door, she stepped quietly inside to be met with a wave of heat. The smell of starch, fried potatoes and sweet perfume combined to give the room a strong, female fragrance. She thought about the cooler air outside, wishing she could sleep there but decided it was too late to make any changes now. Her sleeping bag was under Sparkle's bed and getting it out would wake everybody up. Shutting the door quietly behind her, she tiptoed to the back, careful not to step on the creaky spot on the floor next to the sink. The bedroom door was open and she slipped in, putting her feet down softly. In the dim light coming through the little window, she could make out the outline of Birdie's head. As she moved forward, she tried to remember if she had left her nightgown on the bed or if she would have to get it out of the cupboard that squeaked whenever it was opened.

Wham.

She stifled a yelp as her knee slammed into something in the dark, overcrowded room. She heard the crunch of glass under her heavy work boot and she lifted it quickly, hoping to change what had just happened.

The room was silent for the space of a few heartbeats then Birdie's voice cut through the darkness.

"What was that?" Sleep was over for the inhabitants of the sweltering trailer.

"Somebody get the lights, would you? I can't see a thing."

Moments later, the interior was cast into stark relief as the overhead light came on. Annie saw the drawer under Birdie's bed had been left open several inches and realized she had managed to crash right into it. Pushing aside the clothes hanging by a frayed rope strung across the room, she shoved the drawer closed with her foot.

The remains of Birdie's eyeglasses lay where the sole of her boot had trod. With a terrible sinking feeling in her stomach, she realized that they were ruined.

"Oh no, my glasses!" Birdie's wail was loud in the otherwise silent room, her brown arm reached out of the bed as she groped for the crushed spectacles inches from her hand.

Turning slowly, Annie saw that for a change, all three of her roommates were in residence. Gloria's unfocused, pale blue eyes peered from a break in the covers of her bed and Sparkle sprawled on a pile of light sheets thrown to one side of her lumpy mattress. No air was moving in the hot, sultry interior. Annie felt an itchy, close feeling and took a deep breath, trying to ignore the strong urge to turn and flee the overcrowded room. The silence seemed filled with condemnation. She finally cleared her throat.

"I'm really sorry, Birdie. I couldn't see anything." She stopped and chewed on her upper lip.

"Oh I know you din't mean it but another pair is gonna cost a fortune. I could feed my kids for three weeks on that money. It's gonna set me back bad. The darn things must'a fallen from the cupboard." Birdie had risen to a sitting position on her bunk with her arms tightly wrapped around her legs, rocking back and forth. She was looking up at the high shelf she normally put the spectacles on at night, safe but close at hand. Until tonight.

Annie's mouth was dry and she felt much bigger than her six-foot-two, one hundred and seventy pounds. She tried to think of what a new pair would cost, and what would happen if Birdie couldn't send her mother-in-law in Georgia enough money.

"I'm really sorry. Do you have a spare pair?"

"Sure woman, every po' color'd girl got a spare pair of glasses just settin' around."

Annie did the quick calculation of her savings in her head and spoke slowly. "I'll pay for a new pair. It's my fault."

The response was quick. "Ah'm not takin' charity from nobody."

"It's not charity, I broke them, I'll pay."

Gloria had jumped down from her bed and chimed in. "Birdie, it is not taking charity when someone ruins your things. It is just right."

"Nope." Birdie's voice was flat and cold. Annie opened her mouth to insist when she was interrupted by a voice from the front of their little metal home.

"Would you shut up? Some of us are trying to sleep here." Sparkle's voice was muffled as she pulled a thin, striped coverlet over herself.

Birdie threw her legs over the side of the bed. "Who you tellin' to shut up woman? You got no bis'nes bein' rude."

Sparkle rose from the bed, throwing the coverlet angrily off to the side. "I'm telling you to shut up, that's who. I just got to sleep and I'm tired. And another thing, I don't want to hear one more word about how bad off you are, or how much it takes to feed your brats! Fer' Christ's sake, there's a whole lot more in this world than just you and your stupid family."

Annie turned to say something and saw Gloria, her fist covering her mouth and eyes worried. Annie was at a loss. If this fight were between her brothers and herself, someone would start punching and the one with the luckiest hit would win. She didn't know what to do with these women snarling at each other. She shook her head. The low-level bickering that had been going on for the last month was finally out in the open. Gloria remained frozen, half on and half off her bed. She didn't seem to have any better clue as to what to do.

Small hard hands and knees pushed at her, trying to get by. Annie turned to clear the aisle and found Birdie ready to go after Sparkle. Startled by the short ball of fury, she held up her arm thinking that this was more like her kind of fight after all. She moved back into the aisle to restrain the charging figure.

"Hold on Birdie, I'm sure she didn't mean that. It's just so hot tonight. Let's . . ."

Birdie's angry voice rolled right over Annie's words. "Get outa' mah way. Since she started it, ah'd like to know how come she's so tired all the time. Where's she been getting to all these nights? How come she comes crawling in at all hours smelling like cheap perfume? And how come she got all those nice clothes and jewelry and stuff? Don't think she makes any more money than the rest of us."

Annie turned to Sparkle, careful to keep her full frame in the aisle blocking Birdie and preventing bloodshed. She felt like a dog between two fighting cats. Guiltily, she realized she was interested in hearing Sparkle's response to the rude question. She didn't have long to wait.

"Who do you think you are, my mother? Don't you be asking where I'm being, you trashy bitch. Just 'cause you're not in Georgia any more don't mean you turned white all of a sudden, niggah. And it ain't no bis'nes of yours where I get my stuff. If you hadn't been so stupid having all those kids maybe you'd have something other than some man's undershirt for night-clothes."

Annie's stomach tightened and she held up a hand as if to protect Birdie from the bruising words. Small fists pushed from behind again, harder and more demanding.

Birdie didn't appear to want or need protecting. "Ah might not have no pretty nighties, but at least I ain't dressing like no slut! You can see right through that outfit you got on now. And ah'm sure not too many peoples are lining up for the job of being your mother."

Annie smothered a grin. Her quick glance at Sparkle confirmed the analysis. The short woman stood there in the sheerest of nightgowns, her pale skin showing through the silky gauze. The long fluid line from shoulder to ankle was highlighted by the dark background and glaring light. Sparkle's appearance was definitely what her mother would have called 'unseemly'. She looked over at Birdie and saw Gloria's face go from a question mark of surprise to a faint smile.

"Slut! I'll show you, you bitch. As soon as I get past this big horse I'll take you down a notch or two!" Sparkle's voice had risen to a shriek and she began pushing on Annie's chest, her hands clenched in fists even harder and more demanding than Birdie's at the back.

Annie tried to get a hand on either one of the enraged women with no success. There was no room to maneuver down the middle of the trailer. With both women pummeling her she couldn't get herself into a position to stop either one.

"Bitch!" Birdie's voice had risen to a screech. "You let me past. You ain't saving that white trash no more."

Annie felt Sparkle back off slightly as if in response to the threat from Birdie. The pause gave her enough room to grab Sparkle's flying hands and hold on. They shuffled backward like two drunks while Annie tried to get Sparkle seated on her bed. Two steps away, she was hit from behind with a powerful wallop. They all went down in a pile of arms and legs and falling clothing.

Annie was in the middle. Sparkle on the bottom screaming, "You're squashing me! Get off . . ." and Birdie on top, still pounding away.

Annie tried talking with Birdie who was the more reasonable of the two. "Birdie get off, this isn't helping anything."

"I'm gonna kill her. She can't talk to me that way. Who does she think she is anyway?" Each breath was accompanied by more pounding on Annie's back.

"Oh gracious. Oh my word. For heaven's sake. Stop this minute." Gloria's voice was charged with hopeful authority. The only person not engaged in the fight was apparently trying to mediate.

They all stopped moving at the sound of the new voice and Annie felt Birdie cease her attack. Sliding carefully from between the two sweaty bodies, Annie rose. Only the pile of sheets on the bed separated Birdie and Sparkle. She stood on shaking knees, ready to put herself between the two if it looked like the battle would resume. Birdie's face had changed. She was looking at Gloria and Annie could have sworn the short woman was stifling a laugh.

Gloria continued speaking. "Now, this is better. We're all act-ing more civilized. Why don't we sit down and have a nice cup of tea and talk this whole thing through?" The girl's voice had taken on a syrupy, triumphant tone as she moved to light the tiny stove in the middle of the trailer. Her embroidered cotton bathrobe was cinched tightly around her waist.

That was all it took, Sparkle was galvanized. She rose from the bed as if starched by a overzealous cleaner and sprang for-ward on the attack, after the peacemaker this time.

"And who the hell are you to talk to us about anything? You with the wardrobe from hell. It's your fault Annie stepped on the glasses. This place isn't big enough for all four of us and you bring in enough clothes for an army. We can't use the end of this bed because of the your goddamn box full of 'little things'. Jeez woman, you're a nightmare to live with."

Annie was about to retort that she was getting tired of Sparkle's hair-trigger temper and her penchant for always voic-ing her opinion when Gloria stuttered out a response.

"Uh . . . Well, I did not think that . . ."

"That's the problem woman, you don' think 'bout anything but yourself. Just look at all that makeup you got hanging in the bathroom. It's enough to make even Annie pretty."

The room was suddenly still and Annie felt tightness in her throat, her jaw muscles squeezing hard.

Birdie cut in quickly. "Now there ain't no call to be rude there, Sparkle. There's nothing wrong with Annie that a good haircut and some nice clothes wouldn't cure." As soon as the words were spoken, Birdie's eyes widened and she gasped. She turned to Annie apologetically. "Now don't you be worryin' that I don't think you're pretty enough. I didn't mean that a t'all. It's just that . . ."

Annie swallowed. "It's okay Birdie, don't apologize. I know I'm no beauty. Most of the time it doesn't matter much. My fiancé thinks I look all right so I guess I'm not too bad."

CHAPTER THREE

The room was suddenly quiet again and Annie was aghast to find a slow trickle of tears running down her cheeks. She had no idea why she'd brought up Howard now. She scrubbed at the tears and tried to continue.

"Really, it's all right. Let's talk about something else. How about a beer? I think there's two left. They're cold and we could split them."

Birdie's mouth made a round little *o* of surprise and Gloria's forehead was vee'd so severely she looked like a deeply troubled squirrel. Sparkle had eased herself back so she was sitting on the rumpled sheets covering her bed.

Sparkle spoke first. "You have lived here, what, almost two months? And this is the first time you've mentioned you have a 'fiancé overseas?' Were you ever going to tell us? What the hell is this about?"

Birdie's voice sounded hurt. "Why didn't you tell us? You tol' us all about your momma and papa and brothers. Now you tell us you got a fiancé?"

Gloria was last. "Annie how could you? We are your friends."

Annie didn't know why she hadn't said anything before. At first it had somehow embarrassed her. And then it just never seemed the time to bring it up. She tried to think of some way that made it sound better than it was but finally settled for the truth. Her face started to feel warm.

"Well, it just never seemed to come up I guess."

"A fiancé who just never came up?" Gloria sounded hurt.

"Well, I guess I mean I didn't really know what to say about him." Annie's voice sounded funny in her own ears.

"Start talking woman." Sparkle commanded as she settled back in her bed against the red checked pillows.

"Yep. You got a lot of explaining to do." Birdie hoisted herself onto the portion of the bed not used by Sparkle. Annie felt relief begin to pierce through her guilt. These two, who were about to kill each other a minute ago, now seemed to have turned their interest on her in the blink of an eye.

Gloria had moved to the refrigerator and was holding out a coffee mug half filled with beer. "Here, Annie. Talk."

Annie gratefully reached for the mug and took a long swallow. "All right. His name is Howard and he has two children. We were going to be married before he left for the war but he was called up early and had to leave. He's a very nice man and his children are wonderful." Annie sighed and looked at her friends, rather pleased that it was finally out. She leaned against the cabinet and smiled.

Sparkle cocked an eyebrow. "That's it. His name is Howard and he has two children. And he's nice? You are not going to bed until you tell us all so you might as well just pull up that chair and one for Gloria and get on with it."

Annie looked at Birdie and Gloria. They agreed with Sparkle. She still couldn't believe how quickly this had changed from near war to interrogation. She shook her head, got the chairs from the back as ordered, and sat down. After taking a deep breath, she started her story. After every sentence or so, one of the three chimed in with a question or remark.

In the end, she told them the whole thing. It was a tale of a spinster who gauged her chances of getting married right next to the likelihood of her ever fitting into a size four skirt. It wasn't that she was so keen for marriage, it just seemed the logical thing to do. Mostly, it was of grave importance to her mother, that loving woman who, in equal measures, drove her crazy and made her yearn painfully to be just like her. She told them what she knew about Howard, a good man who thought it honorable to marry a friend who would be both a companion to him when he returned from the war and a mother for his children. Tidy and respectable. And he was a very good man. She told of him asking her to marry him. The occasion had been short on romance and incredibly long on a kind of tenderness that she'd grown to appreciate. When she was finished, her friends were quiet.

Finally, Sparkle shook her head. "I don't know what to think, girl. That's about the least romantic thing I've ever heard."

Annie felt a pang run through her and wondered if she'd made Howard sound too boring. She started to protest. Sparkle held up a hand, her red colored fingernails reflecting the dim light over the stove.

"Now, don't get your pants in a twist. I'm not saying anything about the man. Just seems like a strange thing that you've never mentioned him before. And when you do, you can't wait to get done. Kinda makes you wonder, don't it?" She'd turned her head as if to check on Birdie and Gloria's opinion. The dual nods of assent were quick and positive.

Annie's surprise had become annoyance. She should defend Howard. But on the other hand, she was very tired and the trailer seemed homey and comfortable again, so she just sat back and smiled. The three women would never be able to appreciate what a good friend he had always been. They didn't understand how hard it was to have first one friend, then another marry and start families and be left with no offers, not even one she could turn down. Howard had done her a mighty favor. It just seemed awfully hard to explain to her roommates.

"Birdie what is this . . . this . . . stuff?" Birdie laughed at the look on Gloria's face. With her mouth puckered and nose wrinkled she looked like a puzzled two year old.

"It's chicory coffee. You git used to it after a spell. Kinda spoils you for the real stuff." A feeling of quiet settled on Birdie and she put down the pot. A warm breeze came through the tiny window over the kitchen sink and slid past her.

They'd been together in the trailer over two months now and Birdie could feel herself relax more each day. She'd finally gotten the hang of bucking and was beginning to learn riveting thanks to Annie and Jonathan. She was good enough to hold her own and didn't have to worry about losing her job. Harder to accept was the fact that Annie had indeed, paid for her new glasses. She still wasn't comfortable with it, but when it became apparent that she couldn't see well enough to work, she'd been forced to take the money and get another pair.

And, she'd begun to do the cooking in the trailer. She liked the warmth of real smiles when the other women ate. Annie had talked the other two into letting Birdie skip paying her share for the food, as long as she made some sort of breakfast and dinner for all of them. She grinned when she thought about the tall redhead. Now there was a woman with a good soul. Birdie wondered if Annie would ever get past being so shy and reserved.

She was pretty happy with the sleeping arrangements. Annie was an easy roommate; generally quiet and mindful of her own part of the bedroom. She could tell that the tall woman wasn't used to having a Negro around. She sort of tiptoed about her and tried to act natural. But she worked at being fair and that was quite a bit more than most people. Since the battle three nights ago in the trailer, she was beginning to think they were going to be all right. Birdie was very pleased she hadn't ended up sleeping in the bed made from lowering the tabletop. Sparkle was often woken up when someone came home late.

It tickled Birdie to watch Gloria try to think of something nice to say about the chicory coffee. The girl was such a mixed-up mess of straight-laced worry about other people's feelings that she seldom said what she meant about anything. She tried to remember if she was that flighty at nineteen but decided the idea of measuring her life against the rich girl's was silly.

Gloria let out a sigh, rose slowly from the tiny dinette table and reached for the sack of groceries she had just carried home.

"I do not think I am likely to be spoiled for real coffee anytime soon, thank you. I hate to shop and then have to carry everything home by bus. These sacks are heavy. What are you cooking? It smells awfully good. I sure wish one of us had a car. And look at this." She spread the remaining coupons on the table. "I think I mixed up the coupons again. I thought it was every other day that we got meat but the man said no, we could get more today if I wanted to but you didn't put it on my list so I didn't get any. And another thing, why is coffee rationed?" Gloria sounded peevish. "It is just a few beans for heaven's sake. Metal, sure, we have to make planes and bullets, but why coffee?" The girl was angrily pushing the cans into the tiny cupboard.

Birdie hid a smile. It wasn't often that they would see Gloria in a bad temper. "Whoa girl, I'll put those away. I need them in one piece, along with the cabinet." Gloria made a sniffing noise but stepped over to the dinette and sat down, pulling her knees up and wrapping her arms around her legs. When she was settled and Birdie was done with putting the supplies away, she moved to the other side of the table and sat down, taking a long swallow of her own coffee before trying to explain rationing.

"I'm cooking beef stew with the smallest pieces of meat in the world and a bunch of 'tatoes. The reason coffee is rationed is that it takes men and ships to grow and move the beans. What we're doin' now is using those men and ships to grow and haul only the things that we need to survive and win the war. Coffee just ain't one of them."

Birdie sighed, once again thinking that, for an educated person, Gloria seemed to have trouble putting all the pieces together. The only one of them with part of a college education and it appeared she'd never had to think much before. But, Birdie did appreciate the girl's easy good manners and cool head. They were a Godsend in this trailer of strong personalities.

Chicory coffee was as common to her as early morning and the smell of wisteria on the front porch. She put a hand over her mug to catch warmth from the steaming liquid. The afternoon was losing the soft edge of heat and she shivered, wondering if she'd ever be warm again. She longed for the long, hot evenings of her Georgia home.

The sound of heels clattering on the steps announced that Sparkle had returned. Birdie pulled her mug from the table and stood back from the door. She and Sparkle were miles from being friends. It was a shame really, under all that bluster the little spit-fire was a pretty good person. As Birdie watched, Sparkle threw open the door and surveyed the two occupants of the trailer.

"So what are you two doing sitting around here moping? It's Friday night and you haven't even changed out of your work clothes yet. Are you planning on staying here like a couple of lumps all night?"

Sparkle stood in the doorway, one hand on her hip and the other planted on the doorframe. Birdie tried not to stare. Sparkle's blouse and skirt were the same material and cut as lots of women at the plant, but a few tucks here and there and the outfit molded to the woman's remarkable frame, making you blink when you saw her. It amazed her what Sparkle could do with that old sewing machine. Birdie couldn't imagine when she'd changed her normal work shoes for high heels.

Gloria's voice was soft and calming, in contrast with Sparkle's mocking tone. "No we are not going to sit here all night. Annie is coming after her shift and we're going to the movies. We are going to see that new James Cagney film, *Yankee Doodle Dandy*. And we are not moping. Birdie was just having me try this wonderful new coffee. Here, take a sip, I think you will love it."

Birdie looked at Gloria sharply. The girl's face was smooth and free of any hint of guile. She could have sworn Gloria did-n't have it in her. Stifling a snort of laughter, she reminded her-self not to underestimate people.

"Coffee huh? Where'd you ever get it? It's been weeks since we've had any."

Sparkle clicked her way to the stove and grabbed a blue mug sitting on the drainboard. Putting it down on the counter she poured herself a full cup of the brew, then sat where Birdie had been earlier and propped her feet up against the red box containing the cleaning supplies for the kitchen.

With a sigh, she breathed in deeply. "This smells more like charred wood to me. But it's been too long since we've had any. Time we got some."

She pulled the cup from the table and put it to her lips, taking a drink with a smile of anticipation on her face. The look changed immediately to something else and her feet hit the floor with a thud. Her lips puckered tightly into a funnel of disapproval and Birdie thought for a moment that Sparkle was going to spit the whole mouthful onto the table. Gloria let out a gasp of laughter.

Birdie stepped back, afraid she might be hit with the spraying liquid. Finally, with a huge effort, Sparkle swallowed.

When the blond found her voice, her tone was harsh. "Which one of you idiots made this horse piss? And what the hell is it?" Sparkle's mouth was pursed and two deep lines ran from the sides of her nose to the bottom of her face, accentuating the tongue sticking out. Her rude, accusing words had the effect of squelching Gloria who grabbed for the white hanky tucked in her blouse pocket and dabbed at her eyes.

Birdie cleared her throat and tried not to grin. "Cain't believe you don't like it, Sparkle. Comes from down home and its called chicory. Supposed to take the place of coffee. I sort of like the taste myself. I guess this means you don't?"

"Got that right. Shee-it, that was really awful." Sparkle pushed the offending cup to the middle of the table and put both elbows on the surface, placing her chin on her hands. "I can't believe you two never want to do anything more exciting than drinking rotten coffee and going to the movies. Don't you get bored? You'd think the three of you were joined at the hip or something. There's a party going on tonight at Lou Purcell's. Why don't you come along and have a little excitement for a change?"

Birdie saw Gloria's face pinch tight and had to agree with her thoughts. The shabby white Purcell house was about four blocks from them on California Street. People were always coming and going and there seemed to be a perpetual party at the residence. She'd heard they made their own rum in a bathtub just like they'd done during prohibition. She didn't object to the booze as much as the type of people. She'd known their sort and was familiar with the kind of trouble they attracted.

Scowling, she faced Sparkle. "Not likely we're going there. Them's some trashy people. We'll just wait for Annie. You run along, though, don't let us slow you down."

Sparkle's head whipped around and she glared. Birdie stared back, keeping her gaze level. This state of affairs reminded Birdie of a dog they once had, ready to bite at any time. If you showed fear, the dog would go for you before you could blink. They'd handled him by ignoring the growls and not turning their backs on him. After a couple of years he'd finally decided they weren't going to beat him and relaxed. She hoped it wouldn't take years with Sparkle.

Finally Sparkle lowered her eyes and shrugged, turning to look at Gloria. "So, why isn't your precious Annie here now? It's five thirty. Her shift's been over for over an hour."

Gloria had recovered from her fit of laughing and was composed again. "I am not sure why she is late. I wish she would hurry. If the line is too long we might not get in." Gloria twisted around in her seat and peered out the window, as if Annie might suddenly appear because they'd talked about her.

Sparkle's voice was jeering. "I'll bet she's still working. Thinks she's hot stuff, working two shifts in a row. She's just really big and dumb is all."

Birdie bit down on a hard nugget of anger. Before she could speak, Gloria cut in. "That is not fair. Annie is one of the smartest people I know. Just look at how she fixed the toaster and the outside steps when they started wobbling."

Sparkle's mouth went flat and a cynical line appeared above her eyebrows. She stared at Gloria. Birdie thought about her old dog and decided she couldn't back down.

"Gloria's right, you got no call to be sayin' Annie's stupid. And the reason she works extra shifts is that she can and feels it's her obligation. Most of us are so tired we can't see straight after one shift. She's just been steppin' in when someone doesn't show up is all." She paused and slowly placed her cup in the sink. "Someone like you. Didn't you miss a night las' week?"

"I did not." Sparkle spoke before Birdie got the last word out. "I was a couple of hours late but that's it. What you doing woman, watchin' me?"

"No. It's just hard to miss that somebody's still sleeping when her shift is startin' in less than an hour." Birdie tried to keep her voice calm. Their talk was going nowhere. She motioned for Gloria to move over so she could sit at the table. Ever since Sparkle had accepted a position on the night shift drilling holes for the rivets, she'd been acting as if she were somehow better than the rest. Birdie couldn't stop herself from needling the woman. Annie had heard about the position and encouraged Sparkle to apply. Birdie had thought about making the same change but decided she'd had quite enough trouble just doing the riveting and didn't need the extra pain trying to learn a new job.

Sparkle's expression changed from an angry frown to a calculating one. "Well, I think Annie's expecting something special from the big boys."

Birdie sighed and looked at the other woman. "More likely she's doing somebody a favor. Seems to me she tries to carry around the 'sponsibility of the whole war on her shoulders. Mos' times the woman is too soft. She looks so big but any time somebody needs something or can't get the work done themselves, there's Annie, he'ppin out."

"And another thing," Gloria didn't want to be left out of the defense of Annie, "she never tells anyone, just does the job and goes on. She stopped to help the Gonzales out when their car was broken down on the road. They told me she spent over two hours helping them. And never told us anything about it. How many of us would do that?"

Sparkle sat back on the bench seat, her mouth settling into a flat line of annoyance then let out a sniff. "Well, how many of us could? And it's just swell being so noble but where does it get her? Like tonight. I'll bet you she's late and you end up going to the show without her. Why doesn't she just tell them she can't? Doing favors for people doesn't get you anywhere."

A crooked line of sunlight from the window moved and fell on Sparkle's face, then the clock behind her. Birdie looked at them both and jumped.

"Golly, it's after six. Gloria, go change your blouse or whatever you need to do and let's try to catch the quarter pas' bus." Gloria started to say something but Birdie waved her hands and told her to get going. As the girl hurried to the back of the trailer, Birdie turned to look at Sparkle still seated at the table.

"You know you could come if you wanted to." Birdie wondered if Sparkle would ever let down her defenses enough to trust anyone. "But I surely don't want you to be bored."

For a moment it looked as if she might join them. But then Sparkle's eyes narrowed and she waved her hand for them to go.

"Nah, you go ahead. It'd ruin my image to be seen in the company of the likes of you two."

Cain Adamson rubbed the back of his neck, trying to work out the knots. Not for the first time in his life, he wished he were a bit shorter. On school teams, he'd been chosen first because everyone thought he should be good at sports, even though he'd never demonstrated any particular ability. In the war the tallest man made a fine target for the enemy. Right now the worktable he and John had commandeered to spread out the plans was too short and caused him to bend over just to make out the lines on the paper. The long table was pushed close to the first in a series of rows of B-17 tail sections and although the overhead lights were bright, this area of the shop always seemed a little darker. The real problem was that this particular set of plans didn't seem to have any relation to the sections beside them. He'd laughed at the joke about having the guys making up the plans actually build the plane to their specifications. Some of the planners were good but the man who had drawn this one probably had never built anything in his life.

John Fielding, his friend and co-worker, was talking but Cain was listening with only half his attention. Glancing over, he noticed the large cuffs on the bottom of John's pants and grinned. His friend wore the typical khaki work clothes but the sleeves and pant legs were turned up almost a foot to accommodate his bulky frame and short stature. John's constant grin had caused crinkles like tiny bird tracks, at the outer edges of his eyes. As opposite as they were in physical appearance, they enjoyed many of the same things. They both liked the challenge of making things work and both hated the speed with which the war mandated they complete these projects. They were methodical in nature, wanting to be sure everything was perfect before letting the project go. Someone once said if it were up to the two of them to get the planes out the door, the war would be over and they'd still be measuring one more time before cutting. He took a deep breath, remembering the look and feel of the pine furniture he'd made for his mom back home in Montana. Every cut was precise and every dovetail fit perfectly into its counterpart.

Cain shook his head and reached for the package of cigarettes in his shirt pocket. Remembering where he was, he sighed settling for the promise of a smoke at lunch. He could see that John was expecting an answer and realized he hadn't been paying attention at all.

"What?"

John let out an exasperated grunt. "Sheesh man, where were you? I want to know how come you got off that cushy trainer job? Sounded like swell duty to me. Lots easier than this."

"Have you ever tried to train someone?"

"Well, no."

John stood back from the table and pulled out a stool that was rounded off on the sides from the hundreds of rear ends that had rested there. He eased himself onto the seat and rolled his shoulders backward and forward.

"Nobody ever asked." His tone held a trace of injured pride.

Cain looked at his friend and wondered why no one had asked him to train new workers. He was certainly capable, probably more so than Cain. He was decidedly more patient.

"Trust me buddy, it's not so easy. Eight hours of swinging a hammer never made me that tired. After a full shift of trying to teach people how to rivet, drill and buck, I nearly didn't make it home some nights." He remembered that first week of being an official trainer and drew in a deep breath. He still couldn't believe the questions like: Which end of the bit goes in the drill? Why do I have to plug it in? When do we get a break? Why do we have to fill all the holes, couldn't we just do every other one? Just keeping up with fourteen inexperienced people had almost driven him nuts. The only thing that had kept him moving during that time was the thought of a stiff shot of Jack Daniels when he got home. That and the fact that during his last week of training, he'd met Annie Tosh.

He reached up and ran his finger down the scar on his face then stretched out his leg, trying to relieve the cramps that plagued him after being on his feet too long. He took a deep breath then smiled as he thought again of the tall redhead with the soft brown eyes. There was a puzzle for you. Smoothing his mustache with a forefinger, he stared at his friend.

"John, what do you know about Annie Tosh. Don't you work on the same crew as her roommate?"

John smirked, his eyes wide and mocking. "That Sparkle, now there's a pistol for you. I thought at first she was just another skirt but boy, don't mess with her, she'll rip you apart. I wondered when you'd get around to asking me about Annie. She's something isn't she? About as big and strong a gal as I've ever met. Kind of good looking too in a tough way. Damned smart female too."

Cain looked at his friend in surprise. "Annie? Tough? I don't think so." His impression had been quiet and somehow powerful in the most female way he'd ever seen. He thought of the last time he'd seen her in training and felt a rush of heat course through him. She'd been helping Birdie drill out holes in an area so awkward that Annie'd had to bend almost double to help. While leaning over, her blouse had slipped open far enough to reveal the smooth white top of her breast. He'd been immediately aroused and had to turn away, thinking furiously of his mother's eternal lectures on the proper protocol with women. When he'd looked back, she'd been upright again, her blouse adjusted to its modest closure just under her collarbone. Relief and disappointment had hit him at the same time.

He'd been happy to know that his body still worked as it should. He didn't remember a time in the last six months he'd been interested enough to look much less get excited. Not at all like when he was younger. He'd been a hell of a randy buck back then, deserving of the lectures from his mother.

He'd watched as Annie'd drilled several of the holes before returning the tool to Birdie so quickly that no one but he was aware there'd been any helping. She'd worked calmly, bestowing her slow quiet smile on those around her. The combination of the sight of Annie's powerful female body and her smooth handling of the situation had given him an unsteady, almost light-headed feeling.

He'd dated many women in his life but it had always seemed as if he had lots of time to make a decision about marriage and children, until the war had loomed. After the attack on Pearl Harbor, he'd been in such a hurry to get into the action that he'd asked his girlfriend of four years, a tiny blond named Bitsy, to wait until he'd returned and then they could have the wedding she'd always wanted. She'd cried but he'd been insistent. She'd always talked about a huge ceremony in the Methodist church on the hill with all their family and friends. Besides, he'd told her, once they got in, old Jerry didn't have a chance. They'd all be home in no time.

Along with the letters from his Mom he'd gotten a windfall of letters from Bitsy every time they stopped long enough to collect the mail. Then on a fine spring morning when they were bivouacked in a dusty valley outside Bizerte in Tunisia, the

Jeep carrying all the mail had unloaded six letters from Bitsy, a jackpot. He'd carefully read them in date order. The first five told him how much she loved him, the sixth said that she'd met someone new and would be marrying within the month. Even now, almost a year later, his hand shook and his mouth went dry when he opened any letter. This damned war ruined everything. He knew Bitsy would never have done anything remotely like that if it weren't for the war. It just plain scared everybody. His manner of dealing with it had been to sign up instantly. Her method had been to find someone and try to hang on to him.

He picked up a pencil sitting next to the plans and drew several quick, rough lines around the areas that he didn't understand. He tried to shake off the bitter memory but it didn't want to leave. The image of the day he'd received the batch of letters was a clear picture in his head.

By that spring morning, the wedding had been over for a week. He'd nearly choked when he'd read the last one and tears of helplessness had overwhelmed him so he'd had to turn away from the group. It was a betrayal of the very worst kind. The others in his platoon had just laughed. Not only wasn't he the first, they'd insisted he wouldn't be the last. Orville had even said they'd all be bachelors by the time this war was over. Their motto had been lucky in a fight, unlucky in love. It was the fourth 'Dear John' letter their group of eight had received since they'd left home. They'd all met in boot camp and then been stationed in the same platoon in Africa. As the war progressed and they were in more and more battles, they became superstitious about the fact that none of them had been injured badly enough to warrant a trip home. They were pretty sure their number of kiss-off letters, as Paul called them, must have been a record.

He wished he hadn't started thinking about Bitsy. After he'd caught the shell piece in his leg, it seemed that everything that happened was determined to add to the helpless feeling he'd had when he'd received that letter. He made a promise to himself he would never again make the mistake of waiting too long. But since coming back to the States, nothing had been easy. The

look of swiftly concealed pity on his nurse's face when she saw
the awful scar the shell had left on his leg was indelibly print-
ed on his mind. He walked to minimize the limp but he knew
people didn't look at him the way they used too. The worst was
the hollow, black feeling that always lurked, ready to strike
when he least expected it.

Noise from someone drilling inside a tail section behind
them brought him back and he focused on John. "What do women
think of a guy with a limp?"

The creases beside John's eyes became deeper. "My sister
thinks they're romantic. But then, my sister is twelve."

Remembering the look on the nurse's face, he gazed at John
and said aloud something he'd thought about but never spoken
before. "I hate it when people pity me. Makes me sick."

John stopped smiling and tapped his foot lightly on the
table. "I know what you mean. I get something like that because
I'm so short. Sometimes people stare at me like I'm strange."

Cain felt his eyes widen. He couldn't think what to say. It
had never occurred to him that being short was that much of a
deal. Finally he just said the only thing that came to mind.

"Yeah, I guess it's not so great being different from the aver-
age guy."

Mostly, Cain didn't care what people thought of him. He figured that if the pain would go away, he could handle anything.
But talking about the tall redhead made him wonder.

"Annie is something though, isn't she? Do you know where
she's from?"

"Some place in Oregon. I overheard Sparkle talking about
her with a guy on the crew. Seems she's engaged or something
to a petty officer in the Navy."

Cain let out a breath while a cold finger of disappointment
traced down his back. The scene John's words brought to mind
was hard-edged, black and white. Cain did not want to be interested in this woman.

John spoke in a bemused tone. "The way the roommate tells
it, the guy's not much and Annie just told him she'd marry him

to be nice. Kind of a shame with a woman like that. Sparkle says Annie's pretty straight. Won't even think about going back on her word."

Just about everything he'd heard about this woman intrigued the hell out of him. He wondered if the 'not much' guy might be back home anytime soon. He thought about it for a moment and then decided he didn't have anything against somebody changing her mind, he just hated the idea of being thousands of miles away and getting a letter that didn't give you a chance to compete.

He hadn't had the energy to be attracted to anyone for so long that he was surprised he was interested enough to try to figure a way around a fiancé. For just a second, a dark thought snaked through his mind and he considered if the fiancé were in the heavy fighting and if he would even make it home. He shook his head. He thought of Annie then wondered how she would feel about being friends with a gimpy Montanan with some nasty scars. Friends at least until the fiancé showed up.

"What say we take these back to the shop and find out what the heck they mean?" John spoke loudly. "We could stand here forever trying to figure it out ourselves."

Cain looked again at the plans and realized he hadn't actually been seeing them for awhile. "Okay. I don't know if they can help but maybe just moving around will. I don't seem to be able to concentrate."

John snorted and gave his friend a quick punch in the arm. "I think you're concentrating fine. Just not on work."

Cain smiled then rolled up the plans. "You might be right." As they walked toward the front of the plant he tried to ignore the familiar knife of pain that gripped his leg. When the throbbing eased up, he moved a little faster and caught up with John.

At two o'clock in the morning, Sparkle was having trouble focusing on her drilling. For weeks now, she'd been working the graveyard shift at Shop 301 and she was so tired from not being able to sleep during the day that she had to think about everything she did. There simply wasn't enough noise and action on this shift to keep her attention. The plant hummed with workers, but not at the same intense pace as the day shift. She did enjoy having the daylight hours off even if she was always weary from not getting enough sleep.

She pushed hard on the drill and forced one more hole through the aluminum skin then stopped, thinking of the day that she'd refused to accompany the others to a movie. For some reason, she was having trouble clearing the incident from her mind. She'd never been comfortable around a bunch a gabby women. They generally made her throat tighten up and her head ache, but this group was different. If it wasn't that they had to live nearly on top of each other, she thought she might get to like them.

All except that Birdie, of course. She'd told the others right out. That nigger needed to go. Didn't need to be living with white women, but they wouldn't listen. Didn't even really seem to care and that sure bothered her. She may not know much, but she sure knew that she was better than any blackie. That was about the only thing her sorry mother had taught her. The thought of her mother brought her back to the present like a step into that cold Wyskogy River.

She shifted where she was kneeling on the side of the fuselage and tried to get blood running through her legs again. Moving her arms forward, she attempted to lean into the drill but it was no use. The angle was so awkward that all she could do was use what little muscle power she had in her hands and fingers, just enough to keep the drill bit going in with agonizing slowness. And just about the time she thought she had the damn thing in, sweat would run into her eyes and she couldn't see what she was doing. She put the heavy drill down for a second and looked up at the scribe marks telling her where to drill along the exterior of the center section. The line seemed to go on forever. She yawned and wished it were closer to the end of shift.

It felt like she'd been drilling rivet holes her whole life and the smell of greasy dirt and reused oil kept getting stronger as she climbed up and over and around the aluminum skin of the fuselage. Her nose itched and she felt a sneeze coming on only to retreat after a minute, leaving her irritated. Trying to get herself into a more comfortable position, she lost her footing and nearly slipped into the neat row of Clecos just installed behind her.

"Watch out, I don't want to have to do those again." Ethel, the woman putting the holders in, gave her a shove forward. Sparkle knew she was tired, she didn't even react to the rude words or the push. She'd decided that this shift would probably kill her. Annie was right, she was learning something new. Drilling holes was a different skill from riveting or bucking. But the only extra money she was making so far came from the increased pay for working the late shift, not from any pay increase for the new job responsibilities. She and Ethel were just finishing up on this set of sections and then the day shift would work on them in the morning.

She hadn't realized how easy bucking or even driving rivets home through the damn Cleco tubes had been until she found herself trying to make the hole in the metal skin for those tubes. Making sure that she drilled the exact spot where the stringers and formers met was frustrating, even with lines to follow. She wanted to give Ethel a kick just on general principle, but decided that it would take more energy than she had.

With an effort, she straightened up and gazed at the row of center sections ahead, each looking like a metal skeleton imbedded in a floor of gray scaffolding. Those structures of wood and metal seemed to stretch on for miles. And just when you thought that was more unfinished work than you ever wanted to see in your life, a row of tail sections started and it went on for more miles. Leaning her forehead against the cool surface of the metal, she decided that she just wouldn't look at them anymore. Straightening up, she yawned then stretched out her arm, positioned the drill and pulled the trigger, only to have the drill kick backwards into her hand. She swore then checked the tool to find that the bit had snapped off almost clean against the tightened jaws of the chuck that held it in place. She turned to Ethel who was waiting, her mouth set in a straight, tight line, to put in more Clecos in the holes Sparkle hadn't drilled yet.

"Looks like it's just about time for lunch break anyway. I need to get another drill bit. You coming?"

"It's ten minutes early."

"Who the hell's gonna notice? We're here almost by ourselves with a coupla' million holes to drill. What's ten minutes? And we can't do anything until I have something to drill with."

Ethel stood with lips pursed and cheeks sucked in. Sparkle could see she wasn't about to break any rules, she'd be standing in the same spot with no holes to fill for the next ten minutes, no matter what Sparkle did. The sour looking woman wasn't really that bad to work with, she was quiet, but she was simply unable to do anything that she wasn't told to do. Suppressing an urge to yell at the woman, she shoved the drill into the holder on her tool belt and turned, making her way along the scaffolding. She grabbed the handrails flanking the shaky metal steps and climbed down to the floor of the plant fifteen feet below.

She stopped and drew a deep breath of the fresher air. Grabbing the tool again, she tugged the key for the chuck from its position taped to the drill and unscrewed the jaws holding the broken bit. As she dropped the round piece of metal into her pocket, she felt the spiral cut in the bit. Why in the world was the mechanism holding the bit in place called a chuck? Reaching for her pack of cigarettes, she shoved aside the long cord connecting the drill to the air source. She pulled the red-labeled cigarette package out, feeling an overwhelming urge to relieve the tightness in her lungs.

"You're not supposed to be smoking in here you know."

Sparkle turned to find Nate Thorne, the fifteen year old apprentice close to her. He alternated work and school, two months at the plant, then high school for the other two. He was a big boy, well over six feet tall and showed signs of being good looking once the baby fat left his frame. Thick, blond hair hung over one eyebrow and his blue cardigan sweater was unbuttoned, giving him a casual look. His face was a mixture of hope and leer.

"Maybe you'd like to come outside with me and we could, you know, spend a little time together."

Sparkle's fingers tightened on the drill. His knowing look made her stomach sink. He must have heard the rumors about her. Her shoulders ached from the continuous drilling and her head throbbed from too many hours of screeching metal and not enough sleep.

She scratched her arm and tried to wipe off the thin film of aluminum dust. "Nate, you're a nice kid but I don't need this right now."

When she was younger she'd taken on these young ones, sometimes even for free. It had been sort of fun. All that intense excitement in so short a time. But after months of heavy work in the shop and only the occasional trick, she was too tired to want anything more than a hot bath. She was surprised that she felt bored with men in general. When she first got into the game, it had been the most exciting, powerful thing she'd ever done. Now, it seemed to be a bother.

She began to walk away, trying to finger one cigarette out of her pack. Nate moved just enough to block her path. His hips pushed forward and one hand was wrapped around the metal leg of the scaffolding. She could see a fine film of sweat on his cheeks.

"Joe said all I needed was money and I've got that, see? I wouldn't, like, expect this for free or anything." He fumbled in his back pocket for his wallet.

Sparkle's teeth clenched. She looked past his arm to see if anyone was watching, angry at the thought of someone seeing her being backed against the wall by a kid. Nate had pushed her just far enough under the steps and up against a solid wall to be in the shadows thrown by the huge overhead lights. With a start, she realized that she would really like to leave her past behind.

The closest men stood twenty yards away and were bent over a worktable with pieces of a rivet gun spread out in front of them. She would bet money that Ethel was still standing above, watching the clock for the exact second that the break officially started. She would take care of this without an audience. Her arm muscles tightened. Feeling the press of wood from the scaffold steps on her shoulder, she addressed the boy.

"Move it, would you? The grown-ups are working here." She started forward again, her heart beating faster than normal, a sure sign anger was about to take over. He shuffled back a bit but not enough to give her room. She snarled at him. "Godammit kid, I said get your butt outta my way."

Nate hesitated, his eyebrows raised in a question, then he leaned forward, pushing his chest near her face. She could smell hot, anxious sweat as he dropped the other arm onto her right shoulder. He was so close that it was impossible to squeeze past.

She tensed her leg, about to raise her knee when she realized she still had the drill in her hand. Her mouth turned upward in a smile as she pushed the open chuck of the drill into the loose weave of his sweater and pulled the trigger, for once enjoying the kickback of the unit. In seconds, Nate was gasping and backing up, his mouth open and eyes wide. Sparkle felt a rush of satisfaction as the tool turned, catching in layers of yarn as it wound around the chuck.

"What the . . .." Nate's voice was high and anxious and his hands batted at Sparkle as if to push her away without getting near the still turning drill. He stumbled and his head thudded on the stairs now blocking his way.

In seconds, the sweater had turned and twisted, pulling forward on one side and drawing up tightly on the other. Nate's face looked bleached and his lips made little sucking noises. She could feel the drill begin to labor as the material filled the chuck. She let up on the trigger and watched him try to squirm out of the cardigan.

"Don't ever, ever try that kind of shit again. This time it's a sweater. Next time might be your pants. You're way the hell outta your league, buddy." Nate's mouth had stopped moving and his head turned from side to side. Obviously it was his turn to see if anyone else was watching.

Pulling backwards, Sparkle tried to untangle the yarn from the chuck only to have it twist worse as she did. Disgusted, she let the gun drop from her hand. It landed with a thud on the floor, stretching the sweater farther and pulling Nate with it. She didn't look back as she shoved him from her and stepped around, making her way toward the plant's main exit door and pulling the cigarette loose at the same time.

She wondered if it would ever stop. For the first time since she'd been paid the huge sum of ten cents to lay with Joey Coyle, her stomach churned at the thought of one more man. Maybe it was time to quit the game. It had been exciting at first, watching men turn from strong and all-powerful to needing her, even begging sometimes. But for the last couple of years it had been just the money.

A little jar of recognition ran through her. Even though she was pretty sure her roommates might have guessed that she'd been a whore, they didn't know for sure and she would really like to keep it that way. She was quite happy that these women accepted her. If she stopped now, the three of them might just forget it. She had a feeling that Birdie would be all right. She'd been around enough to know that things and people change. Gloria would go whichever way Annie went. She took a long, slow drag on her cigarette. Annie was brutally honest and Sparkle figured the situation was a first for her.

A thought struck her. She had no idea how much money was enough. With a sigh she dropped the cigarette to the ground, grinding it out with her heel and wondered just how she was going to figure that out. She thought about her roommates. They all seemed to have some idea of what they wanted to do. She didn't have any idea how to make up a plan, but now she had some women she might consider asking.

CHAPTER FOUR

The warm July air felt soft on Annie's skin and for once there wasn't a cloud in the sky. Annie stood apart from her section group and watched as they laughed at another of the never ending war jokes. She enjoyed the momentary peace from the noise inside the plant. Gazing around, she thought that half the plant must have decided to spend lunch breaktime outside. She breathed in and caught the scent of newly cut wood. A crew had begun cutting up a packing crate and sawdust lay around the area in little mounds. She wondered idly what they were planning to do with the four-foot lengths they'd created.

Annie spotted Cain Adamson in the crowd, standing alone. He was leaning against the rough metal of the plant exterior, knee bent and his foot placed on the wall. His eyes were closed and she gazed at him, noting the way his shoulders and chest stretched the red plaid of his shirt. Thin as he was, the round curve of muscle was apparent under the material. The gentle afternoon sun fell on blue-black hair, making it shine like glossy bird wings. Quick warmth ran from her chest down to her belly. She shook her head and tried to ignore the sudden sensation.

It was ridiculous. There was something about the comfortable way he stood balanced with shoulders and one foot braced against the wall that made her want to touch him. She couldn't understand the feeling. It made her anxious and excited at the same time. She looked back to see that he had not moved. His hand, balanced on the raised leg, held a cigarette.

She felt her face flush. Even thinking about the incident at the training session made her want to hide. Annie should talk with him. She had promised her roommates, the night Gloria had told them about her troubles, that she would speak with Cain. The talk they'd had with Gloria's own shop steward had been a joke. He'd looked at them as though they were telling him a very bad, off-color joke. He'd seemed embarrassed and asked them not to spread this kind of talk around as it was bad for morale. They had tried for the next two weeks to find someone else who might be able to help. At last they'd given up and voted that Annie should speak with Cain. He was also a union steward. They'd thought he might be able to help.

Taking a deep breath, she started forward, ignoring the sudden feeling of weighted legs. As she neared him, she cleared her throat, not wanting to startle him. He jumped and the foot resting on the wall hit the ground with a thud while he bent forward, arms thrust ahead in what looked like a defensive position. The cigarette flipped from his hand, landing in the dirt two feet away. Annie stepped back.

He straightened and muttered something unintelligible.

"Pardon me?" Annie could feel heat coming from her neck and rising to her cheeks.

"Oh nothing." He moved forward and ground out the smoldering cigarette. When he looked at her, his face had a rueful smile. "Did you want something or did you just come by to watch me jump out of my skin?"

"I'm sorry . . . I . . ." Annie stopped and took a deep breath. "I hate to bother you but I didn't know who else to talk to. Do you have a minute?"

He looked tired, the line over his brows was deep.

"Sure." He glanced at the battered watch on his wrist.

"It's like this. One of my friends is having trouble with a guy who works with her. You probably know him. Ed Bartell?"

He looked at her, one eyebrow raised slightly. "Sure."

"Well. We're wondering if you could have a word with him. He keeps pinching her and backing her into corners and . . . making it hard for her to work."

Cain's eyes widened. "Has he hurt her?"

"Not really." She didn't know how to say what she meant. In the end, she just said it straight. "Sometimes what hurts doesn't leave a mark."

He settled back against the wall and slowly nodded his head. "I know something about that. But what I think doesn't matter. You need to have her talk with her own shop steward."

Annie snorted. "We've tried but he was embarrassed and acted like it was her fault."

Cain considered her remark a moment. "Well I can see his point. Lots of guys think that. When you put women and men together at work, that kind of thing is just bound to happen."

Annie tried to squash the quick knot of irritation that materialized in her throat. "Most of us figure a way to stay away from guys like that or at least keep them at a distance. But she's only nineteen and not very tough yet."

"Sounds kind of like you girls need to help her figure out what to do."

She could feel her teeth begin to grind. "We've tried. Now they've asked me if the union could help. Something to do with that International Association of Machinists deduction every paycheck and what it's for."

Cain squinted at her. By now he'd lit another cigarette and smoke drifted past his eyes.

"What do you want me to do? I've got to tell you, the IAM guys will think she's just looking for attention."

"How can they say that? Everybody knows that Ed bothers all the women. He's always grabbing somebody."

"Annie, that's just how it is with some guys."

She felt the back of her neck begin to warm. "Well, maybe you could just get her transferred to another crew?"

"Well, uh . . ." Cain ran a hand through his hair. "Maybe I could say something but I don't know how much good it will do. Some of the guys think you women get too much now."

"That's silly. Anyway, if you can't transfer her, how about you transfer him?"

Cain paused and looked at her for a moment. While she had him thinking, she continued. "Why don't you see if you can get him on one of those crews that's mostly men? Maybe you could figure out how to have that other crew request him. He's a pretty good worker when he's not grabbing somebody."

Cain's mouth was raised in a half smile as he looked at Annie. She stared back and they stayed like that for several moments, neither speaking. Annie's anger was fading and she felt the urge to smooth her hair or take a quick look in a mirror. She wished she could get rid of the dirt and grease she'd accumulated during the day. With an effort, she brought her mind back to the issue.

"So, can you do anything?" Her voice was lower, throaty, almost as if she were trying to sound seductive. She coughed to cover her embarrassment. Thank goodness Cain didn't seem to notice.

"I don't think so. I'm assuming you're talking about Gloria Westfall and you know I trained her, but I'm not her shop steward. It will look like I'm interfering."

"But you're the only one I know. What good is it to have a union if you're only going to listen to the men? We pay our dues, just as you do." Annie could see that he had made up his mind. He couldn't or wouldn't help her. Without thought, she pointed her finger and poked him on the shoulder, as she would have done with one of her brothers. His eyes widened, then he put his hand up to rub the spot where her finger had been.

Her breath came in a harsh gasp. She couldn't believe what she'd just done. She felt a sudden urge to laugh. There must be some sort of law that said she had to do something dumb every time she was around him. He was most certainly not one of her brothers.

"Oh my gosh, I'm sorry. I didn't think . . . oh no." She reached forward to touch him, to let him know she didn't normally do that kind of thing. He moved aside, putting a hand up protectively.

She looked around, wondering how many people had seen her poke him. With a sigh of relief, she realized that most of the others had gathered in the sunshine at the front of the plant and had missed the display.

"I really am sorry, I don't generally do that. This is just so frustrating. She didn't want me to talk to you but I said that you might be able to help. Ed is really becoming impossible. He won't leave her alone."

"You need a woman to run for steward."

Cain had shifted and was now leaning against an upright box. Annie couldn't tell if he was beginning to smile or frown. A tiny shower of debris fell from the top of the crate on to the shoulder of his work shirt. She had the urge to reach up and brush it off, but stopped herself in time.

"What did you say?"

"Well, I meant it as a joke, but it might be a good idea. Why don't you convince some woman to run for steward?"

"Why?"

"I couldn't say much in a meeting about what you women need that would make any sense to these guys. Maybe a woman could."

The idea was so foreign that Annie had trouble taking it in. "But there aren't any women stewards. And would any of the men vote for her? We'd have to get more than the women's votes."

"I'd vote for her."

"You would?"

"Sure, I figure you'd hit me if I didn't." His face seemed to soften a little around the hard edges.

Annie got an unfamiliar feeling of warmth in her chest that seemed to have nothing to do with anger or embarrassment.

She looked him in the eye, trying to decide if he were making fun of her.

"Are you serious?"

"Well, like I said, I wasn't at first, but now that I think about it, it's not a bad idea. I could get you an appointment with Slattery. That's where you'd need to start."

"Do you think we could get someone elected?"

"I don't know. I think something in the bylaws says women can't even run. I'll ask, maybe I could do something about that."

"Would you?" Cain's face was turned from her and when he looked back she saw that the deepening lines around his mouth were definitely the beginning of a grin.

"My pleasure."

A pleasant sensation ran through Annie. Then, as if on cue, she thought of Howard and the feeling seeped away. She'd certainly never treated Howard like one of her brothers. She knew he would not want her to run for steward. She felt like a traitor comparing the two. She'd convinced herself for some time that she was really in love. And now, well, now it all seemed different. She stepped back and tried to clear her thinking.

"Thank you for your help. It looks like we'd better get going now." She waved her arm to indicate the row of workers entering the plant door and put a foot forward to follow the crowd. He raised a hand as if to stop her then dropped it and they separated. As they entered the plant, Annie wondered what he'd left unsaid.

Annie entered the trailer almost too exhausted to move. It had been another long day in a string of interminably long days. Sometimes she wondered if she was going to make it. She envisioned herself melted right into the ground beside a Fort some day, Clecos and rivets spread around her every which way.

She removed the scarf she'd worn all day and placed it on the bench seat of the trailer. Sparkle gave her a bad time about it. She said you could spot Annie anywhere on the plant floor just by looking for a bright red hankie on hair nearly the same color. Sparkle's remarks often hit her where Annie was most vulnerable and she would feel like crying or hitting the woman. But Annie was beginning to understand that Sparkle didn't mean to hurt anyone. She'd simply grown up in a world where good manners were not considered much of an asset. And Annie appreciated the fact that Sparkle never held back saying something because it might hurt your feelings. It was a trait Annie had come to value more and more.

She sighed then sat down stiffly on the green bench and eased her legs out in front, trying to loosen the muscle knots and kinks that were a natural outcome of a full ten hours of work. She could hear Gloria and Birdie talking in the back bedroom, their voices barely audible. The smell of something heavenly came from the oven. She had a momentary thought of going to see what it was, but couldn't quite work up the energy. Bending over, she grabbed her leather shoelaces and methodically unwrapped them from the boot hooks.

A white envelope, nearly hidden by her scarf, caught her attention. The characteristic tidy printing on the return address made her smile. Father used his weekly letter to keep everyone up-to-date with what was happening in the family. Her mother hated to write and did so only in the direst emergency.

She picked up the envelope, tore off one end and blew into the opening. With two fingers, she extracted several pages, enjoying the slick feel of onionskin paper. After she'd pressed the creases to make the letter lay flat, she sat back and began to read.

> July 6, 1943
> Dear Annie:
> Hope this finds you well. Your mother and I miss you and your brothers, the house is just too quiet without you all coming and going. Mom wants you to know that she's reorganized your bedroom and it's now full of bandages. I told her that it was fine, you weren't likely

*to be stepping off the bus and needing it anytime soon
but she's worried you would be upset if you came upon
it unprepared.*

Annie knuckled an errant tear from the corner of her eye
and felt the sameness of home wash over her. No matter what
happened in the rest of the world, her mother would fuss that
one of her children wouldn't feel welcome if they arrived unexpectedly. As if Annie might be upset having to push over a few
bandages.

*I heard from Phillip, and I was right, he was
definitely at Guadacanal. You remember his letters were
so blacked out at the time that we couldn't piece much
together. Mrs. Johnson had to eat a little crow on that
one. She said the Saratoga wasn't involved. I'm glad we
didn't know for sure Phillip was there when it was going
on, I don't think your mother could have stood knowing
her son was in such a battle. Apparently there was some
discussion about moving his group onto the Wasp when
the Saratoga was torpedoed in August. Thank goodness
that never happened. A lot of good men were lost on that
boat. Remember Anthony Spencer from school? He was
part of the First Marines and was killed some time in
December. There was some sort of snafu and we didn't
hear until just yesterday.*

Annie's stomach lurched and she tried to swallow. She pictured Tony, a short, stocky boy whose ears stuck out like cabbage leaves on the sides of his head. Fast and strong, he had
played shortstop on their high school baseball team for three
years and held the record for the number of beers downed in one
sitting at the Wet Pig Bar. Annie sat back and wiped her eyes,
fighting an urge to slam her hand on the table. She thought of
his two young sons as she'd last seen them at the county picnic.
They were energetic little carbon copies of Tony, short, wiry fellows with ears that stuck straight out. That damned island had

claimed three people she knew. The white pin inserted on the map had come at a very dear price. Taking a deep breath, she waited until her vision cleared and continued to read.

> *We got a letter from Roger last week and he says it's so hot where he is, he's thinking of importing some of our West Coast rain. He may still be in Tunisia but I think his division is part of the force fighting in Sicily. I can only hope not. The news is bad, it appears there are heavy losses. Of course Mrs. Johnson says . . .*

Annie put the letter down. Frankly, she didn't care what Mrs. Johnson said. A wave of relief slid through her like a cool river. Both brothers were safe. Leaning back, she stared out the window of the trailer and watched the Bradford twins playing swords on the grassy space between the trailers. Her hand dropped to the tired fabric of her scarf. With a savage movement, she grabbed both ends and ripped the material in half. She stared at the fabric hanging from her hands then balled up one piece and threw it as hard as she could toward the back of the trailer. Its light weight didn't allow the fabric to carry far and it rolled out onto the linoleum, red and white threads hanging from the torn edges.

Quickly, she relaced her boots, stood up and strode from the trailer wiping tears with the back of her hand, her tired feet and aching back all but forgotten. Somehow, someway, they had to win this war, even if it meant her spending every waking hour at the plant. How she hated losing one more person. She wanted it to be over right now. The waiting and not knowing was just too hard.

Cain pulled his car into the driveway of number nineteen Plum Lane and braked to a stop. Resting his fingers on the worn door handle, he stared at the trailer and replayed his idea to stop by and see if Annie were home. It had been five days since they'd spoken at the plant and he was curious about her decision. More than that though, when he'd gotten up this morning she was the first thing he'd thought about. On this warm Sunday, when he had his first day off in weeks and could do anything, he'd found that the only thing he wanted to do was see Annie again.

He reviewed his plan. Just a friend stopping by, wanting to know if she had decided to run for steward or not. It had sounded like a good plan earlier.

He'd never met anyone like her, not even at home in Montana. He could see that she was attracted to him. He could feel it when he was around her. But nothing she deliberately said or did would have led him to believe it.

His plan to get to know her better and be friends hadn't gone anywhere. He'd decided it was too much effort when he'd seen her the week before and she'd asked about her friend Gloria. After that he couldn't stop thinking about her. When they'd ended the conversation, she'd looked at him with her mouth turned up slightly off center and her eyes softened on the edges. And all that topped by the ridiculous mop of red hair. He'd had to take a deep breath. He was crazy not to try whatever he could.

Sighing, he pushed down on the door handle, swung the door open and stepped onto the running board. A familiar dull pain in his leg reminded him to square his shoulders and start out walking on the outside of his foot. He'd been told the limp was less conspicuous when he did that.

A short, blond woman with a cigarette in one hand and a red ribbon tied in her hair came from behind the trailer. When she caught sight of him, she slowed her hurried walk and sort of swayed toward him, her stare open and interested. When she finally came to a halt not a foot away, he had to clamp his jaw tight to stop his mouth from dropping open. The woman barely came up to his shoulder. She wore a bright green dress with red apples flung at random across the material. The dress was stretched tight enough to show the lines of her underwear and the top of her breasts were pushed up above the folds of the green material. He tried to look at her face but his eyes kept straying to the sight of so much unrestrained cleavage. She raised a hand and took a long drag on her cigarette, exhaling the smoke from slightly parted lips. When she spoke, her voice had a deep whiskey-cigarette edge.

"You looking for someone?" One arched eyebrow seemed to emphasize the question.

"Uh . . . uh . . ." He stammered, then tried again. "I just stopped by to see . . . uh . . . Annie Tosh. Is she here?"

She looked him over with a slow, deliberate gaze. "Nope, not right now but she's due soon. You can wait inside." She placed a light hand on his wrist and began to walk toward the steps to the trailer home.

As they moved forward, he felt his eyes drawn again to the expanse of soft skin showing above the green dress. He had to admit; she was something. Not pretty exactly but with a hard edge of challenge and availability. Frankly, she scared the hell out of him. He'd met a few women like that overseas. They were desperate for a man, any man. When they'd taken what they could from one, they'd look just as hungrily at the next. He peered down the road, hoping to see Annie. When she didn't miraculously appear, he held back and let the blonde's hand slip off his wrist, then followed her up the steps. He wished Annie would hurry.

"C'mon in." The rough, deep voice had a suggestive overtone. "She'll be home in a few minutes and madder'n hell if we let you get away."

He wasn't so sure about that. As the woman opened the front door, he took a deep breath then smiled in surprise. The tangy smell of barbeque wrapped around him and drifted out into the evening air, reminding him of picnics back home.

His mom and sisters would pack up the salads, beans and marinated beef and haul them in the old pickup out to whatever pasture the men were working that day, either branding or running fences. They'd wash up in some creek close by then dig in to some of the most satisfying food he'd ever eaten. His mouth began to water and he realized that he hadn't eaten since breakfast. With a start, he thought that it had been a long time since he'd been this hungry. Army food, hospital food, now John's cooking were all designed to keep a man alive, but never really satisfied.

He stumbled at the doorway, his bad knee catching him off guard, then glanced up and stopped. His first look at the interior took his breath away. It was so crowded and strongly feminine that he felt as if he should surely be barred from going any farther. He swallowed hard, trying not to look at anything too closely. Silky lingerie hung next to brassieres and lacy nightwear on a cotton line to his left. Tiny high heels of every color lined a shelf above the dangling wisps of clothing and the dinette table on his right held a box filled to overflowing with bottles and things that he guessed had something to do with hair.

Birdie Jones and Gloria Westfall, Annie's friends from the training class, were in the trailer. Birdie stirred a battered pot on the lone burner and Gloria was folding clothes on the kitchen table. As they entered, Birdie turned and looked at him, black eyebrows raised in question. Before she could say anything, though, the blond moved close enough for him to smell her flowery perfume. When she spoke, she raised an eyebrow and looked at him knowingly.

"Look who I found outside. It's Annie's friend, Cain, from work. Isn't he just the cutest thing? I think if she doesn't get home soon, I'll just keep him for myself."

He felt the hair on his arm rise and a shiver run down his back. And once again he found his eyes drawn to the mound of breasts. He looked up with a jerk and met Birdie's gaze, the sides of her mouth crinkling up on the corners. She turned to the blond and peered over half glasses.

"Cut it out Sparkle, yer' embarrassin' the man. Now turn loose of him." She looked back at Cain. "Here, have Gloria move over and take a seat and let me get you a glass of lemonade." After speaking, she turned and took a couple of short steps toward the rear of the trailer. With a flick of her hand, she unhooked one end of the laundry line and let the armful of clothing slide into a basket below. "That's that. Cain't believe you'd bring the poor fella in while yer stuff is hanging everywhere."

He gulped and glanced at Gloria. She smiled cautiously and blushed then moved over so he could sit. He nodded at her then looked quickly at the woman named Sparkle, wondering how she would react to the colored woman speaking to her like that. When she didn't seem to notice, he let out a breath and turned to take a seat at the table. As he squashed himself between the bench and the table, he figured out what was bothering him. This place was so small and crammed with things and people that he couldn't believe Annie lived here. She must surely feel, as he did, like Alice down the rabbit hole without benefit of being shrunk first.

Birdie had turned to the square refrigerator door on the wall opposite the stove and opened it to reveal three shelves stuffed with bowls and food wrapped in waxed paper. She reached in and pulled out a glass pitcher and poured him a mugful. Placing it in front of him, she smiled, showing even white teeth.

"Is Annie expecting you? She's usually home now but today I know they had a problem so she might be a little late."

He could feel heat begin to rise on his neck. "Well, no. We don't really have a date or anything." The warmth continued upward to his cheeks, he certainly hadn't meant to say date. He looked up quickly at Sparkle and saw that she had noticed, her smile was knowing. "I just wanted to talk to her about some stuff that's going on. I thought I'd take a chance."

Birdie was quiet for a moment then spoke in that slow, syrupy twang that he was beginning to like. "Well, whyn't ya just stay fer dinner while you're here? Lord knows we have plenty. Jes set fer a minute, then you can he'p bring everything outside to the table. Lots more room there."

Cain opened his mouth to say no but just then she turned and pulled open the oven to reveal a large pan of golden cornbread. The odor was wonderful and his stomach growled. He didn't want to think about it any longer.

"If you're sure there's enough. I don't want to impose but it does smell good." As he spoke, Sparkle slid into the seat opposite him, her knees brushing his on the way. He shifted his legs, trying to put some inches between himself and the woman. He wished she would stop pushing at him.

The woman's face smoothed and one side of her mouth curled up, reminding Cain of a predatory cat. When she spoke, he had to swallow hard. "Now isn't this cozy? And if Annie doesn't get home soon, there are lots of other possibilities."

Sparkle tapped her fingernails on the windowsill, enjoying the little staccato sounds they made. She leaned forward and pushed a hand through her hair. "So, do you think he's interested in Annie?"

"Cain't think of any other reason the man would stop by a strange house when he wasn't sure she was here and brave talking to you until she got home." Birdie's voice was light but the words cut. Gloria giggled nervously.

Sparkle sucked in a sharp breath. Sometimes she absolutely hated this nigger. The woman just couldn't seem to figure out her place. "What do you mean, talking to me? I was perfectly . . ."

"You were perfectly awful, as usual. If the man had'a been a horse, you'd a rode him right into the ground. If I was you, I 'd go a little easy on this one, don't 'peer interested in you."

Gloria's eyes widened and she placed a hand over her mouth. Sparkle turned to snarl at Birdie but the other woman was already back staring out the window intently. Her words were muffled as she spoke into the glass.

"Mah question is, how int'rested is Annie?"

The three women were kneeling on the bench seat of the dinette and peering past the checkered curtains at Annie and Cain in the front yard. Gloria was on Sparkle's left, leaning forward toward the glass, her hand pushing the red and white material aside. Sparkle was in the middle and feeling crowded. She tried to elbow Birdie over an inch or two but the dumb broad wouldn't budge. She felt the hot, tight flash of blood and nerves that generally paved the way for a fight. She turned to yell at the woman but found that Birdie wasn't paying any attention to her. All her rapt attention was focused on the two out in the lawn.

The whole idea of Annie being interested in a man other than the absent Howard was grand. Sparkle couldn't understand the redhead's loyalty to a man who was so obviously just a friend.

Cain had one foot on the running board of his car as if to leave but his torso was arched back slightly toward their friend. Annie stood with arms crossed and feet spread apart, her jaw set. Sparkle wished that there had been time to help Annie pull something together other than the checked flannel shirt and dark slacks that seemed to constitute most of her wardrobe.

Annie had a great figure, it was a shame she didn't show it off. The only woman's skill that Sparkle's mother had taught her was sewing. For years she'd dragged around an old Singer, designing and constructing most of her own clothes. She'd learned to turn the cheapest of material into something special. She had the machine wrapped in oilcloth under the trailer and hoped that would be adequate to protect it from weather and dirt.

She increased the pace of the tapping of her long red fingernails on the sill, anything to calm the jittery feeling of her nerves. "Gawd, why doesn't she just say yes? You know he's asking her out, what's she waiting for?"

She could feel the bench shake as Birdie laughed. "You sure got a one-track mind. She's engaged to a man that's been at war these past two years and tryin' to make the best of it. Our Annie's got principles."

She made it sound like that was something good. All this holier-than-thou stuff just irritated Sparkle. Breathless, Gloria let out a little sigh.

"I think it's so romantic. Just think, she's made a promise and she is going to fulfill it, no matter what. You are right, Birdie, her ethics are impressive."

Sparkle snorted. "Ethics don't keep you warm at night." Pausing, she became distracted, staring at Cain's physique. "And that man could surely keep you all heated up. He's mighty good looking."

Birdie laughed and shifted from one knee to the other on the bench seat. "Gotta agree with you there, he looks mighty nice in his clothes. Would kinda like to see him out of 'um."

Sparkle couldn't believe what she'd heard. She stared at the colored woman. It was difficult to tell, but the merest twitch of Birdie's upper lip showed that Sparkle'd heard her right.

"But, did'ya see the way he couldn't take his eyes off her, not even when you was waving yer chest in front of him? I liked that."

Sparkle was jerked back with a great tearing thrust, the feeling uncomfortably like embarrassment, running from her face to the ends of her fingers. Her words came out in a rush "I was not waving my chest in front of him. When I do that, no man's gonna look at somebody else. I was just trying to make him feel at home so he would wait a little longer for Annie."

Gloria sat back on her heels and looked at Sparkle, her mouth slightly open then let loose a most unladylike snort. "Sparkle, you are terrible." She cocked her head to one side, a tiny smile turning up the sides of her mouth.

An itchy flush began to work its way up Sparkle's neck. She glared at Gloria. She looked back at Birdie when she heard the woman laugh.

"You bet. Just trying to make him feel at home. That's why you offered to keep him for yerself."

Hot, quick anger flooded Sparkle and she turned, raising her hand to slap the woman. But she stopped midstroke. Birdie's face revealed dark skin drawn taut over cheekbones, and eyes gone flat and icy. The checkered tablecloth and smell of cornbread disappeared and she was back on the street. A shiver ran through her gut.

She could feel Gloria move away from her, farther down the bench seat. The colored woman's voice struck her flat and hard. "You won't be hittin' me woman."

Sparkle's mouth was dry and she felt lightheaded. She didn't know what had just happened. She cleared her throat, trying for her normal tough edge. "And just why not?"

"'Cause I'll smash your pretty little face in and you won't be lookin' nearly as good as you do now. Nobody hits me no more."

Sparkle sat back. This was a side of Birdie she'd never seen before. "I can fight . . ."

The words hadn't left her mouth when she saw Birdie's hand shoot out of nowhere and snatch the red ribbon from Sparkle's hair, pulling out several strands caught in the knot. Jerking backwards, she hit her rear on the dinette table.

"Ouch, what the hell?" Sparkle raised a hand to her head and touched the now tender spot, then moved it down to the sore place on her behind.

"You don't have to fight anybody here, girl. I won't hurt you." Birdie's face was set in strong, hard lines.

Sparkle swallowed hard. She started to tell the stupid fool she wasn't scared of her but stopped again. The unblinking brown eyes were dead straight on her. She felt the open, boiling stink of fear tear at her gut. They glared at each other for several moments, then Birdie held out her hand with the ribbon laying on her palm like a knife cut.

"Someday you and I are gonna have to come to some sort of understandin' or jez kill each other, I suppose. 'Til then, we might as well try to figger out how to get along. What do you think?" The freezing, deadly look had disappeared and the muscles in the woman's face formed the beginning of a smile.

Sparkle didn't know what to think. She hated the woman for being colored but other than that, she didn't have much against her. And she was a hell of a cook.

"Is it going to be all right?" A small voice broke her attention and she turned back to Gloria. Both she and Birdie had forgotten the girl during the altercation.

"Well, don't look to be no bloodshed right now anyway." Birdie's voice was calm again with no hint of its earlier unmovable core.

Sparkle shivered then caught her breath. She seldom ran up against someone she couldn't bluff. With a shaky breath, she decided that the whole thing didn't seem that important anymore. She shrugged, her stomach beginning to settle. She reached out with two fingers and picked up the ribbon from the russet-colored hand.

"I guess like you said, we'll have to figure it out. I think it's going to be all right, Gloria."

Gloria looked from one woman to the other, apparently deciding that there wasn't imminent danger. Birdie looked straight at Sparkle then nodded her head. Sparkle studied Birdie's face and there didn't seem to be any anger there, only a straightforward confidence. Sparkle shifted on the seat. It was cold and she attempted to pull her skirt down to cover the exposed skin.

She turned back to the window, having to push both Gloria and Birdie aside to see at all. They watched the two people in the front yard in silence for several minutes. Cain put a hand on Annie's arm, as if to gentle a wild horse. Their tall roommate moved back a half step but didn't try to pull his fingers from her sleeve. Then Annie turned and Sparkle's breath caught in her throat. Annie was smiling a shy, private smile that Sparkle was sure they'd never seen at the trailer before. She recognized the language of their movements; his body determined and bent forward, hers wary and and leaning back. Not too far and certainly not wanting him to leave. The world's oldest dance routine. Almost boring. Only watching Annie, Sparkle had this uncomfortable confusion of feelings. First Birdie, now this. Shaking her head, she turned from the scene and flounced down hard on the seat.

"I can't stand it. She's gonna lose her chance with him. She needs to make her move now. Anyway, he's too darn shy for me."

Birdie was silent for a moment, then turned around and joined Sparkle sitting on the bench. "I don't know if she wants a chance. She could cut it off now, you know."

"Cripes, she doesn't love that Howard at all. She just made a deal with him 'cause she didn't think she could do any better, being so tall and smart and all. Things change. That's a deal nobody should be held to."

Gloria put her hand lightly on Sparkle's arm and spoke, her voice hesitant. "But that is not how it works. She is supposed to wait patiently until he comes home. When he does, she will see that she really does love him and they will be married."

Sparkle looked at her, started to say something then stopped. For a moment she'd forgotten that Gloria was only nineteen. She shook her head. She wasn't sure she was ever that young. The look on Birdie's face was thoughtful.

"Honey, things don't always work out all that tidy. We're just gonna have to wait and see what she decides. I kinda like how she tries to stick to her guns."

Sparkle felt a smile begin and realized she agreed with her roommate. As she gazed at Birdie, an idea took hold. "I think we should help her change her mind."

Birdie turned and looked at her directly, one eyebrow raised. "And just how do you think we should do that? No funny stuff now."

Sparkle tried her most innocent look. "Me? Funny stuff?" As she watched, Birdie's mouth curved up on the edges and a glimmer of amusement showed in her dark eyes.

"Well, for right now, I'm gonna feed that man, then we'll see what our Annie does. Want to help?"

"Yes." Gloria and Sparkle spoke in unison. They laughed and the tight feeling in Sparkle's chest eased.

"Sure, we'll help. But there's something I want to talk to you about while we work."

Birdie smiled with her whole face this time. She gave Gloria the spoon to stir the barbeque sauce then handed Sparkle a bowl and a head of cabbage. "Cut this up and I'll make some dressin'. What did you want to be talkin' about?"

Sparkle grabbed a knife from the rack and walked to the tiny counter. After she'd begun to make equal slices of the cabbage, she thought about the clothes she'd made before the war then took a deep breath and started speaking.

"Well, I have this idea that women like to have something new when they go to dances and out at night. When the war's over it's going to take a while for the manufacturers to start making something other than uniforms and work clothes. You know I've always been able to whip up a dress in a pretty quick hurry. And it looks great when it's done. I'm thinking that maybe I could open a little shop. Charge a little more than a dress at the store. I could call it Sparkles or something."

She had gotten so involved in the telling that she'd forgotten that this was the first time she had actually spoken about the idea. When she looked up from her cutting, she saw that Gloria was staring, her hand frozen still holding the spoon in the barbeque sauce, her mouth slightly open. Birdie had turned back from the tiny refrigerator she'd opened and slowly shut the door.

"A dress shop?" Her words were croaky, just short of disbelieving.

"Yes, maybe a little one downtown, or out in Fremont. What do you think?"

Birdie cleared her throat. "I's a little confused. You're gonna make dresses for all them society ladies. The ones you're always sayin' are silly?"

Sparkle cocked her head to one side and thought about Birdie's question. "No, not them. I think there's going to be more women with money after the war, not just those society dames. Women who will keep on working. I think women'll be looking for something to make them pretty. I can do that."

Gloria continued to stare at Sparkle but her hand had started the spoon stirring again. "My mother spends hundreds of dollars on clothes every year and they don't do that much for her. If you could really make them look better, you could charge a fortune."

Sparkle laughed. "It's not women like your mom who will be my clients. I think there's going to be women like us, women with more money than they had before the war."

Birdie had closed the door to the refrigerator, her hands still empty. "Ah think maybe that would work. I've seen what you do just to make your work clothes fit. But you know not everyone wants to dress so tight or have that much skin showing."

"She does not have to do that. She does have a good eye and I will bet she could just make them a little a bit looser but still fit well, it would be fine."

Gloria's tone was firm now, as if she knew just how to do this kind of thing. Birdie walked slowly over to the table and sat down, an eyebrow raised in thought.

"If Gloria's right, be kinda fun to see what you could come up with. How you going to pay for it?"

Sparkle finished her cutting and laid the knife down before she spoke. "Well, that's where I thought you might help. How much money do you think I'd have to save to start something like that?"

Birdie touched the rim of her glasses and cocked her head to one side. "Hmm. First we'd have to think of where's the best place."

"Well the best place sure, but one I could afford so it can't be too fancy."

Gloria had stopped stirring completely and had joined the other two at the table. "And we will have to work on your grammar."

Sparkle felt a flash of annoyance. "What's wrong with my grammar?

"Nothing particular. Some things you say just need some revising. Remember, you will be a businesswoman and you will need to sound like one."

Sparkle was ready to say something about that but stopped. Gloria went on as if she hadn't noticed.

"The location should not be too fancy, Sparkle, but you can not be skimpy on that. It will be important at first that women be able to see the shop. After you get a reputation for good work, it will not matter that much but it is vital at the beginning. And we need to figure out whom we could use for your models. We could take pictures and everything."

Birdie looked at Gloria. "Whom?" With a shake of her head, she turned back to Sparkle. "This should be interesting."

CHAPTER FIVE

Annie felt like a wart on the end of a witch's nose. She stood beside the office door, waiting behind two short, old men for a chance to speak with the union boss, John Slattery. Cain had been as good as his word. He'd been over to dinner only three days ago and now she was waiting for her turn to talk with the IAM boss. A fluttery sensation filled her chest when she thought of Cain. It seemed silly that she should react like this to the simple act of the man carrying out his word. The hall they were standing in was narrow and none of the late evening sun had managed to work its way into the dusty interior. She thought they certainly didn't need any more heat inside this cramped space but a little more light would have been nice.

Her mouth was dry and she slid her tongue over her teeth, wondering as she did if there were any chance that John Slattery would listen to her more than two minutes. She wished now she hadn't been so brash as to volunteer for this operation. The door opened and the men in front left to enter the office. Annie jumped when she heard a raspy voice behind her.

"How come you're here 'stead a shoot'n in them rivets?"

Annie turned to find the shop janitor, Otis, standing behind her. He was only five feet tall but seemed to overfill any area he occupied, layers of fat wrapping around him like a friendly quilt. Most people avoided him because of his size or because his thinking was slow, but Annie found him endearing. She under-stood his permanently unrealized desire to join the armed services. The news of Tony Spencer had made her wish she could jump into a uniform and put herself on the line. She was certainly as big and strong as many men and she had no children to leave without a parent. She told herself the work she did at the plant was important but sometimes it didn't seem like enough. Not for the first time, she wished she were born a man. She was tired of staying home and 'helping' instead of being on the front line. She smiled at the janitor.

"Oh, Otis. You startled me. I'm here to speak with Mr. Slattery. What are you doing here?"

Otis thought on that question for a moment, then smiled widely, revealing a gap where several teeth had been.

"I'm here to see Mr. John, myself. Need to report in."

Annie wondered why a janitor would report to this man. Or maybe Slattery was a little like her, humoring Otis instead of sending him on his way. If so, he would certainly gain her respect. From what she'd heard, he was hard but fair. She was curious what he was like in person.

"What do you see him for?"

"Oh, it's really 'portant stuff but . . ." Otis' brows made deep lines on his forehead and his chubby pink cheeks hollowed out slightly. "I can't tell you."

"What?" Annie started to ask him what was important but he had turned away, shuffling his feet on the polished linoleum.

"Annie Tosh?" Annie jumped, almost colliding with John Slattery, standing only inches from her. It was their first meeting and she was startled by his size. Here was another man who took up more room than his height warranted. But, unlike Otis' slack, bread dough kind of physique, his was muscle and broad bones.

Because of his reputation, she had expected someone much taller. His shirt was snug over his shoulders and Annie wondered if he were even able to secure the top button. His neck looked about as thick as a pillar on the front of one of those southern mansions she'd seen in pictures. There seemed to be a force about him that was formidable. She chewed on her bottom lip for a moment. She wasn't used to anyone with such natural authority. She rather liked it even though it made her a little nervous.

"Yes." Annie gulped then thrust her hand forward. He took it, his square face close to hers. He pumped her hand up and down twice, dropped it and then stood back, looking her in the eye. He nodded as if making his mind up about something, turned on his heel, entering the room quickly and leaving a trace of the clean scent of pine behind.

Annie turned and saw that Otis was looking at her again. She smiled and followed Slattery, her shoes making clumping sounds on the floor. Swallowing hard, she recited to herself why she was here. Something had to be done about moving Gloria to another crew. The foreman, Bartell, was still making her life miserable. He couldn't seem to stay away, even when she'd repeatedly told him she wasn't interested. Annie had to convince this man that Gloria or the foreman, needed to be changed to another crew. She had decided before she came that she was not going to bring up Cain's idea of the woman shop steward.

Annie surveyed the office. She saw a plain room with a utilitarian desk flanked by cabinets on either wall. Gray binders lay on top of the filing cabinets and the desk surface was littered with stained coffee cups and an ashtray with stubbed-out cigars.

The smell reminded Annie of her father's den where a humidor and a collection of cigars were placed next to the decanter of port. Some of her earliest memories were of her father's stories laced with the leathery smell of the ever-present cigar. Her mother hated it, but Annie found the scent oddly comforting.

John Slattery had seated himself behind the desk and gestured for her to sit in the straight-backed metal chair on the opposite side. The planes of his face were hard and straight, as if someone had used a chisel to hone the edges. She swallowed. She wanted to do this right and wasn't sure how to start.

Annie eased into the seat and placed her hands carefully on the legs of her trousers, folding the crease between two fingers.

Breathing in, she looked directly at the union leader and decided that it would be best to let him speak first. The man pulled a cigar from a box on his desk, bit off the small end and spat it into the trash. Then he put the cigar in his mouth. She waited but he didn't search for a match. Just seemed content with it stuck in his mouth.

He faced her and smiled, his square face softened by two surprising dimples appearing on either cheek. His eyes seemed to change with the light, one moment piercing blue, the next an indigo color. Annie decided that her worry was unfounded. He didn't seem nearly so intimidating sitting behind his own desk with a cold cigar in his mouth.

"So, I understand you have plans for our little union?"

Annie hesitated. She'd never asked Cain exactly what he'd said to get this appointment for her. Slattery's question made her realize she should have been better prepared. The man sat back in his chair and exhaled slowly, one eyebrow raised. She took a deep breath and opened her mouth, hoping she could speak without sounding like a strangling chicken.

"There is one thing you might be able to help with. One of the women I work with is having a problem with her foreman and we thought maybe you could help us resolve it."

"What kind of problem?"

"Well, he keeps bothering her, generally making her life miserable."

Slattery's voice was measured. "And that's all?"

"What do you mean?"

"Has he hurt her? Attacked her?"

"No, but he may since she keeps telling him no."

Slattery moved the cigar from one side of his mouth to the other. "I know that some of the boys are a little rough around the edges but this is an airplane factory for Christ's sake, not a tea party. If she hasn't been hurt, I don't know what I can do. Many of the boys don't want you here at all."

Annie felt her chest squeeze tight. What he said was the truth, even if it wasn't fair or right. "All you would need to do is transfer her to another crew. Or him. It wouldn't take that much of a change. And you would be a hero to the women."

"What did her own shop steward say?"

"He said she shouldn't be talking about it, almost as if it were her fault. The man is an idiot." She stopped on the last word, realizing what she had just called one of his union's representatives.

"An idiot?"

She swallowed and the back of her neck began to prickle. "Well . . . yes."

"Hmm . . . ." Slattery sat back in his chair, steepling his fingers just under his chin. "The boys don't think they need you here at all. They've been working like hell just to get the wages up to near what the shipyards are making." He paused. "But if you're right about a pretty quick fix . . . ." His voice trailed off. Then he sat forward and slapped one hand on the desk. Annie jumped.

"Okay, if Adamson was right, the girl is that little mouse on Bartell's crew." He shook his head. "Can't figure. Why anybody'd be after her is hard to tell. What's her name? Gloria West . . . something?"

"Yes, that's right, Gloria Westfall. We would all certainly appreciate it."

"I'm not promising anything, but I'll see." He sat back in his chair again and this time opened the drawer and pulled out a book of matches. With a practiced movement, he lit the cigar, blew out the match and tossed it into the green metal garbage can beside him. "And why were you chosen to be the one to bring this up? You don't look like you'd have much trouble with the men."

Annie gulped and tried to think how to answer that. "Well, because . . . ." This had not been part of her rehearsal. "Well, we just thought it would be better if someone who didn't . . . oh that's not it either." She gulped and decided to stick with the truth. "Oh hell, it's because I'm so big they thought you wouldn't yell at me."

A twitch started at the corner of his mouth, then he opened it wide and laughed loudly, shocking her with the noisy intensity. It was as if this were the first funny thing he'd heard in a long time. He stopped laughing finally and gazed at her.

Rich, sweet cigar smoke filled the room and Annie suppressed a cough, wishing the windows were open. The smell was overpowering in such a small room. He'd leaned forward and his eyes had changed to the piercing blue of a hawk.

"I'll tell you what. I think you and I can work together to solve this thing."

Annie felt a thrill run through her. That was precisely what she wanted, someone else to show an interest. She bit on her lip to deter the huge smile that wanted to be born.

"Do you women have other grievances we need to look at? And while we're talking about that," Slattery tapped his fingers on his desk, "Adamson said that the two of you talked about having a woman be shop steward."

Annie stared at him, her momentary delight replaced with a growing uneasiness. This was what she had feared. She wasn't ready. Her mind raced to come up with a response. She took a moment to think, looked down at her feet and saw that her boots were dusty and scuffed. She wished she hadn't looked. She lifted her chin.

"I don't know about that. We just talked about that a bit. I think it's a good idea. I'd certainly like to have a woman steward. Is it possible?"

"Haven't thought about it before. Might not be a bad idea. Why don't you let me see what the bylaws say?"

"All right."

"Now you can do me a favor."

She was startled but nodded her head.

"I need to know what's happening out there and I need people to keep their eyes open and report back to me. Tell me if there is something I should know about."

Annie felt a clutch of panic. "But sir, I couldn't possibly spy on my friends."

He stood up and smile lines framed his mouth. "I'm not asking you to tell me when someone says I'm a fool or if someone's not working hard enough. What I want is a person with a brain out there to keep her eyes open. There's a war going on and I need to know if there's something happening that you don't think is right. You be the judge, Annie. I don't expect you to come to me with little things."

Annie thought about that for a few minutes and finally nodded. "I could do that."

Slattery moved around the desk and offered his hand. Annie jumped to take it, a bit startled that the interview was over. She felt foolish that she hadn't stood first. This was a very busy man and he had already given her more than she had expected of his time. She shook the rough hand then turned quickly to leave.

"You'll keep me informed?"

"I will. Thank you for your time." She walked carefully out of the room, knowing her face was still scarlet, but giddy with relief that it was over.

The faint sound of a guitar glided through the trailer court, its hesitant melody indicating the musician's amateur status. Clouds had gathered during the night and the air felt warm and close, a warning of the hot August day to come. The early morning Saturday light bathed the trees and grass with a hazy sheen. Annie was pretty sure that there wasn't a better time in the world than the morning with a full day off ahead of you.

She was seated at the picnic table with the small loom she'd brought from home resting on the rough boards of the tabletop. Her fingers guided the shuttle filled with crimson yarn through warping strings. The only sound was the quiet swoosh, swoosh of the shuttle. She'd come before anyone else was up, unable to sleep with the thin stream of yellow sunlight sneaking through the shades and onto her pillow.

She stopped just for a moment and pulled out the latest letter from home, picturing her father's blue fountain pen making the perfect swirls and lines of the sentences. If she closed her eyes, she could almost touch the striped material covering the table on the porch where her father sat in the summer.

> *August 1, 1943*
> *Dearest Annie:*
>   *The yellow roses outside your bedroom window are in full bloom and your mother keeps saying that you should be here to enjoy them with me. I don't recall that you were so crazy about them but she has a different recollection. I do remember the time you and Phillip cut the pink rose bush down flat so you would have a clear run to the pond. It's hard for your mother. She doesn't seem to be able to get very far from her worries. Sometimes I wonder if she'll ever get her sense of humor back. It's like she's trying to hold all of you tight to her by worrying more.*

Annie took a deep breath and then let it out. She remembered the fine lines that had deepened on her mother's face since the war began. A dull pain began behind her eyes and she blinked to stop the tears. Her mother exasperated her at times but she was also the dearest, most caring person Annie had ever known.

> *But enough about that. Your mom says that I have to tell you about Joann Smalley. She gave birth (yes, almost three months early!) to a two-pound girl they named Miracle. They have her in the oven and it's a problem getting her to eat but it looks like she might live. You just wouldn't believe it. She's no bigger than my hand and has wisps of curly brown hair just like her dad. And she keeps smiling and smiling. Everybody*

*says it's just gas but your mom says it's because she is
so pleased to be alive.*

*The ladies have been trading off going over and
helping out. Joann is feeling pretty poorly and it might
be several weeks before she can take care of the little
thing by herself. I'll let you know how things go - keep
your fingers crossed and be sure to put in a good word
for her in your prayers.*

*I'm enclosing Roger's letter. They get shorter
and shorter as the fighting becomes more intense. He
talks about not being able to sleep and jumping at every
noise. The vets from the last war say that's only the
beginning, it gets worse when you get home. I don't
think. . .*

"Why aren't you going this time?"

The voice startled Annie and she dropped the letters as she
turned to find Sparkle standing close behind her. She bent
down, picked up both letters and tucked them back in the pocket of her shirt. She squinted at Sparkle, not in the mood to have
her lovely morning interrupted. Turning back to her weaving,
she passed the colored yarn through the taut threads with great
concentration.

Sparkle ignored the obvious snub and sat down next to Annie
on the wooden bench. A whiff of heady perfume filled Annie's
nose and she wanted to ask Sparkle to move down a bit. At the
sight of the 'outfit of the day' though, she had to stop. Sparkle's
short cotton blouse rode up high enough to reveal most of her
midriff. Her blue shorts covered enough real estate to save her
from being arrested but not much more. It made Annie shake
her head. She too was dressed in shorts and a cotton blouse, but
there the similarity ended. Her own shirt was modest, short-
sleeved seersucker, cut loosely so as to reveal only a little skin
and no cleavage and her shorts were loose and had enough
pockets to carry an army's equipment for a week.

"When I think about it, you never go. How come?"

Annie stopped for a moment in her easy, rhythmical shuttle throw. As usual, the query seemed just one step from rude. She realized Sparkle was referring to the USO dance to be held that night at the school. She sat back and flexed her hands to ease the stiffness in her fingers.

"I don't care much for dances. I told you that last night. I don't normally have a very good time."

"How come? It's one of the few times we can loosen up and really have some fun. Why'd you want to sit here, doing nothing? Besides, you might meet someone."

"Why would I want to meet someone? I'm engaged." Annie could feel the defensive edge to her tone.

"Woman, you might say you're engaged, you might think you're engaged, but really, you're no more engaged than I am."

Annie felt the back of her neck tighten. Sparkle was doing it again. The woman was a master at getting under her skin.

"What are you talking about? Of course I'm engaged. As soon as the war is over, we're going to be married. I've told you that as well."

Sparkle snorted. "You have told me that, but I can read you better. You've got no feeling for that man at all. The only ones you seem to care about are his kids. Look whose pictures you have up."

Annie felt a twinge in her chest. Sparkle was right. She would never say so out loud, but she occasionally forgot what Howard looked like. Not that he was bad looking. He had that square, Scandinavian, rather forgettable face. If not for his height, he could have passed unnoticed on the street. She squirmed a little, wanting Sparkle to quit talking about him but not wanting to make the change too obvious. She didn't like having Howard maligned, especially in his absence.

"I just think his kids are cute. That's why I've got their pictures up. And I do have feelings for Howard." A quick memory of his photograph, forgotten on her bedside table at home, made her wince.

Sparkle's mouth curled up and she slapped a hand on the tabletop. "Right. So come to the dance anyway. It's gonna be fun and it sure beats sitting around this pokey trailer all night."

Annie thought about it for a moment, then looked at her roommate now carefully half-seated on the end of the table with one leg still on the ground and one on the bench. She was bent over, examining her scarlet painted toenails.

Staring at the woman, Annie tried to think how to phrase her answer. The habit of turning down any occasion like this dance was ingrained. Too many years of standing like a tree stump in the corner watching others enjoy themselves had taught her to avoid those hours of trying to look interested but not desperate. Somewhere in her early twenties, she'd given up hope that she would find someone at one of these functions. She was about to brush Sparkle off again when she felt a pang of honesty.

"I don't know. I've given up trying to compete at one of those things. Only the tall guys ever ask me to dance and there are so few of them that it's just not worth it. Let's face it, there aren't many eligible men around now. I'd be trampled in a stampede of women if I even talked to one."

Having answered the question, she went back to throwing the shuttle with slow movements from left to right, then right to left. The cloth on the loom was to be a runner for their small table in the trailer. She was working on the center section, now sliding pale yellow strands, to be followed by a brighter, lemony color. The outer bands were grayed greens and blues. Annie had studied the sunset one evening and was trying to reproduce the feeling.

Sparkle stared at the cloth taking form under Annie's hands. "You know, for a really artistic person, anybody would think you'd be able to do a little of that on yourself."

"What do you mean? All I'm doing here is putting colors together. It's not that hard."

Sparkle snorted. "Right. Just putting a few colors together. Look, why don't you do the same on yourself? You never wear anything that isn't basic gray, black or white. What's wrong with a few colors? You always look like you're practicing for a funeral."

Annie's shoulders hunched and her mouth went dry. She hated anyone scrutinizing her this closely. With an effort, she straightened and looked at Sparkle, trying to speak in a normal tone.

"Dressing anyone as big as I am in bright colors is a mistake. Instead of just looking big, I look like a giant pumpkin or gorilla or something."

"Who says?"

"I say. My mother says. I've tried that and it just doesn't work."

"I think maybe you weren't trying it quite right. There's nothing wrong with your shape. Don't you know you never listen to what your mother tells you? You're not fat, just tall."

Annie laughed remembering how her mother used to talk about buying clothes to 'minimize' her size or 'camouflage' her height. A little rivulet of sweat started down her back.

"Just tall. Like it's not much. Do you have any idea how much I wanted to be small and petite and just the right size, like you?"

Annie couldn't believe she was telling this to Sparkle. It had been years since she'd thought of the teenaged pain of being different. A faint smile played across Sparkle's mouth. Annie rushed to explain further, she wanted her friend to get that look out of her eyes.

"Or, if I have to be tall, then at least thin. A size that wouldn't make men scared. Someone . . . oh, I don't know. Just someone who looks a whole lot better than me."

She glanced up at Sparkle, now wishing she'd kept her mouth shut. Instead of getting rid of the gleam, it seemed to be increasing. Sparkle straightened up, looking directly at Annie now.

"Woman, you missed the boat somewhere. Just because you're not little doesn't mean you can't be a knockout. You're just not packaging yourself right. Instead of dressing to hide yourself, why not dress to show that body off?"

Annie couldn't stop a gasp of surprise from escaping. "I think my 'packaging' is just fine." She looked at the excess of skin showing on Sparkle and gulped. "Thanks. I don't want to hurt your feelings but . . . well . . . I don't really want to start dressing like you."

Sparkle jumped up from the table and paced over to Annie, each step making a crunching noise in the brown grass. She put her hand on Annie's arm.

"Did I say dress like me? Honey, I've been wrapping myself up for sale for eight years, I dress to get the job done. That don't mean that I don't know what you're supposed to wear. Let me think a little here."

Annie laughed, a dry, strangled sound in the quiet morning air. She wished Sparkle would leave her to her work. "You have a real problem here with a sow's ear. Don't bother, it's just not worth it."

She went back to her weaving but from the corner of her eyes she could see that Sparkle's face was speculative. After a minute, she lifted her hand from Annie's arm and walked into the trailer. Annie felt relieved. She hated it when someone fussed about her appearance. It made her feel even larger, as if she were swelling up. Hearing the door of the trailer slam, she relaxed.

For a moment she wondered how Gloria was doing. The day before had been the girl's first day of work in the office and she hadn't spoken with her since. Annie's talk with Slattery had paid off even better than she had hoped. Gloria had been called into the office and asked if she would be interested in a clerical job. Although no mention had been made of the union or Slattery, they'd known immediately who had initiated the offer. The job was perfectly suited to Gloria. Most importantly, it got her away from her supervisor. She'd been hired within the hour, taking her off the line and into something that she could do easily with very little drop in pay. Annie sighed contentedly and let her mind return to the pleasure of the sight and feel of the soft cotton in front of her.

Several minutes later, she was startled when all three of her roommates exited the trailer. Gloria had thrown a light wrap over her nightgown and was rubbing her eyes. Annie was surprised to see her awake as she rarely rose before she had absolutely had to. Birdie had apparently been up for a few minutes because she clutched a chipped ceramic coffee cup in her hands.

As they approached, she studied their solemn faces then cleared her throat, which had suddenly gone dry. "What's this, a management meeting? You all look terribly serious." She felt a tightening in her chest. "Gloria, how was your first day?"

"Oh fine." The girl's voice was soft, preoccupied.

The other two ignored her questions. Sparkle, who appeared to be the ringleader, went first.She held up her hand and seemed to assess Annie. She turned finally, looking at the other two.

"What do you think? I believe we have some real possibilities here."

Birdie hummed off-key and stared at Annie. Gloria circled the picnic table, her face still showed signs of fatigue but she cocked her head thoughtfully. Sparkle's jaw was set in a determined line.

Annie stopped her weaving, her shoulders tightening. "What are you three doing? What's going on?"

"You didn't tell her?"

Sparkle shook her head. "Nope, thought I'd talk to you first." They looked at each other for a moment and nodded as if in agreement.

"We just need to do a little reorganizing." Sparkle's brows pointed downward in the middle. For a moment, she resembled a witch.

Laying the shuttle down carefully on the warp threads, Annie pushed the picnic bench back as she stood. She could feel her heart hammering uncomfortably fast. "All right, you can stop right there. I don't know what you're thinking about, but it better not have anything to do with me."

Sparkle put one foot on the picnic bench and looked Annie in the eye. When she spoke, her words were sharp and clear. "Birdie's going to cut your hair. Gloria's the makeup gal and I'm doin' the dress. You're going to the dance and you will be beautiful."

A clutch of fear tightened her chest. She started to speak but Sparkle was still talking.

"And don't worry, the dress I make will be perfect. Maybe not as great as the one I'd make for myself, but we don't want you to be too attractive, now do we?"

Annie's face flushed. "I am not going to sit here and let you turn me into a clown. Just because you think . . ."

The group didn't hear what she had to say. Sparkle put one hand on Annie's shoulder and pushed away from the bench. She turned and started for the trailer with Gloria and Birdie on either side. They were all talking at once.

"Not too bad a job if I do say so. Even though ah'm the one that did it." Birdie's voice was quiet and a smile curved her mouth.

Annie felt a blush warm her neck. Seven hours had passed since her friends had left her in the yard. Now she stood in the center of their cramped trailer, trying to see all of herself in a square foot of mirror hanging on the closet. Birdie sat on one side of the dinette with her feet tucked up under her and Gloria lay on her stomach on the other side, her legs in the air, elbows on the seat and chin resting on her open hands. They gazed at Annie in silence.

Where before her red hair stood out like random sprouts of hay, now it feathered softly against her face. Birdie had taken the shaggy, chin-length mop and cut it into layers, then used pincurls and lotion to make it behave. Annie decided that she liked it and put a hand over her mouth to conceal a grin. It seemed silly to be so pleased with her own reflection.

She felt a wrinkle of unease as her gaze dropped lower to the dress she was wearing. Sparkle had found several yards of grease stained, cotton-linen material that had been used to wrap heavy machinery. Several dips into a bleach bath, then a short hang on the line in the bright sun had dried the material and changed it from a muddy cloth to a soft, ecru colored fabric with artistic swirls of dark brown. The dress, pinned in places with unfinished seams and still unhemmed, seemed to float on her like warm light. Still, she was sure that there was something wrong.

"Look at me, there's just not enough fabric or something." Annie felt her breath catch in her throat as she peered in the mirror.

Sparkle stood behind her, pulling on the waistline of the dress. She took the pins from her mouth and spoke sharply.

"So, what's wrong? There's not too much skin showing, right?"

"Well not exactly too much skin, but it seems to hang funny, like it isn't really covering me."

"It's not too tight?"

"No, that's not it."

"And lady, you got a great set of bazoogies. You been hidin' your light under all those droopy clothes too long. It's time to do some advertising. We could even make it a little lower."

Annie clutched at the fabric and held out a hand to Sparkle. "You wouldn't." In the next moment she saw a gleam in the short blonde's eyes and relaxed. "Oh, I don't know. Gloria, what do you think?"

Gloria looked at her with one eyebrow raised. "Sparkle, I definitely think that you are going into the right line of work. How in the name of heaven did you put that together? She looks like Aphrodite. Gracious, the men will be all agog."

Annie felt a queer rush of pleasure. Not only had men never been agog before, she'd never had anyone be more than mildly passionate. With a little thud of her heart, she had to admit that Howard belonged in the latter group. Squinting into the mirror again she thought that maybe she had never looked this good before. Sparkle somehow read her thoughts about Howard.

"It's not like you need to be loyal to a fiancé who talks about his kids, his mom and dad and his hunting dog before he gets to you. Shee-it, that's pretty lukewarm if you ask me."

Annie tensed, then let out a slow breath. For some reason, she couldn't conjure up the necessary energy to rush to the defense of Howard. "Let's not talk about him now, okay?"

Sparkle shrugged and seemed willing to leave it alone. Gloria kept staring at Annie, as if unable to match this image with the one she'd had of her.

"You know, with that dress, I wonder if I should use different colors, maybe a little stronger. Hmm. . .. The girls at college used more eyeliner than I have on her. I think that just a little more . . .." Her eyes held a speculative gleam. "I will need to use my tweezers too. Have you ever plucked that awful line of hair between your brows? Gracious, it makes you look angry all the time."

Annie felt a shiver down her back. "Doesn't it hurt to pull them out? One by one?"

Gloria let out a most unladylike snort. "So says the lady who lifts those wooden crates full of wing parts without waiting for help. Is this same lady now scared of the little eyebrow tweezers?" Gloria waggled the offending apparatus in front of Annie's horrified face then touched her gently on the arm. "This will not hurt much more than a broken leg." Annie could feel her face begin to pucker in anticipation.

Gloria stopped waving the tool and went back to contemplating the dress. "How short are you going to make the hem? And is it going to take you longer than we have to finish all those seams? It looks like way too much work to me."

Sparkle pulled on Annie's shoulder and turned her around to face her. There was no room for two people to pass in the tiny hallway. She grabbed a handful of material at the front of the skirt. "I have an idea, instead of just cutting it off at the knee, I was thinking about cutting it short here at the seam line, then letting it hang a little across the front, then end about here." Sparkle used her hands to hold the cottony material in place at the hipline.

Annie looked down and gasped. "Sparkle, that's too short. I couldn't wear anything that . . ."

A wicked grin cut across her friend's face. She lowered the fabric three inches. "I know, just getting your goat. Worked didn't it?"

"A little too well. But Gloria's right. How can you possibly get this done in three hours?"

"It's going to take about four hours on my old machine, but it's okay. You don't want to get there early anyway. You'll make a grand entrance around 8:00 o'clock. Everybody'll be there by then." She turned her again and began to unpin the side seam.

A chill made its way down Annie's back. It seemed like so much work for just one evening. And she had to admit it, she was still worried that no one would ask her to dance. Perhaps this metamorphosis wouldn't inspire the excitement in the male species that her friends expected. She chewed on her lower lip. She didn't want to let her friends down.

Sparkle's hands were warm on her back as she worked and Annie's anxiety subsided. Even if not one darned man looked at her, attending the dance with this bunch of friends was going to be an adventure. She'd never had this much fuss made over her. After a thoughtful moment, she decided that she quite liked it.

Cain watched the swirling lights and laughing people and wished mightily that he hadn't come. The USO dance at the gymnasium had sounded like a good idea when John talked him into it, but now all the laughter and noise just made his head hurt.

Ever since the mortar shell had exploded not twenty feet from him, he'd felt disconnected from society. The doctors and nurses told him that this type of malaise was common after a disaster. The doctors didn't understand the half of it.

The dance floor in front of him transformed from brightly colored party dresses to the brown drizzle of the Tunisian countryside. He remembered how the cold, wet mud of the African December surprised them all. They'd expected dust and sand dunes, not rain and quagmires of muck. And they surely hadn't been expecting the shell that came out of nowhere.

It hadn't been much of a fight. Five minutes prior they'd all been sipping coffee in a derelict building. Joe, Frank, Orville, Lester, Joshua, Fred and Peters were inside, stretched out and enjoying the momentary respite from the constant sound of bombing. He'd gone outside to get more water from the old hand cranked well. Paul had followed him, leaning against the cracked wall of the abandoned structure. The screaming shell had made only a dull whomp in the clammy countryside air. Then, as if crushed by a giant's hand, the roof caved in, its unholy grip pulling the walls down as it went.

Cain took a deep breath, shoving his hands deeper into the soft interior of his pockets. He tried to warm himself and push the god-awful memory away at the same time. It didn't work. It never worked. It was as if the motion picture had a life of its own, always playing the story out to its bitter end. Paul's face was there, in the front, terrified. In the next moment, the building blasted apart, sending pieces of brick and wood everywhere. Dust billowed out and obliterated what was left of the house and the trees close-by. He'd gone in to check for the others first, filled with the crazy hope of a fool that the luck they'd had still held.

It hadn't. All seven were dead. He'd pulled Paul out of the hideous wreckage and used his belt and bare hands in a vain effort to stop the flow of blood from the numerous wounds.

Not willing to believe what had happened, he'd cradled his friend's head in his lap, crooning softly as he'd remembered his mother doing when he was a small boy. His mind blocked from thinking . . . about his friend or the bleeding of his own leg and face.

When the medics tried to take the lifeless body from his arms, Cain was wiping Paul's face with a handkerchief, trying to clean the dirt and blood from his lips. He raged and fought, insisting that he would save this man. Somehow he held reality at bay while he still touched his friend. He could still feel the grit and sticky blood under his fingers as they pulled his hands away. The medical aid he'd wanted for Paul, was given to him instead. A shell fragment had lodged in his leg and a sharp piece of something had sliced diagonally across his face. Neither injury disturbed his blazing anger at the quixotic fate that left seven friends dead and him alive.

An overhead beam spotlighted a woman in black lace twirling on the dance floor and his attention was brought back to the dance. He rubbed his forehead, trying to clear his mind of the shadows. It had been six months and he still didn't know why he hadn't been killed. He realized that there were tears forming in the corners of his eyes. The familiar guilty, sick feeling in his gut rose when he felt the surge of relief that he was still alive. He was blinking furiously when he heard a voice behind him.

"What the heck are you doing, man, standing there like a stick? This is some great dance. Look at that row of female talent just waiting for a stud like you." John was standing close to Cain, his strong breath and slurred speech indicating that he'd found a bottle somewhere.

"Yeah, this is a nice dance. I'm sorry buddy. I just can't seem to get into it. I'm going outside for a smoke. Thanks for bringing me, maybe I'll see if I can catch a ride home."

"Cain, it's only eight. Why not hang around a little longer? You never know what might turn up. Have a drink. Loosen up. Let me introduce you to Olga. She's the blond over there in the purple dress and great legs. She's just dying to meet ya." John's face took on an expression of good-natured leering.

The blond in the purple dress had a desperate look that made Cain's back teeth hurt. He patted John on the shoulder as he pushed past him. The music started again, this time a quick, swing tune and people were heading for the floor. As he moved forward, he noticed a tall woman with a smooth cap of red hair. She looked vaguely familiar, but since recognition didn't come immediately, he continued walking. And then, as if drawn by an unseen hand, he searched for the woman again.

He nearly stopped breathing when he located her. It was Annie. He stood perfectly still, his mind having trouble taking in the change. The music and the crowd of dancers dimmed as he stared.

More than just her hair was different. She was flushed and smiling. The dress was some sort of wizardry. He'd always admired Annie for her strength. When a lot of the women were simply not physically able to handle the big pieces of steel, Annie would quietly move the parts. He'd admired her for her caustic wit and for fending off sarcastic comments from male co-workers.

And he'd certainly thought about that body under those baggy shirts and trousers. He gulped, realizing his imagination hadn't even begun to do it justice. He moved toward Annie who was now smiling at a circle of men all intent on catching her attention. He kept walking forward, unable to reconcile what he was seeing with his earlier impression of her. He stumbled when he felt a hand on his elbow and turned to find John facing him.

"Hey man, you look like you saw a ghost. What's going on?"

Cain pointed at Annie. John grinned when he saw the object of Cain's interest.

"Oh, ain't that something? Who would a thought a gal that big could look so good? There's nothing about her that's rationed, that's for sure. It's a wonder she hasn't been fighting guys off all the time. You're the one always said she was pretty. You sure were right. Just look at that bunch of idiots around her."

Cain's breath momentarily caught in his throat. He became aware of the group surrounding her. The tall, well-built officer with a patch over one eye, the foreman from the Everett shop handsome enough to be a movie star, and a slick, well-dressed fellow each staking out their territory. He stopped.

The record player filled the warm, crowded room with thumps, trills, and the occasional inspired horn solo. Cain took a deep breath and strolled forward. Or anyway that's what he hoped it looked like. He was trying to minimize the limp and appear nonchalant at the same time.

When he reached Annie he stood quietly for a moment, waiting for her to notice him. When she did, a wide smile lit her face and the men surrounding her did a little adjusting, trying to cut him out of the circle. When she stepped forward to greet him, he caught the angry looks from her admirers but ignored them.

"Hello Annie. You look wonderful."

She bit her lip as if embarrassed. He reached out and touched her hand. She jumped but did not pull it back.

"Would you like to dance?"

Again, the broad smile. She nodded to the men and excused herself with a few gracious words. The next moment he found himself on the dance floor. He placed his hand on her waist, held out his hand and she took it. He smiled, there was no awkward bending with her, she fit perfectly. He felt a strong tingling down his arm and fought the urge to run his fingers farther than the acceptable hand-sized area around her waist. He pulled her closer, hesitating, wondering if she would resist. When she didn't, he relaxed and tried to concentrate on his footwork. He could tell by the tense feeling of her arms and back that she wasn't comfortable. He couldn't tell if it was because she didn't dance much or because being this close to him made her uneasy.

He glanced up to see her friends at the other end of the hall and tried to steer her in the opposite direction. He wanted very much to have her to himself right now. There was that brassy woman named Sparkle who had scared him to death when he'd gone to the trailer the first time, Birdie, the short, colored woman who could cook like an angel, and Gloria, the well-dressed society girl. He'd never tell Annie but he thought the four of them made a strange group.

He counted carefully, feeling awkward. His leg still gave him fits and every time he thought he was getting it right, he'd stumble or step on her foot. He hated the sporadic weakness in his leg. John had told him to concentrate on the music but it seemed like it was just too fast. Strange, he thought he'd built up a wall that would keep not just the war but also the whole world at bay. But he'd been wrong about that. So wrong that he was out here making a fool of himself on the dance floor.

With a jerk, he realized that he had grazed her foot again. He felt Annie tense and tried to take a deep breath, but it didn't help. He felt the hot flush of embarrassment creep up his face.

"Let's go outside a minute." His voice sounded harsh but he didn't care. This hot, crowded room was making him nearly sick. He dropped his arms and turned, then strode from the dance floor, taking her with him.

The cool evening air filled his lungs and he stopped at the edge of the wide porch. Gripping the rough wood of the handrail, he drew in deep draughts of night air. With a shaking hand, he reached up and yanked the handkerchief from his pocket, wiping his forehead now dripping with sweat.

After a couple of minutes, he felt a hand on his shoulder. He swallowed hard. Annie stared at him, her forehead creased in lines of concern. When she spoke her voice was low.

"I'm not crazy about dancing either. Why don't we just stay out here for awhile?"

He noticed how intensely brown her eyes were. And how the little crinkles at the edge of her mouth gave him a quivery feeling in his chest. He wished mightily that he hadn't reacted so strongly to the crowded dance floor.

He cleared his throat and spoke through a dry mouth. "I'm sorry, I don't normally . . .." He couldn't think what to say. "I'm not . . ."

Annie put up a hand and placed her fingers gently on his lips. "It's all right. You don't have to explain. My brother Phillip writes that it's a little like having a monster perched on your shoulder. When you least expect it, there it is, stomping around in your head. Says he hasn't had a decent night's sleep since he left for Africa."

Cain let out a long, slow breath and the tension eased from his body. He felt for the first time in a long time that it might really be all right.

"Do you want to go back in to the dance? I think I can do it right this time." He tried to sound enthusiastic but it came out much less than that.

"Why don't we just stay out here? It's cooler and I could use a break."

He sensed that there was something else on her mind. The August moon was so bright it made the upper branches of the fir trees glow with an eerie white hue. Several couples were seated just beyond the perimeter of yellow light from the open double doors and the smell of cigarette smoke was strong. Cain shivered. The contrast between the hothouse atmosphere inside and this cool night air was strong.

He turned to the woman beside him and the chill disappeared. Annie Tosh was woman enough to warm anyone. She had told him, the night he'd stopped by her house, that she was engaged but he'd noticed there was no ring on her finger.

"Cain?" Her voice was quiet, soft, but he jumped slightly. "Yes?"

"I need to talk with you before you get the wrong idea."

He felt an uncomfortable knot in his stomach. He was quite sure he didn't want to hear what she had to say. "And what's this you need to tell me that's so important?"

Annie's face was partially hidden in the shadows but he could see a thin line across her brow.

"I told you I'm engaged to Howard Gray. We're to be married as soon as he gets home. I came to this dance because my friends insisted it's good for the morale of the troops. I'm not looking for a man or a date or anything like that."

He wasn't sure he believed her. He knew she thought she was speaking the truth but something about how she said it made him wonder. He could hear John telling him about the 'not much' fiancé. She expected him to say something so he spouted the first thing that came to his mind.

"So, you're in love with this guy, Howard?"

The thin line on her brow turned into a furrow and her mouth curled downward.

"Certainly, why do you ask that?"

Cain wasn't much good at reading people but he had an idea from her tone and the way she drew back farther into the shadows that she wasn't being entirely straight with him. He paused.

"All right. But while he's gone maybe we could see each other, just as friends?"

She was quiet, her face shifting as emotions he couldn't read played across it. When she spoke, it was without a hint of a smile.

"Cain, I'd like to be your friend. You just need to understand that it's not like I have a choice. I've given my word to Howard. If I gave my word to you, you wouldn't want me to go back on it, would you?"

Cain's jaw tightened. Her logic hurt. If she'd made a promise to him, he'd kill any guy who thought he was going to change her mind. Especially while he was off fighting. He understood exactly what she meant. But the shot of heat that ran through him was certainly not a friendly feeling. He turned toward the door, frustration making his voice shake.

"Sure, I get it, we'll just be friends. Want to try another dance?"

She hesitated, then moved toward him and put her hand on his arm. He paused, trying to steady his breathing. He wasn't sure if he could wait until Howard got home and they could have it out, man-to-man.

CHAPTER SIX

So, why didn't you tell us you met someone at the dance? How come we had to find out from that stupid Jeanette three days later?" Sparkle's voice sounded loud even in the clatter of the noisy noontime lunchroom. Gloria winced and looked around, concerned that they would be noticed. She had been picking at her gravy and potatoes when Sparkle roared in and dramatically flounced onto one of the creaky wooden chairs at Gloria's table.

Gloria felt her face flush and wished she'd left just five minutes earlier. Sparkle could be so loud sometimes. Remembering the dance, her heart did a little dance in her chest. She'd been so interested in getting Annie ready for the event, she hadn't had time to prepare for it herself. She'd grabbed a year-old dress patterned with tiny flowers and pushed her hair back with simple barrettes. She had expected to spend most of the evening helping the women pour punch and talking with her friends. Instead, she'd met a boy, actually a man if she thought about it since he was in the Navy, and her world had been sort of pink and fuzzy ever since.

Sparkle snorted. "So, I suppose you're going to wear something boring? Something beige?"

A sliver of unease shot through her and she wondered if Lester would think she was pretty enough. Her father had said a hundred times that she needed to be sharper, more aggressive. Said she'd never make it being such a shrinking violet.

She stared at Sparkle. "Well, I had not really thought much about it. He said he would like to go out to a movie or something. Does it matter a great deal?"

Sparkle's laugh made several people at the table next to them turn their heads, then turn away quickly as Sparkle glared at them. She lowered her voice but the words were no less alarming.

"How do you expect to catch a man wearing those boring clothes of yours? My God, are you nuts? I've got that red number with the black lace on the bodice that might look good on you."

Gloria's throat felt dry. She remembered the red dress. It was skin-tight on Sparkle and made of some pre-war silky material that shimmered when you walked. "That would never work, it is just a picture show for heaven's sake, not a big date or anything. Really."

Sparkle's mouth tightened. "My dear, they are ALL big dates. Now if you think the red is too much, how about the black dress with the yellow trim on the waist and neck?"

Gloria spoke quickly. "Sparkle, I do not want to scare him to death. He just needs someone to talk to, he is leaving for the Pacific in three weeks and he is lonely." She thought about Lester again and how grand he looked in his uniform and the light, cotton candy feeling returned. She noticed how much better the plant lunchroom looked today. She wondered if anyone had thought about adding some curtains to the blank windows.

Sparkle's voice interrupted her thoughts. "You won't scare him to death if you just look good. How's this, you could wear that pair of brown slacks you have, they show off your body and I'll loan you my yellow blouse. That should make him sit up."

She held up her hand as Gloria began to protest. Sparkle's mouth made a straight line and her eyebrows pulled together above her nose. "It's never going to look the same on you as it does on me, darling, you just don't have the equipment." As Gloria watched Sparkle tapped on her front teeth with her spoon. "Yep. I think that will work. The color is just right for you."

Gloria gathered her dishes to put on the dish return stands. As she rose to leave, she felt Sparkle's hand on her wrist.

"You don't have to rush. None of the men get back till ten after. Now let me think."

Gloria looked at Sparkle, torn between the need to rush back to her job and the thought that she might be able to make herself quite appealing to Lester. She eased back in the chair and listened as Sparkle talked.

The late afternoon sun had gone behind the alder trees on the lot adjoining the trailer park and now cast flickering gold shadows across the picnic table. Gloria fingered the beige and green silk scarf at her neck and sighed. Her other hand was resting under Lester's on the rough surface of the picnic table and the feel of his skin next to hers gave her a most unusual, quivery feeling all over. She didn't know if the yellow blouse had anything to do with it, but this first date was turning out to be much more than she had hoped.

She'd been embarrassed at first. Birdie had been so obvious, gathering up Annie and Sparkle, insisting there was something that needed doing in that hot, stuffy trailer. Sparkle had even given her the thumbs-up sign behind Annie's back where Lester couldn't see as they'd trudged off. But she and Lester had been alone almost an hour now and it felt just right. He talked with her as if she were the only person of importance. He seemed quite content to listen.

They had been discussing doing something like a movie next when he smiled, his pale blond mustache rising on one side.

"Why don't we go to the zoo? I've never been to a real one, have you?" Lester's voice dropped slightly at the end of the sentence, giving Gloria that drippy, honey feeling through her limbs. She giggled and then put her hand over her mouth to stifle it. Giggling was something her father abhorred. Looking up, she found Lester's face wreathed in a smile that reached from his eyes to his mouth. It even seemed to include his ears. She suddenly did not care what her father abhorred. And Lester was so proud of the car he had borrowed that she really did want to go.

"That sounds grand." Rising from the picnic table, Gloria found herself almost skipping to the trailer.

Lester's driving was smooth. Gloria loved the way his hands held the wheel. After maneuvering through downtown, they turned onto Aurora Avenue and Gloria admired the concrete work on the bridge as they crossed the structure. She thought she could have driven forever with this man.

He parked the car and they began walking through the zoo, holding hands. When Gloria saw Monkey Island, she was so surprised at the tiny animals scampering around that she dropped his hand and ran ahead.

"Lester, come quick. Just look at the darling little creatures." He caught up with her and although he tried to act as if he saw this kind of thing all the time, she could tell he was as amazed as she. The island where monkeys lived was surrounded by a ten foot water moat. The wall holding back the visitors also allowed them to watch with no bars interfering with the view. Gloria was sure she'd never seen anything like it. One little fellow was perched on his mother's shoulder and kept trying to grab another monkey or one of the trees. Just as he seemed about to lose his grip, he'd fling both hands back onto his mother then chatter in what Gloria was sure meant that mom was supposed to hold on to him, not the other way around. She and Lester stood close together, shoulders touching and laughed.

As they crossed the dirt path to the next exhibit, Gloria stopped when a girl about her age walked by wearing a zookeeper's uniform. "Lester did you see her? I can not believe it, that was a girl zookeeper. Could you see me feeding bears and cleaning up after lions?"

Lester shook his head, his hair falling into his eyes and smiled in his slow, easy way. "You'd be great doing whatever it was you wanted to do. You'd probably look darn good in that uniform too."

Gloria stared at him and by some wonderful accident his lips touched hers. His mouth was gentle and electric at the same time. For several moments she lost track of everything but his spare, strong body pressing against hers. When they stepped apart, she felt a chill and he pulled her close again, his arm around her shoulder.

They passed clumps of salal and ferns as tall as they were. Pine needles crunched under their feet and the green smell mingled with the sharp odor of wild animals. They passed the commissary. They found a flat rock that had been warmed by the sun and Lester spread out his jacket for her. They sat for a few moments in silence, watching the light change as the sun made its way down toward the horizon.

It seemed to Gloria that Lester was the first person she had ever been with who was so solidly with her every moment. She glanced sideways at him and felt the jolt of pleasure that was becoming familiar. It was as if he had all the time in the world to be with her, rather than the few short weeks that were allotted them before he had to leave for the war. Gloria pushed that thought resolutely from her mind.

"Golly. It's like one of those picture postcards or something." His arm reached out to encompass the forest and people and exhibits. His voice was quiet and deep and made Gloria's heart beat a little faster as he spoke.

She had an urge to reach up and touch the strands of hair that spilled onto his forehead. His eyes were brown and soft and made his otherwise unremarkable face glow. As he moved she remembered the feel of hard muscles under her hand when she'd danced with him. An involuntary sigh escaped her lips and he turned to her and smiled.

"Are your folks still in Portland?"

"Yes. I have been here two months already. It does not seem that long." Gloria thought that this was probably the first time she had met a man who did not know about her family. Lester was not aware just how rich and powerful her father was. She had told him only the barest essentials of her life and now felt a shot of satisfaction that her family's wealth was not an issue here. "In a lot of ways, I feel as if I have been here all my life."

"I know what you mean. Being from Texas I didn't know there was this much water and green stuff anywhere. This must be the prettiest place in the world. Kinda makes me wonder why my folks didn't do any traveling. That Birdie friend of yours told me that you weren't working at the plant anymore. How come?" His accent resembled Birdie's, but it was a little less drawn out. When he talked, she thought of lazy, hot evenings on a front porch swing. It was strange, as she had never had any of those evenings but it was pleasant to think about.

"Well, I am still at the plant, but now I am upstairs in the office. I was not much good at the other kind of work. I am working for Foreman Colfax. Annie helped me get the job. I do filing and stuff like that. He wanted someone who could type and did not have a beau or husband or was pregnant or anything so she would not leave in a few months like the last two." She smiled.

Lester was quiet for a moment and Gloria turned to look at him. He held out his hand and took hers, the ghost of a grin touching his mouth. "I guess he wouldn't be hiring you now would he? If it's all right with you, I'll just take that job of beau."

Gloria put her hand on his chest and felt his heart beat. She thought that maybe hers was beating just as fast. A distant roar startled her and they both jumped. Lester put his arm around her shoulder and pulled her closer. "I heard they have two lions called Gilmore and Lionhead. One of those two would like to get out of his cage and join us."

Gloria shivered and slipped her arm around Lester. The thought of lions could not scare her much when she was with him.

August 10, 1943
Dearest Annie:

  The paper says it's pretty warm there in Seattle. I hope that the plant is cool. I know how hard it is to concentrate when it's too hot. The weather has been great for the garden. Your Mom has filled the pantry with quarts of everything from green beans to pear chutney. She could tell you exactly how much of each but I lose track when she tells me. She thinks we'll win the victory garden award this year. I hope she starts giving some of the preserves to the rest of the county before I have to build a whole new room for the overflow.

Annie sighed and eased herself down onto the tiny patch of grass next to the trailer. They'd finished dinner, she, Birdie and Gloria and it was Gloria's turn for the dishes. Sparkle was working an extra shift and that left Annie completely alone for the first time in many days. She savored the relative quiet of evening in the trailer park. Her father's letter had been waiting on the table for her when she'd arrived home but she liked to read them in private before sharing them with the group. She was always a little frightened that the news might be bad and she relished the connection as she read them. It brought her closer to her family.

I haven't heard from Roger in two weeks, always a concern, but I think it's because the fighting is so heavy. Your mother is very worried but trying not to show it so I won't be worried. If it weren't so frightening, the whole thing would make me laugh. She's looking kind of tired but I guess we all are. Phillip's letter is enclosed. Or what is left of it. It's so shredded we decided the censor must have thought the letter contained Hitler himself.

I'm glad to hear that you are working with the union. It sounds like that Slattery fellow is pretty sharp. You be careful, though, and mindful of the men's positions. I don't think it's a great idea for you to run for steward. There are just some places that women aren't welcome and I don't want to see you get in a bad situation. It's not that I don't think you're capable. I'm afraid some men will take your running for office the wrong way and try to get back at you.

Annie felt a quiver of anger. She wasn't running because she had some overwhelming desire to make men look bad. Heck, they did that all by themselves. She thought it wise to have a woman listen to other women's problems and she was sure most men didn't want to do that. She heard the quiet chatter of birds and began reading the letter again.

Miracle is living up to her name. Apparently she's eating like mad and making an awful noise when someone doesn't hold her. She seems to have the whole neighborhood wrapped around her tiny finger. I don't know if I told you but her daddy, Carl, is with your brother in Sicily. Joann hasn't heard from him lately either and that doesn't make it easier for her recovery. She's better but it looks as if it's still going to be a spell before she can take care of the baby full time.

Your Mother sends her best.
Love,
Dad

Annie sighed, her eyes stinging with the threat of tears. The thought of the tiny creature fighting to stay alive made her happy. She felt that as long as the little girl lived, there was hope for the whole world.

I can't give up ten percent of my pay for the danged bonds. That's crazy." The voice was stringy and waspish in the momentary quiet of the meeting room. "I'm just as patriotic as the next person but I can't pay my bills if I do that."

Sparkle watched Trudy Harris speaking, the skinny riveter from swing shift. Her odd, puffed out cheeks were the only part of her that looked well-fed. She stabbed the air with a finger as if her complaint would be heard more clearly that way. The dark green walls of the room made the place seem smaller than it was and Sparkle felt as if all forty of them were crammed into an undersized bedroom. She yawned then looked again at Bertha, the woman supposedly in charge. All she'd done so far was start the meeting and ask for questions.

Sparkle flipped her hand irritatedly at a wasp buzzing around her head, wishing she'd been smart enough to sit closer to the door. She'd be delighted to slip out right now. If she had to hear much more of this complaining she would scream. The dented clock on the wall proclaimed that it was after eight p.m. This meeting of the 751 Aerettes had been going on for over an hour and the late afternoon sun had dropped enough that it was shining right into her eyes. She absently scratched the side of her neck and stared hard at Annie, willing her to get up and get things organized again. Her friend was the only one who could make these women stop griping and start thinking about what they could do instead of always complaining. It looked like Bertha wasn't going to do anything but look worried.

Trudy was still talking. "I don't think the International Association of Machinists can do anything right."

Sparkle gave an annoyed grunt. Trudy never shortened it up to using the initials of the union, IAM, as the rest of them did. She had to agree though. The men did talk a lot more than they acted. She looked over to see that Gloria's eyes were beginning to close and she gave her a nudge. When the tired girl sat up with a start, Sparkle made a face at her. The young woman smiled at Sparkle then yawned in bored solidarity.

Near the back, a woman stood and spoke, her voice almost too quiet to hear. Someone yelled at her to speak up.

"We keep paying union dues but I don't see any raise in pay yet. All we do is pay, pay, pay. Look at the shipyards, I heard the men are making ninety-five cents an hour now."

There was a collective gasp, followed by whispering and louder conversations as the group took in the information.

"The sixty-two cents our guys make doesn't seem like much when you hear that. And then what we women make is a joke." A shrill voice echoed what the women were thinking.

"I do know something about that." The room quieted and Sparkle smiled. Annie was on her feet finally and it looked like she would be reining in the group.

"Our guys have been working like mad to get the wages raised." Her voice was steady, loud enough to hear but not over-bearing. A few jeers in the back made Annie look at the culprits and stop talking until they were quiet. "I know it doesn't seem like they're doing anything but they've been working with the RWLB." She looked around. "Do all of you know what that is?"

There was much nodding of heads but several 'no's were heard.

"It stands for the Regional War Labor Board. It's made up of guys from our own 751, some delegates from Boeing and I think a couple of representatives from Seattle. The first of this month the board presented the company plan to our committeemen. They agreed to it and now it's back with the RWLB for final approval. If it goes through, our men will be making over eighty cents an hour. Our wages should go up about the same amount."

Sparkle sat up straighter. Now this was something she could get serious about. Most of the other complaining had concerned stuff she didn't give a hoot about. But money, that was some-thing else. She had begun saving for her own store and any extra dollars would be more than welcome. A wave of chatter filled the room. Questions were shouted but there were so many Sparkle couldn't hear clearly. Trudy screeched the loudest.

"How come we never heard about that?"

A flush crept up Annie's neck. Sparkle let out a quiet snort. Knowing a few of the Union bigwigs was obviously keeping Annie better informed than the rest.

"I don't know why they don't tell us. I think they don't want us to be too involved."

"They take our dues but don't want us knowin' anything. Don't seem right." This time it was an older woman way off to the right speaking. Sparkle agreed. They only really wanted them to fill positions, never help with decisions.

Annie's mouth tightened and she walked toward the front of the room. "I know it isn't fair but at least we'll share in the pay raise, it's not just for the men."

An uneven cheer rippled through the room. Sparkle started to join in when the wasp made another run at her. The tiny bug was so close to her ear it sounded like a miniature B-17. She swatted at it, trying to encourage the insect to take its flight pattern elsewhere but only managed to hit her finger on the side of the chair in front of her. For the next moment, all she could think of was how badly one little finger could hurt. When she looked up, the women were all raising their hands, trying to talk at once.

Once again, Trudy's shrill voice rose above the rest. "That's great but I'd like to know a few other things too. Like how come we can't make closer to what the men do? And how come we can't get breaks during our shifts? We get off for lunch but that's it. My brother works in Portland and he gets breaks."

Next a woman wanted to know about a place to lie down during a shift. In case one of them wasn't feeling well. A third wanted to know why no one seemed interested in starting a place near the plant for children of the workers.

Annie held up her hand, the look on her face thoughtful. "These are things we need. But remember, we've got to win this war or nothing we do is going to be worthwhile. I'll try to talk with the fellows again. Maybe if you write down what you want, I can bring up your ideas."

There was a general shuffling as women grabbed in their pockets and purses for paper. Sparkle could see Annie sigh as order descended and all that could be heard was the scratching of pencils. When they'd passed the notes forward, Annie carefully folded the scraps and laid them on the small table.

"So, what about the ten percent of our salary that we're supposed to use to be buying bonds with? I can't do it. And they're telling me it's mandatory."

Annie stared at her for a moment, a thoughtful look in her eyes. "We need to win this war and that takes money." Trudy's mouth twisted downwards. "On the other hand, you're the one who has to pay the bills. If you can't give that much, there's nothing you can do about it. Has someone been giving you trouble?"

"My boss tells me I'm going to single-handedly lose the war."

Sparkle joined the ripple of laughter that ran through the room. Everyone always had a better idea for your money than you did. Annie grinned, then addressed the unhappy woman. "Let me see what I can find out. If some of us give more, a few folks should be able to give a bit less."

Sparkle jerked upright. Now this might be a problem. She glared at Annie, wanting her to know that she would not be giving more than ten percent. Annie gave her a quick nod. There was a murmur and Trudy looked hard at Annie and then sat down apparently satisfied with the compromise.

A few more remarks were shouted from the back but Annie just held up her hand. "Let's call it a night. I know most of you need to get up early so let's see what we can do about getting answers to these questions then deal with the others later. How about two weeks from now, same place, same time?"

Sparkle led the round of grateful yes's. She rose slowly, her leg muscles having worked themselves into kinks while she sat. As she walked toward Annie, she wondered why her friend looked uneasy. With a shrug she decided that was Annie's problem. What she wanted to know was exactly how much more money it looked like they would be getting. She needed to plan what she could put away.

Gloria decided that the metal skin of the small trailer must collect heat from the ninety-five degree September day, swallow it, and then dispense it inside like sticky fog. The week had started cool but by Wednesday, the temperature had risen past ninety. She lay prone on the bench seat of the dinette. Sweat trickled from her too hot skin onto the slick vinyl surface.

Even her lightweight seersucker dress seemed heavy, sticking to any part of her body that it touched. She raised her legs to get air under her skirt and smacked her knee against the metal trim around the table. Uttering an oath, she sat up, swinging her feet to the floor.

A haze clouded her vision and she let her head drop onto her arms now crossed on the table. She wondered if the slight nausea she felt meant that she were coming down with the flu or a cold. She was seldom sick. Memories of the cool, ordered spaciousness of her parents' home filled her with a longing she had not had since she'd left there.

With an effort, she lifted her head off the table and blinked. Sparkle stood in the doorway wearing green shorts and a halter top, her blond hair tied back with a rust colored band. Gloria thought that the material was the wrong color for Sparkle. It made her hair look brassy. She wondered if she should tell her but decided she was too hot to make the effort.

She did remember something that she needed to ask though. "Sparkle, can you help with plane spotting duty on Thursday night? Joe Welch can not make it and I am his backup."

Sparkle shifted her weight from one foot to the other, then lifted her damp pony tail from the back of her neck. "I don't know. I'll have to see if anything better comes up." The way she stood showed that she couldn't have cared less about what Gloria needed.

The scent of Sparkle's thick, cloying perfume drifted across the small space between the two women. Taking a shallow breath, Gloria tried to quiet her rolling stomach by looking elsewhere. Unfortunately, her gaze fell on the untidy pile of women's clothing and lingerie, mostly Sparkle's, on the other side of the table.

Taking another careful breath, she turned back. Sparkle still slouched against the doorframe, her halter top sliding open and showing the top of a lacy black bra. Gloria swallowed, clamped her teeth shut and knew that she had to say something. She could not stand another moment of Sparkle's presence.

"Why do you always have to dress so . . . so . . . so tight?" The last word came out high and anxious. Gloria swallowed and tried again. "Can't you dress like everyone else just once in a while?"

Sparkle turned her head, opened her eyes slowly and stared at Gloria, one eyebrow raised.

"Honey, I am who I am. Sorry if the competition is too much for you." Gloria felt herself shrink as she remembered the last dance she and Lester attended together. She'd caught him twice staring at Sparkle, unable to pull his eyes from the woman. Gloria could not get enough air to breathe when she thought of her own pale, tidy appearance next to Sparkle's obvious charms. It was a contest she did not even want to enter. If Lester felt that way, she may not even want him.

She took a deep breath. "Why did you have to flirt with Lester? He was leaving in a week."

Sparkle gave her a startled look, then grinned. "Did you think I was flirting with little old Lester? You can't be serious. All I did was talk to him. He's all yours, dearie."

Of course, that was the problem. Sparkle was not after Lester. It was just that if he got interested in her, there would be no looking back at drab little Gloria. And Sparkle did not even have to try. Jealously boiled up so strong and ugly that she wanted to kill Sparkle, wipe her off the earth. Or better yet, steal some man from her whom she really wanted. But Gloria did not know how to do any of that. So she just said the first thing that came to her mind.

"Do you know how you look to other people?"

"No. How?"

Gloria hesitated and felt tears sting her eyes. Rubbing them so the other woman could not see, she gulped.

"Well, you know, cheap. Like a lady of the evening or something."

Sparkle hooted and slapped one hand on her exposed thigh. "Well now, doesn't that just cut it. So what's wrong with looking like a 'lady of the evening'?"

Gloria felt her face flush and she splayed her hands out on the table in front of her, hoping for some feeling of coolness against her skin. "Because that is just not the kind of person anyone wants to live with. Sparkle, you are my friend but I do not want to have to worry about Lester every time you are around." She pressed her lips together watching her roommate.

Sparkle stood up straight, her eyes blazing and face screwed up as if to spit something out.

Gloria felt another uneasy roll in her stomach. What she'd said was true but certainly not kind.

Finally, Sparkle shrugged and bent over, pulling first one high-heeled pump off, then the other. She sat down next to Gloria leaving a space of six inches between them.

"I've been this way so long I don't even think about anybody else. What if I promise to behave when Lester comes back? I don't want you worrying about him. He's not interested in me you know. And if it means that much to you, I'll be glad to help you spot planes or whatever you need."

Tears slid down Gloria's cheeks in earnest now and mixed with the sweat making her feel like a salty, slick mess. This sudden concern of Sparkle's was harder to take than her normal caustic attitude. She wanted to thank the woman but felt her stomach rise into her throat instead. She rose from the bench but knew she was not going to make it to the bathroom in time.

The hard rooftop provided little comfort. Sparkle stretched her legs out seeking some anyway. She gazed at the sky above, stars making bright holes in the darkness. It was warm enough to be out with only a sweater. September in Seattle. She had to admit it was almost perfect. The scent of mown grass and just turned dirt was heavy in the air. Too many years in too many cities made her uneasy with this outdoorsy stuff. She was terrified of bugs, spiders and anything that moved quick and sideways.

"I suspect that if a Jap zero went over right now," Annie's voice interrupted Sparkle's reflection. "I couldn't tell him from a low flying duck. What is in that bottle? Pure alcohol?" Her tall roommate's voice was measured and deliberate as if each word were an effort. Sparkle smiled. The mighty Annie Tosh, lying on her back, drunk as a skunk.

Lighting a match, Sparkle coughed, then held the flame to end of the cigarette, enjoying the smell and feel of the tobacco as she inhaled. She sat back a little and watched her friends. Birdie leaned against Gloria and held up her hands, making an outline against the night sky with her fingers.

"So what is it Annie, a zero or a duck?" She collapsed against Gloria in a pile of giggles and her round form jiggled with barely controlled mirth.

Gloria pushed herself back up and whispered to the group. "Shush up you two, what if someone comes up and catches us with this liquor? They might throw us in jail or something. And what if an enemy plane comes by?"

"I doubt anybody's going to come up to this stupid plane-spotting post now. It must be after 11:00."

Funny, Sparkle realized that right now she preferred this rooftop with its fresh air atmosphere to a comfortable, smoky bar with lots of potential customers. The last few months with her roommates had worn off some of the edge of panic she'd kept secret. It had been there since she was eleven and her mother had thrown Melvin out of the house. He'd been the only man to stay with them over six months, in fact he'd lasted four years until one night her mom had gone on a toot and returned with a merchant seaman in tow, saying that Melvin wasn't 'fun' anymore.

She studied her friends who were now in various stages of intoxication. It surprised her that she was here, tough, street-wise Henrietta Collins lying on a roof with three other women and actually enjoying it. Ever since she'd renamed herself Sparkle Melody at sixteen, she'd pretty much been on her own and avoided the company of women, her mother in particular.

She had begun to wonder recently if she might have missed something.

She looked over at Annie again and grinned, then reached for the bottle. Gloria, Birdie and Sparkle sat on thin mats in a semicircle while Annie sprawled out flat on her back on the top of Marshall tower, the highest building in West Seattle. Sparkle moved the binoculars and the identification chart farther from her reach and thought that any Jap pilot coming by tonight would have to be pretty stupid. Spotters all along the coast would be able to see them with no problem.

Gloria's light, lisping voice interrupted her thoughts. "Uh, I want to thank you for helping out since the other spotters had to work. It is awfully nice of you. I am sure you would rather be doing something else. I apologize for not bringing any food or coffee. I am not at all sure that we should be drinking this . . . this stuff." Gloria had consumed only a cupful but the effect was apparent. "We never had any of this white lightning stuff in college." Gloria's voice was a mixture of disdain and excitement.

Annie interrupted Gloria's recital. "Would it be possible, just for a few minutes Gloria, for you to stop apologizing? If we did not want to be here we wouldn't. Just leave it at that, okay? We all have to take our turn at this. It's important for the war effort. And we know you're lonely without Lester hanging around every time you have a free minute."

Each word was enunciated carefully. With a grunt, Annie pulled herself up to a sitting position and rested her shoulders against the only stanchion on the roof. Her dark form, not five feet from Sparkle, was outlined against the night sky.

"I am sorry, Gloria, if I sound rude. I believe I have had too much to drink." A loud hiccup verified Annie's assessment.

Sparkle pulled the blanket closer around her shoulders. An occasional blink of light from the city would flash, only to be quickly extinguished. The red glow from the end of her cigarette gave her comfort.

She heard a sound of snuffling and let out an exasperated sigh, knowing it came from Birdie. The colored woman had

gulped the first few drinks from the bottle when they sat down
and ever since she'd been switching between tears and laughter.
Sparkle assumed that whatever was in the letter from home
had been bad. She felt the smile leave her face, replaced by a
grimace.

"Can't any of you make that nigger shut up?" As soon as she
said it she stopped. She'd meant it lightly as a joke, not at all
the way it had come out. She knew that she'd overstepped the
precious boundaries of her roommates again. For once, she did-
n't want to get in a fight about it and hoped that no one had
heard her. As soon as Gloria spoke, she knew she hadn't been
that lucky.

"Sparkle, you must stop saying that. It is not polite and it
makes Birdie feel badly. She did get the letter in the mail today."
Gloria's soft 'peacemaker' voice made Sparkle itch to take a
poke at her.

She took a quick swallow of the bottle and felt her face flush.
She wished she could think of someway to take it back. Just
when she was beginning to feel included, she'd said the wrong
thing. She hurried to mask her discomfort.

"Well, I don't see as it makes any difference. It's what she is
after all. What's wrong with calling a spade a spade?" She
gasped and then started again. "Ah shit, I didn't mean that. I'm
not saying she's a rotten person or anything." The familiar feeling of needing to defend herself before she got hit was strong.

She heard a scuffling sound and turned to see a large dark
form rising up in front of her. As if a chill wind found the back
of her neck, shivers ran over her skin. Knowing in her head that
the form was Annie didn't help her since her gut had already
mistaken the shape for one of the devils of her childhood. Those
shadowy figures had held bruises and pain in one hand and tender, smelly affection in the other. She watched as the tall woman
pulled herself upward on unsteady legs.

Annie's words were stronger, as if the situation called for a
clearer head than she had. "This is the way it is Sparkle. You
cannot use that word anymore. It does not make any difference

what you think. It only matters how Birdie feels." Her sentences ran together and she went from high to low pitch for no apparent reason, but the message was clear. "How do you feel, Birdie?"

"Don't want you defen'dn me. I c'n take care of myself." Birdie's voice was nearly as slurred as Annie's, tears choking off words.

"I am not defending you. I am telling Sparkle how it will be. No more of that talk. This is between . . . her . . . and . . . ah . . . me." Annie's words ran down at the end like an unwound music box.

Sparkle flung out a challenge. "Y'know I could move out of here, move in with just about any guy. Any one of 'em would have me, even ol' Jack down the street. Then what would you do for the other part of the rent?" A small smile of triumph crossed her lips. She knew Birdie couldn't pay more.

Annie took in a long breath. "We will miss you Sparkle but it wouldn't take more than a word at the plant to get us another roommate. There is not enough space in this city." Annie voice was calm as if she were at the end of a conversation.

Sparkle heard a gasp from Gloria. She felt the sound echo in her chest and wondered if she'd have to make good on her stupid threat. Jack smelled like a goat and chewed tobacco in bed.

Her voice held a shake she couldn't stop. "You mean you'd rather have her than me?"

This time Annie's voice thundered, as if tired of explaining. "Sparkle, it has nothing to do with what we want. It has to do with what's right. Quit saying that stupid word and everything's all right. Nobody is asking you to move out. You are the one threatening." Annie ran out of steam. "And frankly, if I've got to choose, I'm going to choose someone who can cook." She sank to the roof, her dark form leaving the sky open in front of Sparkle again.

"Dammit, don't you think I've tried? It's not so easy, you know. People where I come from wouldn't even stay in the same room with her, no matter what she's like, much less live with

her. I can't just change overnight. And who says I can't cook?"
Sparkle hated the pleading note in her last question.

She waited for someone else to speak. The minutes dragged
on and she pulled the cigarette from her mouth, burning her
fingers on the short end. She dropped it quickly on the roof, then
stood up and carefully ground the butt out with her heel.

As she thought about the situation, she had an idea. "Tell
you what Annie, I'll quit saying nigger if you quit saying you
love Howard."

As Sparkle watched, Annie's head jerked up like it had been
yanked. Audible gasps came from Birdie and Gloria and the
silence stretched out interminably.

Annie finally sat up straight and wrapped both arms around
her legs. The question seemed to have a sobering effect on her.
"I don't think that's the same at all."

Sparkle began to warm to her subject. "No? Well I think so.
Saying that word is just something I do without thinking.
Saying you love Howard is just about the same thing, you've
just been saying it so long you think that makes it true. Tell me
straight out that you love the man."

"Well." Sparkle could tell that Annie was struggling. The
woman didn't have a dishonest bone in her body. Annie took a
deep breath. "Maybe I'm not sure what love is."

The rooftop was quiet again and Sparkle decided she would-
n't press her point. Instead, Birdie's southern drawl interrupted the night's darkness. "Speakin' of your cooking, girl? You is a
worse cook than my Aunt Penny an' she couldn't even pour salt
right. But that's not 'portant right now. Y'r jes being stupid, but
that's nothing new. Right now, I gotta figure out how to get my
kids out here. It's jes not gonna work any longer to have them
back home until the war gets over or I get enough money to go
home. They're missin' their mama and I'm about dyin' with
missin' them. My Beau's momma is jes' too old and I'm afraid
that Letty is gonna be gettin' in trouble."

"I am not stupid." Sparkle felt her face flush again and
pressed her fingernails into her hand. She decided to try anoth-

er tactic. "Well they sure as hell can't stay with us. There's hardly enough room for anyone to sneeze in the trailer, much less put four kids."

If Birdie was serious about bringing her kids out, maybe it was a good way to get rid of her and save face at the same time. "You should talk to Maggie. She's trying to get someone to help her run the Blue House."

"How would that help? Birdie's got no more time than the rest of us." Annie's voice was muffled.

Sparkle spoke quickly. "The Blue House is a boarding house. I heard that Maggie's looking for someone to do the cooking. She's so drunk at night that she's servin' raw potatoes and meat like glue. Some of the boarders have already left. I'll bet you could make some sort of deal for a room or two. Maybe try to get a graveyard shift at work then cook the supper." As Sparkle talked her own idea sounded better and better.

Gloria's voice startled her, as if she'd read Sparkle's mind. "I wonder if there are any extra rooms there. I could help Birdie out and maybe learn to cook at the same time." Gloria's voice was timid, as if she were asking permission.

Sparkle quickly revised her idea of getting back into the bedroom. "Why the hell would you want to live there? At least you get a little bed to yourself. I'm up there in front of God and everybody."

"Yes but sometimes I would like a little privacy too. A whole bedroom to myself would be nice."

"I kind of like the idea myself. Do you know how many of the rooms are filled now?" Annie had straightened up and spoke clearly.

Sparkle gulped, pulled her lower lip in between her teeth and started to chew. Her great idea was starting to backfire. "Now hold it just a minute. If all of you move out, there's only me left. That's not going to work. Why can't we just get Birdie moved out?"

Annie cleared her throat. "Because we like Birdie and she is easy to live with. Besides, it sounds like a good opportunity."

Sparkle began to chew earnestly on her lip. "That's crazy, let's just forget the whole thing. Forget I said anything. It was dumb idea. We'll just leave it like it is."

"But that means you're gonna have to live with a niggah." Birdie's voice was soft and Sparkle couldn't tell if she was joking.

"And an idiot with too many clothes." Gloria leaned closer and began to tug on the blanket still hanging from Sparkle's shoulders.

"And a darned big giant."

Sparkle tasted blood and she released her lip with a start. Her own fear was strong. She gulped and spoke quickly. "This isn't funny you guys. I was just trying to help. Now you're making it all worse." She fumbled in the pocket of her jacket for her cigarettes. Her hand was shaking as she scraped the match head against the rough surface.

Annie chuckled. "Depends on your point of view. You might have just had your finest idea ever. If it works out Sparkle, why don't you just come too? Stop saying that word and it'll be just like it is now, only we'll have more room."

"That is a great idea, Sparkle. It would not be the same without you." Gloria's lisp was stronger than normal in the cool night air.

"Yep. Can't imagine a morning without trying to get you out'n the way so we can get going." Birdie's tone was teasing, light.

Sparkle couldn't quite catch her breath. She was tingling all over and a little trickle of tears started down her cheeks. They weren't throwing her out. In fact they wanted her with them. She started to speak and realized she couldn't say a word without blubbering. Finally she just sat back and smiled.

CHAPTER SEVEN

Birdie and Gloria stared at the Blue House. The faded, peeling paint on the exterior emphasized the right half of the front porch, painted haphazardly in an eye-popping bright blue color. It appeared to Birdie that someone had started to paint but given up when they found out what a long, hard job it would be. She was sure that at one time the two story house had been well-built and then cared for but now the gingerbread trim hung loose in spots and the lawn had gone back to weeds. The front porch sported a sagging couch and lopsided curtains hung in the upstairs windows.

Gloria coughed, then spoke in a whisper. "I wish we could have called first, it is hard to tell if anyone is here or not. I do not want to interrupt."

Birdie laughed. "Don' think we need to whisper and sure don' think calling would have helped. Looks to me like this place always looks empty." She moved forward. "Won' be getting a job standin' here. Let's get moving." She could hear the tap of Gloria's shoes on the stone path as she climbed the three stairs to the porch.

She rapped on the screen door, then 'yoo-hooed' into the interior. When that didn't work, she pulled the door open and stepped in, Gloria following closely behind. Her first sight of the front room, filled with old but comfortable looking chairs and tables, made Birdie want to pick up a dust rag.

Her next yoo-hoo produced grumbling and hacking behind a door to the left. Then the door swung out and a woman appeared.

Her weathered, stork like frame oddly matched the dilapidated condition of the building. A cigarette hung from two fingers and the skin on her face lay folded in deep grooves. She coughed again and spoke in the deepest, raspiest voice Birdie had ever heard in a woman.

"What-cha-want? Got a room open but I don't have no women here now and I don't want no trouble." Her words came out like rough boards rubbing together and Birdie had to concentrate on what she was saying to understand.

"My name is Birdie Jones and this is Gloria . . ." The girl moved from behind Birdie to stand at her side. ". . . Westfall. We heard you might like to have some help with chores and cooking. I'd like to apply for the job."

For a moment the woman was absolutely still, then her mouth opened wide and she brayed. Really brayed, like a donkey, loud and long and at the end. Finally, Birdie realized she was laughing.

"Well you two girlies come right on in here. Let me tell you a little about this no-good place." She'd just come through the open door and led them into the kitchen.

Greasy pots and pans and containers were stacked high in the sink and against the coarse wood siding of the backsplash. The kitchen was dark and hot and smelled like boiling socks. Maggie sat down and rested her head on the back of a green rocker, the only seat in the room. An ashtray, overflowing with butts, balanced on the arm. When she spoke, her voice sounded like the rough side of an old barn.

"Y'know I can't believe they're doing this to me. After all I done for them. Workin' my fingers to the bone. Now they're c'mn in here and saying I don' run a good place. Sayin' I don' serve a decent meal. They jus' been listenin' to them whiners. Jeez, you'd think they's paying thirty bucks a month to stay here. They're always saying 'Maggie wha's this stuff? Maggie how come there's lumps in the 'tatoes?'" The words dribbled off and the old woman's eyes closed. As Birdie watched in horror, the ash from the burning cigarette held in Maggie's tobacco stained fingers, wavered then fell precisely into the middle of the ash-tray.

Her eyes opened again and she hacked a couple times. "I think the reason is cuz they's a man owner. You know, I don't believe I ever met a man I really liked. Well, 'cept there was Joe back '21 . . . thaz the summer of '21, I didn't stay with the bastid long y'understan. Anyway . . ." As she talked, Maggie's mouth puckered and wrinkles pointed toward the center, as if an invisible cigarette remained in residence. It occurred to Birdie that in her youth, Maggie had probably been tall and willowy. The bones were still there, but over the years the flesh had sagged and withered, leaving a scrawny, creased copy of the original. "Did I tell you I been runnin' this place for twenny years?"

Birdie stared at the woman, her brain going as fast as a peach orchard boar, trying to put together the pieces of her idea. This boardinghouse arrangement looked like the best chance to bring her children up north and she wasn't about to give up before she'd given it a heck of a try.

Maggie was speaking again. "Ungrateful, slimy bastids. Said they were going to drop in for a visit." The last words were higher and sing-song.

"Who's dropping in?" Birdie was confused.

"Owners." Maggie's tone made it sound like poison meat.

"Say they's gonna check it out. I know what they're gonna do. They're coming to fire me." The old woman gulped on her water glass full of dark whiskey and sucked on a cigarette then her head dropped forward on her chest.

"Good gracious." Gloria stared at the woman.

Birdie paused only a moment. "Get back to the trailer and see who's there. Tell 'em we need help, lickety split."

Gloria looked at Birdie with almost the same expression as she'd given Maggie.

"Get going, girl. I got an idea and we got a dinner to fix." Birdie was determined not to let this chance pass. She had to convince the boarders there were better things coming and quiet the fears of the owners, all in three hours. She shooed the girl out the door and told her to hurry. Then she turned back to Maggie.

Birdie nudged the woman's arm and saw her blink. "Um, what did you say was for dinner? I could maybe help you get started." She leaned forward in her straight backed chair and looked directly into Maggie's red rimmed eyes

"Beef and 'tatoes and other stuff." Maggie's head slid forward again and this time she burped, then made a slow bone-settling move into the rocker. Birdie felt sweat begin to trickle between her shoulder blades. Gazing around her, she took a deep breath and rose to see what she could find.

She tiptoed to the stove and peeked into a pot. Whatever was in there seemed to share the watery looking broth with seeds and sticks. A quick look into another pot revealed potatoes swimming in milky water. She rubbed her hands up and down on her skirt and moved forward in her search of something edible. She spent several minutes trying to decide what kind of meat was in the pot and just what she could do with it. She was checking another pan when the sound of a slamming door made her jump and she dropped the lid back down with a clang. Turning she saw Gloria and Sparkle entering through the back door, followed shortly by Annie and Cain.

"What the heck's going on? Gloria's got us all confused."

Sparkle's loud voice sounded like cannon shot in the quiet room. Birdie put her fingers to her lips and made shushing sounds. Birdie pointed to the woman snoring and muttering intermittently in the rocking chair. Gloria moved closer and whispered.

"So, did you get the job?"

Birdie put her head close and spoke softly. "Ah dunno, we didn't get to that part yet. But in two and a half hours there's gonna be some people out there lookin' for food along with the owners of this place who are lookin' to fire Maggie. If I can show them I can put together a meal for everybody, maybe they'll give me the job." The friends gazed at Maggie as she settled further into the chair and made sporadic snorting sounds.

Birdie kept her voice soft and the others leaned forward to hear. "Ah've decided that we can serve it. Mostly it's cooked. I can fancy it up a little, make a few more dishes and you-all can hep' me. We just need to keep Maggie out of the way for a while."

Sparkle snorted and they all turned back to gaze at Maggie's loose-jointed form. Annie's eyes grew wide and she stepped back a couple of paces.

"She's really drunk."

"Smells like a distillery in here." Cain muttered.

Birdie squared her shoulders and looked at her little army. "Now listen. If we got any chance of pulling this off, we got to all work together. I need to figure out the menu. Don't remember ever seeing meat like this before but I'm gonna make it so's you can eat it." She gulped when she noticed the alarm clock sitting on the white enameled top shelf of the old stove. "I'll 'splain while we work. C'mon." She moved her arm in a 'follow me' signal and they shifted into the heart of the kitchen and away from Maggie.

Twenty minutes later Birdie was standing by the stove and stirring thick red sauce in a battered pan that rested on two or three points of its bottom. Maggie's snores were reduced to an occasional rumble in the background and Gloria was pouring water off the potatoes. Annie had gone into the dining room to set the table and ward off any curious boarders. Cain was on the floor with his head thrust in a cabinet searching for serving dishes and Sparkle was emptying cans of green beans into a pot. The front doorbell rang. Birdie's stomach did a quick flip.

"The boarders wouldn't ring the bell and it's too early for the dinner group."

Gloria's forehead was wrinkled. "It's got to be the owners."

Annie pushed open the swinging doors and stuck her head in. "I guess they're early. I'll try to hold them off."

The bubble of hope Birdie had been nurturing while they worked, burst as the door swung shut after Annie. Shaking herself firmly, she stabbed the meat from its gray looking broth and placed it into the pan with her own red sauce.

"This isn't the best barbeque sauce I ever made but it should help this poor old meat out some. Gloria, stir this a little will ya while I whump up some biscuits." Birdie kept her voice low, trying to cook, talk and think at the same time. She kept repeating to herself. 'I can do this. I been feedin' folks all my life. This is just more of the same'. She looked up at Sparkle who stood with one hand on her hip and stared at the rest of them.

Silence filled the room as Birdie concentrated on finding flour and baking powder, opening and slamming doors shut in her search. The kitchen door banged again and Birdie took in such a sharp breath she almost choked. Annie stood in the doorway, eyes wide.

"They want to see Maggie, and they want to talk to her. I told them she was sick, maybe the flu, but they're being stubborn. Any chance of sobering her up?"

Birdie snorted as she gazed at the sleeping woman. "Well, I guess it's time." She pushed the damp hair from her eyes, straightened her back and marched into the sitting room.

A man and a woman standing beside an overstuffed couch, looked up as she approached. They were brother and sister apparently, both tall and lean looking with blond hair and thin lips. Birdie nodded at them and smiled.

"Hello. I'm Birdie Jones and I came to see if Maggie could use some help. I can see that things aren't in too good a shape here. I'd like you to give me a chance at cookin' tonight and maybe runnin' this place. I've got my crew in the back hep'n me make dinner now. I b'n working at this kind of thing all my life, you'll see I can do it." She swallowed hard. She figured the worst they could do was say no.

The man raised one eyebrow, pursed his lips then shook his head. "Hello, Mrs. Jones. I'm Mark Wellington and this is my sister Jewell. I'm sorry but I don't think we could let that happen. You've probably discerned that we were about to let Maggie go. There have just been too many complaints. We're thinking pretty seriously of selling this place and this looks like as good a time as any."

Birdie could feel her chances slipping away. She pictured her children and her fingers itched to grab the man, make his listen. "How about you let me finish supper? That way, nobody's gonna be mad at you for making them go without eatin' and you can decide then if you want to give me a chance."

Mark shook his head again and began to speak. "I don't think . . ."

His sister interrupted him before he could refuse. "Hold it. She's right, what have we got to lose? I say we give her a chance."

Birdie looked hopefully at Jewell's brother but saw that he was about to shake his head again. Just at that moment, Cain pushed open the kitchen door.

"Birdie, I can't find the forks and stuff." He stopped when he saw the visitors. "I'm sorry, I didn't mean to interrupt. Hello, I'm Cain Adamson." He held out his hand to Mr. Wellington.

As Birdie watched, the expression on Mark's face relaxed. He shook Cain's hand. "Are you on Mrs. Jones' crew?"

Cain blinked then smiled. "I guess I am. For tonight anyway." He glanced at Birdie.

She talked fast. "Cain, the Wellingtons were 'bout to give us a chance at cooking supper tonight. Isn't that grand?"

A small grin appeared on Jewell's face as her brother studied Cain, then nodded his head.

"Yes, that's right, I'll be interested to see what you can do."

Four hours later, Birdie shut the door behind the owners and let out a huge sigh of relief. Her feet were killing her, her head hurt and she had specks of food all over. But that didn't matter. She stared out the window at the Wellington's retreating figures and let the wave relief spread through her.

She heard a chuckle from behind her and turned to see Cain, Annie, Gloria and Sparkle standing there. They all looked much like she felt, exhausted, happy and surprised.

"Well boss, that was some evening. Don't think I've had that much fun since the war started." Sometime during the rush, Sparkle had acquired streaks of flour on her cheek.

Gloria shook her head. "I had no idea you could feed that many people so quickly. You're a marvel, Birdie."

She was pleased the girl thought she was that good but shook her head. "I hate to tell you, that was the easy part. From now on it's gonna get hard."

Sparkle snorted and held up a hand. "I'll tell you something right now, I'm not going to be working every night feeding a bunch of folks. I've got a job."

Birdie felt a gnawing of uneasiness. Her plan would include all of them, at least for the first month or so.

"Don't complain until you hear what Birdie has in mind." Annie's voice was calm.

Sparkle looked at her and scowled, then shrugged her shoulders and said, "Okay, tell us the plan Birdie, but remember, I may not like it."

Birdie just looked at the other woman. "Let's sit down, this might take a bit."

They settled themselves on various couches and chairs and Birdie gathered her thoughts. "Well, I've got the job and I need to thank Cain for hepin' out. When he talked with Mr. Wellington after dinner, the fella decided to go along with his sister and let me have a chance. " 'Preciate that."

Cain nodded, his cheeks red.

Birdie moved forward on the couch. "I'll need to change to graveyard at the plant. The rest of the time I'll work here."

"Are you going to give up sleeping?" Sparkle's voice was sarcastic. She still wasn't buying the program.

"I figure I can get about six hours sleep a night. That should be plenty. Better than when the children were babies. Anyway, that's only part of it and I can handle that. Now this place has four boardin' rooms and right now two are empty. I said we'd take the two rooms."

"You did what?" Sparkle's voice was amazed.

"Look, we all said we'd like more room. Right now a couple of you are going to have to share a room, but it's sure more space than the trailer. The only hitch is that it's September 27th now and I told them we'd be in by the first of October.

"You did what?"

"That's only three days."

"I don't believe it."

"I know it's going to be tough but look. If we're out of the trailer by the first, we don't have to pay October rent there. We can start paying here and the way I figger, it's gonna be cheaper. We get more room and don't have to pay as much. I'm going to need help with dinner, but if I've got it figgered right, we can split it up so nobody has to put in more than an hour or so a day." Birdie was speaking fast, trying to convince the group what a good idea it was.

The room was silent for a few moments and then Annie rose and began to pace. "Can we look at the rooms?"

Twenty minutes later they had examined all but Maggie's and the two boarders' rooms and were back in the sitting room. Annie was talking. "I think Gloria should take the small room next to the bathroom. Sparkle and I can share the larger one. Birdie's right, it's going to work. But what about Maggie?"

Birdie sighed. "She told the owners she would be out by tomorrow. She has a sister here in town. She said she's going to get a job at Boeing. Said it had to be easier than this. Hope she don' get a job buckin' with me." They laughed and then Birdie voiced her real concern. "I'm wonderin' how we're gonna get moved in three days."

Cain shifted forward in his chair. "I think I can borrow a truck. Can we make the move after work or are we going to need to take time off?"

"Ah think we can do it after work." Birdie was so relieved to hear that they were going to go along with her plan that she would have carried all their possessions to the Blue House on her back in the dead of night if she had to.

Gloria was smiling. "I will start a list. If you get the truck, Cain, I will try to figure out a time schedule."

"I want to talk about the rooms. I think I should get the single room." Sparkle was still pitching but Birdie knew she would end up sharing the room with Annie.

"Did you hear why this place was painted blue in the first place?" Birdie and the other three turned to Cain and shook their heads.

"Mark told me. I guess the first owner was rich, old and nearly blind. He painted it the brightest blue he could buy. Some people said that when the moon was just right, the house glowed. He told the neighbors that he wanted to find it when he came home blind, staggering drunk, which I guess happened pretty regularly. When he sold it, the new owners converted it into a boardinghouse, but stayed with the color. Said it made it noticeable. That new paint on the porch is about the same color as the original."

They all laughed and Birdie sat back in her chair and wondered what her Beauregard would have to say when he saw it.

The aroma coming from the open door of the Blue House almost made Annie cry. It was incredibly good to be home. She smiled. It was strange to call this new place home. It had been only five days since the first dinner at the Blue and they were already beginning to settle into their new residence.

During the last two hours of work Annie hadn't been able to tell which was worse, her need for sleep or food. She knew she didn't need any alcohol. Since their night of drinking on the roof, she still felt a little queasy when she thought of anything with spirits.

She wondered what her parents would think about the incident. She knew the boys had spent some uncomfortable time out in the shed with their father after episodes like that. If her father could only see her now.

Low clouds hung over West Seattle, leaving wispy patches of sunlight on the ground and over the houses on West Roxbury. One of the things she did like about this new place was that the bus picked her up right outside the door, not five blocks away like Plum Lane. She was also very pleased with the rooms they all had. She and Sparkle were sharing and Gloria was happy with the little side room. Birdie, though, was the happiest. Off the kitchen was a large bedroom with a little side room. She told them when she brought the children to the Blue House she would be able to fit all of them in her two rooms. Annie offered to build bunk beds to save some space. Annie lifted her arms wide and yawned nearly hard enough to crack her jaw. Running her fingers through her hair, she found a thick blob of grease.

"Yuck. What the . . .."

Birdie stuck her head out the front door and caught sight of Annie. "Thought we could have some pot roast for dinner. You c'mon in here and get cleaned up. Supper's gonna be ready in about a half hour."

Annie's mouth watered and she wondered if she could find anything to eat right now. She examined the grease on her hand and decided she must have gotten too close to the nose of the ship while the crew was putting in the engine. She looked down at her dungarees. She'd been hit by spraying oil at least twice in the last eight hours. She wiped her fingers on the already greasy material. Another giant yawn attacked. She stopped with one foot on the wide front porch enjoying the luxury of not moving for a few moments.

What seemed like seconds later, the sound of Birdie's voice brought her up sharply and her eyes flew open. "Ya gonna spend all night holding down those steps or come in here and get cleaned up?"

She laughed then stepped inside and walked into the kitchen savoring the smells of pot roast, cornbread and something else she hoped was Birdie's apple pie. Reaching for the oven door, she felt the slap of a kitchen towel on her arm and pulled back quickly.

"No peekin'. You know bettern' that." Birdie stood beside the stove, guarding her domain. A sigh escaped Annie and she pushed her way past Birdie and headed upstairs toward the shower on the second floor.

A half hour later, she sat next to Gloria at the dining table relishing the feel and smell of clean hair and clothes. The room was quiet although the table was almost full. Their two remaining boarders, Matt Parker, a balding man in his fifties, and Joseph Robletto, a dark complexioned fellow with longish black hair sat at the far side of the table. Four other men, two of them 4F and the others too old for service had introduced themselves as Paul, Jim, Ben and Joshua almost as if it were one name. They waited quietly, but with forks raised, as if expecting food to arrive momentarily.

Gloria was still dressed in her work clothes and Annie looked at her with envy. She was wearing a white blouse with lace around the collar, a blue skirt with a red belt and red flats. Since Gloria had been working full time in the shop office, her wardrobe had become quite splendid compared to the rest of them. Sitting next to her, Annie felt bulky and awkward with her extra large flannel shirt and wrinkled slacks. She stared down at Gloria's tiny red shoes and tucked her own size twelves farther under the bench. They all had large iced tea mugs in front of them. Annie's was nearly empty. Gloria had brought the glass to her lips three times, only to pause, then set it down carefully on the blue checked tablecloth without drinking anything.

Annie felt a twinge of surprise. "What is the matter?"

At the sound of Annie's voice, Gloria flinched.

"Nothing. Nothing. I am fine." The girl's words were hurried and breathless, almost as if they had caught on her prominent front teeth.

They were interrupted by Birdie coming through the swinging kitchen door. A huge apron was wrapped around her middle and she squared off with her hands on hips.

"C'n I get some help?" Annie jumped up and headed at a trot for the door. She could hear Gloria following with slower footsteps. Annie saw that two of the men had come half out of their chairs. "No, it's all right, we can manage just fine." The two seemed happy to be relieved of any domestic duties and sat back in their chairs.

Annie was handed the platter with pot roast and potatoes, while Gloria received the cornbread and butter. Annie felt a smile start as she caught sight of the apple pies cooling on top of the empty pans lining the sink. It looked like Birdie had taken no time at all to become comfortable with the layout of the Blue kitchen. As usual, every surface was covered with assorted pots, pans, food containers and a dusting of white flour.

Annie laughed. Her mother's kitchen was always pristine, no cooking paraphernalia or containers left out and never, never would flour be allowed to settle on any surface. Myrtle Tosh had turned out thousands of meals from the huge kitchen but nothing like the pure heaven of tastes and smells that Birdie was able to produce from the tiny trailer kitchen or this overgrown, awkward jumbled up workspace.

It took less than twenty minutes for the men to finish their meals including two apple pies. Birdie had saved portions of these in the kitchen for the four of them. As soon as the men left, Annie and Gloria cleared the table and Annie set forks on the picnic table at the side of the house. They much preferred eating outdoors as long as the weather allowed and today was one of those Seattle surprises, a balmy October evening.

A loud slam indicated Sparkle's arrival and a black Ford sedan shining with wax and chrome pulled away from the driveway. She sat down with a breathless sigh. Her red skirt was hiked up to mid-thigh due to the snug fit and her starched white blouse struggled to stay buttoned. A filmy crimson scarf floated around her neck, anchored precariously in her cleavage.

"You hanging around with that man again?" Birdie's voice was flat and directed at Sparkle. Annie had noticed that the argument on the roof had cleared the air. The two women seemed to be on an even footing, even though they still didn't see eye to eye on much.

"Mind your own business, woman. It ain't no concern who brings me home long as he don't stay." Sparkle returned the answer briskly.

Annie felt her teeth begin to grind. "That's enough you two. Absolutely nothing is going to spoil this evening. If you need to argue, go somewhere else. Pass me the pie, would you?" She put her napkin firmly in her lap and nodded expectantly at Gloria, who was closest to the pie plate. Sparkle looked mutinous for a moment, then shrugged.

Annie looked at Gloria whose face was chalky white. Her eyes were so wide they showed white all the way around the pale blue iris. A funny gurgling sound came from her mouth. She clapped her hand over it, rose from the bench and ran toward the house.

Annie's jaw dropped open as she watched Gloria. "What in the world?" She started to rise from the table when Sparkle put a hand on her arm.

"Don't bother, this is something she's going to have to do on her own. She's been up the last couple of mornings."

"Oh no." Annie felt her face go slack with surprise. "You mean?"

"I think that she and Lester the Lover were doing more than talk." Sparkle put a spoonful of honey on her cornbread and sat watching it melt into the yellow surface.

Annie could feel her heart begin to race and she looked in disbelief at the other two women. "What in heaven's name are we going to do? They're not engaged. Lester doesn't even know."

Birdie put down the rib she was working on and spoke slowly. "We are going to have us a baby, that's what."

"Or not." Sparkle's voice was flat.

Birdie shrugged. "There's always that I suppose. Kinda hate to see it tho'."

The look that passed between Sparkle and Birdie was old and wise and Annie felt left out and angry and confused all at once. She chewed on her bottom lip.

The slamming of the screen door brought the three of them up short. Gloria walked with a measured stride across the weeds and grass that made up the side lawn and she had taken some effort to put her face together. As she neared the others at the table, she stopped, looking at them with eyebrows raised in question.

Annie wanted to break the silence, hoping to soften whatever Sparkle might come up with. "You're pregnant, aren't you?"

The carefully composed face dissolved and Gloria took the last two steps to the bench as if she were a million years old. She seated herself carefully, smoothing her skirt with trance like movements. Huge tears slid down her cheeks. She slowly lowered her head onto her arms and for several moments all they heard was a low wail of despair. Annie's arm went around Gloria automatically, Birdie put her hand on the sobbing woman's shoulder and Sparkle sat back quietly.

When the tears subsided, Sparkle's calm voice broke the silence. "Your parents are going to be pretty mad, aren't they?"

Gloria blinked. "Oh yes. You know they were not happy about my coming up here. Especially about living with all of you. They'll never forgive me for this."

Annie pulled her tighter, wanting to draw out some of the pain she felt in her friend. Gloria turned and looked at her with knitted brows. Annie tried to sound reassuring.

"This isn't the first time someone's gotten pregnant without being married."

"Oh, that part is not so bad. My cousin got pregnant a couple of years ago and she married the boy and everything was just fine." Her lisp was more pronounced when she was upset.

It was Annie's turn to be puzzled. "Then what's the problem?"

"I'll bet your cousin hooked a rich one, didn't she?" Sparkle was staring at the row of trees behind them.

"Yes, that's right. It was a really good match." Gloria rubbed her eyes with the back of her hand, making red marks across her cheeks.

Annie took her arm from around Gloria and sat back slightly. She was confused. "But you said yourself, Lester is a wonderful guy, much nicer than anyone you'd ever met at home. I think he'll make a great husband and you really do love him."

Now Gloria and Sparkle shared a look that Annie understood no better than the earlier one between Sparkle and Birdie.

"You don't understand. Les is nobody. He came from Texas and his parents are farmers. I can't imagine what my parents will think. I can't marry someone with nothing. My family is too important for that." A thin wail escaped from Gloria and tears were threatening to fall again.

Annie looked at her plate and realized that her appetite was gone. She had no idea what to say or do. After a moment, she pulled Gloria back close to her.

"I guess we'll just figure this out as we go."

The two other women nodded and went back to eating as if this were the most common thing in the world.

CHAPTER EIGHT

Dark clouds scudded across the evening sky and played hopscotch between the trees. Cain wondered if they might be in for more rain. The last two weeks had brought them nothing but gray days and assorted rain in the form of mist, downpour, scattered showers, and the occasional drizzle.

He shifted and the truck lurched sideways then bounced hard as he tried to get the transmission to behave. The Ford truck, borrowed from John, was a nightmare to drive. His car would certainly have been more comfortable but it was unable to carry the larger pieces they needed to haul. He cursed quietly and pulled the steering wheel around to straighten the vehicle's forward progress. The violent movement brought Annie closer to him and she put her hand on his leg as she steadied herself. He felt a moment of loss when she removed it.

The road was rough but his inept driving of the temperamental vehicle was certainly exacerbating the situation. The bed of the vehicle was loaded with tires and scrap metal destined to become bombs and bullets. The material had been gathered by the small army of children and old people who lived in the neighborhood surrounding the Blue House.

Annie had asked him to help her move this heavy load of material from the empty lot on the corner to the transfer station on the waterfront in Tacoma. Apparently, at the last minute, the man in charge had been called to work an extra shift leaving Annie the whole job. She told Cain she could load and unload the metal but needed someone else to drive since she'd never learned. He'd been glad to say yes. He welcomed any excuse to see or be with her. John had warned him about the eccentricities of the fifteen year old truck. If he had known sooner that he would be driving, he'd have tinkered with the clutch some.

Another rough shift and he glanced at the woman beside him again. The late evening light caught Annie's hair reminding Cain of campfire flames. Fiery strands wrapped around his thoughts and burned into his dreams. He couldn't understand it. He'd always been drawn to small women with tiny frames and big breasts. And certainly no brains. Here was a woman of raw power, awesome size and a mind that scared him. Well, at least she did have great breasts.

He shook his head and put the hand that was reaching up to touch her hair back on the wheel. He didn't trust the rising surge of longing that attacked him whenever he saw her. Anger and confusion warred within him.

"Why did you say you would do this alone? This is almost a two man job, much less one woman. And how come you don't drive?"

She turned to him, her jaw jutting forward defensively. "Do you think that I'm not capable of doing the work? Not strong enough?"

Cain gritted his teeth and watched her face to see if she was serious. That wasn't what he'd meant at all. He was about to say something when she continued.

"And I don't drive because . . . because . . . because I just don't that's all. Are you offering to teach me?"

Her words were a challenge and he winced when he thought of a novice driver in his car.

"Aw c'mon. Don't take it wrong. I just meant that this is a two man job at least. There's a limit to what even you can do."

He didn't know what to say about her driving so he looked ahead again. Sunset had begun to work its magic on the western horizon and soft bands of color bathed the dark trees and bushes with red gold. He sighed. Every time he got close to

Annie he said some dumb thing that he wished he could take back later. The lethargy he'd been plagued with after returning from Africa had begun to lose its grip on him. Since he'd met Annie, he was beginning to feel like his old self again and he wanted that feeling to stay.

Cain grabbed the gearshift and worked the clutch until he had the truck in second gear again. They weren't making very good speed, but in this lower gear he figured that they would at least get there.

They were in sight of the transfer station, metal and tires lying in piles like untidy children's toys, when they hit a huge rut. Annie's head struck the top of the cab with a thunk. He tried to gear down quickly. The truck pitched forward and she was thrown roughly to the left, ending up sprawling over Cain. He felt her pull herself backward when his foot slipped and the motor coughed and died.

The truck rocked forward and they finally came to rest. He grabbed her arms to pull her up only to find that she had become wedged between the gearshift, steering wheel and him. Annie tried to struggle free but succeeded only in forcing them closer. Cain caught a faint scent of something clean and flowery as he laid his hand on her shoulder to still her for a moment. The feel of her skin warm and alive through the material of her shirt made his heart begin to beat uncomfortably.

"Hold on a minute. Let's figure this out or we'll be stuck here all day." They were struggling to become untangled when a white face peered in the window.

"What's wrong buddy? I told you to pull forward. Are you two all right in there?" The man staring at Cain through the half rolled down window sported a face like a hound dog with enough extra skin to cover two people. He was missing three or four teeth in front, giving him a dim, sort of Ichabod Crane look. Wrinkles of concern on his forehead were replaced by a startled expression as he took in the scene in front of him.

"Uh-oh. You guys got trouble?" The cigarette, which had been firmly clenched between his teeth moments earlier, dropped unnoticed from slack lips, leaving an ash trail down the front of his dark clothing. Cain felt a bubble of laughter as he realized what the other man was seeing.

"It's okay. Your road and this old truck just tossed us around a little. Give me a couple of minutes to get us sorted out and I'll pull forward."

The man went back to his work and Cain again tried to extricate Annie. This time his tugging worked and between them they managed to get her upright. She was seated now in the middle of the truck, still very close to him.

"This is nice." Cain was surprised. He'd been so busy directing his thoughts away from her presence that he was amazed how quickly his physical response took charge again.

Annie's face, only inches from his, turned a pretty shade of pink. "It is much better. Who was that man?"

"I suppose he works here."

Annie looked at him with a quizzical expression. He hoped she didn't want to move away from him.

He put his hands on her shoulders and lowered his face just enough to graze her lips with his. For a moment, he remembered Howard and then pushed the thought aside. When she didn't pull back, he pressed harder, this time feeling her lips part and answer his with a quickening eager excitement. Her strong body strained against his, her lips aggressive and soft at the same time. His chest tingled and his body responded to hers like a schoolboy, no technique, no conscious thought, just a fierce drive. He could hear a roaring sound in his ears.

He felt Annie's hands on his chest and shifted his weight, trying to ease sideways to allow them more room. As he moved he felt Annie pull back and look at him, her eyes dazed and her mouth a startled 'O'. He gritted his teeth and tried to gather Annie back to him at the same time she moved to come forward. Their heads crashed together.

A loud 'ouch' escaped him and Annie reached up to touch her forehead where they'd collided. Cain pulled back and saw Annie's lips twitching. She finally let loose a full blown belly laugh. Cain felt a flicker of consternation in his chest. Her next words dispelled his fear.

"I think we're dangerous together."

"To each other anyway." Cain's voice was rueful. She still had not moved away from him and he studied a small scar under her lower lip and wondered how that had happened. Her reserved expression was gone, replaced by something softer, more vulnerable.

His hands felt slick and his chest was suddenly filled with too much air. A familiar ache had begun between his legs. Annie's cheekbones were highlighted by the light coming in the window of the pickup and he raised his hand to touch her face. Her skin was soft as his fingers traced the line from eyebrow to jaw, lingering on the faint stripe under her lip. He leaned down to kiss her again when a loud knocking interrupted them.

They jumped apart and she settled on the other side of the cab. His hands shook slightly as he grabbed the worn handle and rolled down the window.

"If you're all set, you can drive over to the right there. See that big pile? I need to have you put your stuff there. Now where is that lazy boy? Henry!" He yelled loud enough that the noise rattled around the interior of the cab.

Cain looked at Annie. Her lips were pressed firmly together with barely controlled laughter. He started the motor and pulled the truck forward smiling.

"Thanks, fella. We'll be glad of any help you can give." Cain was careful to ease the clutch out gently this time. When he had backed up as close as he could get, he turned to Annie and found that she had sobered considerably.

"This isn't much like being friends is it?"

Frustrated, he jumped down from the truck quickly, and walked to the other side to open the door for Annie. His heart longed for the ease of the previous minutes before. As he opened the door, he found she was smiling.

They worked quietly, unloading the unwieldy pieces of metal and tires. Henry never did show up, but they completed the task in less than twenty minutes.

When they returned to the cab, Cain attempted to think of something to say to bring them back to the earlier intimacy. With a shrug of his shoulders he realized that wasn't going to happen. He looked out the smeared window of the truck and then had an inspiration.

"Would you like to go somewhere and learn to drive now?"

She gazed outside at the dark beginning to fold around them and then back at him with a slight frown on her forehead.

"Well, not right now. But maybe sometime."

He felt the tension in his shoulders ease. Friends they would be. He admired her commitment and he made a promise to himself that he would do his part to honor it.

Annie stretched her arms up and yawned wide. Seated with Gloria, Sparkle and Birdie in Cain's coupe, she was beginning to think that her life had developed an ironic twist. First nothing happens to you for a hundred years and you yearn desperately for any kind of change at all. Then everything happens at once and you wish it would just slow down.

In the last three weeks, Birdie had organized the Blue House and had made a list of who would help her and when. She cracked the whip harder than any supervisor Annie had ever worked with. The only problem was that Birdie herself couldn't seem to get to work at the plant on time. She'd been late three days last week and they'd all begun to worry.

And now, it appeared they were embarking on the craziest thing of all. Gloria had decided it was time Annie learned how to drive. She kept insisting that Annie didn't look competent enough to be elected to the stewardship position if she couldn't even drive. It was as though pregnancy had given Gloria some sort of motherly status that was maddening and endearing at the same time. At first Cain seemed reluctant to loan them the car. Annie wasn't sure if he wanted to teach her himself or was worried about her wrecking the automobile but after Gloria had turned on her charm, he'd folded without a whimper.

Now they were in a mown hay field and she could hear the grass stubble brushing underneath the black '35 Ford coupe. Evening light made long shadows of the fir trees and the crisp, cold scent of frozen grass filled the car. Learning to drive at the spinsterish age of thirty was damned near the most terrifying thing she'd ever done. She laughed. All she had to do was get behind the wheel of a car and she started sounding like Sparkle.

She tried to raise her foot slowly from the clutch, as she'd practiced in the front yard of the Blue House, but the easy forward progress was ruined as the vehicle shuddered and lurched. Behind her Sparkle yelled "More gas, more gas." She stomped on the pedal but it was too late. The car pitched forward hard then died with a cough.

"Shit."

"Now do not be upset, that happens to everyone. You just need to relax."

"Ah think we all should kinda brace ourselves back here. This might be a little rough." Birdie's slow drawl was edged with a chuckle.

Annie felt her breath coming in short little gasps. She gritted her teeth, then carefully pushed in the clutch, pressed the starter button and squashed the gas with enough force to keep the motor going. When it didn't move forward, she pushed harder but heard only the sound of the motor racing faster and faster. She looked at Gloria helplessly.

"Um . . . you should probably put it in gear."

"Oh." Her face felt hot and she swallowed a lump forming in her throat. She tried again, this time remembering to put it in gear first.

"Now, let the clutch out very slowly as you press on the gas. Now that's better. See, you are already driving." Gloria's voice had the soothing tone of a mother with a young child.

The car rolled forward and she tried to get some feeling for the right amount of pressure to apply to the gas pedal. Looking down, she marveled at her hands on the steering wheel. She was actually driving. With a surge of warmth in her chest, she saw that the speedometer was nearing five miles an hour.

"Ah . . . yer gonna need ta turn soon." At the sound of Birdie's worried tone, Annie twisted around to look at her in the back seat. The movement was met by screeching.

"Girl, look a-head-a-ya, not backwards."

"Eyes forward, Annie. Turn the wheel."

Jerking her head back around, she realized that a stand of trees was approaching much too quickly. Trying to think and act at the same time, she slammed her foot on the brake, turned the wheel and shrieked "Omigod".

The car pitched a few times then stopped dead in the grass, the engine coughing and belching before it died. Annie wiped her hands on her trousers and gave Gloria a sideways glance, trying to ignore the giggling from the back seat.

Smiling, her friend patted her shoulder. "Now don't you worry, we all started out this way. Just put the clutch in next time you want to stop, that way the car won't die."

"Poor car's gonna be permanently dead with ol' Rocket Racer at the wheel." Sparkle's words were long and drawn out.

Birdie spoke again. "Y'all think we maybe shoulda brought some pillows?"

Tears threatened as Annie's heart returned to thumping at a slightly less frantic rate. "I can't believe people do this all the time. I'm sorry I can't get it right. " She shifted her weight, wanting desperately to relinquish the driver's seat to any of her three friends.

"Now you sound like Gloria, apologizing for something that isn't your fault. Is that stuff catching?" Sparkle was sitting behind Gloria and Annie could see the lacy edge on her snug blue blouse in the rear view mirror.

Annie sniffed and asked, "What's that smell?

Ignoring everyone else, Gloria smiled at Annie, her eyes wide with encouragement. "That is just the silly clutch getting a little hot. The car companies need to take lessons from us on how to build things. Don't worry. We lived through Sparkle making dinner, we will live through this too. Now start it again, would you?"

Annie laughed and let out a breath she hadn't known she'd been holding. She put the car in gear, pushed in the clutch, pressed the starter button and the motor caught the first time. Pressing gently on the gas they moved forward. This time, Annie was careful to watch the uneven field in front instead of her friends in back. A happy grin curved the side of her mouth.

After a couple turns around the field, the pitch and roll of the auto became easier to judge. The feeling of rushing forward too fast lessened and Annie pushed harder on the pedal. As the car went faster, she noticed a whining noise. Soon the sound filled the car and she wondered if she were doing something wrong again.

"It's time to shift, Annie, you need to get out of first gear into second. Now, it's just like first, ease the clutch out. Oop . . . oop . . . not so fast. Yes, that's better. Now change to second. No, no that's third. Here, I'll help." Gloria put her hand on Annie's and directed the gearshift into the correct position. "Now let the clutch out very slowly and hit the gas at the same time."

Annie did as directed, amazed when she saw the speedometer register fifteen miles an hour as the ruts in the meadow threw the car up and down at will.

"Kee . . . rist." Sparkle's voice vibrated like a warped record. "I can't believe it, first we can't get her started then we can't stop her. Kinda like a guy I used to . . ." Her words were lost as they struck a substantial pothole and she and Birdie hit the headliner with twin thumps.

Annie grinned at the momentary silence from the back seat and turned the wheel slightly, angling the car back toward the middle of the field. She liked the feel of control as the vehicle responded to her touch. A surge of warm excitement ran from her belly to her throat and made her laugh.

Birdie sounded like she was on the same wobbly record as Sparkle. "Ooh . . . ah think . . . she's tryin' to kill us for all the tall jokes. We give up Annie. You're not too tall, yer jes perfect." She giggled between words and when Sparkle joined her, the laughing and shrieking sounded like an enthusiastic chicken party.

Annie watched the speedometer as it crept toward twenty miles an hour. "I think we should move to the road, don't you Gloria? I think I'm ready."

Gloria was hanging onto the door handle and looking at Annie with wide eyes. "I'm not so sure, I think we should go around a few more . . . ."

Her friend's words trailed off as Annie pointed the car toward the end of the field and the beginning of the road. She hit the gas harder and just as the field ended, the front of the automobile went down sharply and the wheels stuck fast in a dip in the ground. At the same time the back of the car rose up, then came down and hit the grass with a loud thud. The rattling ceased and the coupe coughed twice before dying, a faint smell of gasoline noticeable.

Silence filled the car for a moment.

"Ditch."

"Must be."

"Can't drive over those ditches, Annie."

Birdie started laughing and Sparkle yelled. "I've got it! We have a new secret weapon. We'll send Annie over to drive for Adolf. He won't last a week."

The four friends climbed slowly out of the car and stood in a row surveying the vehicle now resting uncomfortably, its nose pointing down into the ditch. Annie couldn't see any damage but her mouth was dry and her hands shook.

"Do you think it's hurt?" Her voice sounded faint even to her.

"No, I think the car's fine. I think we're the ones that are hurt." Sparkle was rubbing the top of her head cautiously.

"Maybe we could sorta push it backwards. You know, it can't be that hard. I see guys doing it all the time." Annie's stomach felt like mush and she wanted to do something, anything. Sparkle stopped massaging her head and slapped Birdie on the shoulder.

"Annie's right. We can get this thing out of here. Gloria, why don't you get in and start it up and we'll push?"

Annie felt a wave of relief that these women were her friends. Gloria jumped into the car and started it, Annie and Birdie pushed on the front and Sparkle on the side door handle. Soon the car moved a little backward, then forward. After several efforts the car came to rest on the stubbly surface of the field again. Gloria stepped out and they surveyed the damage. The smell of gas was strong but otherwise a look under and around indicated that the vehicle seemed no worse than its pre-ditch condition.

Annie gritted her teeth and decided that this was probably like a horse, get right back on when it throws you. She put her foot in the car and started to get behind the wheel when she looked up to see her friends turning toward her like puppets attached to the same string. The chorus of 'no's was very loud.

After several moments of silence, Gloria put her hand on Annie's shoulder and smiled. "That's okay. I'll drive the car to the middle of the field. You need a little more practice before you're ready for the road."

Sparkle jabbed Birdie in the ribs and the two piled into the back seat. Their explosive laughter filled the evening air.

Cain blinked, then looked around in irritation. Loud voices and the sound of riveting below had interrupted his train of thought. Schematics for the fuselage section were spread out in front of him. He was trying to decide if the half installed aluminum piece next to him was cut wrong or if the framework of alloy rings and aluminum strips making up the structure was off a whole inch. Neither seemed likely, but they sure weren't fitting properly. He shook his head and tried to ignore the ping of rivets and the screech of drills, but it was no use.

He straightened up and glanced around, struck once again by the sheer size of the plant. No matter how often he looked, the place still had the power to amaze him, rolling on for what seemed like miles. The huge platform scaffolding he was standing on held four center fuselage sections, all looking more like skeletons than plane pieces. The crew making the noise was working on the next set. These sections, skinned with the alclad aluminum sheets, had been separated from the original platform used to construct them and now rested on the smaller pipe supports with wheels. These wheels fit on tracks and as each section was completed, it was rolled to the next area to begin the attachment to the nose and tail sections.

He smiled when he caught sight of Birdie stretched as far as she could reach, trying for one more rivet before moving the ladder. She'd moved to the graveyard shift almost three weeks before and he enjoyed her slow, easy smile when they passed each other. He could see Sparkle working on disassembling scaffolding just a little farther down the line. They seemed to be having trouble because Sparkle was using a cutting torch to free a connecting bolt that didn't want to come apart.

He looked down at the plans again, trying to concentrate. Leaning forward, he kept both hands on the sides of the paper to keep it from rolling inward. Gradually, the sound of rivet guns and drilling receded as he remembered Annie. It was certainly a good thing that she didn't work in this shop. If she were here to distract him, all these middle sections might end up crooked. Her memory brought with it her clean, flower scent and a longing so strong he had to swallow hard. Straightening he allowed the plans to roll into one hand.

"Woman, how come you cain't figure out which rivet goes where yet? You're the goddamdest slowest person on this line."

The group of five or six workers had stopped and every head was turned, watching the burly supervisor lean close to Birdie who was now off the ladder and standing perfectly still.

Cain couldn't believe his eyes or his ears. He'd heard someone say that Zachary Waskom occasionally flew into rages but he'd never seen it himself.

"Cain't you get anything right? Goddamn you is one dumb nigger bitch." Birdie's gun fell from her hand and hit the floor with a crash. Loose rivets clinked on metal surfaces like tiny bullets in the sudden quiet.

Waskom's threatening form crowded within inches of Birdie, his fist raised over her head. She was now backed as far as possible against the fuselage and Cain could see her hands protecting her face. The crew near them seemed frozen, unable or unwilling to move or intervene.

Cain let out an involuntary "ah . . ." then yelled, "Waskom don't!" but either the man didn't hear or didn't care. They were so close that his first impulse was to jump over the scaffolding side and go after Waskom. But he was over eighteen feet up, just too far. With an effort, he pulled himself from the sight and lunged for the stairway down the far side. The sound of Waskom's angry voice followed as he took two steps at a time.

He skidded around the corner of the scaffolding, sure that he would find Birdie lying on the ground. He stopped cold and stared, trying to sort out the scene in front of him. Instead of Birdie crumpled up on the ground, he saw Waskom leaning backwards over the fuselage, his mouth pulled taut and eyes wide. The thin blue flame of Sparkle's cutting torch was right next to his face, not quite touching the skin. Her tiny form seemed to grow taller as the supervisor shrank from the threat of his own flesh burning.

Sparkle's voice was low and deadly. "The woman's been working two jobs and she's got a right to go a little slower. You got no call to be going after her like that." She thumbed the flame lower but still kept it close his chest. "You gonna back off now?"

As Cain watched, the foreman nodded. His face had gone from red to chalky white, heavy eyelids blinking like a reptile.

Sparkle stepped back and turned off the flame. For a moment, no one moved or spoke. The only sound came from other rivet guns down the line. Waskom straightened up but seemed unwilling to move, his gaze fixed on the small woman. Birdie stood, still pressed against the section, her eyes wide and mouth half open.

Cain couldn't believe what he'd seen. Sparkle sure as hell was gutsy. It wouldn't take them long to fire her. Even though the action was warranted, he knew it wouldn't help. The minute she'd gone for a superior with the open flame, she'd kissed her job goodbye.

Cain finally reached Birdie and looked at her anxiously.

"Are you all right?" She nodded her head slowly then tried to smile at someone behind him. Turning, he faced Sparkle. She raised an eyebrow.

He answered the unspoken question. "I don't think he touched her. Just scared her. But we've got trouble now. It's not good, you know. Waskom will be screaming bloody murder the second he gets upstairs."

She nodded and then grinned. "Worth it. I was looking for a job when I got here."

Birdie sat down on the scaffolding steps and put her head between her hands. Sparkle came to stand beside her, protectively. Waskom was leaning against the airplane section, his face still white. He drew a handkerchief out of his pocket and wiped his face. He straightened and began to walk forward, obviously heading for the office. Cain held up his hand and yelled at him.

"Waskom, hold on a minute." The large man looked at him and blinked, then stopped.

"Waskom, we need to talk." The man followed Cain as he walked away from the rest of the group and the production line. They stopped at a small alcove on the side. Cain spoke slowly, trying to control his anger.

"I see you're going up to report what just happened. I don't think that's a good idea."

Waskom's mouth dropped open and his huge shoulders rolled forward. His face shone with moisture and became redder as Cain watched.

"What do you mean, that's not a good idea? You saw that bitch. She tried to kill me. Was gonna burn me, she was. You saw the whole thing. She's gonna be fired in about five minutes."

Cain swallowed, trying to control the urge to just beat the man until he couldn't tell anyone anything. "I know what I saw. I saw a woman being threatened and another woman protecting her. That's about it. No one deserves to be fired for protecting someone."

"Oh Christ, I wasn't threatening her. I was just tellin' her to move faster. Dumb broad." Waskom started to push his way past but Cain put a hand on the thickset man's arm.

"This is the way it is, Waskom. I'll tell my story right along with yours. You're going to look like a fool when they hear what you did to start it."

Cain saw a twitch along the man's jaw line and stepped back onto the balls of his feet, ready for anything the man might throw at him. Cain watched Waskom's eyes and recognized a flicker of fear. He suspected that this man was like a lot of bullies, tough with someone who couldn't fight back, but not much when it came to someone his own size. When Waskom spoke, his words were slow and full of menace but Cain knew he was hearing the bluster of a coward.

"I'm not a man to cross, Adamson. I won't forget. I'll get even."

This time he shoved passed Cain, pushing him as he walked away. Cain let out a breath and walked back to the group. They were waiting for him, all seven that had seen the incident. Cain cleared his throat. "I know you saw what just happened. What do you think?" His question took in the whole group but he'd directed it mostly at Joel Bartsmith, the lead man on this piece of the ship and a brother in the union.

Birdie spoke first. "He deserved it, Cain. He was going to thump me. If anyone gets in trouble it should be me, not Sparkle."

"Don't worry about me, girl."

Cain looked at the others and several were nodding in agreement with Birdie. He looked at Joel. "I told Waskom that I saw him threaten Birdie and Sparkle stopped him. That's it. I told him that if he said anything about the torch I would back up Sparkle. If he wants to try to get her fired, fine, but I would have my say. What do you think, Bartsmith?"

The man tapped his fingers on the side of his pant leg. "I guess I agree. Waskom's a pretty bad apple and that's not the first time he's gone after someone. I'm worried about what Waskom can do to the rest of us."

Cain looked at the seven. "If we stick together, there's not much he can do. It's up to you folks."

Several heads nodded then a small, mousy looking woman spoke up. "I'm all for it. Maybe he'll think twice before he does it again." She turned and addressed the others, "What do you say?"

One by one they said yes. Cain spoke to Sparkle. "It looks like you're off the hook for now. But next time you see something would you let Joel or me know? It would be a whole lot better if one of us took care of him."

Sparkle smiled. "Sure."

From the look on her face, Cain knew she would do exactly the same thing again for a friend.

The incident bothered Cain for a week. He eventually heard that Waskom had not gone to his superior. He'd complained and ranted to friends but that was as far as it looked like he was willing to go. He'd apparently believed that Cain would support Birdie and Sparkle. Cain wasn't sure if that was good or bad.

The room was small and at least twenty women had crowded in to listen to what Trudy Harris had to say. Annie shivered, pulling her coat closer around her. November had finally shown its winter promise and the temperature had been in the low forties all week. It wasn't much better inside. She sat on an old brown folding chair and stared at the back of Sparkle's head, wishing this were over. Birdie had come to give her support but she knew many women wouldn't want her there so she sat as close to the rear as she could. Annie had told the group that she'd spoken with Slattery and he'd promised to look into their grievances. Unfortunately some of them, led by Trudy, wanted faster action. Now the woman was trying to get the rest of the group to agree with her.

"I don't care what Annie says, I think it's time we did something about it."

The room was quiet after Trudy's pronouncement. Everyone looked tired. They'd been talking for an hour and they didn't seem to be getting very far.

Sparkle sounded exasperated. "We agree that it's time, Trudy. Complaning gets us no place. What we can't seem to agree on is exactly what it is we need to do.

"All right, we agree that something needs to be done about safety, right?" Heads nodded. Some women just sat, their faces a mixture of puzzled and anxious. "And we'd sure like to have some say in getting rid of Ed Bartell and other guys like him, right?" The nods were quicker this time. "And every time we try to say something or make a suggestion, both the managers and the union just brush us off. It's like we're here but everybody that counts is just waiting for the war to be over so we'll leave and let them get back to their jobs. Right?" This time she had a unanimous murmur of approval. "So, all we have to do is come up with the best way to be heard."

Annie sat forward in her chair with her elbows on her knees and rubbed her temples. It wasn't that she didn't agree with Trudy, it was just that whenever she talked, Annie had an urge to clap a hand over the woman's mouth. Trudy had the heart of a warrior. Unfortunately, she also had a fishwife's voice and the subtlety of a grizzly. If she wanted you to do something, she just threw you on the ground and beat you up until you did it.

Looking around, Annie could tell from the restless shifting of feet that others felt the same way. Several had started to give indications of leaving. When Trudy took a breath, Annie stood up. The thin woman's cheeks puffed out but she finally gave Annie a reluctant nod and lowered herself uneasily to her chair. Annie thought she heard a collective sigh of relief as the women settled back.

She wished someone else would do this. She still didn't like speaking in a crowd. Taking a deep breath, she looked around and saw that right now she was definitely the only one willing. "Well first, there are a lot of things we can't solve tonight and what I think we need to do now is just make a start. Why don't we take a vote? Let's see which we like best. There are three options we can pursue."

She held up her hand and raised one finger. "First, we could stage a slowdown." She raised another finger. "Second, Trudy wants to have a walkout. And last," the third finger was in the air, "some think that we need to try to work through the union. Is that about all of them?" A whisper of assent rippled through the room.

"Now remember, we need to be ready to do whatever it is we vote for. Okay, all in favor of a slowdown?" Four eager hands went up. "All right, now who's in favor of a walkout?" The same four hands went up along with two or three tentative others.

"This isn't going to work if you keep voting for all of them. Now just vote for one. Again, who's for the slowdown?" They voted again. This time there were three votes for a slowdown and three for a walkout.

Annie was surprised, six women voting for these ideas had been so vocal that earlier she'd have sworn there were many more.

"Who wants to work through the union?" This time the hands were numerous and she counted at least twenty. "It looks like that's the course we want to take. Now Trudy, you're good at this and you probably have the most knowledge. Why don't you help us try to figure out how we're going to make that happen?"

As she looked at Trudy, she could see a hard edge of anger cross the woman's face and then a thoughtful look as if mulling over the last part of what Annie had said. Annie sat back in her chair and felt a momentary pang of guilt that she had pushed the vote. With a shrug, she decided that it was more important to get this group rolling. With Trudy in charge, they might just blow up the plant to make a point. She knew this was important to the skinny riveter and that she really did care about the people. It was her manner that rubbed everyone the wrong way.

Trudy cleared her throat and spoke. "You heard Annie, how are we going to do that?"

"Annie has talked to people and she knows what we need to do." Birdie was standing but looking slightly panicked.

Trudy looked at Annie again, her jaw muscles tense. "What's she doing here? She sure can't be part of the union, she's colored."

Annie sighed and stood again. "I know she's colored. Heck, she even knows she's colored." Light laughter came from the back of the room. "That's part of it. Along with us trying for better working conditions and more voice in the union, we need to see that Negroes are working right beside us, doing the same job, and they don't have any representation at all. At least they give us women lip service." Annie could hear murmuring from the back of the room.

"Okay, I know not all of you agree but I think it's the right thing to do." She could hear more whispering but couldn't determine how the women felt. She was startled when Sparkle rose to speak.

"I think this is about enough talk. It's time we get a woman in as shop steward. That's a start anyway. What did you hear about that?"

Annie nodded, grateful for anything to be moving them forward. "I know that the by-laws say that women can't hold office. We can hold a position in the women's auxiliary group, but they don't do much of anything except supply food for the parties. So what we need is to get that by-laws changed and then get a woman on the ballot. John Slattery is willing to try both at the same time, but he says it will be pretty hard. It's going to take all of the five months until the election for him to convince his people to give it a try."

She sat down quickly and Trudy looked relieved to resume control of the meeting.

"If you're finished, we can get on with the meeting. Who do we want to run?" One of the audience raised her hand and nominated Trudy immediately. Trudy shot Annie a smirk. Annie sat back carefully and rubbed her temples again, wishing she were home in bed.

Half an hour later, Annie found herself outside the meeting room with a small group of women surrounding her.

"We think you'll do just fine."

"You're the only one we think has a chance."

"Would you believe how Trudy acted when we elected you? She looked like she'd swallowed a grapefruit whole."

"But you know, I think she'll work hard for us even if she lost the nomination. I just think she was surprised."

Annie let the words flow around her and waited for the lovely warm glow to subside. She was more surprised than Trudy had been. She'd been embarrassed when Sparkle'd nominated her. But now, even though she tried to be calm and remind herself the odds were against her name ever being on the ballot, she couldn't stop smiling. It amazed her that these women trusted her enough to let her try. But the most extraordinary thing was that Trudy had offered to be her campaign manager.

As the women talked and laughed, Annie realized that she wasn't really paying attention any longer. The person she really wanted to talk to was Cain. After all it was his idea that had started this whole thing.

CHAPTER NINE

Annie shifted her weight to the side of the chair without the crack, trying to distance herself from the pinch of wood. She was glad to be inside, away from the dark and rain. This cold weather made her wish she'd brought her wool coat up north with her. The heavily painted surface of the small table felt soft where she leaned her elbows and the smell of frying steak and chicken made her stomach growl. The tiny cafe was only half filled but everyone seemed to be talking at the same time. It had been five hours since she'd eaten her lunch at work and she was more than ready for dinner.

This was the first opportunity she'd had to tell Cain about the women voting for her to run for steward and she was anxious to hear what he would say. At first she'd felt awkward about their decision to be friends but now it was beginning to feel like a natural part of her life. They'd had the one incident at the transfer station, but had agreed that wouldn't happen again. He'd picked her up at the front gate of the plant in his Ford, the car looking no worse for the wear as a result of her driving lesson.

Cain was at the counter, putting in their order, a sandwich for her and chicken-fried steak for him. She watched him and sighed. She still got a fluttery feeling in her chest when she saw him and hoped that would stop once they were firmly in the habit of being friends. With two male siblings she'd learned early how to hold her own and give it back without even thinking. Even her association with Howard was comfortable, almost brotherly if she admitted it. Friday night dinner at her parents, Tuesday night dinner at his, usually a Sunday walk with his children after church. It was a pleasant way of life but no one had ever made her feel quite as giddy as Cain.

She shook her head. She had to continually remind herself of her commitment to Howard, particularly after Cain had kissed her. Part of her insisted she should never see him again. The other part threw his name and face up persistently in her consciousness.

And for no good reason she could identify, she'd spent the last twenty minutes of her shift in the bathroom washing the dirt from her face and applying liberal doses of water to make her unruly curls lie flatter. All the while she tried to convince herself they were just friends and to calm the light, goofy feeling in her chest.

"Is a sandwich and coffee going to be enough?" Cain's voice startled her. As she turned to look at him she felt her face flush. He appeared to be doing much better at this friendship thing than she was.

"Yes, that's fine."

He sat down in the opposite chair, with his stiff leg sticking out in the aisle. The waitress arrived with her coffee. Annie lifted it and sipped the steaming liquid. She watched him out of the corner of her eye, wondering again what had happened to him in the war. The story behind the scar on his face and how he'd hurt his leg interested her. She'd almost said something two or three times, but hesitated. Since he'd never brought it up she decided again to let him tell her in his own time. She realized that he was speaking to her but his voice was so low she had to lean forward to hear.

"I hear the women elected you to run for shop steward."

"Nuts. I wanted to tell you." She eased back in her chair. "Well, you did suggest it. And there's just a lot of things that need to be changed." She stared then took a deep breath and continued. "First there was Gloria. I know that's fixed now but I had to speak with John Slattery. That should be something we can work out. And then there's the fact that we get no breaks and there's no child care close by and reasonable. I think the union should be addressing these issues, don't you?"

He smiled. "Yes, I suppose."

"And look at Birdie, being attacked by Waskom." Annie hesitated. "That man should be in jail. Instead we're all just thrilled to bits that Sparkle didn't get fired. It's just not right."

Cain's eyes were kind and she felt the tension begin to slide from between her shoulder blades. She tried to make her voice light. "And we want to know why we get paid less for doing the same jobs as the men."

This time Cain's eyebrows raised and he sat back. "Wow, you're taking on a lot of things. I need to warn you Annie, there are an awful lot of grievances out there that haven't been handled yet. I know I have four or five that we don't seem to be able to get anywhere on. Things like ratings not being changed when they should, not being able to make lead man when you're already doing the job. You need to pick your battles carefully. Your issues are so major that if you take it all in at once, I think you're going to lose them all. Maybe you need to start with one or two."

"That's what I told them but some gals are ready to start walking out or slowing down now. They're as patriotic as the next person but they feel if we wait, nothing will ever get done. They want the changes now."

Cain drew his leg back to let a waitress pass, his lips thinned and a frown marked his forehead. "What do you think?"

"Actually, the way I see my job is to get everybody settled down. I'd like them to decide for themselves that a slowdown is not good for the war effort. Let's face it, the most important thing is to get the war won. Most of them don't really want to do anything drastic. It's just a few hotheads who get everybody worked up. My first instinct as far as bringing up the things we want to change is the same as yours. Too much all at once will kill all the ideas. My second is that if we only get heard once, I want to make sure they get all of it." Annie put her hands around the thick coffee mug in front of her and rotated it slowly.

The sounds of the diner had faded and Annie felt as if they were on a tiny island by themselves. She shifted in her chair and swallowed hard. A mix of emotions warred in her chest. She wanted so much to have Cain understand how she felt. It was important that these women feel they had a voice in their own management. Even if they were turned down, it was better than feeling so helpless.

How she wished she could forget everything and think only about how incredibly blue his eyes were. With a start, she realized that she was wandering off the subject again. Her own thoughts seemed to be more than willing to sabotage this new tender friendship.

As she watched, smile lines crinkled the sides of his mouth. "If I had a white horse, I'd put you on it. You're a corker Annie. I guess what we need to do is get your name on the ballot. Did you talk with Mr. Slattery about that?"

"We've talked about it a little but I haven't told him for sure yet. I wanted to talk with you first. I think he has to get the by-laws changed." Annie looked down at her coffee mug, not wanting to see his reaction. He put his hand on hers and she looked up. His eyes were calm, warm.

"I'll be glad to talk with him if you like. But there's really a bigger issue. Even if every woman in the plant voted for you, you can't get elected if the men don't. How do you plan to make that happen?"

Annie's grip tightened on the mug. The sound of utensils clinking and conversation intruded into their little world again. She cleared her throat.

"Well, they have some crazy idea about campaigning for me, talking to the guys who are all right with women working there. Sometimes I wish they'd chosen someone else. I don't think I'm all that good at this kind of thing."

Annie jumped as the waitress put two plates down on a table next to theirs, the dishes clanging as they hit the surface. The two men opposite tucked napkins into their shirtfronts and began to eat. Her mouth watered as she watched them. She looked up to see Cain staring at her, one eyebrow raised.

"I guess it's up to you if you want the aggravation. I don't think I know a woman who has a better chance than you. There's enough time before the election to maybe get people used to the idea, I think it's at the end of May and we're halfway through November now. You know the position of steward doesn't carry that much weight. I'm not sure you can make a dent in all the changes you want. You'd have to hang on and go for a position on the board if you really wanted to make something happen."

"I know. But it's a start. We don't want to change everything, we would just like to have a say." She picked up her coffee and took a swallow.

He sat back in his chair and appeared to be thinking about what she'd said. "As long you know the score. Here's a question for you. I can understand why they want to be represented, but why you? Why not Sparkle or that Trudy woman?"

"Because they don't think they could even get the women to vote for either of those two. The group keeps saying that it needs to be someone with more . . . well . . . somebody . . . with, oh nuts . . . they say I have more appeal. It's ridiculous, I have about as much appeal as a rivet gun."

Cain pushed himself forward, a lopsided grin relaxing his face. "Well, I've got to tell you that I never wanted to hold hands with a rivet gun. You don't give yourself enough credit. I'd certainly vote for you."

Annie found herself chewing on her lower lip. "Well, you're different."

"How's that?"

"We know each other."

"Okay. I know lots of people and I wouldn't vote for very many of them. You're different." As Cain spoke, he leaned forward and almost put his hand over hers, stopping at the last minute.

Annie felt a sense of loss. He was keeping his end of the bargain. She wished her emotions would let her keep her side as admirably.

Sparkle put her fingers over her mouth to keep from smiling. They, all four of them, were playing cards at the big dining room table. The two remaining boarders were gone for the evening, so they had the place to themselves. With everyone so busy working, helping Birdie around the house, and now Annie out talking with people about being shop steward, they were seldom in the same place at the same time anymore. For the first time this old house was beginning to feel as homey as the trailer. Odd, because she would have sworn that what she really wanted was time away from all of them.

Shifting her position on the old chair, she folded her cards together then leaned back brushing accidentally against the curtains. Her good mood was interrupted by Gloria's nagging voice. "You're pushing those curtains open again Sparkle. I'm sure light is showing outside."

"Play the goddamn card and don't try to weasel out of it. You're going to lose this hand." Sparkle watched the girl and when she didn't play the card, she moved herself forward dramatically and let the blackout curtain fall shut. "My God, are you going to win the war single-handedly by not letting even the teensiest sliver of light show?" Sometimes it was all she could do not to shake the girl, she was so damned nit picky.

"I don't think that is funny. Somebody has to watch out for that kind of thing. If we were all as careless as you I'm sure we'd all be eating raw fish and speaking German right now."

Sparkle felt a warm flush creep up her neck. "Now that's just not true. I'm the one who saw that whole line of missing rivets in the tail of that ship and stopped the line until we could get them back in. I'm the one . . .."

"We know what you did Sparkle." Annie's voice was tired. "We've heard it before. Could we just finish this game? I need to go to bed. I have to be at the plant at four tomorrow and I've got a headache."

Annie's uncharacteristic tone stopped Sparkle. She looked up to see that the tall woman had placed her cards on the table and was rubbing her forehead with both hands. The unflattering light overhead made her look almost gray. Sparkle's run of good luck at pinochle had eased her aggravation at the incessant November rain pounding outside. She turned away from Annie's tired face and carefully folded her own cards together. She looked hard at Gloria.

"Well I'm not the one whose turn it is. The pregnant Little Miss Perfect is holding up this show." She waved her hand in Gloria's direction, checking the condition of her nail polish as she did. She decided that one more coat would hold her until the weekend.

When she lifted her eyes back to the group, her heart sank. She'd said too much again. Gloria's lower lip was trembling and her eyes were filled with tears. As she watched, Gloria got up from the table with an effort and wobbled toward the kitchen, her hand covering her mouth and her shoulders heaving with sobs.

Annie looked at Sparkle. "Do you ever think before you speak?"

The constriction in her chest grew and she looked at Birdie, hoping for some backup. Birdie was yawning and pulling down the sleeves of her old black cardigan sweater. When she looked up and found Sparkle staring at her she shook her head and shrugged her shoulders.

"Don' look to me for no hep'. Annie's right, you could screw up a train wreck. The girl needs a little leeway now. She's pretty tender."

Sparkle began to feel her shoulders droop and she straightened them with an effort. "You're both too easy on her. Lots of pregnant women don't get catered to all the time. Why is she so special?"

Annie gave Sparkle a long thoughtful look, then placed her elbows on the table and rested her chin in her cupped hands. "You just don't get it, do you?" Lines appeared in Annie's forehead and she let out a long sigh. "Have you ever had a good friend? Somebody you don't tell they're wrong even if they are? Gloria's okay, you know. And it doesn't hurt to have somebody paying attention to what we're supposed to be doing to keep the war effort going. So what if she gets a little carried away?"

Sparkle began to chew on the inside of her mouth. She hated conversations like this. She never knew what to say. Once again she felt the pinch of never having had a real female friend. Men were the only ones she really trusted, and she only trusted them because she knew exactly what they wanted. The familiar heat of anger coursed through her.

"Nobody's going to forget anything with the Purely Perfect Princess always around. She just makes me tired. She's always had everything her own way and now you two are acting like she'll break or something. Look at that family of hers always pushing money on her, the high and mighty Westfalls of Portland. And her being so righteous and not taking it. Shit, it's enough to make you choke. She's been spoiled rotten from the day she was born. I wouldn't be surprised to see her mommy and daddy show up here pretty soon when they find out she's pregnant and yank her home and wrap her up in cotton until the miraculous birth happens."

Birdie slapped on the table just loud enough to stop Sparkle's outburst. She lifted her hand and pointed her finger directly at Sparkle's nose.

"That's enuff. That girl is doing more than her share helping out here. And just 'cuz you got money don' mean your family's happy. You think 'cuz you had a crummy upbringing, everybody else's was better. Let me tell you girl, there ain't nothing meaner than a rich person when they think the money might be goin' away. I know."

Sparkle felt her defenses rising. She pushed the cards away with a thrust of her hand. "Now I suppose you're going to tell me how hard you had it? Look here . . .."

"Birdie's right." A quiet voice from behind the three women startled them all. "Just because you have money doesn't mean anything about your life is that good."

As Gloria neared the table, Sparkle moved aside to let her sit down, feeling guilty that Gloria had heard what she'd just said, even if it was the truth. She put her finger up to her mouth to chew on a nail then stopped herself.

Gloria sat back on the cushion. She was pale and plain looking, her hair damp around her face. Sparkle could see that she had lost her makeup in the recent flood of tears.

"My family is not that much of a treat. Remember that camp I told you about? The one I went to every summer with horses and swimming?"

Sparkle felt herself holding her breath, watching Gloria. The girl had never said anything bad about her family before.

"Well for three straight years I ended up in the hospital because I was so homesick. The damned counselors would call my father and he would tell them not to let me fool them, that I was just a ninny, looking for attention." Gloria ran her fingers through her hair and sat back. "I was five years old and scared to death! It generally took about a week and then I was okay. But I hated that place until I was ten."

Sparkle had never heard Gloria swear before. She'd assumed that the girl felt she was better than the rest of them with all that money. Now she wondered if she'd misjudged her, just like Annie'd said. Letting her breath out slowly, she waited for Gloria to continue. When she didn't, she asked quietly.

"What happened when you were ten?"

"I decided it wasn't going to change so I'd better. I started making a few friends. Decided to quit fighting them. Like when my Mom made me go to college. Well, it wasn't like a real college. It was how to dress and how to set a pretty table. We had some classes that were hard, like art and sociology and literature. But mostly, we studied sewing and deportment. They called it a finishing school. It was pretty easy, even for me. I hated school but my mom and dad did not want me around."

Sparkle felt a flash of annoyance. Here she was, buying into this sad sister's 'poor me' story. "Why did you think they didn't want you around? They didn't give you enough money or something?"

Gloria looked at Sparkle with her mouth set in a flat line and her eyes narrowed to a tired, knowing look. "I know because they have shipped me out whenever they could. That message is pretty clear. And anyway I do not want any of their money."

Birdie reached out and covered Gloria's hand with one of hers. "We best be looking ahead 'stead of back. You're pretty well off now. You got a job and you got friends."

"Yes, and if I keep this job after the war, I'll bet I could get my own place and everything. That way, when Lester gets back we'll have someplace to call home and this little Junior here," she patted her stomach, "and I will have something to live on."

This time Sparkle didn't hesitate. "You're thinking like a child. You are going to have to ask them for money before long. It won't be long until they fire you. The minute they find out you're pregnant, you'll be gone."

Gloria's mouth worked from side to side, showing a flash of teeth. "I will have to figure something out, that is all." One tear began a gentle slide down her cheek.

Sparkle raised her eyebrows in bewilderment and looked at the other two. Annie shook her head but Birdie leaned forward and squeezed Gloria's hand, smiling. "You'll be fine. We'll work something out." The colored woman turned and scowled at the Sparkle and Annie, then changed the subject. "So, what is it that your daddy does to make his money?"

More tears began and Gloria raised her hand and pressed it too her face. After a moment, she dropped it and faced the women. "He cheats and lies and steals."

Sparkle felt her mouth drop open. She stared at Gloria.

"Oh I know, it's strange, a big businessman like him, but he's a crook really. I used to help him with his business after school. At first it was just file this and type that, but in my senior year, he decided since I was family I could help with the books. His factory makes engine parts, you know. It wasn't so bad before the war, but as soon as he started receiving the big orders from the government, he would pad every order instead of just a few. You know, adding a few hours to the time we turned in, pushing up the price of materials. I told him that pretty soon they'd catch on and go someplace else but they haven't. His factory is one of the few that makes the parts.

"And you didn't tell anyone?" Sparkle's voice was doubtful.

"He trusted me not to tell his secret. Said I wasn't to spoil it for the family. Told me we had a sweet deal that it was a lot better than those guys who sold the inferior metal. They get people killed doing that. He gets richer and the government loses a few bucks. I finally told Mom, but she said that everybody did it and that I had better get used to it. She just told me to shush, it was business."

"My God. No wonder you left. You're such a straight shooter that must have been pure hell." Sparkle shook her head and looked past Gloria to Annie. She didn't know what to say.

Birdie patted Gloria's hand again and murmured. "Ah think this is the best place for you, darlin'. Y'r right, you don't need to be around y'r family at all."

Sparkle nodded in agreement and Annie made it unanimous.

"We're going to have to call him something other than Junior. What do you think of 'Benjamin'?"

Birdie watched as mud slid over the top of her shoes. Only three more feet and she would have made it to the front steps of the Blue. She jammed her lips together and rubbed her eyes, darned if she'd cry now after holding back for so long. She'd have to wash the shoes and hope the leather would dry without cracking. It was a laugh, only fifteen days until

Christmas and she'd decided she didn't have much to celebrate this year.

This dreadful dark, cold night with its relentless downpour and strong sideways wind was making her feel as if what'd happened in the supervisor's office only two hours before was the beginning of a slippery downhill entry into hell. She shook her head and looked up at the lights from the house. Thank God, only a few more feet and she'd be inside and warm.

Taking a deep breath, she carefully moved her umbrella to her right hand, trying to keep as much of the soaking fabric over her as possible. She then began pulling her foot free from the ooze. As she did her other foot, the one holding her weight, slid backward and leaving her off balance. Pumping her arms forward, with the umbrella waving like a sword in front, she moved faster and faster but went nowhere. Then, abruptly, she tumbled forward into the water. With a thud, she landed first on the hand she was trying to catch herself with, then fell hard on her side. The umbrella, caught by the wind, flew out of her hand and into the night.

As the cold and wet hit her, she breathed in, swallowing a mouthful of dirty water. Choking, she rose to her knees. The tears she'd held back since leaving the plant began to course down her cheeks. Her hands were so cold she could hardly bend her fingers.

With a shriek, she pulled up a handful of the mud and threw it with all her might. The clod fell with a plop only a few feet away. It was like everything she'd been trying so hard to do, just plain foolish. The only things she really wanted in life were to have Beauregard home and bring her children north and both those plans seemed to be vanishing like just so much smoke and hope. Zachary Waskom had taken care of that.

A picture came to mind, so vivid, of her little William, only three years old, throwing a ball with the same result as she had just had. For just a moment she was standing in the early morning Georgia sun, the rays coloring their home with yellow light and tinting the ivy trailing over the stone chimney with gold.

William and his sisters were piling on top of Beauregard, his deep laughter joining their high-pitched screams and filling the soft warm air like brown sugar in beans. A cold ache replaced the choking fire in her chest and she sat back on her heels and wept.

"What the hell you doing rolling around in the mud, woman?"

The voice came from behind her and Birdie didn't have the energy to yell at Sparkle. That woman never failed to catch her when she felt her lowest. She felt like she couldn't breathe and bent forward, trying to bury herself in the puddle in front of her. She was just too tired and heartsick to care anymore.

Immediately hands pulled her up and out of the muck. A slash of north wind caught them and Birdie recognized Sparkle's newest scent *Evening in Paris*.

"Don't be pulling me aroun' woman. I be perfectly happy down here." Birdie knew she was being ridiculous but she didn't care. She just wanted to curl up and die. The other woman paid no attention to her and together they stumbled up the steps. Sparkle was wearing the black boots and brown rain slicker that were kept next to the front door. Birdie felt herself being handed off. Annie took her jacket and sweater and Gloria pulled at her shoes. Annie told her to stand still, then unbuttoned her skirt and peeled it off. Birdie felt the roughness of dry towels then Sparkle told her to hold up her hands and slipped Birdie's old work skirt over her head, tying it around her waist. When they were done, they finally let her settle into the overstuffed couch and covered her with blankets.

Gloria came over to her. "Birdie what happened? Annie and I finished the supper as you requested. We thought you were coming to help but when you didn't show up we decided we must have made a mistake about what you told us and you had to go to work early. Then when we arrived and Sparkle came home she said you didn't meet her after work so we were really worried. And it's such an awful night and everything."

The expectant mother's words ran together. Birdie could hear the worry in her voice. She pushed back the towel Annie had thrown over her head in order to see. The blood began to return to her hands and she used the towel to wipe the inside of her mouth, trying to rid it of the grass and dirty water.

"Where have I been for the last three hours?" Birdie sighed and settled back into the couch. "I's been gettin' fired. Me 'n Sparkle worked this extra day shift today to sort of make up for the times I been late or gone. If I coulda left right after my shift, I would of made it home in plenty time to put supper on. But Mr. Johnson jez come and got me at the end of my shift. He took me to his office and tol' me I was late too many times and the company had decided to fire me. I tried to explain to him I was tryin' to work things out here at the Blue House and wouldn't be coming in late anymore but he jez shook his head. I told him I'd do anything but I got to keep my job." Birdie could feel her voice rise on the last sentence and didn't attempt to staunch the flow of tears.

After she'd managed to clear the mud and water from her eyes, she saw her roommates standing in a circle around her watching as if she were crazy. Sparkle was covered with mud down her front where the slicker hadn't protected her and Annie had smudges on her pants and shirt.

Annie was the first to speak. "I don't believe it."

"He said he didn't need no niggah woman comin' in late every day and not doin' a good job. When I left his office, I saw Zachary Waskom standing outside the door just grinnin' at me. I guess he got back at me after all for that trouble we gave him. I know it was his idea that started this." Birdie coughed. "He said I could stand in line to service him later. He hadn't been with no dark sugah for some time and maybe I could make some money that way. I decided I needed to clean up there in the puddle jez from talkin' to him."

Annie handed Birdie another towel. "Did you talk to John Slattery? He might be able to help."

"I tried to but Mr. Johnson said they'd already tol' him and he'd agreed. No point talkin' to him. Then I had to catch the fifty-four bus home cause that was the only one still running. It drops you off on Delridge, must be twenty blocks from here." She bit her lip, trying to stop thinking about the awful smile on Waskom's face as she'd left the office. She hunched her shoulders as a chill ran down her back.

"God damn it all." Sparkle's words shot out like hard pellets. "This is awful."

Gloria had sat down beside her and placed her arm around Birdie's shoulder. The warmth felt so comforting she had to blink away more tears.

"But you know maybe it's for the best. Since you'll be here all the time now, I'm sure we can work something out to bring in more money. I know we can get more people to come for dinner and that would help. Maybe you could start cooking breakfast. It is not the end of the world. You're always saying things have a way of working out."

Birdie had an hysterical urge to laugh. She used to believe that. Now, she wasn't so sure. As she looked around, Birdie saw Annie and Sparkle both standing poised and ready. Ready to warm Birdie with their own bodies or murder Waskom, whichever she wanted.

Annie stepped forward and handed her another blanket. "You're freezing. You'll be catching pneumonia if you're not careful. Here, let me wrap this around your legs."

As the tall woman moved, they heard a knock at the door. Sparkle murmured, "Who the hell is knocking at this time a night?"

Moments later, Sparkle opened the door and Birdie looked up to see a bundled form. Water streamed from a yellow fisherman's hat and a dark topcoat protected his body from the wet. Sparkle assessed their visitor then looked at herself covered with mud. With a shrug, she grabbed his hand and pulled him in with her to the sitting room.

"He says he needs to speak with you, Birdie." The man moved forward reluctantly, leaving a trail of puddles to combine with those on the already wet floor.

"Excuse me ladies. Which one of you is Mrs. Jones?" He unbuttoned his coat, reaching for something inside. As he did, Birdie caught a glimpse of the uniform. For a moment she couldn't place it, then recognition came wrapped in a gray shroud. The Western Union emblem stood out like a dagger on the fabric.

The messenger was young, blond, and uncomfortable. He started again. "Mrs. Jones . . .."

The room was suddenly very cold. Birdie stopped breathing. She found herself trying to listen to his words but the darkness was strong and inviting and she was sliding into it.

"The United States government regrets to inform you . . .."

CHAPTER TEN

Annie stared at John Slattery and felt her cheeks flush. Her mission had sounded so simple but, like a lot of things, somewhere it had become difficult.

"All right, she was late a few times. I know that's not good but it's not the type of thing someone gets fired for, is it? Certainly not during a war when we need every person we can get on the line."

She could hear her voice rise at the end of the sentence and cleared her throat in hopes of sounding more confident when she spoke again. She knew pleading wouldn't help but that's just how she felt.

"Well, if it goes on and on, yes. But that's not the real problem. I knew she was your friend so I tried to help but I'm afraid there's nothing I can do either." The ever-present cigar quivered and then steadied as Slattery leaned forward. His eyebrows were pinched together and his face had lines of concern marking the sides. Annie felt her back relax. She didn't know why she always got herself into such a stew when she had to talk with this man. He really was concerned.

"Then you did try to help?"

"Well sure, like I said, I knew she was a friend of yours. But Waskom seems to have some sort of vendetta against her. Says she made him look like a fool. And he's convinced her foreman to back him up in saying she's not reliable. I tried to talk them out of it but that didn't do much good. He'd pretty much made up his mind."

"But . . . but . . ." Annie couldn't defend Birdie. She had been late too many times. What a mess. "You know she's just lost her husband. It's a terrible time for her."

"I'm sorry, but there are a lot of widows out there now."

Annie could feel her teeth clench and tears were threatening to spill over and ruin everything. She wanted so very much to change his mind. "But that's what I thought the union was for, to straighten out these kinds of problems and make sure everyone is treated fairly."

The union leader gazed at her for a moment, then smiled, weary and humorless.

"That's what we're supposed to do but don't forget what we have to work with. We're just people who listen and make sure that most of the time, things go the way people think they should. You've got to understand, particularly if you're going to try to be a steward, there are some battles you can't win. If you get in one of those and make too big a stink, your own people begin to doubt you and pretty soon you can't get anything done. This is one of those times. Waskom's got some good ammunition in the fact that Birdie's been late so much in the last month. I can't help her. And neither can you. If you really want to do something, tell your friend Sparkle to watch out. Waskom's got it in for her too."

Annie wished she'd talked with Cain about this. Maybe he would have known if there were something more they could've done. She just didn't know enough about how things worked to make a difference here. She rose and extended her hand still fighting tears of frustration.

"Thank you for talking with me. I appreciate your time. It's just that she is pretty low right now and we don't quite know what to do. She has that other job but it doesn't bring in too much money yet. She's still on a trial basis."

"Well then, maybe it's for the best. She can devote all her time to the other job and she won't get fired there." He shook her hand. One thing she didn't like about Slattery were his moist hands. She pulled back as quickly as she could and felt an embarrassed twinge. It wasn't his fault he had sweaty hands. Looking at him again, she wondered what the point of being a boss was if you couldn't do something you felt was right.

The bus ride home was quiet, she was between shifts and it felt good not to talk with anyone right now. She had hoped that she could do something for Birdie but since she hadn't said anything about going to see Slattery, she didn't have to mention that she had failed.

Two days later, Annie pulled her coat closer against the cold air and walked a little faster. She'd laughed when someone had first mentioned that it felt like snow but now she wondered if they might be right. It was the middle of December and she supposed it was possible. Pushing up her collar, she wished she'd remembered to bring her hat and gloves. She walked faster to keep warm. She'd tried everything she knew with Slattery and it hadn't helped. It was certainly going to be rough for Birdie.

Entering the house, she hung her coat in the closet and breathed a sigh of relief. Birdie must be out shopping and the boarder, Matt Parker, was dozing in the big green chair, the lamplight shining on his bald head. There was no sign of the other boarder, Joseph Robletto, Gloria or Sparkle.

It had been three long days since the news about Beau's death. After crying through most of the first night, Birdie appeared the next morning bright and early, just as usual. She had closed a door on her grieving and thrown herself into a cleaning and cooking frenzy. Annie felt awkward, as if they should be talking about him more. Maybe Birdie should be in her room crying while the rest of them took care of the house. Instead Birdie wouldn't even mention his name and had insisted they all go to work as usual, she would handle things. And she'd handled them to the exclusion of everything else.

With a guilty start, Annie realized she was relieved to be away from her grieving friend for a spell. Her mother had always taken care of this kind of thing, getting together with the neighbors to bring casseroles and sympathy with an ease of purpose honed by years of practice. Annie felt useless watching Birdie bustle around the house like a madwoman. Her offers of help were rejected with a brisk wave of the hand.

Annie pulled out her budget book and began to check off what needed paying this week, enjoying the peace of the moment. Ten minutes later she sat staring at the numbers on the small page in front of her. It was the same book she'd started eight months ago, except now there were many more entries, and the total made her smile. For the first time in her life, she had over two hundred dollars that she could call her own. After her share of the rent, food, war bonds and union dues there had been between five and seven dollars a payday that was promised to no one. She took the notebook and closed it carefully, her fingers running over the worn edges. The numbers gave her a feeling she couldn't quite describe. It was like a bubble, rising gently in her chest. Every time she made a deposit the feeling grew stronger and she found herself humming and smiling. She wasn't sure what she was going to do with it, but the independence it represented opened more doors in her imagination than she'd thought possible. She could even help out some folks in need if she got the chance.

The thud of the front door startled her. She put the notebook in the pocket of her shirt and looked up to see Birdie standing at the door, her face wet from tears or rain and her arms filled with wet sacks. Annie rose and hurried to help her. As she took the bags one slipped and in a moment, cans and wrapped packages fell with a crash to the floor. They both bent over to retrieve the items and bumped heads. Annie placed her hand on Birdie's shoulder to steady her and found that her friend was shaking. Tears ran down Birdie's brown cheeks. For a moment Annie hesitated, she wished someone else were here, she wasn't any good at this. Then, because it felt like the most natural thing to do, she pulled Birdie to her and just stood there, holding her friend as waves of shudders racked her. When Annie looked up, she saw that the boarder had disappeared.

After several minutes, the onslaught subsided and Annie led Birdie over to the couch. Giving her a handkerchief, she sat holding her hand, waiting for things to quiet. She tried to think of something to say, but looking at Birdie, just waited.

When she finally spoke, Birdie sounded choked. "Don' seem like I can get past this thing. You know it might happen, almost expect it sometimes, but when it does . . .."

Her words trailed off leaving a heavy shadow of pain behind. Annie squeezed her friend's hand and waited.

"I guess if the children were here, it might be easier, but I just cain't seem to figure how that's gonna happen. Seems like it's not meant to be that I bring the kids up here to live." Birdie sighed and sat forward. "This is a whole lot better place to bring up the kids, especially now with no man to help. Money is the biggest problem in the world. I just don' see how I can do it now."

Annie felt the air leave her chest. Her friend's words hit her like physical blows. She knew exactly what she should do. In fact she'd know for the last month. The realization that she had the means to help Birdie was terrible. She didn't want to do it. The hollow feeling in her stomach came as much from her reluctance to give up her this newborn feeling of independence as from sympathy for Birdie.

She knew what her father would say. The hardest path was the best choice. She'd never realized how difficult that rule would be to live by. Her stomach muscles knotted and her mouth went dry. The longer she sat looking at Birdie, the worse she felt.

She sighed, a deep thing that let loose some of the hesitancy that had plagued her. It didn't seem to be doing her any good to hold on to the money when the pleasure it gave her was so mixed with guilt. She couldn't relax any more than Birdie could. Closing her eyes for a moment, she made a decision. She hesitated, not quite sure how to say what she wanted.

"Birdie, let me give you the money to bring your children north." She'd debated offering it as a loan but was afraid Birdie might not take it then. She sat back on the worn sofa and smiled. She'd said it at last.

"No thanks, ah'm doing fine."

"But you just said that you weren't even close to having enough money."

"When ah get it, they'll be coming up here or I'll be going home. That's all."

"I don't understand, why don't you take it? I don't need it and it's just sitting in savings."

Annie sat forward, a cold jolt of anger at the back of her head. She was ready to get it over with and go on, ready to feel good about herself again. She wasn't prepared to have to talk this stubborn woman into it. Annie turned her head, catching the outline of Birdie's face.

"Ah told you, ah'm not gonna be beholden, 'specially to someone like you.

Annie felt the muscles in her stomach tighten.

"Ah been making my own way since I was twelve and ain't gonna stop now. Don' want to talk about it no more."

On the last word, Birdie rose and began picking up the scattered groceries, the outline of her back stiff and uncompromising. Annie felt rooted to the sofa and knew her mouth was open.

"What do you mean, someone like me? What's wrong with me?" She rose to help, her anger slipping away.

"You're not family or nothing." Birdie's voice was clipped, offering little room for argument.

"But I'm you're friend. That must count for something."

"Sure. Best way to get rid of a friend is borrow money."

"I told you, I'll give it to you, no strings attached."

Birdie spun around, the grooves in her face now set like hard, dark marble. "Don't want no charity. Cain't you hear good? No. And that's final."

Annie bent over to pick up a can of beans. For just a moment, she'd caught a glimpse of courage so strong it stunned her. Stupid. Idiotic. Dumb. But oh so very brave. She shook her head. She didn't understand Birdie. But she had to respect her determination to do things her own way. People often had the same complaint about her.

As Birdie took her armload into the kitchen, Annie had a thought. There was certainly more than one way to get this job done and if Birdie didn't like it. Well too bad. A little organization, a little letter writing, and her harebrained idea just might work. Annie wondered if she should tell Gloria and Sparkle. Perhaps she'd keep it to herself.

Cain watched the door, waiting for the familiar tall frame and red hair to appear. They had agreed to try this new place for dinner but he wasn't sure Annie knew exactly where it was. He wished she'd let him collect her. They'd invented some shaky rules about how this friendship would progress and her meeting him at the restaurant or the movie was part of it. Afterwards he always felt as if he'd only been able to take a tiny bite of the apple when he really wanted the whole thing. He had to keep reminding himself, it was still better than no taste at all.

When she did come in, he almost missed her. She was wrapped in a heavy blue wool coat with a scarf around her neck and a stocking cap pulled down over her head. The weather had hovered around forty and was dropping a little lower each night. He'd overheard some children asking if it would be a white Christmas. In Montana you were pretty much assured of that. Here it was unusual.

He waved a hand and when she saw him, she pushed her way through the crowded tables, dragging her hat off as she moved forward. Her brow was creased and she seemed to be trying to tell him something but the clatter of dishes and pitch of the chatter in the café made it impossible for him to hear. He marveled again at how much he liked seeing her and being around her.

When she got close, he finally caught her words. "Sorry I'm late. I hated to leave the Blue House. Birdie's been having a pretty hard day." She let out a sigh as she settled on the chair he'd pulled out for her. Her nose and cheeks were red and shiny and her eyes shimmered from the cold. "Would it be all right if we went there for dinner? I feel really uncomfortable leaving her. She seems awfully, well . . .." " Annie stopped and looked at him, tiny brackets of worry edging her mouth.

Cain felt a twist in his chest and coughed. He liked Birdie and thought she liked him or at least approved of his friendship with Annie. He'd had a warm spot for her since she was the first of the three friends to accept him.

He leaned over and spoke close to her ear to be heard over the din, "Sure, no problem. Birdie's got it rough right now. If you think you need to be there, let's go. It's no sacrifice for me to eat her cooking. Just let me pay for this cup of coffee."

When they got to the car, Annie reached over and touched his shoulder for a moment and smiled. "I appreciate this. I know it's silly but she scares me. One minute she's scrubbing a bathtub like a madwoman and singing some spiritual and the next she's bent over double crying. Sometimes she can't even breathe right. So far she's managed to get the dinner on the table on time but I worry every night. We keep offering to help but she only lets us when she has to. It's like she thinks if she does everything herself she won't have time to be so unhappy."

Cain pictured the days after the shell had killed his friends. The sick smothering feeling had made him feel nearly dead inside and he knew it would be months before Birdie could really laugh or enjoy herself without feeling stings of guilt and pain.

"It's tough. I guess the only thing I'd suggest is that you keep doing what you're doing. Just be there if she needs you." He put the car in gear and drove slowly toward Roxbury Avenue thinking about how hard it must be to lose someone you'd thought you'd spend the rest of your life with.

When they got to the Blue House, the table was set and five people Cain didn't recognize were there. The two boarders and the group filled up the worn couches and chairs, their impatience clear by the fidgeting and scuffling of feet. As usual, the smell from the kitchen was wonderful and Cain could feel himself growing restless as his hunger pangs became more evident every minute. Gloria came out of the kitchen with a huge bowl of mashed potatoes and put it down in the middle of the table.

"You can wash up for dinner now. It will only be a minute before we have everything on the table." The group of men trouped off obediently, a couple of them looking at their hands suspiciously, but Gloria's tone of voice brooked no disobedience.

Supper was a quiet affair, the interest concentrated more in eating than conversation. As Cain watched, he could see what Annie'd meant. She and Gloria would try to help, only to have Birdie leap to her feet and rush for a refill on the chicory coffee before they could even get properly started. During the clean up, she couldn't get it done all at once so the others were able to give her a hand. In fact, Cain found himself drying dishes as Annie handed them to him.

He stole a glance at Birdie now and again. Most of the time, her face was closed and stony but occasionally her lip would tremble or her eyes fill with tears. She would wipe them away quickly and go on. After the cleanup was done, Gloria, Annie and he sat at the long kitchen table with cups of coffee. Birdie looked at them and started to leave when Annie put a hand on her arm.

"Birdie, won't you sit with us a minute?"

The grieving widow stopped midstride and looked at the three of them at the table, her expression strained.

"You don' be need'n a sobby ol' woman. You just sit here and enjoy yerselves." She started to march out the door when Annie rose and stood in front of her, blocking her exit.

"Birdie, sit with us a minute. Let me get you a cup of coffee or some hot chocolate."

The colored woman's face was mutinous and Cain thought for a moment she was going to refuse. Gloria stood to stop Birdie's exit.

"Stay Birdie. We haven't sat together once since . . .." A stricken look crossed her face and she started again, this time slower. "Well it seems like you're always busy since . . .." The girl's eyes were wide and she stopped, then added, "Birdie, we miss you."

Birdie's face went through several changes but finally, with a sigh, she dropped into the seat Annie offered and put her hands, palm down on the table.

"It's okay girl, you can say it. Since we heard about my Beauregard." Her voice trembled and she paused then took a deep breath. "It's been a little over a week now. But I'm sure Mr. Cain don't want to hear about all this."

Cain was startled and when he spoke, he was almost as rattled as Gloria. "Miss Birdie, I'd be honored to have you sit with us. Just so you know, I was speaking with Mark Wellington the other day. He told me how pleased he was about the job you were doing here. Said if he had ten of you, he'd buy nine more boarding houses. You're a valuable person, Birdie and I'd be glad to hear whatever it is you have to say. I can't begin to know how you feel, but I do know about losing someone."

Her gaze was cool but she seemed to accept him after some thought. During this exchange Annie had given her a cup of coffee and they'd all settled back in the well worn kitchen chairs. For several moments it was quiet. When Birdie started speaking, her voice was low.

"It's just that I can't stop thinking about him. Every minute of every day. If I scrub a toilet, I remember the little outhouse back home that I fancied up with checkered curtains and Beau said it was the fanciest outhouse in the county. And if I cook cornbread, I remember that he would brag to his mother that if we ever entered a piece in the county fair, I'd win hands down." Tears slid down her cheeks making them glisten in the overhead light.

Annie had passed coffee around for all of them and Cain took a swallow trying to ease the painful lump in his throat. The tick of the black and white kitchen clock was the only sound other than Birdie's sniffling.

"And when I see a man, just about any man, I want to smash him cause he's not my Beauregard." She looked at Cain and he noticed a faint hint of her old smile. "It's okay, I think you're safe."

Cain wondered what Annie was thinking and saw that her lips were pressed tightly together. She was trying to hold back tears and wanted to comfort her.

"Is there anything we can do? We're your friends and we want to help." Annie's voice sounded choked.

Gloria murmured agreement and Cain, unsure of what was expected of him, settled for what he hoped was an earnest smile. Birdie took a blue handkerchief from the pocket of her apron and wiped her eyes then blew her nose. She was calmer than before.

"Since I got so much time on my hands, don't need so much help around here, I guess. I don' know, just seems like everything hurts, even you folks. Jus' can't stop missin' him. I'm not sure anybody can help." She raised her chin a bit and looked around. "Maybe jus' keep up doing what y'r doing and I'll keep tryin' to not be such a crybaby."

Annie reached over and put her square, freckled hand on Birdie's and Gloria placed her pale slender one over the other two. When she spoke, tears filled her words.

"Birdie, you cry all you want. Nobody's got a better right. But you have to let us know when and what we can do. All right?"

Birdie nodded. Cain watched as the three women cried and wondered if there was any end to the pain the war would cause.

CHAPTER ELEVEN

Annie strained to hear the last of the radio report but the scratchy voice of Elmer Holmes Davis kept fading in and out in the quiet kitchen of the Blue House. Gloria had put a string of popcorn and green and red paper ornaments on the tiny tree the boarders had brought in and set up in the front room. She'd pasted some of the extras in the kitchen, giving it a lopsided festive appearance. "Reports are coming in from . . . It looks like it won't be a Merry Christmas for our troops . . . ."

"What did he say? I can't hear him." Gloria's voice was more lispy than normal, anxious.

Sparkle reached up and gave her a nudge on the shoulder. "Nobody can hear him with you talking. Be quiet."

Annie shook her head. All of them, except for Birdie were on edge because the war news was so confusing. Birdie's interest in the war was almost nil with Beau gone. But the rest of the country was anxious. It was as if the European winter ice had frozen the news as well everything else on that continent. The tension rose at home as the days passed with no real word about what was happening.

Annie hated to listen but couldn't stop. She was scared to hear that another battle had begun, as she would imagine her brothers involved in the bullets and bombs again. She ran her fingers through her hair and then stretched her arms to release the tension in her shoulders. Sitting back, she noticed that the four of them were arranged around the kitchen table much like they'd always been around the dinette in the trailer.

"Annie, read that letter from your Father again. At least that makes me feel better."

Gloria was twisting yarn around knitting needles. She was certainly not making anything yet, but she was trying. Annie shifted in her seat and reached for the letter, sitting with others in a stack beside the refrigerator. "Okay. One more time."

December 18, 1943
Dearest Annie:

I hope this letter finds you all snug in your new home. The weather here has been terrible. We've had some snow and your mother keeps me hopping clearing the paths around the house. She won't let me use the heavy shovel but does insist that I keep moving. She has me using the scooper you had when you were little. I think I've shoveled a couple of thousand tons of snow with the teeny little thing.

We got another letter from Roger and I think he's still in Sicily. The newspaper makes it sound like they just breezed through there but I think it's been a terrible battle. Roger sounds pretty down. One of his high school friends, Brad, got home the other day. He got injured enough to bring him home and keep him out of the war. His mother doesn't seem to be concerned that his arm will be stiff the rest of his life but I think it bothers him quite a lot. He was with the Eighth Air Force in London and tells me that the Fortresses are being shot down at a terrible rate. Apparently, the fighter escorts have to turn back before they get to the target. I'm sure we're working on a long-range fighter right now but it can't happen soon enough. Of course, Gladys Johnson thinks we're doomed and we'll lose all the planes. The woman is a terrible pessimist.

And speaking of not happening soon enough, Miracle is almost five months old and every day she

*smiles a little more, especially at me. I end up taking
care of her once in a while when your mother has a
meeting and we get along just fine. I'm still not crazy
about diapers but I guess that's just baby business.
Tell Birdie I'd like to come up and see the Blue House.
It sounds like she is really taking hold. That's a heck of
a job and I'm glad the rest of you girls can help out.*

*Your mother sends her love and we're looking
forward to having all of you children home soon.*

Love,

Dad

Annie heard a sniffling from the back and saw Birdie wiping away tears. No one spoke. It was hard to stop thinking about the war. Any minute they might hear their troops had failed to hold the enemy and they were being pushed back again. She was grateful that she'd decided to work at Boeing. It made hearing the news more bearable. It had been so easy at first, thinking that it was just six months or so and the war would be over and they could all go home. Now, it seemed like it might go on forever. Looking at her friends, she wondered if any of them would go home after it was over. And even if they did, would it really be home after what they'd been through? She shrugged. Her legs were twitchy from sitting in one place too long. As she rose to go upstairs, Sparkle jumped up.

"Oh Annie, I can't believe I forgot it. Here's another letter for you." Sparkle took the envelope from the heavy brown bag she had used for shopping.

Annie felt the pleased smile on her face dissolve when she saw the return address. Howard's square, firm writing was on the outside. While she ripped off the side and pulled the letter from the stained envelope, the others remained silent.

Reading his words, her stomach churned. When she looked up, all three women were staring at her, waiting. She dropped the letter on the table stunned.

"Howard has been reassigned. He'll be here in a couple of months. He wants to know if I want to get married here in Seattle or in Coos Bay."

Annie was finding it hard to breathe. The girl standing on the front porch of the Blue House looked to be about an eleven year old version of Birdie with uneven tufts of hair surrounding her head. Three shorter children, a boy and two girls stood behind her, looking tousled and sleepy in the cold morning air. They stood together, not holding each other, but as if their courage and determination depended on that closeness.

Annie shut her eyes and tried to rid herself of the vision of an imminent train wreck. Five minutes before she'd been sound asleep when she'd heard an insistent knocking on the front door. She'd ignored it at first, but when it appeared no one else was going to answer she got up. It was Christmas Day and they all had the day off. Except Birdie of course, she would be cooking. Annie had planned to sleep until ten if she could, then help Birdie with dinner. Birdie must have gone to Mr. Quincey's house to get the fresh eggs he'd promised her if she got there early. The knocking didn't cease. She looked over at Sparkle's sleeping form and shrugged. As usual, Sparkle could sleep through an earthquake before noon. Annie made her way to the front door, pulling her robe closer to ward off the chill.

The girl's voice was clear and steady.

"Is you Annie?"

"Um, yes."

"Well, we's here."

"I see that. And you are . . .?" She let the question hang as if hopeful the answer might not be the one she knew was coming.

"I's Letty." She dragged forward a shy boy of seven or so with dark freckles scattered across his cheeks. "This'n is William. The big girl is Elzbeth and the littl'n here is Hepsah." The two girls obediently stood clear of the group for a moment, then slid back into the unit. The youngest was dressed in a nightgown top and long pants and the older one wore a long coat and tattered woolen hat.

"You're Birdie's children?"

"Why 'course. What'd you expect? You sent the money. We come."

"But I sent the money to your grandmother." She stopped, unwilling to continue in front of the children. She had indeed sent the money to Birdie's mother-in-law but she'd sent enough for five tickets, one for the woman to accompany the children. She had expected them a month or so from now. Plenty of time to prepare Birdie.

"I didn't think you'd . . . ." Her words trailed off again and she stared at the children, still perplexed that there seemed to be no adult with them or vehicle that had brought them or any more than one small satchel between all three. With a gulp, she realized that it was seven o'clock on a cold Christmas Day morning and there were four children on the porch needing food and warmth. She smiled at the little band and put her hand out to take the satchel, a silly, happy feeling running through her as she did.

"Well Letty, welcome to Washington. Come on in. Your mom is really going to be surprised. Sit here on the couch a minute. Let me get some help. This may take a couple minutes. Sparkle!"

The children trooped in and sat on the couch, lined up with feet together like tiny soldiers. Annie strode into the bedroom she shared with Sparkle and put her hand down to shake the bed as she passed. The bedclothes didn't move so she grabbed the blankets and pulled, exposing a great deal of skin and a very little nightgown.

"What the hell?"

"You need to get up. Birdie's children are here and I need you to help me get them something warm to eat and then figure out what I can tell Birdie about who sent the money for them to come." Annie eyed Sparkle. "And put some clothes on, you look a little bare."

Sparkle's face was blank. She was having trouble getting her eyes to focus. As Annie watched, gradual awareness dawned. She started to speak and Annie could tell what was coming.

"You didn't . . .."

Annie leaned forward and put her face next to her roommate's. "I did. We'll talk about it after you get up."

Fifteen minutes later the children sat at the kitchen table. They'd used the bathroom and Letty had washed their faces and slicked down the various heads with water, giving them all a newborn puppy look. Sparkle stood at the stove stirring the warming milk for hot chocolate and wearing a loose robe. Her brows were drawn together into a straight line and Annie ducked the occasional dark look that was directed her way. She sat at the table with the children, trying to get the story straight.

Annie took a deep breath. "Tell me again, how did you get the money? I sent it to your grandmother." Her voice sounded faint in her own ears.

"I stole it. She went to noddin' off and we figured we'd had enough waitin' around for my mam to send the money for fare. We're tired of bein' in Georgia and Granny's so old she don't let us do nothin'. So I just had everybody pack what we could carry and we grabbed the money and ran."

"You stole the money from your grandmother and then you bought tickets for the bus and then you all came up here from Georgia all by yourselves?"

"You bet. My mam always said wasn't much use hangin' back when you're ready to go. Lef' ol' granny a note and here we be."

"And how did you get here?"

"We took the bus from Sweetwillow. Had to change a few times and Wil'm there got us lost once 'cuz he needed to go to the bathroom and we missed the bus. But we's made it to the big station in Seattle, finally. Then there was a nice man with a truck fulla winter squarsh what let us ride in the back. He felt sorry for us 'cause it's Christmas. Tol' him to drop us off at the Blue House, he knew right where that was."

"With the squarsh . . . um squash?"

"Yep."

"Well . . .." Annie stopped.

"What's going on? Who's here?"

Gloria stood at the kitchen door dressed in blue striped pajamas, her belly showing as a noticeable lump now. Annie felt her throat tighten. She was sure she had put her friendship with Birdie in jeopardy with her rash act.

"Gloria, meet Letty and William and Elzbeth and Hepsah, Birdie's children."

Sparkle looked up from her stirring, a lopsided grin on her face. "Sit down, Gloria. We're about to hear Annie's explanation to their mother. I can't wait. Probably gonna get pretty hot in here."

Annie was sure she was right.

"What's going on in here? I could hear y'all outside the house." The kitchen door opened and Birdie stood there, a basket of eggs held in her hand.

The next sound they heard was the crash as the container hit the floor. Birdie threw her hands up and ran to wrap her arms around the closest child, which happened to be Hepsah. It was hard to tell who was more excited, the child or the mother. All five of them were hugging and crying and laughing and dancing around. The noise in the kitchen was almost deafening.

As Annie stood watching the scene, she blinked away tears. It wasn't going to make any difference to her how long Birdie was mad. It was Christmas and this was the best present she'd ever given. And bunk beds were not that hard to make.

Seven hours later, Annie looked down the table and couldn't stop smiling. The boarders, Matt and Joseph, were seated at the far end of the table, both a bit bemused to be joined by four colored children. Each child was trying hard to be well-mannered. They were not succeeding particularly well when excitement overcame them. Gloria and Sparkle were seated beside Annie. They were trying to outdo each other in praise of the chocolate cake. The eggs were not all broken and Birdie had been able to make a cake that could make an angel cry. Or anyway that's the reason Annie gave for the stinging in her eyes every time she caught the glow on Birdie's face.

Cain sat opposite Annie, his face still red from playing outside with William and Hepsah. Cain had arrived at four, his arms filled with presents for all four women. Annie had been embarrassed, because all she had for him was a scarf that she'd woven. He'd been exceptionally pleased by her gift and that had embarrassed her even more. She'd been thrilled that he had carved a six-inch bear for her, the detail of which took her breath away. He'd given Birdie and Sparkle boards with hooks that he said he would mount on the wall so they could hang their coats. As large as the Blue House was, it boasted few closets. For Gloria, he'd made a box with carved toys for the baby. Birdie's children had been allowed to pick out a toy from that box and they'd been ecstatic.

She could tell he'd been startled by the presence of the children, but had recovered quickly. They'd found a cot in the cellar and he'd set it up in Birdie's room for Letty. He'd also found an old, sagging double bed that he and Annie had managed to get in the door of the smallest bedroom assigned to Birdie, a job that left them both laughing. The three youngest would sleep there until she and Cain could build them bunk beds.

Annie looked at him now as he tried to follow a complicated story William was telling and felt a wash of happiness paint her soul. The strong square line of his jaw gave her a surge of longing for something other than just friendship. For a second she thought of Howard's letter and then pushed the image away. For right now, everything was perfect.

Birdie sat at the head of the table, a position Gloria had insisted upon as soon as the food was served. Her face was alternately filled with joy or exasperation as one or the other of her children jumped up and raced to the front to give her a hug. They seemed to need the reassurance of actually touching her to be sure she was real. She would occasionally glance down at Annie and smile.

After the initial excitement of the arrival, Birdie had been quick to question Letty. Since Annie had been unable to formulate a story with her, the girl had given her mother the unabridged version of their trip and who had made it possible. Silence had descended for a few moments and Annie feared her friend was going to be very angry. But Birdie had surveyed her little group again and then come over and hugged Annie. Her words had been only for Annie. "I was an idjit. I need these kids. But I'll pay you back every penny, ya' hear?"

CHAPTER TWELVE

Sparkle picked up a small, well-worn shirt from behind the couch and tossed it into the basket in the middle of the room with a snarl. Saturday night. She had the night off. And by God here she was, helping clean up the Blue House for the regular onslaught of hungry diners.

She bent over to pick up a shoe when the glint of dull metal under the couch caught her eye and she lay down on the floor, pushing her arm as far as she could underneath. Her fingers just touched it and pushed it further under. With a grunt she shoved herself forward and grasped the object. When she had pulled it out she found it was a metal car, part of a small set of toys Cain had brought over for the children. William had been so excited he'd taken several pieces to bed with him. Now a month after they'd arrived, she was apt to find their toys any-where.

Sparkle tossed the small object into the basket filled with other clothes and flounced down on the couch, trying hard to be angry. Although she wouldn't admit it to her friends, she had just about lost the urge to go out in the evening. It surprised her that she didn't seem to care that much about men anymore. They didn't fit in any of her plans right now. But it also didn't seem right that she was here, cleaning a house that wasn't hers and picking up after someone else's children on a Saturday night.

Her quiet was interrupted by the slam of the kitchen door. Hepsah, which Sparkle now knew was short for Hepsabeth, was standing at the doorway, her short legs wide apart and hands on hips like a ship captain. The tiny four year old wore a hand-me-down skirt that was rolled up almost double on her waist and a too small shirt that had once been white. Her hair had been braided and tied with colored ribbons earlier but now half of them had come loose and looked a bit like sprouts of wheat. When the girl saw Sparkle, she shot forward.

"Sparkly, Sparkly. Have you seen me green flowerdy shirt? My mam says I gotta wear it tomorrow at church and she's gotta wash it first. Hab you seen it?"

Sparkle kept her mouth straight and looked sternly at the little girl. "How many times have we told you to put your clothes in the bedroom in your mama's clothes hamper? How come you have to keep looking for everything?"

The girl looked directly at Sparkle, her head cocked to one side and completely ignored the question. "I think you got it and are yer trying to tease me. My mam says you're a teaser."

For the first few days after their arrival, whenever Sparkle spoke to the girl, she'd run behind her mother. After a week, that had changed. Instead of being scared of Sparkle, the child now ignored Sparkle's tough attitude and almost seemed to like her. The girl had renamed her Sparkly when she'd had trouble pronouncing the word correctly. At first Sparkle had been upset, she was not used to children and didn't know how to deal with them. Certainly four at once was overwhelming. But as the month progressed, she'd begun to look forward to coming home from work to their laughter and excitement.

Hepsah ran to the couch and jumped up next to Sparkle, shaking the whole structure. She put a hand on the girl's leg and frowned. After she had settled down, the child caught sight of the missing shirt in the basket and bounced up snatching the top and racing into the kitchen.

"Mam, Sparkly's teasing again. I got my shirt, Mam." The door closed, blocking out Birdie's answer.

Sparkle grinned. She surely did like that spunky little girl. Her sister Letty too. She had to admit, any kid who could orchestrate getting herself and three siblings from Georgia to Seattle in less than a week was one sharp little lady.

The front door slammed. Gloria was home. Her face looked tired. She sat in the same spot recently vacated by Hepsah, put her head back and groaned.

"In a minute I'm going to have you undo this girdle. Right now I'm too tired. I cannot believe how much work there is to do in that office. Sometimes I wonder if somebody goes in the back room and manufactures paper just to make more work."

Sparkle looked at her but didn't say anything. She had no idea how hard office work could possibly be, she'd never done any. It seemed that throwing around a rivet gun or any of the hundreds of jobs on the shop floor had to be more work.

Pretty soon Gloria pulled herself forward and lifted up the back of her blouse to reveal an old fashioned corset-type girdle that was tightened at the back by crisscrossed strings. It was the only thing they'd found in the last month that held the baby in enough to make it impossible to tell if Gloria were gaining a little weight or pregnant.

"I can't stand it, undo this awful thing would you?"

Sparkle obliged by unknotting the strings and letting more slack through the eyelets. Gloria let out a sigh of relief. When the kitchen door swung open, she quickly pulled her blouse down in back. Annie and Birdie came through one right after the other. Sparkle could hear Elzbeth telling William how to arrange bread on a plate. Apparently he wasn't doing the job to her specifications.

"Oh good, you're home." Annie spoke in an absent-minded manner as she greeted Gloria with a little wave. Birdie pulled her apron off, fanned her face then sat on a hardbacked chair from the dining room.

Annie sat on the overstuffed leather chair with the broken spring. Sparkle wondered what this meeting was about. She hoped it didn't have anything to do with assigning any more work for her. When Annie spoke she looked at Gloria.

"Okay, here it is. Gloria, Birdie and I think you need to see a doctor."

The girl's face went quite pale and Birdie broke in. "No, it's all right. We don' think there's anything wrong with you or the baby but you're gettin to be better'n five months along and we want to be sure everything is just like it should be."

Gloria relaxed visibly sitting back on the couch and putting up her feet on the worn ottoman. "But I don't have a doctor. How can I go to one? I don't have a husband to bring along. And I can't lose my job yet."

"We've been talking about that and this is what we think. First, Birdie has a wedding ring you can use. We'll just say your husband is overseas. That should work out all right." Annie was warming to her subject, using her hands to show the direction overseas. "And I know of a doctor in Ballard. I don't see any reason he should connect a pregnant lady from Roxbury with a woman working in an office at Boeing. I'll get the phone number and you call and make the appointment. I'm sure we can borrow Cain's car for the trip."

"But what if someone finds out?" The girl's tired look had changed to one of apprehension and Sparkle could see her tense up on the couch once again.

Birdie spoke quietly. "Then you get fired a little earlier than we figured and you start helping out here. But no one is going to find out."

As they nodded in agreement, the front door opened and Cain entered. William and Elzbeth, both grinning and shuffling in their new boots, followed him closely. They'd owned no cold weather clothes when they'd arrived and it had been a matter of secondhand stores and some judicial shopping by their mother to get them outfitted. The results weren't exactly pretty, but the children were warm.

William and Elzbeth stopped when they saw their mother and carefully backed up, removing their boots and heavy coats. They hung the coats on the low branches of the coat rack Cain and Annie had put together and put the boots in a box beside the door. William's face was a study in concentration. His sister followed his lead but her coat dropped on the floor when she turned around. William shook his head and picked it up, placing it carefully on an empty wooden arm. It was difficult for Sparkle to keep a straight face. She could just imagine William growing up with his three sisters. He wanted things to be right, wanted people to behave properly. One sister or another always seemed to be upsetting his applecart.

The bong of the old grandfather's clock reminded Sparkle that she was supposed to have the house picked up and the table set before the diners arrived. Some nights now they had fifteen people for supper, not counting any of them. There wasn't room for Birdie and her children, Gloria, Annie and her to fit with the others at the table any longer. Birdie organized mealtimes so they fed the diners first, then they would eat in the kitchen. Sparkle liked it better that way, it gave them time to talk and catch up. Things were so hectic lately that it was one of the few times they could be together. She jumped up and began her search. The others followed suit, Birdie heading for the kitchen giving instructions as she went. Gloria got to her feet and followed Birdie and the children.

That left Annie and Cain sitting opposite each other. Sparkle knew it was Annie's night off from tasks at the Blue House. Sparkle was pretty sure if Cain kept on showing up so regularly Birdie would assign him some chores as well. The two of them talked in low tones, then got their coats and went out the front door. Because she didn't hear Cain's car start up, Sparkle assumed they were going for a walk.

Sparkle watched, still amazed that they maintained the illusion of being friends. You could almost feel the heat from the two of them when they were together. It surprised her that some people made life so complicated.

As Annie walked next to Cain, she wondered if she would ever feel as if she'd had enough sleep again. Her work schedule, union meetings and then the few hours she was able to give to the Blue House were unrelenting. He looked at her and smiled, the easy grin making her come awake completely.

He spoke quietly. "Let's say we walk toward the water. It's awfully noisy in that house."

The sound of his throaty voice made her blush and she was glad for the early dusk in this late part of January. Ever since she'd told him about Howard's letter, the friendship the two of them had carved out somehow seemed in jeopardy. Sometimes they were reserved and polite around each other and then other times much more aware and emotional.

They walked slowly down the road, turning at the path to the beach. Fir branches interlocked above them scattering the moonlight. His hand on her arm mingling with his fresh, masculine scent made her chest tighten in a rush of longing.

He stopped in mid stride, pulling her around and closer so her face was only inches from his. The strong feel of his body started her heart racing and he bent down, pressing his mouth to hers stopping her thoughts completely. She began to float, a soft easy feeling accompanied by little charges of electricity that ran through her.

All her words proclaiming that they were just friends, that they weren't going to do this were drowned out by the sound of blood pounding in her ears. No matter what she'd said, she felt her body responding, her lips parting and her hips pushing against his. She could hear her own quick gasp as he took his mouth from hers and began kissing her lightly on her neck and then down farther. Slowly, with enormous care, he unbuttoned her blouse. The feel of his hand on her skin made her nearly blind with longing. When his hand found her breast above the cotton of her brassiere, she didn't want him to ever stop.

His voice was hoarse. "Annie, I want you so much. I don't think I can stand it."

Her thoughts were so badly scattered she barely heard him. She wanted to take this feeling and wrap herself in it. Her body ached for him. And then, almost as if her brain would let her go just so long, she remembered Howard and the cold, guilty thought made her shiver. Her promise to Howard was still valid. She put her hand on Cain's chest and pushed, not believing as she did that she could stand to end this. When his hand left her breast she shuddered with the sudden cold. She pulled her shirt together in the front with shaking fingers.

"Oh Cain."

He'd stepped back, his jaw muscles tightened and his arms held stiffly at his side. "Annie, I'm sorry. Sometimes it's just too much. I want to be your friend but I want more too."

"I know. We shouldn't be together but I don't want to lose you. What can we do?" She was shaking now, her body craving the warmth of his. She tried fastening the buttons of her blouse but her hands felt like icicles, unbending and frigid. She looked at Cain. His eyes were sad when he spoke.

"If Howard were here and we could have it out, things would be so much better. Annie, I can't trust myself around you, not the way we've agreed anyway. Maybe we can't be just friends. I don't think it's going to work."

Annie's body knew the answer but her mind seemed to be in charge right now. "You're right of course. I can't see any other way. I can't keep telling you no, it's too hard."

"That it is, that it is." He touched her face so gently she thought at first it was the wind. "Annie, I think I know what you want. But you'll have to make the decision in your own time." He let out a long slow breath. "If you need me you always know where I am."

Then he offered her his arm and they returned to the Blue House, silent as strangers.

"I can't breath anymore. I almost passed out twice today. What am I going to do?" Gloria rested in the rocking chair in the kitchen, a cloth placed on her forehead. The cool dampness of the material was in direct opposition to the churning hot feeling that came in waves and threatened to overwhelm her. Tears slid down her face and she didn't care. Right now she didn't care about anything but the awful way her feet swelled and her back ached. The day had been so long and now she just wanted to die rather than go back to work tomorrow.

She didn't think she'd ever felt so cranky. The children had been with them about six weeks now. She liked having them around, but whenever she moved, it seemed that Hepsah or William or Letty or Elzbeth were there, sometimes in the upstairs bathroom where they weren't supposed to be, sometimes in the kitchen, but always around, like puppies. Fun if you were feeling good, exhausting if you weren't. It seemed as if every time she wanted to take a bath, one of the boarders would decide he needed to use the facility right then. Sometimes she almost missed the trailer, at least there they'd worked out a schedule. So far the way it worked at the Blue House was first come first served.

Little things angered Gloria in a way that surprised her. She'd never been that way before. She thought about her room at home and sighed. This bedroom was small, even for the Blue House. She felt as if she were trapped in a medium-sized box.

She wished Annie were around more but it seemed that Trudy had her talking with people every moment she didn't have something else planned. She wished it could all be like it had when they moved into the trailer before they all had something so important to do. She wished she weren't pregnant because it was too hard.

She felt the cloth on her forehead being moved and replaced by another piece of fragrant cotton. Birdie's soft words reached her as if from far away.

"One thing's for sure, you ain't wearing that damned girdle anymore. Don' care what Sparkle says, it's not good for the baby and it shore not good for you. The doctor tol' you last month, seven months is too late to be wearin' that thing. We cain't be worrying about who knows."

Gloria sat up quickly. Glittery stars and see-through circles of blue and green jumped across her field of vision. "You won't tell anyone will you?" A gasp caught in her throat and she choked as she reached out to put her hand on Birdie's leg.

"No, I told you I wouldn't, darlin'. But I'm not going to let you hurt yerself or the baby."

"Oh Birdie, why couldn't it have been different? Why did Lester have to leave so soon? If we'd just had another week . . . .."

Gloria felt a sharp pain next to her heart and she wondered if she were having a heart attack or maybe if the baby was coming. She grabbed the washcloth that had fallen on her lap and scrubbed at her face fiercely, trying to distract.

"Just you remember that at first you said he wasn't good enough. Said you didn't want to marry him anyways. Why you so upset now?"

Birdie moved over to the sink and ran water into a pot, then set it on the stove to boil. She picked up the peeler and a potato and began the rhythmic movement of paring off the skin. Gloria felt a stab of annoyance at Birdie's unflappable logic and memory.

"I didn't say that. I said I didn't know for sure if I wanted to get married to somebody like him. Now I know I do but it's too late and I can't do anything about it. He's going to get killed and I'm not ever going to marry anyone and my folks are going to disown me and I'm going to be on the street with my baby and no one is going to want to help me and I'm going to be just like those beggar women on First Street." She ran out of breath on the last of her list of problems. She was sitting upright now and could feel the baby kick hard on one rib, the one that seemed to be its favorite target.

"Sounds ba-ad." Birdie stopped her peeling for a moment and looked over the top of her glasses at Gloria, smiling slightly.

"Do not tease me. It is bad." Tears slid down her cheeks in a slow trickle.

Birdie put the peeler down and moved toward her, only to be interrupted by the sound of an automobile door slamming in the driveway. She changed directions and pushed the swinging kitchen door open. After a moment Gloria heard her speaking in a puzzled tone.

"Now who do y'all suppose that is? Don' recognize the car." Gloria rocked forward and stood up then moved slowly to follow Birdie. She caught sight of the car through the front window and inhaled with a frantic whoosh.

"Oh no." Her throat was nearly closed and she had trouble getting words out. Birdie looked at her with an eyebrow arched, then shrugged and started for the door in the front entryway. The horror of the situation flooded Gloria and broke through her frozen dread. She grabbed Birdie's hand before she could get out of reach. The two women stared at each other wordlessly. A loud knocking made Gloria's already quick beating heart escalate to thunderous proportions.

"Who?" Birdie's eyes were dark and questioning.

"My mother and father."

"Omigod."

"Yes, definitely."

"I'm gonna have to let them in, they can tell somebody's here. Maybe you want to go to the bedroom and I'll say you're out?" The two women's faces were inches from each other and Gloria caught the faint scent of lemon.

"I don't think it's going to help. They must know sooner or later." She chewed on her bottom lip then sighed. It was inevitable that this would happen. She thought that she would like to be anywhere but here. It wasn't going to do any good to prolong the meeting. "Might as well let them in."

After Birdie opened the door, Gloria could hear the voices in the front hall, the loud imperious ring of her father and the lighter, wispy sound of her mother's voice. Soon the two people, clad in large, wool overcoats and hats were standing in the entryway shaking off the light mist of rain that had settled on their coats on the walk from the car to the house. Birdie had come and placed her hand on Gloria's shoulder. She could feel the warmth along with the thudding of her heart.

Her father, Michael Westfall, stepped forward first and removed his coat, then took his wife's and turning around, finally placed them on the shabby couch. A frown creased his forehead.

Suddenly, Gloria felt as if she'd never left home. His suit was a dark gray pinstripe, well cut to disguise his short stature but spoiled by a thin trail of cigarette ash snaking down the sharply cut lapel. Gray, slicked-back hair framed a swarthy complexion and mustache. His body bristled with barely concealed energy. Her mother stood quietly next to him and, as always, reminded Gloria of a well-trained dog just recently returned from the grooming parlor. Each sculpted brown curl blended into the next, the whole resembling smooth waves on a lake. She was dressed in warm beige tones that enhanced the color of carefully applied makeup. She stood slightly away from her husband, shoulders tense.

"What happened to you Gloria? It looks like you have been crying for a week. And you certainly have not been missing any meals."

Gloria was terrified. Her stomach lurched and her hands began to sweat. Her mother stood absolutely still with her mouth hanging open. Her startled squirrel expression was riveted on her daughter's belly. Michael stood surveying the living room, a hand on one hip. His chin was up and Gloria knew he had immediately assessed how much this house and furniture were worth.

"Why didn't you tell us this place was nothing but a second rate boarding house? I could have found a better place in a minute."

His eyes were icy and his lips thinned down to a slash mark. Gloria looked with new eyes at the home she had lived in for the last month and felt fear clutch her heart.

"Dad, this place is fine, I told you I have never been happier. Why didn't you let me know you were coming? I could have met you in town."

"Because we wanted to see where you were living. We have been wondering. Particularly when you changed addresses. And you have made a point of never inviting us."

He looked around the room. His bushy eyebrows pointed downward like sticks of charcoal. Pacing, he stopped to look at the worn couches and tattered chairs. He made a full circle, returning to wife and daughter and finally became aware of his wife's total attention on their daughter.

"What is wrong with you, Ruth? What are you gawking at?"

A shaky arm rose and she pointed a finger toward Gloria's belly. "You are preg . . . preg . . . preg . . . ." She coughed, unable to finish the word, then took a lace-trimmed handkerchief from her pocket and placed it over her mouth.

"What are you talking about?" Her father's words stopped abruptly and Gloria could see anger forming in his eyes. She felt her muscles tense. She backed up, afraid of the battering words that normally followed the storm. Gloria could feel her father's eyes on her and she tried to cover her stomach with her hands. She knew that he could see right through her clothes to her awful secret. Sweat trickled down her spine.

The man drew back and looked directly at Birdie. "I am sorry ma'am. My daughter seems to be unable to perform normal courtesies. I am Michael Westfall, Gloria's father and this is her mother, Ruth. Maybe you could make some coffee while we speak with our daughter? We need to have a conversation in private."

Gloria felt her teeth clench and grabbed for Birdie's arm. Her mouth was nearly too dry to speak. "Daddy, Birdie is not a waitress. She is the manager. And she is my friend." Her last words sounded more like a plea and she took a deep breath to calm herself.

Her mother had been standing back during the conversation, letting Gloria's father do the talking. Now, she moved forward as if pulled by a wire, her eyes never leaving Gloria's stomach.

"How? When? Who is the father? I always told you I wanted a wedding at St. Patrick's, how could you do this to me?" She stood and stared, her mouth twisted and her foot tapping the floor, the closest she ever came to showing anger. "It is too late to have a reception but I could probably put something together with some of the women from the garden club. I am assuming the father is in the war somewhere." She stopped and took a breath. "Are you eating all right? Gracious, you look peaked and there is so much to do. Michael, ask her when she plans on coming home."

"Mommy, I am right here." Gloria took another breath. "I am seven months pregnant. The father is Lester Thompson. We are not married, he had to leave for overseas and he doesn't know we're going to have a baby. He's in the Navy. And I don't know when he'll be back. He writes every week. He's wonderful and I love him."

Her father snorted and she could see the small muscles around her mother's jaw line tense as she reached out a hand, almost touching Gloria. Her voice sounded like dry leaves. "Not married? And a baby." As Gloria watched in horror, her mother grew incredibly pale as if she were going to melt.

Birdie stepped forward and took the woman's arm, easing her down onto the couch.

"Whoa there. Let's get you down, easy now." Birdie positioned Ruth's head on a pale green cushion. Westfall had stepped to the center of the room, his face set in angry lines. "Gloria, get some cool water on that cloth we been usin' on you. Bring it over here quick like." Birdie began to straighten out Ruth's arms and legs. When Gloria returned with the cloth, her father spoke, his voice cool and clipped.

"Look what you have done now, little girl. I cannot believe I sent you to college just to have you get in trouble with the first rube sailor you meet. You should have called me. You know I could get him out of the service. Goddamn, I could have saved you a lot of trouble." He stepped back and seemed to realize something for the first time. "And why the hell have you been living with a nigger?"

His words exploded in the living room like rifle shots. Gloria
knew he used that word on purpose. All she could think of was
the night the four of them got drunk on the roof. Gloria felt her
eyes sting as if she'd been slapped.

"Daddy, stop. She is not a nigger. She is Birdie. And Lester
and I are in love. He is going to come back when the war is over
and he is going to marry me."

Her chin began to tremble and she knelt down beside the
couch to be closer to her mother. Her shoulders were hunched
and her breathing reduced to jagged gasps of air. She didn't
think her father meant to be so cruel but he'd never been able
to handle anyone in his family disagreeing with him. She
almost laughed. Moments before she'd been worried her father
would disown her, now she rather hoped he would.

Ruth's eyes had come back into focus and five minutes later
she was sitting upright on her own, drinking the hot tea that
Birdie had prepared. "Mother, are you all right?"

Michael Westfall had placed himself at the window of the living room right after his wife had threatened to faint away and
now stared out at his shiny 1940 Oldsmobile and smoked a cigarette. Gloria felt his disapproval sliding over her like a gray,
living thing. She shuddered. His silences were worse than the
outbursts. They waited for Ruth to recover.

Finally, Gloria's mother spoke, her voice stronger. "Gloria,
you must come home. You have to see that. You cannot possibly
take care of the baby here. We will get a nurse. You can finish
college. We will keep it very quiet. I will call everyone and tell
them you have had some sort of breakdown from all the hard
work here in Seattle. It will be fine, no one but the doctor and
the wet nurse needs to know. I will just help you get your things
together. This does not have to be the end of your life as it was
mine. If you will help me up, Michael?" The words were said
with calm, easy assurance but cut into Gloria's mind and soul,
as if fleshy parts of herself were being torn away. She wondered
if she did know what was best for her own baby. She desperate-

ly wished Lester were here. She swallowed hard and looked at Birdie.

Her friend's face was set and her eyes glittered. "What do you want, Gloria?"

Gloria's father turned from the window and strode to Birdie stopping within a couple of inches of her and towering nearly a foot over her. Birdie stood her ground, never flinching while he glared.

He spoke through clenched teeth "The point is not what she wants but what is best for her and the baby. We can provide for them better than you or anyone else living in this . . . this . . . this . . . dump." He seemed hard put to come up with any words bad enough for the house they called home. Gloria tasted bile as she stared at her parents. Her father's face highlighted by the cheap overhead light was dark and glowering, contrasting with her mother's pale, timid face.

Gloria was struck by the fact that all Michael Westfall's power came from intimidation and fear. Never from being a leader. Never from the need to work for a cause bigger and better than one person or even one community. His force was without heart. She shivered then looked back at Birdie.

"I think I'd rather stay here, Birdie, if it's all right. I want to wait here for Lester. You said we'd figure a way." Gloria's words were brave, but her hands shook as she spoke. She clutched them together to stop the quaking.

"Then that's the way it will be." Birdie turned to look at Mr. Westfall. He stepped even closer. The difference in size was almost ludicrous.

"Listen here, this is my daughter and I do not want to hear you say another word. We are taking her home." His wintry tone grated on Gloria. She remembered its soul withering effect on her all too well. She moved forward, hoping to insert herself between the two. She put her one hand on her father's shoulder and the other on Birdie's arm.

"Please don't fight. We can work this out. Maybe I should go home with them for awhile, just until the baby is born or something."

Birdie looked Gloria in the eye. "Is that what you want?"

"No." Gloria dropped her voice to a whisper. "But I don't want you to get hurt."

"I can handle this. Me and your daddy gonna have a few words then they'se gonna leave." Birdie turned back to the man now icy with fury.

"How dare you? Do you know who I am? I could have you fired tomorrow." The man's words came out like rocks.

Birdie's face was set in hard lines. "You're not going to do nothin' less you want the world to know about the little deal you and yer boys got set up. Ah think that people would be mighty interested to know jes how come your company pads the bills." The room was so quiet Gloria could hear her father's harsh rasping breath.

"No amount of dragging people 'round by the hair is gonna' help. You not gonna' get me fired or anything else 'cause I don' work at the plant no more. You ain't in the catbird seat here. Gloria is. She's a woman grown and it's time you figgered it out. She got her mind made up on that man of hers and she's staying here. She been taking responsibility for this whole thing without yer help." Birdie stopped for a moment and took a breath.

"Now, let's talk turkey here. I don' care one way or the other about your bisness. All I care about is Gloria. You take off now and leave us here. Nobody needs to know but you and your conscience. I'm not gonna say nothing and neither is Gloria. Just go and let us be."

The man's face was glaring red and his hands were clenched together into hard knots. He finally turned to Gloria.

"You want to stay here? With this . . . this . . . this person?"

"Yes, I do." She wanted to explain, somehow make it easier for him. She wanted to make her mother not look so crestfallen. But she knew that would be a mistake.

"Lester and I are going to be together and I'll wait for him here." Her words came out soft and breathless. She felt something steady within her. Something she hadn't known was there. Finally, she repeated. "I will stay here."

Her mother's body seemed to droop, crestfallen. After several moments she smoothed back her hair and straightened her dress. Her father's face had lost all the red and now appeared carved from stone. "Just like your brother. Ungrateful pup." He turned on his heel and a quick thrust of his arm brought Ruth to his side. She looked pleadingly at Gloria, then scurried to follow him out the door.

Silence followed and Birdie and Gloria stared at each other. "Are you all right, honey?" Birdie's face looked worried.

Gloria's stomach churned and dipped. "Not right now. But I think I'm going to be fine." A little smile passed between them and Gloria felt her shuddering heart ease. The mention of her brother Fred reminded her that he was free. It was time now for her to be.

CHAPTER THIRTEEN

T he smell of chemical solution was so strong Annie's eyes watered and she had to keep wiping them with her shirt-sleeve. Birdie was giving Sparkle a permanent and Annie almost wished she were at work. It was the middle of a gray Sunday afternoon in March. Only a few rays of light came through the tiny kitchen window left open to let out the ammonia odor. She felt a sneeze coming on. A bowl sat on the table and another on the floor beside her. Peelings went into the first bowl and the other was nearly filled with nude potatoes.

She reached up and rubbed the back of her neck. The niggly anxious feeling that had been chasing her for the last couple of months had developed into a full blown pain since she and Cain had determined that they couldn't be alone together. That meant no dinners, no movies, no walks. It had been two months since that evening and sometimes, particularly late at night, a longing strong enough to frighten her, would seize her. Fortunately, he had become so much a part of their little group that he was still at the Blue House at least twice a week. Although it almost killed her to have him so close, the thought of not seeing him at all was worse. She'd been thinking a lot about her home lately. She wondered if her mother had been correct after all. Maybe Annie should have stayed home. At least she wouldn't be having this awful dilemma of wanting someone she couldn't have so badly that it colored every waking moment.

She'd only had one letter from Howard since the first one saying he was coming home. The last letter indicated that his plans were delayed. It now looked like it would be early April before he would be in Seattle.

Gloria was looking out the window watching the drizzly evening turn into night. "Are you ever going to be done with the permanent?" Her voice held a tired, whiny edge. A green construction paper tree with tiny white cutout balls hung on the cabinet beside her, no one had taken the time to remove it yet.

Sparkle sat next to the huge sink on a straight-backed chair, her neck wrapped in towels and strips of blond hair twisted around silver curlers. Birdie had taken one curl loose and was examining the lock of hair.

"Well girl, ah think y'r about cooked. Looks to me like it's time to put on the neutralizer stuff. Here stand up and stick y'r head in the sink."

As Sparkle rose, Annie had to smile. Her friend had on one of Annie's old plaid shirts and it hung to her knees from under the red towels. Birdie had loaned her a patchwork skirt, which wrapped nearly double around her and draped to the floor. Annie thought she looked like a gypsy and a logger had collided.

Birdie dragged the kitchen storage box they'd brought with them from the trailer over to the sink and stood on it while she poured the milky solution from the little jar over each hair wrapped curler. Annie shook her head. It seemed like so much work for a few curls. She'd like to have given Sparkle her own curls and saved the house from the smell and work of this every two month ordeal.

She put the last cold potato in the bowl and wiped her hands on the towel laying on the dinette table. As she did, the unease she'd been harboring returned. Breathing deeply, she decided that she wanted to put this thing behind her. Looking at her friends, she thought she would ask them the question now. Hopefully she could slip it in and make it seem like it wasn't such a big deal to her.

"I have a question about . . . well . . . about men."

Sparkle's head popped up and Birdie nearly dropped the bottle of neutralizer on her. Gloria turned around, her head tilted to one side. Annie could feel all eyes on her and realized that she hadn't been as subtle as she'd hoped.

Birdie pushed the curler wrapped head down into the sink. "Don' you even think about sayin' anything until we're done here. Hold on there Sparkle, you're not goin' nowhere lest you want to be hairless on part of yer head. I gotta get this stuff all over. Annie, you jus' keep still a while. This sounds like something we'll all want to hear."

Annie picked up the bowl of potatoes, fingering the flower pattern on the sides and wished she'd kept her mouth shut. She wanted the answer to her question and she wanted it from her friends. She just didn't want to go through the teasing and pointed questions she knew it would take to get to the answers.

While the rest of them got organized, she reviewed her question. The few minutes she'd spent with Cain in the woods had unnerved her. Not because she hadn't enjoyed it, just the opposite, she didn't think she'd ever enjoyed anything quite as much. In fact, it was her strong reaction to him that pointed out her problem. It had made her realize that she wasn't willing to compromise. During these difficult last two weeks she'd made her decision. Since she'd given her word to Howard, she'd made a commitment to him and she'd better get cracking on making that work. Cain was going to have to be one of those war memories you simply tucked away.

Ten minutes later, Gloria, Sparkle and Birdie were seated at the table. Sparkle's hair was wrapped in a towel and Birdie sat with her hands folded carefully. Gloria's mouth was pursed and her eyes squinted as she tried to thread a needle. A blouse with a missing button lay in front of her.

"Okay, we're ready. We got a lotta experience here, lady. Ask away." Birdie was smiling but it wasn't helping Annie feel any better. She realized she was just putting off the inevitable.

"My question is simple. I've never actually made love. I need to know what it's like and I need to know what I'm supposed to do." If she hadn't been so nervous, she would have laughed at the look her three roommates gave her. Sparkle's face was scrunched, making it look like her mouth was trying to meet her eyebrows. Gloria and Birdie appeared to be startled bookends with wide eyes and mouths slightly open.

Sparkle recovered first. "I think we're all going to need a shot of something here. This is a serious subject."

With a quick movement, she pulled herself free from the table and elbowed Annie out of the way. Pulling the towel from her head, she threw it in the sink then bent over and extracted a bottle of red wine from the rack on the wall and placed it on the table. Next, she motioned for Annie to pull down the wine glasses from the wooden shelf next to the window. Moments later, Annie had joined the others seated at the table and they all had a glass sitting in front of them. Sparkle poured a generous amount for each. The room was quiet and now that the pressure was off to ask the question, she sat back with a sigh, curious about what her friends had to say.

Sparkle took a swallow. Her face was young looking without her usual makeup. Her blond hair was curled ferociously in even ringlets all around her head.

"So you want to know what it's like to be with a man? They're all pretty much the same. The trick is to let them think they're special, not just another fool with plumbing."

Gloria let out a sigh. Her face had gone red at Sparkle's words and she was studying her hands folded in front of her. "Now just a minute. I don't think you can say they're all the same. Lester is special."

With a snort, Sparkle sat back, her face smooth and assured. "Is that from all the experience you've had? My God, you've been with one guy, I've been with . . . well . . . more. Anyway, if Annie wants the best idea of what it'd be like with a man, I think I should be the one to tell her."

Gloria let out an exaggerated sigh and folded the blouse, placing it on the table. "Well, you may have had lots of experience but you don't even like men. That's no way to start out."

"Missy, I may not like 'um much, but I do know what makes them happy. So let's start with the male parts."

"Sparkle!"

"You can't be an expert if you don't know the equipment. Let's start with . . .."

Birdie was laughing as she held up one hand.

"That's enough. You two are lookin' at both ends of the dog, one's got the nose and the other's got the tail, but what's in between is what' important. Now, this guy's been married before right?" When Annie nodded, she smiled and took a sip of her wine. "Then I don't think you're going to have to worry about what you have to do. They seem to know what the procedure is."

The sound of Sparkle's fingers drumming on the table was loud. Birdie held up her hand again.

"This is about Annie, not about how many fellas you've been with. Ah'm thinking here she needs to get a little better feel for what to do when she and Cain . . .." She paused as Annie opened her mouth to protest. "Okay, then when she and um . . . Howard, do it for the first time, right?"

"Yes. And you know very well his name is Howard. I can't stop thinking that he's met some French women and he'll think I'm a hick. Maybe he'll feel badly that he's saved himself when he finds I don't have any . . . well you know . . . experience."

Sparkle let out a bark of laughter. "Well, it's one way or the other you got to worry about. Either he saved himself or he found a French tart."

Birdie frowned at the blond. "You be quiet there." She turned to look at Annie. "You grew up on a farm right?"

Annie felt her face grow hot and she nodded.

"Okay. So we don't need to be gettin' into how the parts fit together. The two of you must have been close enough to be sure you were interested in each other, right? You know the feeling."

The back of Annie's neck grew hot and she took a deep breath. She couldn't lie to her friends. Her stomach did a roll and she swallowed, trying to think how to tell them.

"Actually, we have a . . . friendly relationship. We don't, well, we never did do anything but kiss a little."

Birdie raised her eyebrows and swirled the red liquid around in her glass. Gloria's mouth was set in a small circle. She had taken about three ladylike sips. Sparkle had chugged the glass in a couple of gulps and was stopped mid-pour on the next glass when she heard Annie.

"You're kidding, right?"

Birdie silenced Sparkle again with a thump on the table. "Okay, but we're thinking here that those kisses weren't like you'd kiss yer momma, right? When you kissed you got that feeling between yer legs like melting molasses? Kinda like yer knees were made a jelly?"

Annie sat absolutely still. The question was fair and she knew it was part of her problem. She'd certainly had that feeling, but it wasn't when Howard kissed her. The times she'd had that feeling, she was with Cain. Or sometimes even just thinking about Cain. She was attracted to the wrong man and most of her worry came from that fact. It was her own weakness that had started this. She cleared her throat, deciding that this was no time to be gilding the lily. She needed some real advice.

"Actually, no, the kisses weren't much. But I do know what you mean about that melting feeling. I'm assuming that will come after we've been together a while. I guess I need to know how to fake it until I feel something." As the last word came out, she grabbed the wine glass in front of her and took a big swallow, choking and spraying little wine droplets as she did.

Her roommates held up their hands and pretended to be protecting themselves from poison gas or flying bullets.

Birdie pursed her lips and raised one eyebrow. "Well, let's see, every woman fakes it once in a while. Ah think you're jus gonna hafta hold on and smile a lot and tell him how much you like him. Or love him, I guess." She turned to Sparkle, her expression indicating she hated to admit defeat. "But I'm not sure, what do you think?"

Sparkle's mouth was in a smug, pleased line and she pushed the glass into the middle of the table.

"Well, I got to tell you that all the faking you're going to do starts in yer head."

Sitting forward, Annie nodded.

"One of the most important things is to shut your eyes right at first. Makes it a whole lot easier to get in the mood if you don't have to look at the hair in his nose or dinner crumbs in his mustache. I like to think of a song, maybe something romantic. Then I think of somebody I really do like."

Birdie sighed heavily, interrupting Sparkle. "Hell, she can't keep her eyes shut her whole married life. She'll thump into somethin'. We gotta think of something better'n that."

"Hey, I can't tell you what's going to work forever, all I ever had to do was for a coupla hours." Sparkle's words were clipped.

Annie shifted her feet. "We're off the point again. It's really my problem that Howard and I haven't been more romantic. It just didn't seem important at the time. Let's assume that sooner or later I'm going to feel something for the guy. Right now I just need to know how to act that first time."

Sparkle picked up the bottle and poured another glass.

"Okay. So probably the first time is the wedding night. That means you're going to be pretty tired and if there's no sparks between you, you're going to have to plan ahead or it's not going to work out too good. You'll need a nice nightgown, maybe some other things. Let's see."

Sparkle slid out from the table and left the kitchen. After a couple of minutes, she returned with a red silk nightgown that wasn't much bigger than a hand towel and a bra and panties that were made from an abundance of lace but little else.

"What do you think?"

Annie felt heat on her face again and was about to tell Sparkle that no respectable woman would wear something like that when she saw that Gloria and Birdie were staring at the items with serious expressions and nodding.

"Those will work."

"But maybe in black."

"Or white."

Annie caught her breath. "But they don't cover anything."

Sparkle laid the soft pieces on the table and sat down.

"We're not trying to cover, we're just trying to make it look like we're trying to cover and it's not working."

"But why?"

Sparkle smiled at Annie and tapped a red fingernail on her wine glass. "When one person isn't much interested in doing it, it's a problem. But if both people aren't interested, this whole thing is just not going to happen. The solution is to make at least one of you very interested. And because of the way this whole process works, if he's not interested, you're going nowhere."

Gloria giggled, then put a hand over her mouth. "I'm sorry. This seems like so much work."

"Well, it is work for some people."

The room was quiet for a minute. Annie had no idea this would be so complicated. She jumped when a warm hand was placed over hers. Birdie was looking at her, little furrows of concern lining her forehead.

"Don't worry, it won't be that bad. If you come out of the bathroom in a get-up like that, he'll be ready." She patted her friend's hand. "But that's only part of it."

Annie took another drink, carefully.

Sparkle nodded. "She could bring Vaseline. That would work."

"It'd work all right, but she's gonna have to be ready to slather it on at the right time. It might be kinda tricky, this bein' her first time n'all. He's gonna get out'a the mood pretty quick if it looks like she been doin' this a lot."

"Maybe start thinking about something else entirely."

"We don' want him doin' that."

Annie tried to speak and only managed to croak. The sound did interrupt her friend's conversation though and they turned and looked at her as if they'd forgotten her presence.

Licking her lips, she tried again. "Why?"

"Why what?"

"Why Vaseline?" She was pretty sure she knew the answer but wanted to be very, very certain. It seemed important. Sparkle pursed her lips together and raised an eyebrow at Birdie who cleared her throat then paused. Finally Gloria gave a tiny smile.

"It's like trying to run a motor with no oil." She sat back against the padded seat and rested both hands on her stomach.

Sparkle snorted and Birdie raised an eyebrow at Gloria. Annie felt short of breath. The whole idea of the wedding night had started to take on a nightmarish quality.

"It's what we been tryin' to tell you all along, woman. This ain't somethin' to get into with somebody you ain't plum crazy about. There's a heap a stuff that two people go through to live together n' a whole lot if it is just plain embarras'n and messy."

Gloria sat forward, the dim overhead light revealing her face softened and mouth curved up in a blissful smile. "But it's glorious if you love each other. It makes it all worthwhile."

Birdie nodded at the girl and then at Annie. "She's right. With the right man it's the most divine thing in the world."

What they were saying certainly didn't sound divine to her. Sparkle leaned forward and picked up the wine bottle. There was only a little left in the bottom and she upended the jug to get the last of it in Annie's glass. She watched the liquid slide down the surface and felt her new resolve trembling in the face of details of a real live marriage of people.

Birdie hiccuped. "Marriage ain't fer cowards."

Annie was scared, unhappy, happy, and panicked all at the same time. She wanted to get out of here, go somewhere she could think. But after a couple of seconds, her mouth began to twitch and she felt bubbles of hysteria mixed with mirth take over. The other three joined her and pretty soon everything in the world seemed funny. Her own virginity most of all. Every time she would stop, she would picture herself in the little red number, waltzing around Howard, trying to apply Vaseline where it would do the most good and she'd start up again.

Her sides began to hurt but she couldn't stop. Finally, when they'd all managed to slow down, she looked around and took a deep breath. As the others laughed and made pointed remarks, Annie sat back and considered their conversation. She saw with clarity what she needed to do and Howard's coming home soon made it easier. She wondered if she should tell Cain of her decision. It was hard to decide how to handle this.

Looking at the three women, still laughing and carrying on, she decided to forget it for now. The wine was making her relax and her friends had made her laugh at herself. She wondered how anyone made it through hard things like this without really good friends.

Cain pulled into the driveway of the Blue House, realizing as he put the car in park that he was an hour early for dinner. He pulled a cigarette from his pocket and lit it, taking a deep drag then letting the smoke out slowly. He stared at the house. It was dusk and misty rain had been falling all day, making the faded shingles glisten. Light glowed from every window and sent sheets of pale yellow onto the front porch and yard. Bushes lining the walkway were transformed into huge Christmas ornaments and the twisted branches of the old apple tree sparkled. He could hear the sound of laughter from inside the house and knew that everyone would be working to get dinner on the table by six o'clock.

He understood that it was hard on Annie to have him here. Lord knew it was hard on him. The problem was, it just didn't seem to work out that they could stay apart entirely. Things kept needing repair at the Blue House and he'd told Birdie he'd help where he could. And the evening meal needed as many diners as possible to make the budget work out. And then, Sparkle had taken him aside and told him that she would pay for a cradle if he would make one for Gloria's baby. And the truth was, he didn't want to be apart at all.

He stepped out of the car and dropped the cigarette in an ashtray on the front porch. Before he went in, he caught sight of the bentwood rocker that had been relegated to the covered entrance because one rocker was broken. He made a note to fix that on Sunday and opened the door.

"Hi, Cain."

"Hello, Matt." The only person in the large front room, Matthew Parker, sat in the green overstuffed chair with a paper in his lap. Light filtered onto the newspaper from a Victorian lamp with faded material covering the shade and strings of scarlet beads dangling from the edges. Here and there beads or a whole strand would be missing, giving it a gap-toothed look. Matt smiled at Cain then returned to his reading. Cain had talked with him many times but didn't know him very well. Cain had been surprised that he'd stayed after the children moved in. The noise was occasionally deafening but Parker said it was a noise he liked hearing. Cain could agree with him there. After the sounds of war, this was heaven.

Cain took off his coat and hung it on the rack then went to stand by the fireplace. He put his back to it and let the warmth ease the pain in his leg. He moved around to warm his hands when he heard Annie's voice.

"Hello, Cain." As usual, the sound made his pulse rate go up.

He turned to see her standing there wearing a deep green shirt and brown trousers. He liked the new fashion of women wearing pants. They certainly looked wonderful on her.

"Annie." He could think of several more things to say but he was pretty sure she would think they were all inappropriate so he just smiled and nodded his head in her direction.

"May I speak with you outside for a moment?" Annie's question startled Cain, going outside would definitely be considered being alone together. He raised an eyebrow, but she just moved toward the door. Grabbing his coat, he followed her out.

The old chains of the porch swing creaked as she seated herself, then again as he joined her. Silence wrapped around both of them and he began to feel the damp of the seat beneath him as the minutes stretched out.

When she didn't seem inclined to talk, he remembered something John had mentioned. "I heard you had a great meeting last week. Some of the fellows have told me they might even vote for you. They say you make sense." He stopped, then stretched out his leg, the twinge of pain less now. "You seem to be over being afraid of speaking in front of people."

Annie laughed. "Yes, I guess I am. When I spoke up in your first training meeting, I felt like someone should shoot me. Put me out of my misery, you know." Her slow, quiet smile made his heart expand. The light from the window touched her face, making it glow like a renaissance painting. Cain didn't know what a renaissance painting looked like but he was sure Annie was it.

"Did you hear about Gloria?" Annie's question startled him from his thoughts.

"No. What about her?"

"She was fired yesterday."

Cain drew in a sharp breath. "No, I certainly didn't hear that. I'm sorry. I suppose someone noticed."

"In any case, the outcome was that she was fired."

"How is she taking it?"

"All right. We knew it was coming as soon as they found out she was pregnant. But Birdie did some figuring and said that with Gloria's help, she could have at least three to four more folks for dinner. With the extra income, it will almost pay the rent on the room. Sparkle and I decided we could increase our rent payments so we should be all right."

"You ladies are amazing." He had never seen an unrelated group pull together quite as they did. He looked at Annie again. They were alone. He needed to know what this was about. He didn't want to be disappointed again. "So we're out here alone. I guess illegally. Did you have something to tell me or are we going to have to go take cold showers again."

Her laugh was deep and rumbly. "Well not illegally exactly, but not in accordance with the rules."

"Right, the rules according to Annie."

"Yep. Those rules." Annie was calm, almost as if she were teasing him but the look on her face was far from teasing. "I made a decision last week and I want you to know what it is."

His heart did a little jump-start and he reached up to touch her only to stop short. He needed to be sure. "What decision?"

"I've decided that I can't marry Howard. It wouldn't be fair to him. . . or to me."

Cain suddenly forgot all about his damp pants and put his hand on Annie's wrist. "Thank God," he whispered, almost as much to himself as her. The rush of feeling he'd been holding in check began to wash over him in waves of red and yellow and he started to pull her to him.

"But . . .."

He wasn't sure he'd heard the word. He sat back, hands falling to his sides. "But what?"

"I'm sorry Cain. I'm not doing this right. It's the reason I hesitated to tell you until after I had spoken with Howard. But, I mean, I don't want to do anything about us until I do tell Howard. I need to be completely honest with him when he gets here and I can't do that if, well you know, if we do anything before. And after that I need a bit more time before we do anything."

Her eyes pleaded with him to understand. Part of him wanted to but the really loud part wasn't having any of it. "What do you mean time? I've been waiting forever for this, now you say you need more time. Why?"

Annie chewed on her bottom lip and then stared at her fingers. "It's hard to explain. For the past ten years I thought I was going to be a spinster. And that really hurts because I'm disappointing everyone who's related to me or knows me. Then Howard comes along and asks me to marry him. I'm convinced this is perfect. He's a friend and my mom approves. Everyone thinks it's great except my dad. He tells me I need to think about it. But I think, what else could I want? We decide to get married but he has to leave before the wedding takes place."

Annie looked him in the eye. "So then I come here and meet you. And I begin to see what loving somebody is all about. Unfortunately I already have a commitment that I thought was perfect to begin with. So I get this dumb idea that you and I can see each other but won't get too close and we can't ever be alone.

That doesn't work because I can't stop thinking about you. So I make the decision that I can't marry Howard. I'm going to tell him that when he gets here. I need to feel right about what I do so I'm going to ask you to wait until I've told him.

"But now I wonder if this decision is the right one? I was so sure about making a commitment last time, I could be wrong again. Even after Howard gets here and I tell him my decision, I'm going to need more time."

Cain felt like a speeding truck had narrowly missed him. Part of him wanted to slug someone, anyone. The other part only wanted to grab this exasperating woman and hold on until she finally just said yes. Neither part wanted to listen to the logical side that said she might be right.

Annie put her hand on his and looked directly at him, her face golden with the light from the house. Her eyes were a wonderfully soft brown and her wide mouth reminded him of kisses shared. He wished he could find an easier women to love.

"Annie, you ask a lot of a man.

"Is it too much?"

"Close." He paused. "But I guess I can wait a little longer.

As he watched, Annie's whole body softened and he realized she had been uncertain of the outcome of this conversation. That made him feel much better.

As Annie watched, the evening sun slid down through the evergreens, its fiery glow making bright cutouts between the dark trees. The air felt warm on her face and she thought that it might be time to put away the socks and gloves she'd been living in for the last month. Breathing in deeply, she savored the musky clean odor of the beach. She let her fingers run over the letters, 'R' and 'S' that had been carved into the old picnic table years before. She loved this quiet, evening time with no deadlines, no pressure, and no continuous noise of the shop. With a sigh, she straightened up and stretched, pushing her arms over her head. She could see only one other person and he and his dog walked on the beach silhouetted against the sunset's brilliant red and orange colors.

She looked at her watch again. Slattery was late. He had sent a note indicating that he would like to meet with her at this park at six P. M. With a start she realized it was April Fools Day and she wondered if this were his idea of a joke. She didn't think he was a man to make jokes. Perhaps she had read the note wrong. Pulling the paper from her overall pocket, she read the words again. 'Meet me at the waterfront park at 6:00 tonight. I want to talk to you about something important.' As she folded it and put it away, she wondered again why they needed to meet away from the plant or the union office. Taking a deep breath, she decided she didn't care if he never showed up. It was lovely to be here.

She settled back against the rounded wood of the picnic table and thought about the four days since she had told Cain about her decision. She explained that she felt they still should make an effort not to be alone. It was too much temptation and Howard was not home yet. She'd decided they could see each other on a limited basis, as they had before. Then, of course, as if on cue, Birdie had suggested something that would throw them together constantly and they'd jumped at the chance.

She smiled. Birdie had proposed that they put a window in the kitchen. She said she would like to keep an eye on the children when she was inside cooking. She said she didn't think it would cost that much since Mr. Farrell next door was tearing out some windows and replacing them with larger ones. Birdie was sure the owners would pay for any extra wood they needed.

Annie and Cain had begun to look at the wall where Birdie wanted the window. The house was old and Cain was concerned about what they might find when they cut into the painted surface. As they examined it, Annie'd backed up and bumped into the work table. She'd said what this kitchen really needed was another four feet of room. Cain got a funny look in his eye and went outside to look at the structure. Soon they were all at the table with pencil and paper, trying to figure out what a really workable kitchen would require. They'd stayed up until almost eleven, changing things, putting in windows, taking out walls, everything they could think of that would make the dark place lighter and bigger. The plan was magnificent but Birdie worried that they would never be able to pull it off. It would cost too much and she didn't know where she could find someone to do it.

In the end, Annie and Cain had signed on to tear out the wall, enlarge the kitchen by four feet, put in most of the Mr. Farrell's windows along the entire side and put in an eating area for themselves so they didn't always have to wait until the diners were finished. They'd all been charged with finding as much wood and building materials as they could and when they had everything, Birdie would go to the owners and ask for the extra money they would need to buy the rest.

She rose and began to walk, a cool breeze had come up and it sent a shiver down her back. She was just starting to tread on sand when she heard a sound. With a start, she turned and saw that the man with his dog were gone. The sun down, and it was getting dark. She was alone on the beach. Or nearly alone. A sound came from the automobile parking area. This time the shiver that ran down her back wasn't from the cold.

She stood perfectly still for several moments and waited. When it came, she laughed. The sound was 'Annie, Annie' called in increasingly louder tones. It appeared that Slattery did not expect her to walk down to the beach and was reluctant to venture there himself. She started forward, wondering again why he had wanted to meet her in this out of the way place.

His voice was gruff when she arrived. "Didn't expect you to be wandering on the beach. Been here five minutes."

As she studied his face, she thought that he looked out of place away from work and the men who surrounded him most of the time. Her first thought was to apologize for keeping him waiting but she stopped herself. Since living with Sparkle this past year, she found it increasingly difficult to apologize for something she had nothing to do with.

"You wanted to see me?"

Slattery was wearing a hat and it shadowed his face, making it impossible to read his expression. She stepped back a pace, pushing her hands into her pockets.

"Let's sit in the Chevy, it's cold out here." His words were clipped and cool. She hesitated then laughed at herself. For just a moment she'd been frightened of him. She pushed the thought aside. He was just a man irritated that he'd had to wait.

As they slid into the automobile he turned the key and pushed the starter. Soon she felt a bit of warmth on her feet.

"I understand you're getting quite a following with the members." She was startled. She hadn't realized the talk at the women's meetings would reach him. He always seemed to surprise her.

"Well, I don't know about a following but I think a few folks will vote for me."

"More than a few from what I've heard. People seem to kind of like the idea of a woman steward. Anyway seems like a lot of people like you."

Annie felt a blush begin to creep up her neck and was glad the interior of the car was dark. "I hope so, we have put in quite a bit of effort on this."

He was quiet for a moment and Annie wondered what he really wanted to say. When he spoke his voice sounded rough.

"I want you to be careful. I think there are some people who don't want you in that position. They get pretty angry when you women want what they think is rightfully theirs."

"What do you mean rightfully theirs? We work hard too. We're helping win the war." Annie's tone got louder and she knew she wasn't sounding grateful to this man.

"Whoa girl, I didn't say you didn't deserve it, I said some fellows think that way. I just want you to be careful. Watch your back. Maybe do a little less campaigning."

He moved forward and soon she saw sulfur spark as he dragged a match across the rough edge of a matchbook.

"Do you think I should quit?"

"No." The word was quiet. He applied the flame to the end of a cigar and soon the interior of the car was filled with the scent of tobacco. Annie took a shallow breath, then reached over and rolled down the window a half an inch. She shifted her position on the seat, sitting up straighter.

"Then why are you telling me this?"

"Like I said, I want you to be careful. I like you, Annie." He paused and Annie shifted uneasily. He continued after a moment. "I don't want you hurt. I need you to do something for me. I want you to ask your friends if they know or have heard anything about Waskom. Now that you seem to have met everyone in the chapter, you can ask questions without people thinking it's funny. You know Waskom, don't you?"

A quick gasp escaped her lips before she shut them firmly. Did she know Zachary Waskom? The story of his threatening fist as he stood over Birdie was very vivid in her mind.

"What kind of things?"

"Well, I can't tell you that for sure. With him holding a position in the union, he has access to more things than a regular worker. I'm worried that he might abuse that trust. We hear some funny stories about him and I'd like someone, like you, to let me know if you hear anything strange. I'd like to be more specific but I can't."

"But what can I do? I don't know him except as a supervisor. I don't know his friends or anything."

"You're starting to know more people all the time. Most of the workers respect you and the word is that you will probably win when you run. I did figure out how to get you on the ballot without changing the bylaws. It's all set for the end of May. But for now, I need to have you keep your ears and eyes open. Let me know if you find out anything unusual."

A thrill of excitement ran through her. She was going to be on the ballot. She could hardly wait to tell the others.

She could hear the long drawn in breath as he took another pull on the cigar. Too bad this really good news didn't come without the strange warning to watch her back and keep an eye on someone. With an effort, she loosened her jaw muscles and reached up to rub the back of her neck. In a way, she felt sorry for him. She supposed a man in his position had a hard time knowing whom he could trust. Maybe this was the only way he could keep track of people.

"I guess I could do that. I don't know if I'll find out anything more than you already know but I'll try."

"That's all I can ask." He turned. "We can work together. I think you're going to be a big help to me, Annie. And you're not the only one. I have Melvin Anderson keeping his eyes open as well. Don't feel like you're all alone on this."

For a second, he put his hand on hers. Then, as if catching himself, he moved it. She was a little startled. She had heard that Melvin Anderson would do anything for money and that he had killed a man in a back room brawl. Maybe she had the wrong person. She didn't know exactly what he meant for her to do but then she shrugged, deciding not to worry about it. She supposed he would tell her in time. When the silence stretched on she thought that he was done. As she opened the door, he added.

"I suppose I don't have to tell you not to speak with anyone else about this? The less people who know about it the better."

A stab of annoyance jolted her. She didn't like not telling her friends. She shook her head admonishing herself. He'd placed her name on the ballot and here she was doubting him.

"Certainly, I can keep quiet." She had gotten out of the car and started to close the door when he spoke once again.

"While you're at it, see if there are any rumors about Otis."

His voice was so low she stuck her head back into the car to hear. "Otis, the janitor Otis?"

"Yes, that's the guy."

"But why?" She felt panicky, as if she needed to protect Otis. The man was like a child, what could he do wrong? Slattery's next words eased her worries a bit.

"Just let me know if you hear anything, all right? I'm worried about him." He put the car in gear. Annie closed the door and stepped back, shaking her head.

Why was Slattery asking her to gather information on two men who appeared to be working for him? It sounded almost as though he suspected them of some sort of spying. She could certainly imagine it of Waskom, but Otis . . .?

The next day Annie was still puzzling over Slattery's directions with no further insight. She'd told her roommates she'd met with him, leaving out the parts about watching the two men. Sparkle insisted that Slattery was definitely a 'bad actor' and Annie should keep as far away from him as she could. Annie couldn't understand why Sparkle had taken such a dislike to the man. Annie would like to have told them the whole story but she'd given her word to Slattery.

The Blue House was quiet this Sunday morning. The boarders were working and Birdie was cooking. The children were playing a game in the back bedroom and she could hear the occasional loud yelp of laughter or voices as an argument began. Gloria was in with Birdie and Sparkle was still asleep. Cain would be over later and they were going to decide how they could keep Birdie cooking while they remodeled the kitchen. Annie picked up the paper, thinking to read it while she had a moment when she heard a knock at the door. She waited for a few seconds, people seldom knocked, they would just walk in. Finally, she got up and opened the door. Standing on the front porch was Howard, his ordinary face overtaken by a huge smile.

Annie struggled to say something but no words would come out. Howard was thinner and had acquired more lines in his face but otherwise his large frame was unchanged. He reached forward and gathered her into a huge bear hug.

"Annie-bug." He bellowed in her ear. "I can't believe it's you." He released her only to gather her again in another hug and yell something else. When he'd finally seemed to have enough of that, he stepped back and looked her over.

She suddenly realized how she must look. Sunday morning was a time to relax, a day off, nothing to do at the Blue House unless Birdie needed something special, and Trudy had her own family to be with. She'd risen from bed, put on her old green robe, brushed her teeth and was sipping a cup of hot tea while she tried to read the paper. She clutched her robe closer and with her other hand grabbed Howard's arm to bring him in. A fine April drizzle covered his head and jacket with transparent drops of rain.

"Howard for heaven's sake, come in. I can't believe it's you either." She led him over to the couch and had him sit down. "Why didn't you let me know you were coming? I'm a mess." She ran her hand through her hair. It was probably straight up on one side and flat on the other. She handed him the newspaper. "Here, read this, I want to get changed."

"Not a chance, darling. I haven't seen you in three years and you look just fine to me. Now come over here and give me a hug." His voice was so loud she turned her head to see if he was talking to someone else, then remembered how his voice had boomed across the pasture. When she turned back he'd opened his arms again. Something popped inside her. What in heaven's name had ever induced her to say she would marry this man?

A noise from the kitchen made them both look up and Annie nearly cried when she saw Birdie and Gloria enter. They stopped at the door as if they were intruding. Annie jumped up to bring them in. In a few moments she had both women seated, Gloria in the only chair she could still rise from without assistance and Birdie on the couch.

"Howard, I'd like to introduce my friends, this is Birdie Jones and Gloria Westfall." Howard looked slightly dumbfounded but he did manage to nod at both women. Annie realized with a jolt that she'd never mentioned in her letters that Birdie was colored or that Gloria was pregnant. The look on his face indicated that he was certainly having a tough time adjusting to something, she just wasn't sure what.

Birdie broke the silence. "It's nice ta finally meet you, Howard. Annie has told us so much about you." Her voice sounded slow and syrupy to Annie, listening to it for the first time as Howard would. Birdie did not offer her hand. She was careful with white people whom she didn't know. It hurt Annie that

Birdie was judging Howard. On the other hand, she was pretty
sure her friend was correct in her assessment of the man.

"Nice to meet you too, Miss, Mrs. . . .." he stumbled, not quite
sure how to address her. His voice had lost its thundering quality but it still sounded loud inside the house.

"It's all right, I'm still Mrs. Jones, prob'ly always will be.
Would you like some coffee?" Howard turned his head and
stared at Annie. She grabbed his hand and held it for a moment.

"That's a great idea. Birdie please get him something to
drink. Gloria why don't you keep him company while I go get
cleaned up?" She nearly ran from the room.

A half an hour later Annie was back, feeling much more like
herself wearing the slacks and shirt Sparkle had made for her.

When she entered, she took in the scene. Gloria was regaling
him with a list of what they had purchased in anticipation of
the baby's arrival and Birdie was smiling and telling him how
childbirth was the most natural thing and that Gloria had nothing to worry about. William and Elzbeth sat on the couch like
matched statues, staring at him. Letty and Hepsah stood in the
kitchen door giggling and pushing each other. Howard looked
stunned, his eyes going from one person to another with little
shakes of his head in between. She sat down next to him, not
surprised at the relief on his face. She smiled at the group.

"Thank you for doing such a good job of keeping Mr. Mitchell
entertained. Would you mind giving us a few minutes alone now?"

Birdie looked relieved and sprang to her feet, the others with
her as she went. Howard grabbed Annie's hands. Before he
could get going, however, Annie stopped him.

"There's something I need to say first, Howard."

"No siree, me first. You look wonderful. You're like a different
person Annie. You're . . . well . . . you're beautiful." A startled
expression crossed his face.

"Thank you, Howard. I can't tell you how much that would
have meant to me a year ago."

His eyes widened and he started to speak. Annie laid a finger on his lips and that startled him as well.

"Howard, I have to tell you this quickly because I feel so badly about it. I can't marry you." She sat back and took a deep breath. His hurt blue eyes questioned her.

"Why? We agreed."

"I know what we agreed and I'm sorry. I am a different person, Howard. I'm not the woman I was when you left. Lots of things have changed, mostly me. I'm not sure why I agreed to marry you. At the time I thought it was best. I'm so sorry now that I did. You deserve better."

His mouth was slightly open as if he couldn't take in what he'd just heard. He blinked. "But I don't want better. I want you. Why didn't you write and tell me?"

She put a hand on his. "I just couldn't do it to you."

He stood then, letting her hand drop from his and walked to the front window. He stared out at the misty Sunday rain and Annie waited. His large hands clasped and unclasped and she ached to comfort him. Ached to tell him how sorry she was. Tears ran down her cheeks but she didn't care. When he finally turned back to her, his eyebrows marched in a straight line across his forehead and his jaw was tight.

Strangely, this time his voice was quiet. "I wish you had written me. I don't like finding out like this. It's not fair."

Annie sprang to her feet stopping just short of him, wanting so much to touch him, ease his pain but knowing he wasn't that kind of person.

"It's not fair at all and if there were any other way I'd do it. I almost told you I would marry you anyway, even knowing that I don't love you. But that's not fair to you. You're a good, kind decent man and one of the best friends I've ever had. Howard, I would do almost anything for you. But I just can't marry you."

"Is there someone else?"

She'd dreaded this, as much as she'd dreaded telling him.

"Yes. No. I don't know. Maybe. He and I haven't really . . .. Well, we haven't . . .." Annie turned her back on him and stomped her foot. "Howard, I don't know. I put everything on hold until you came home. Maybe now there will be." She dragged a sleeve across her face, trying to wipe off the tears. Minutes passed. Annie felt a hand on her shoulder.

"Annie, I won't tell you this makes me happy in any way. I've thought about you for three straight years and imagined your red hair and laughter over two continents. Now I don't know what to do. The girls are going to be very disappointed. They were looking forward to having a mother."

The tears began again.

"But it doesn't sound like there's any changing your mind so let's just sit down and talk now. You tell me about building airplanes and I'll tell you about fighting a war. I've missed you, Annie. And as much as I hate to say it, I know what you're talking about. You and I were never head over heels for each other. I like you, I like to be around you and in a lot of ways I guess I love you. But with Helen, it was different. I always thought it was because we were young but maybe it's something more. We couldn't stay apart more than ten minutes. And when she died, I nearly died too. Maybe I'll never feel that way again. You deserve the same, Annie."

She gave him a wan smile. He was living up to her memory, a gentleman and a friend. She was the one who felt like a traitor. Three hours later Annie stood on the wide front porch of the Blue House and waved at his retreating back. He'd been hurt but after a few minutes they'd decided that they were mostly sad. They'd agreed it would have been a good marriage, maybe not spectacular but quiet and easy. When Birdie came up behind her Annie was able to answer the unspoken questions calmly.

"It's all right. He's gone. I can't quite believe it didn't take any time at all."

Birdie squeezed her shoulder. "It hardly ever does when it's the right decision. You gonna tell Cain now?"

Annie looked at her friend. "Birdie, I think I'll give it a bit. I've been living with a mistake for a long time. I think I'll just try to figure out what the heck it is I really want."

CHAPTER FOURTEEN

Sparkle grumbled and wished she hadn't volunteered to accompany Gloria on her evening walk. Here it was the last of April and the weather felt more like December. She hated to bundle up and go out into the rain again. The only good thing was that it got her out of the mess and noise of hammering and sawing. Even on these rainy nights, Cain and Annie worked on the kitchen as soon as the diners were gone. Looking to the side, she realized that her angry musing had taken her several yards ahead. Tapping her foot in exasperation, she turned and waited for Gloria to catch up.

"Christ girl, you get slower every night. Pretty soon we'll have old people in wheelchairs passing us. It's colder than a witch's tit out here."

As the very pregnant woman approached, the streetlight shone on her face and Sparkle felt a quick pang in her chest. Gloria was beautiful. Since the morning sickness had subsided and she'd been working with Birdie, her skin had acquired warmth, an underlying flush that heated her normally pale face.

"Oh Sparkle, let's slow down for just a minute. We don't have to be anywhere special and I kind of like taking my time. It's just lovely out here." Gloria spread her hands and gestured, taking in the whole view of dripping trees, mist-shrouded houses and lowering sky.

A shiver ran up Sparkle's back and she snorted her disdain of her friend's beautiful world. Putting her arm through Gloria's, she began to pull her along the sidewalk.

"You'd think a train wreck was 'just lovely'. Take a look around girl, it's cold, dark, raining and we're out here like a couple of fools with no sense at all. This whole pregnancy happy-shit is beginning to make me want to punch somebody."

"Oh don't be mean, it's so wonderful. Just wait until you have your first child. You'll be just as bad." Gloria's voice came out in little puffs as she tried to keep up with Sparkle's quick pace.

Sparkle felt her stomach do a flip. Since Gloria had become pregnant and then Birdie's children arrived, she'd fought jealousy and anger in increasingly stronger waves. An anger directed at herself more than anything. The gnawing feeling of loss would creep up on her when she least expected it. Sometimes even at work, when she needed all her wits, she'd suddenly find herself thinking of a cottage and small children.

She had to laugh. Now that she'd decided she was off men, she would feel an occasional pang for something she'd never thought she wanted. Every time she saw Gloria's idiotically smiling face she wanted to kick something, make somebody feel bad.

Then she would remind herself that it wasn't Gloria who'd caused her problem. It was a man who smelled of cheap wine and had the soul of a pirate that had brought her to this end. Him and that drunk doctor who swore everything was just dandy, right up until the time her blood had started dribbling down the table and off onto the floor. Then he'd sobered up in a hurry and run off, leaving only a scared teenaged girl to help get Sparkle to the real doctors.

Gloria continued to prattle on about the joys of motherhood as the anger Sparkle had thought she had under control began to choke her, making her want to scream. She wheeled around to face Gloria.

"I am never going feel anything about kids. I can't have any and I'm damn happy about that." She yelled the last words. Gritting her teeth, she tried to stop but found she couldn't.

"It's idiots like you who keep having children with no thought of how you're going to raise them or what some man's going to do to them when you aren't there, that shouldn't be able to have any. Like what would you do right now if you didn't have us? You'd be back with that papa of yours trying to figure out how to keep him happy and not paying any attention to your baby. You shouldn't be having any little ones at all without a man."

Sparkle took a deep, shuddering breath and filled her lungs with the smell of cool rain and wet leaves. The fire of anger began to cool. She felt a rush of heat on her face. She'd told no one about this painful part of her life before and she wasn't ready to share it now, particularly with Gloria. Her friend's eyes were wide with distress.

Her voice was strained and whispery. "I had no idea. I am so sorry. How horrible for you. I just don't . . . My gosh, Sparkle, I can't believe it."

They'd paused near a bus stop bench and stood sheltered under the slanting roof, the rain coming heavier now. Gloria pressed her hands to Sparkle's and then pulled her closer. Sparkle felt herself stiffen as the other woman tried to wrap her arms around her. It was an impossible task with all Gloria's belly out front and lack of cooperation from Sparkle.

"Don't you be getting mushy, you hear? And I don't want you telling anyone else. God, I must be losing my mind. Out here in this lousy weather spilling my guts to a child."

Sparkle tried to untangle her friend's hands but the girl wouldn't give up. She seemed determined to give Sparkle a hug whether she wanted it or not. Finally, feeling silly, she gave in and for the first time she could remember, she let another woman hold her. They stood like that for a few moments and Sparkle realized that the water running down her cheeks wasn't rain.

Gloria was murmuring something but she didn't think it was words. Just feelings in sound but it had a strange soothing effect on her. This must be what a real mother did with her child. A mother who wasn't more interested in booze and men than the gangly, ugly child she had borne. A quick look into the possible future told her that perhaps this shy, silly girl might make a better mother than she had imagined. She felt her muscles relax and took a shuddery breath. She wanted to take back the words she'd said.

Stepping away, she rubbed her cheeks. "Don't take anything I said to heart. You know sometimes I get mad at nothing."

The rain had finally subsided and a soft light was coming from the house nearest them. Gloria smiled, her cheeks rosy from the cold.

"Sparkle, I try to never listen too much to you. You are not always nice. But this time I think you might have a reason. I had no idea you couldn't have children. It must be horrible for you. You know, I never thought I even wanted them myself, but now I think it's the most natural, maybe the best thing in the world." Gloria took a breath and sat down on the bench, resting on the rough boards of the enclosure.

"And you're right, it's not fair to the baby, me not having a husband right now but I'm not going to worry about what people say. In fact, for the first time in my life, I really don't care. And Birdie says I can stay and work in the boarding house with her as long as I want. I should be able to have a little nest egg when Lester comes home."

"And if Lester doesn't come home?" Sparkle could have bitten her tongue but she couldn't stop thinking about her own childhood of tavern back rooms and tiny slum apartments. She sat down on the bench and looked at Gloria.

As Sparkle watched, Gloria's lips made a thin line and her brows came together in a dainty groove in the middle. "If he doesn't come back then I'll have a nest egg for me and little Ben. Birdie says we can make it and I think she's right."

Sparkle felt her chest constrict and had a moment of panic for this brave young girl. She opened her mouth to tell her that just being brave and good very seldom made life turn out the way you wanted, but something stopped her. With a sigh, she rose from the bench, pulling Gloria up to her feet as well.

"Well, I'd just like to keep talking here all night girlie but it seems like pretty soon we're both going to catch pneumonia. Let's get a move on." Gloria started to shuffle then moved into a full-blown walk beside her.

"Now you don't have to be telling everybody about this." She linked her arm through Gloria's and pulled. "Oh, what the hell. You can't keep you mouth closed about anything so I guess you can just go ahead. All of a sudden, I don't care anymore."

May 15, 1944
Dearest Annie:

I'm rereading your letters and from what I can tell, the election will be at the end of this month. I wish you well daughter, I think you will make a fine leader. Just remember that you can't change things overnight and the people before you worked very hard or you wouldn't have the chance you have.

Annie felt a clutch at her heart. No matter what he thought, he would support her decision. She pictured him seated at his desk, patiently repairing one more watch. A longing to see him and her mother was so strong she debated buying a round trip bus ticket and going to see them, just for a week or so. She shook her head, with her ten hour shifts and union meetings, she had no time to spare right now. Maybe in another month.

I guess I knew when you left for Seattle that you and Howard would never get together. Heck, I almost pushed you out the door. I still say this is for the best. He's a fine man and you're a fine woman and I know you are friends, but that doesn't make marriage right for either of you.

Annie touched the paper and smiled. Her father had always understood her. Thinking back to the election though, she felt a twinge of anxiety. There were so many people hoping for her to win, expecting it really. She wished that all of them weren't counting on her.

I have some bad news for you. Joann Smalley died last Thursday. We got word that her husband was killed near Casino in Italy (you know, that's right on the Gustav line) in March and Joann just lost heart. She hadn't been doing very well and after that she just sort of slipped away. Miracle is still doing fine and doesn't even seem to miss her mother. It's a terrible shame but your mother and the other ladies have been doing most of the caring for her since she was born. I still watch her when no one else can. I'm going to miss her. I've heard Joann's sister from Portland is coming in a few days to pick her up.

Annie put the letter down. She wished she'd waited until later to read it. It seemed that no one was safe, not even a woman barely hanging on to life in Coos Bay.

Your mother has been feeling a little off lately. Every time I try to have her go to the doctor though, she gets mad at me, tells me I'm an old woman. Sometimes that woman drives me crazy. Oh well, I think I'll make an appointment and just grab her by the hair and throw her over my shoulder and haul her there. This war is hard on all of us but your mother sure takes it personally.

You won't believe it. Gladys never gives up. Now she's saying that we'll be two or three years fighting our way through France and Germany. I told her that it won't be long and we'll be putting those Jerries on the run. I think the bombings in Germany (and yes, it looks like we did get those long-range fighters) have just about broken Germany's back and we're on our way. I think we're in for a big push soon. I pray your brothers will keep dodging bullets for however long it takes.

You're mother says she can see the first buds on the rose outside your window. She prays you will be home in time to see them bloom.
Love,
Dad

Annie stared out the kitchen window of the Blue House. She prayed as well, for her brothers, for her mother and father, for her friends and classmates, and for a little girl with curly brown hair, named Miracle.

Birdie rested her forearms on the peeling windowsill and sighed as she eased the kinks out of her back. A pink cotton haze of blossoms covered the limbs of the old cherry tree in the backyard and scattered the grass underneath with fairy light petals. The Blue House, and the half block of grounds it stood on had a worn, unchanging feeling.

She could hear shrieks of laughter from the far side of the house where her children were putting the strange assortment of junk from the back storage room into two piles; one, things to be kept and the other, things to be thrown away. The throwaway pile was taking on the size of a tank. They had all been amazed at the collection of leavings from the years of boardinghouse guests: one wooden leg, an assortment of spectacles, a stuffed cat with no tail and a Chinese black lacquer chest with a lock so curious they'd probably never get it open. These were only a few of the items that had been jammed in the cobwebby interior.

Birdie breathed in deeply, feeling the familiar band of pain fade just a little. The memory of Beau's death would never go away completely but at least the ache was tinted now by the sight and feel of the children he'd left behind. She thought about

Annie, wondering how she must feel with the election only two days away. There'd been a meeting with the women from the union the night before at the Blue House. They'd all decided they had done as much as they could do. Birdie knew Annie was ready for this to be over. She was not a person who liked to be on display and she'd certainly been there for the past five months.

"Didn't you want a rack for pots over the stove? Annie is putting the boards up now that the rack will hang on and I think you should go down now and make sure it's big enough. She won't listen to anybody but you." Sparkle's sudden appearance made Birdie jump.

"Lordy, don' be sneaking up on a body that way, you coulda killed me."

"It looks like you need to be shook up. What are you doing here staring out the window when all the rest of us are working? You'd better get your sorry ass down there." Sparkle's voice was sharp with command but the crooked smile took the sting from her words. In the four weeks they'd spent working on the remodel of the Blue House, Sparkle had taken to wearing overalls and going without makeup.

"Let's get going, woman."

"That reminds me, I need to talk to you." Birdie had been angry to hear that Letty was going to attend dance lessons around the corner. The girl said she had the money and was going no matter what her mother said. The only person not present at the conversation had been Sparkle. Birdie reasoned that the blonde had to be the culprit, putting up the money.

"Explain why you're giving money to my daughter. You know I don' hold with that."

If she hadn't been dismayed to hear about it, she would have laughed at the look on Sparkle's face, her mouth a startled *o* and her eyes widened with feigned innocence.

"Now Birdie, don't you be getting all uppity. You know that girl's perfect for a dancer, look at her legs. She sure didn't get those from you. And she moves like an angel."

"What are you thinking woman? What about the other parents? Aren't they going to be upset with a colored girl in the class?"

Sparkle's face cleared of all expression. Birdie thought she didn't look all that innocent.

"Now it's funny you should ask that because the woman said there might be a problem but when I told her Letty was better than any of the three-footed, stumbly-assed white girls, she just offered to give her private lessons."

Birdie hid a grin. "Just like that, offered private lessons. How many hundreds of dollars will that cost?"

"Don't you worry. Letty and I have it all worked out. She is helping me with some sewing I'm doing. She's really good at cutting out and pinning. I'm paying her and she's using the money the way she wants, that's all. Now let's get going before Annie comes upstairs and scalps us."

Birdie laughed and followed Sparkle's retreating back, thinking about the changes in all of them since they'd met less than a year ago.

The sight of the kitchen she'd left only moments before made her smile. It was going to be wonderful. The dark, cramped quarters were nearly gone and the room was already only a bony memory of the old one. Cain and Annie had removed all but the supporting braces of the outside wall and had extended the floor area four feet out into the yard. Then they'd put what Cain called a bump-out roof over the new walls and installed the two stoves that had been foraged from the out of business restaurant down the street. Her new kitchen was going to be better than she could have imagined. The Wellingtons were not only amazed at the industriousness of the group, they had offered to pay for new materials. Of course, that was a mixed promise. Finding new building material was difficult if not impossible. Just about everything imaginable was being used for the war effort. They did pay for the new flooring Cain had managed to locate and that would make the place a whole lot cleaner and brighter.

Annie was standing on a board laid across upturned buckets. She had a mouthful of nails and was pounding in strips of wood on the ceiling with a sure hand. Birdie had tried to help but the circle of dimples in the wood around any nail she'd aimed at was so large they'd given up ever making her a carpenter and set her to hauling the old wood outside to the burn pile. After a couple of hours, she'd decided to take a break, only to be caught by Sparkle, probably looking for a place to sneak off and have a smoke herself.

"Ym . . . msfs . . . smmd."

The mouthful of nails was getting in the way of Annie's ability to issue orders. Since they'd started, Birdie had been amazed at the way Cain and Annie had managed to do most of the building themselves but still keep everyone else hopping. The only one off the list for hard work was Gloria. She was so pregnant that short walks winded her and she was useless except for the simplest tasks.

As Annie hammered the last of the nails, she turned and looked around. Birdie knew she'd made a mistake, she was standing right in her line of sight.

"Birdie, why don't you hand me those boards over there one by one? It'll be faster and Sparkle can finish getting rid of the grease cans before we start to put the stoves in."

Birdie laughed, she was lucky after all. The haphazard pile of containers filled with fat rendered from every kind of meat was the last of the cleanup in the kitchen. And certainly one of the nastiest to haul away. Sparkle grumbled but Annie paid no attention to her.

"By the way, what time is it?"

Birdie pushed up the cuff of her shirt and checked.

"One-fifteen. You've only got a couple of hours before you need to get ready for work. Can you make that ceiling strong enough to hold a metal rod to hang the pots on?"

"Don't worry, you could hang a Ford from this ceiling when we're done." Annie wiped her face on the side of her sleeve. "I sure hope it's only one shift tonight." Her voice changed from a conversational tone to a yell. "Cain? Cain?"

"Yeah." His response seemed loud to Birdie as he was directly above her. His hammering on the skip sheeting for the roof momentarily ceased when he heard Annie's voice. The smell of cut wood filled the air and Birdie grinned, still admiring the way Annie and Cain had 'liberated' such a large pile of lumber from the surplus stockpile beside the plant. They worked like a team, as if they had been together for years. Birdie didn't know exactly how things were going with them, but if their smiles meant anything, she didn't think it would be long until they were planning a wedding.

Annie's voice was loud. "We only have a couple more hours. Do you want to finish that or help me get this ceiling done before we quit?"

Her words were matter-of-fact, quite businesslike but her face showed something quite different. A slight smile curled her lips and her eyes had a soft look that made Birdie's heart turn.

With a quick shake of her head, Birdie walked over to the pile of smooth boards and dragged out three that looked better than the rest. Struggling to keep them from hitting any of the clutter in the room, she pulled them through the sawdust and scrap pieces on the floor, moving the sawhorses aside as she did. When she returned, Annie was back to her methodical hammering and Sparkle had recruited Letty and William to help her haul the containers of fat out to the back.

Letty had two fingers on one of the bucket handles and was yelling at William to lift his side higher. Sparkle grabbed a misshapen jug filled with the goo and started toward the back of the house. On her way, she stopped beside Birdie.

"Tell me again why Maggie saved this godawful fat so long." Her voice was pinched and she grunted as she tried to lift more than one at a time.

Birdie stopped in the middle of dragging more strips of ceiling wood across the floor. "You're supposed to be able ta' use the glycerin' in the fat to make explosives. Anyway that's what somebody told Maggie when the war started and she never forgot it. She must have forgotten she was supposed to do something with it though. It's so old now I don't think it's good for anything."

"So what are we going to do with it once I get it out to the hole in the back, cook up some grits?"

Birdie looked at Sparkle. "Might not be a bad idea. You want to start it? Would be a heck of a fire, pro'bly never get the thing out."

"Jeez, can't you take a joke? C'mon William I'll help you with that."

As Birdie watched, Sparkle grabbed the sides of an overfilled bucket and lifted, the grease running over her hand. For a moment she thought her friend would drop it, saving her nails. But she pulled up, evening the load and started for the backyard. William trotted along behind, the smile on his face a clear indication of his regard for Sparkle.

Birdie stepped back and smiled. Things did seem to have a way of working out.

Annie stood at the back door and watched as Birdie's children dragged more things out of the storage area. She and Cain were planning to put up shelves and make it into useful space for Birdie. She needed a place to store all the things necessary for running the house. As she watched, Letty sat with Hepsah and examined the black chest.

"It's coming along all right now. I think it will take us only a few more weekends to finish it up."

Annie turned to see Cain behind her, his black hair sprinkled with sawdust. She tentatively brushed it off, feeling giddy. As usual, his nearness caused her pulse to speed up. She'd told him last week that Howard had come and gone. She'd been holding her feelings back for so long she found it odd now to be able to touch him if she wanted.

"I'm glad. Birdie needs her house back. I keep thinking that people won't want to come to dinner with the mess and all but she had twelve last night. It seems to be growing every week."

"Well, I sure hate to miss a meal here. Have the four of you thought at all about buying the place?" Cain had backed up a bit and Annie took in a shaky breath. When they talked like this, of things of interest to them but not about them, she felt as if they were just biding time, waiting for the real conversation to begin. He was here almost every night and just about every weekend.

"Sparkle mentioned buying it. She said it was a shame to put so much work into something for someone else. The problem is with the work we're putting into it now, it's going to be worth more than it was before. And the way the owners have it set up, the more money she brings in, the more they make."

Cain took a cigarette out of his shirt pocket and lit the end, squinting when the smoke drifted back into his eyes. He leaned against the doorjamb. "You know John's pretty good at this stuff. I wonder if he could think of something. I'll bet you could make some sort of deal with the Wellingtons. I've heard of people using part of the rent money for a down payment. They think Birdie has worked a miracle here and I know they don't want to run the place themselves. I'll bet they'd be interested."

The late May sun shone through the open door on the tall man, making him appear almost golden. Annie felt a wave of goose bumps run down her back. Cain was simply the most incredible man she had ever met. His quiet, easy manner hid talents and thoughts that made every other man she'd ever met pale in comparison. She shivered even though she wasn't cold.

He frowned. "Are you all right?"

She coughed to cover her confusion. "Yes, I'm fine. Must have something in my throat."

He stood and looked at her a little longer, then put a hand on her arm. A thrill ran down her arm and made her skin feel sensitive all over. It was the first time he had touched her since they had talked about Howard. She wasn't sure what to do next. Cain was gazing at her, a half smile curving his lips.

"It's good working with you. You make this job fun."

She didn't know what to say. Part of her wished he weren't quite so wonderful. She shook her head, trying to clear the confusion. "I like working with you too. I love to see an idea grow to something real and useful. It's like magic." She sniffed and ran her hand through her hair. "Now I sound silly."

"You could never sound silly. You're a little like magic yourself."

"Oh Cain." Annie nearly choked. "You're grand. I don't deserve you. Why do you keep waiting for me?"

He pulled her gently to him and she felt the muscles in her whole body melt as if trying to be part of him. Her face was against his shoulder and the clean, male smell of him filled her nose and spread through her body like water on a thirsty desert.

They stood that way for several minutes then he pushed her back, letting his arms fall to the side. "It's simple. I want you."

"And I think I want you. I'm just not sure of anything yet."

"Annie, you may never be completely sure. At some point, you're just going to have to take a chance."

Her voice shook slightly as she spoke. "Let me get through this election thing. I'm sure I'll start thinking straighter after that."

"Well, that's only two days away now. Sounds like I won't have to wait much longer. It's time we got back to work. Birdie is going to be after us in a minute." He smiled and then walked out the door and into the yard, his gait only hampered slightly by his limp.

Annie leaned back against the doorframe. She couldn't understand her own hesitation. Or fear if she were to be honest. Every time she got too close that old voice would tell her that she was too tall, too awkward, too big, too much like a man to be lovable. She stepped away from the wall and followed him outside.

She was going to throw off this indecision. This man wanted her and she knew she wanted to be with him. He was right. She would just have to take a chance.

The voting was over. The two days before the election had raced by like water down a drain and now all that was left was the announcement of who had won. A fine coating of dust covered everything in the small anteroom where the six women who had remained throughout the proceeding waited. At first the conversation had been of shopping, the lack of better babysitters and the need to trade for gas coupons. Inevitably though, the women had started talking about the meeting going on in the large room just a few feet away.

Annie tried to keep her mind on the conversation but she kept thinking of the words of encouragement she'd received after everyone had voted. Men she'd barely spoken to had slapped her on the back and said they'd voted for her. A couple even propositioned her.

Trudy rose and began to pace, pulling her jacket closer around her as she spoke. Her voice was loud in the tense atmosphere. "I don't know why it's taking this long to count a few ballots. I wonder if someone is cheating in there."

Sparkle raised her hand and shussed Trudy. "Now you be quiet. They'll be done soon, just wait and see. This is going to go the right way."

Annie's stomach seemed to have turned to rocks. What she really wanted was for this to be over, either way, just so she could stop being anxious.

Trudy was still pacing. "I won't be quiet. Those guys had better understand that we're never going to be quiet. It's time we had our say."

Annie agreed with Sparkle. She wished Trudy would be quiet but she couldn't seem to get her mouth open to tell her that. They all jumped as the door opened with a screech, noisy hinges indicating that they were used infrequently. Cain entered, his long frame filling the height of the door. His eyes sought hers and the merest shake of his head told her the news.

She watched the scene for the next few minutes as if from another room, the shock of it making it hard to breathe.

"It was a close one. I'm not sure how to tell you this . . .."

"I knew it! See they voted us down. I told you they wouldn't let us in. It's just like . . .." Trudy's voice was so shrill it made the other women jump.

"Trudy, slow down. Let him talk." Sparkle had moved forward, almost as if to protect Cain.

Trudy kept on. "Just tell us, don't draw it out any longer. We can take it you know. Good or bad, let us know."

His mouth turned down at the corners and he spoke slowly. "I'm sorry. I'm afraid the news is bad. They voted for John Olafson."

"They couldn't. That man has only been here three weeks. How can they vote him in? Nobody even knows him. That's not fair."

"I know it's not fair." He shook his head. "No, what am I saying? They have every right to do whatever they want. It's their union. Oh hell, I don't know why I'm talking so much. That's all."

Cain's last words were clipped and he limped as he turned and left the room.

"I can't believe it. Isn't it just like a bunch of men to spend so long and come up with the wrong decision? I think we need to have a slowdown or a walkout. Teach them a lesson." Trudy couldn't seem to stop talking. Her fury was evident in her bulging eyes and straining neck.

Annie finally rose and stood at the front of the group. She didn't think she'd ever been more exhausted in her life. "It's over. I, for one, am going home. We fought a good fight and lost. Thank you all for your hard work. Come on, Sparkle. Let's get moving. Maybe we can catch a ride home with Cain."

She could hear Trudy's voice behind her still arguing as she moved out the door, surprised that her legs were willing to carry her. As Sparkle caught up, she put her finger to her lips. "Not one word. I can't talk about it now. Let's see if we can find Cain. All right?"

Sparkle looked at her, her face full of questions, but she nodded and put her arm through Annie's and they walked away.

Annie stared at the wing in front of her. She was supposed to be spot-checking the rivets but she hadn't moved for the last two or three minutes. She watched her reflection in the wavy aluminum skin. At the start of her shift at 4:00 P.M. she'd been fine but as the evening wore on, she'd slowed to nearly a crawl. She was the only one working on this section. The rest of her crew had been temporarily moved to the next shop. Since she was normally the fastest, she was left to finish up on the two wing sections before she joined them. She shook herself and checked the next few series only to stop again.

The scene from the day before kept replaying in her mind and would not stop. Putting the gun down on the wing, she squeezed her eyes shut, trying to stop the tears.

Later, Cain had told her it wasn't a total loss, they had been very close. If she ran again, he was sure she would win. But she didn't think she could run again. Maybe she would let one of the other women try. She had failed, let everyone down and no amount of kind words could change that.

She opened her eyes only to jump backward, a gasp escaping as she did. Otis stood on the opposite side of the wing, a crooked grin on his pudgy face. His small eyes held a gleam and when Annie's heart slowed down, she smiled back. When he was happy, his whole body appeared happy.

"Where did you come from?"

"Scared you, didn't I?" He giggled, his hand hitting the wing between them and making hollow whomping sounds. "I can be really quiet you know. Some people think I'm too big, but I can be really quiet."

Annie nodded. She certainly hadn't heard him. "How are you Otis? I haven't seen you for weeks." As she finished the sentence, she realized that this was the other man John Slattery had wanted her to watch. She had actually asked around about

Waskom, but the idea of this child-man being a threat to any-one's security was so silly she'd simply forgotten. The informa-tion on Waskom had been pretty much as she'd expected, no one was close to him and he seemed to have only one real interest, the union. In fact, the only person who might have been his friend was Melvin Anderson, someone she knew was as volatile as Waskom. She was still puzzled why Slattery kept asking her to gather information, she certainly wasn't much good at it.

The janitor finally stopped slapping the wing surface and a groove appeared between the thin blond eyebrows. He reached up and waggled a finger at her. She couldn't decipher what that meant and frowned. "What?"

He immediately put a finger to his lips and waved, indicat-ing he wanted her to join him on the other side of the half-fin-ished surface. A tickling sensation started on the back of her neck and she reached up and rubbed it. A vague warning thought entered her mind. She stepped over the rivet gun on her way around the wing piece.

"Now what is it that's so important?"

He made a frantic gesture and looked around, as if many people were hiding in the nearly empty shop just waiting to hear what he had to say.

She lowered her voice. "Okay, I'll be quiet, what is it?" The niggly feeling at the back of her neck increased.

"Them tallies were cooked." He beamed, as if he'd said some-thing momentous. She just shook her head.

"What do you mean?"

"Them tallies. They was cooked." This time he pursed his chubby lips together and scowled at her as if she were the one being dense.

"You mean the election tallies were altered?"

"Don' know about that, but you won. They didn't give out the right count."

She gasped, feeling the shock hit her chest like a hammer. She had won. They had been right all along, their preliminary count of supporters had been over sixty percent.

"Waskom done it." Pieces began to fit into place. John Slattery was right, there was a traitor in his camp and precisely the person he had suspected. Once he knew the truth, the union boss would take care of it. The failure and guilt slid off her like water. Elation was so strong, she turned and gave Otis a hug.

She immediately wished she could take it back. Getting too close to someone of his girth who hadn't bathed in a couple of weeks was overpowering. She tried to stop breathing, or exhale, or something, but the smell struck her nose so strongly she nearly choked. With care, she swallowed, pasted a smile on and stepped back.

"Thank you. I appreciate your telling me. You are a good friend. I just need to tell someone and he'll take care of it."

Red suffused his face, neck and ears. His eyes were round and the pink folds of skin surrounding them stretched to resemble long, chubby pillows. He shook his head quickly from side to side.

"You gotta get those tallies yerself. If you tell anybody, they're gonna be gone."

A shiver slid down her spine and she wondered if Otis could be right. Her inclination was to ignore him but something about the stubborn set of his round face made her stop and think again.

"That's silly." Annie stepped back and leaned an arm on the half-finished wing. Otis leaned forward, grabbing up a fistful of his huge trousers as he moved.

"I tol' you before, I know lots of stuff. Important stuff. You got to get those tallies. They're sitting on his desk. I seen 'um. You could just take them."

"How could I do that?"

"Sunday. Nobody's in the office then and you could get in." He lifted his hand and placed it on hers. "I could get you a key."

"That's ridiculous. I can't break into the union office." She felt as if her world had suddenly decided to turn upside down.

Otis stared at her and smiled. "You can do anything, Annie. You're really strong."

"Being strong doesn't make it right for me to do something illegal."

"But you're the winner. Nobody knows it. You gotta prove it."

Of course, he was right. If she had the evidence, she could just hand it over to Slattery. There would be no questions. She moved her arm, lifting Otis' warm hand and patting it gently before she let it go.

"You might be right. Sunday you say? And you can get a key?" Her own hands started to feel warm and she wiped them on her trousers. She wondered what Sparkle was doing Sunday.

The misty rain that had fallen all day had begun to clear. A cool glow from the streetlight outside filtered through the new windows in the Blue House kitchen, making long shadows of the tall canisters that stood on the sill. Sparkle was seated at the kitchen table, now pushed against a sidewall, to make room for the new stoves. She was getting ready to paint her toenails. The sound of chairs being pulled across the floor came from the front room, a good sign that a card game was about to begin. It had become a custom that some of the diners would stay late to play pinochle. Annie was working swings and Birdie was busy with two children down with the flu. She and Gloria were alone in the kitchen and she was thinking over what Annie had told them the night before.

She couldn't believe that Annie had kept her association with Slattery a secret so long. It made her furious to think that Annie was taken in by Slattery. She'd met the man a couple of times and had the measure of him right at the first. She had to admit though he was good. Coming across like he cared about the women and their mission.

The four women had developed a plan, in fact it had been mostly her idea. Now she regretted making Gloria a part of it.

Running her finger around the grape juice stain on the tabletop, she looked at Gloria and tried again.

"I don't think you should go Sunday. My God, woman, you can hardly walk, much less go on a mission like that."

"Don't you see? I'll be the best cover in the world. No one would suspect that anything funny was going on with such a pregnant lady along. It's just perfect."

"You're crazy. Annie said no last night and I don't think she'll change her mind."

"We'll just wait and see, that's all." Gloria's jaw was set in that firm line Sparkle recognized. "But I do wish she would tell Cain."

"You know how she feels about that. She's right, the fewer people involved the better. You know that if she told him what we were doing, he would want to go, or he may not loan us the car. Annie won't let Birdie go because of the kids, afraid if anything happens, there won't be anyone to look after them."

Gloria was standing at the sink, wiping the last of the pots and pans and occasionally putting a hand on the small of her back. Sparkle had dried most of them but the girl insisted on doing her part. Sometimes she was just plain aggravating.

Shifting her position on the hard chair, Sparkle sighed. She wondered if the red color she was painting on her toenails was too pale. She looked critically at the color again and decided it was fine. She moved the painted foot to the floor and pulled up the other one to replace it on the edge of the table. She inhaled, smiling at the sharp, acetone smell of the polish. After carefully putting strips of cloth between her toes, she pulled the brush from the lacquer, mindful of avoiding drips.

Sparkle peered over her toes at Gloria now making her slow way to the table. She pulled the rocking chair over and sat down, releasing a huge sigh when she was finally settled.

Gloria's voice quavered slightly when she spoke. "Well anyway, sometimes there's more to a situation than just what you want."

Sparkle could feel her teeth start to grind then shook her head and sighed, exasperated with the discussion. She hastily put polish on the last two nails, then propped both feet on the kitchen box. Sparkle turned to see that her pregnant friend was trying to pick up a pillow from the floor next to her. Gloria was turned so all that could be seen of her was the curve of her enormous belly. As she watched, Gloria squirmed on the seat, finally reaching the pillow.

"Made it."

Sparkle smiled. "All right, but I still think you're crazy. Pregnant girl like you needs to be sitting home, not gallivanting around the countryside. What would the doctor say?"

"Well, I have an idea about the dress I'm going to wear."

Sparkle thought she might have underestimated the girl again. "Okay, I'll listen to your idea. Let me put that pillow behind you. How long has it been since you've seen your feet?"

Gloria giggled. "Quite a while."

"Then how about I put some of this polish on those little toenails?"

"Really?" Gloria's voice held wonder.

"Yes, really."

"I'd love that. Oh but . . . .." Her voice changed and held a note of concern. "Do you think that . . . well . . . maybe . . . .."

"What?"

"Do you think you could use the pink and not that awful red?"

Sparkle quit stuffing pillows and let loose a belly laugh loud enough to quiet the card players in the other room for a moment.

"Yeah, you might be able to convince me that we should use pink. But I think you ought to try the red, put a little adventure in your life."

Gloria looked at her, then burst out laughing. "I think there's been enough adventure in my life for a while. Just look at me."

Sparkle chuckled then went to get the kitchen box for her friend to use as a foot rest.

CHAPTER FIFTEEN

This is ridiculous. These trees make me feel like we're in the movies and any minute some cowboy is going to kiss his stupid horse and ride off into the sunset." The sarcasm in Sparkle's voice was threaded with uneasiness. It was Grand Plan Sunday and this was part one.

Annie looked up at the structure over their picnic area. Four by four vertical trunks and two by four horizontal branches held bolts of green and black striped material. To enemy pilots overhead, it was supposed to look like a 'quiet city'. From underneath, the 'trees' covered the ships manufactured in the plant but not yet sent off for delivery. Picnic tables and benches had been set alongside and workers were encouraged to spend their lunch hour there, strengthening the illusion.

Annie breathed in and felt the first hint of warmth in the air. She hoped they were in for more days of the blue skies and warmer temperatures. They were all so very tired of the continuous rain. The only good part of the rain was the incredibly green grass. She'd like to take her shoes off and run around.

She looked at the meal and sighed. Birdie was still taking care of her sick children so they'd made their own picnic lunch consisting of wrinkled hot dogs, underdone potato salad and canned green beans. The only bright spot was the red checked tablecloth covered by blue dishes.

"When did you say Otis would be here?" Gloria's voice was uneasy and Annie noticed that she hadn't touched her food. Her dress was a voluminous paisley loaned to her by a woman at the plant. The excess material had enabled Sparkle to sew a large pocket on the inside, just what they needed for their plan. Gloria was so far along that Annie had not wanted to bring her but the girl had been very convincing that her presence would keep them from being discovered or work as an excuse if they were. On top of everything else, Gloria was not acting right, every once in a while, her brow would knit and she appeared to be thinking of something else entirely.

Sparkle was stretched out on the picnic bench, her skimpy pink outfit rising high on her thighs. She was convinced that if Gloria's pregnancy failed to save them, her overexposure of skin should ward off any problems.

"If Otis doesn't hurry up, we'll never get this done. How come he's always so slow?"

Annie's jaw muscles tightened in annoyance. "Why don't you sit up so it looks more like we're having a picnic and not just hanging around here waiting for a chance to break into a restricted building? He's doing his job."

A moment later, Annie heard "Goddammit!" as Sparkle tried to sit up and hit her head on the tabletop. She squelched nervous laughter and turned, catching sight of Otis' hurrying form outlined against the dark background of the plant. His feet were moving quickly and his arms pumping but the short legs made his actual progress slow.

His face was red with exertion when he arrived. "You gotta hurry. You only got a few minutes. I got to get this key back on the board pretty quick. I think maybe somebody saw me take it. Leave it under the box by the door. I'll come get it later."

A cold chill filled Annie and she wondered if he were having as many second thoughts as she was. What if this grand scheme of theirs didn't work? She certainly hoped they wouldn't be caught stealing the tally sheets. This was a federal base and even if they were able to prove the results were rigged she wondered if they could haul them off to prison. She shook her head. The four of them had been over all this a hundred times and they'd agreed this crazy plan was the only way.

She thought again of Waskom and the arrogant way he had decided to change the results of the election. A shot of anger replaced the fear and she pushed herself up, her mind set.

"Sparkle, pack up the stuff. Gloria, let's get you up and moving, you heard Otis, we don't have much time." Annie could hear Sparkle muttering but ignored her. Suddenly the day was black and white with no grays. She hadn't wanted this, in fact had argued that she could do it alone but they were here now and they might as well get it done. She pulled the girl from her seat at the table and began walking toward the building containing the union offices.

She and Gloria started across the damp grass and Sparkle caught up with them after several minutes, the picnic basket swinging from her arm, a corner of red checks sprouting from one side. The walk to the hall took them no more than five minutes but Annie felt more exposed with each step. By the time they'd reached the big front door, her hands were so damp they slipped on the key and she had several false starts before she managed to get it open. With a quick lift of the wooden box on the porch, she put the key under, hoping that Otis would retrieve it soon. She shut the door behind them and turned to survey the entryway. No one was in sight. The unnatural weekend quiet emphasized the hollow thud of their footsteps and Annie felt a finger of dread slide down her back. She jumped when Gloria put a hand on her arm.

"Which office?"

Her breath came out in a whoosh and she laughed.

"I'm not going to make it as a full-time burglar. I don't have the nerve for it. Follow me." Her voice sounded so loud in the empty hall that she dropped it to a whisper. She led the way to third door. They passed Slattery's office and she glanced in, wondering again if she should have just told him. She shook her head and hurried by. Otis had said the second door was Waskom's. Her fingers on the doorknob, she turned it and entered.

This office was smaller than Slattery's and the lingering odor of cigarette smoke gave her an eerie feeling that Waskom might return at any second. The room was simply furnished. Piles of papers were spread on every surface: the desk in the middle of the room, two long tables pushed against the wall and atop a battered metal filing cabinet. The ashtray was filled with butts from days before. The Sunday afternoon light filtered through cracks in the olive drab blackout curtains and made lines across the floor. On the opposite wall, a door stood ajar revealing a small closet with several empty hangers and a navy blue sweater dangling crookedly.

Sparkle's voice was low. "Good Lord, how are we supposed to find anything in this mess. She set the picnic basket down with a thud.

Annie rubbed her palms on the rough material of her trousers. The threat of imminent discovery and arrest produced an agitated edge to her voice.

"Gloria, sit at the desk and start looking through that stuff. Try to keep it in some kind of order. We don't have to be messy burglars. Sparkle, you start on that batch over there."

Both women moved to their assigned tasks and the room was quiet for several moments. Annie flipped through page after page and then repeated to the others what Otis had told her.

"We're looking for two stacks of tally sheets bundled together, each has about twenty papers or so. The top sheets have the totals. He said the first page of the original set has the words 'fix this' written across the top. The fake set should be right with them. I just hope he hasn't disposed of the original papers yet."

As the minutes passed, Annie lifted her head to check on Gloria and Sparkle, hoping that they were having more luck than she. Five minutes passed, then ten. A bead of sweat slid down her back. Glancing at her watch again, she turned to tell them they couldn't look much longer when Gloria groaned and doubled over on the desk.

"What's wrong?" Annie was beside the girl in two long strides.

"I think it's time." The words came out in little gasps, as if each one were an effort.

"It can't be." Annie spoke the words but immediately knew the truth. "You started when we were at the picnic table, didn't you?" The strange concentrated expression had been the early sign and she had misread it completely. She put a hand on the desk to steady herself, then the other on Gloria's shoulder.

"It's all right, we'll leave right now and get you to the hospital." She had trouble making her words come out, her throat was threatening to close up completely. "Come on." She started to pull Gloria to her feet.

"It's all right. The pains are at least a half hour apart and before this last one, they weren't that bad. Besides, I found the papers. You see, I should have looked in the most obvious place first, it's just sitting here on top. And both sets are here. I'll put them in the envelope." With a quick thrust of her hand, she'd stuffed the documents into a manila container. This should . . . ." The sound of a door slamming stopped her in mid sentence and they stood paralyzed for a few precious seconds.

Annie's heart raced, then she breathed in deeply. "It's all right. I'm going to go out and find whoever is here and tell them we need to get you to the hospital. We can sort this out later." She started for the door but stopped when Gloria called softly.

"Don't please." Annie turned back to find that the girl had risen from the desk and was holding out a hand to her. "I don't want my baby born in jail."

"Oh Gloria, they wouldn't do that."

"But I don't want to take a chance. And anyway, the first baby takes hours to be born. Birdie told me so. I think there's lots of time. Can't we find a place to hide?'

Annie clenched her hands and looked at Sparkle now standing beside the door and peering out.

"Don't look at me, I've never had a baby. But I think she's right. It generally seems to take a while."

Annie turned back to Gloria, whose hand was still held out in entreaty. Swallowing hard, she looked for a hiding place big enough for the three of them in the room. Her search finally took her to the only place possible.

"The closet?"

Sparkle nodded her head in agreement and they hurried forward, stumbling over each other in their haste. Sparkle went first, then Gloria and finally Annie. They faced each other in a close semicircle. As Annie pulled the door shut after them, Gloria's whisper was barely audible.

"The picnic basket?"

"Sparkle?"

"I forgot it."

Annie wanted to scream but forced herself to cautiously open the door. When she saw that the room was still empty, she rushed across the floor, snatched up the basket and ran back. She pushed in again only to find that she couldn't get the door shut with the picnic basket. "We're too big. Sparkle, move farther back."

"There ain't no farther back, I'm squashed flatter'n Skinny Lil. Suck it up a little yourself, sister."

They all breathed in and pressed tightly together. Annie managed to pull the door closed. The basket would only fit sitting on top of Gloria's stomach and wedged between her chest and Sparkle's face. Annie lifted her arm to give them more room and rested it on Gloria's hair. They heard footsteps, then the creak of the office door hinges. Men's voices filled the room.

"What the hell's this door open for? This better be good, Mel. I told you I was up fifty bucks and it looked like Joachum's was about to fold. It's a good thing the game was at Wallace's. It's close enough to the gate that we should only miss a hand or two. Now what the hell's so important that it couldn't wait until Monday?" Annie felt Gloria's quick intake of breath and knew that she had recognized Zachary Waskom's voice.

"I told you, Ed from security said he thought he saw somebody com'n in here a few minutes ago. He's all the way over in the guard station so he couldn't tell who it was, just saw someone come in. He would'a called out his boys but he didn't know if we had something of our own going on. I told him we'd take care of it." Melvin Anderson's syrupy voice took Annie's breath away. This was the other man appointed to watch Waskom. It certainly wasn't doing Slattery any good to have one criminal watch another.

"Well, Christ, man, you can see there's nobody here now. I guess if they were gonna get something they would'a got it. What do you think they'd be looking for? Shit, don't suppose somebody's got on to how we're skimming off dues money do you? That stuff is all in this cabinet. Let me see."

The soft shuffling of paper was all they could hear. Annie had a sudden urge to giggle. A few seconds later she felt a strange tightening of muscles low in her stomach, only it wasn't her muscles.

"What the?" Her involuntary murmur was muffled. Moments later she heard Sparkle whisper.

"You having a pain?"

At Sparkle's question, Annie realized that the muscle spasm she'd felt wasn't her own but Gloria's. It was the oddest sensation, almost as if she were in labor herself.

"Looks like they're all here. Don't think nobody's been bothering 'um. Let's see, all the other paperwork's okay." Annie took an unsteady breath and felt the contraction pass. She wondered again if she should reveal their presence. But now the problem was Melvin Anderson. If he found them, she didn't know what would happen. She hoped the men would leave quickly.

"Oh yeah, what about the tallies from the election? I left them right here on my desk because I was going to talk to Joe. Don't want anybody getting suspicious. Now where the hell . . .?" They could hear the sound of rustling paper again.

"Mel, do you see any a those tallies over there? I could'a sworn . . .." More rustling sounds came from the other room.

"Goddammit, I left those tally sheets right here. You don't suppose those crazy women . . .?" Waskom's voice held more puzzlement than anger.

"Them dames don't have the guts to do somethin' like that."

Annie tried to shift her legs only to be stopped by the closeness of her friends' bodies. She heard a smothered groan and felt another labor pain start.

"I dunno, maybe that Annie woman . . .. If it's them, they couldn't a got very far."

Icy threads of fear filled Annie and she prayed they wouldn't open the closet door.

"Let's check the building, maybe they're still here."

They heard the sound of retreating footsteps then silence and tears of relief formed in Annie's eyes. Opening the door slowly, she tried to see all corners of the room at once. Her heart slowed and she cautiously poked her head out. She saw no one in the hall. Waving her arm for the others to follow, she started out the door only to glance back and find no sign of Sparkle.

"Where?" She looked past Gloria to see Sparkle's pink clad form by the file cabinet.

"Sparkle, what the heck are you doing? Get over here. We need to get out of here now."

Sparkle's muffled voice was barely audible. "I'm lookin' for what they've been doing with the dues money. That will give us something more to use against 'em."

"We don't have time for that. We have to leave now." Annie's voice rose to a whispered crescendo.

She could see two or three white sheets of paper yanked out of the drawer, then Sparkle joined them. "He'll never think it was us. You heard him, he thought we didn't have the guts. Fool."

Annie motioned Sparkle and Gloria forward and brought up the rear, trying to will Gloria to move faster. Their shuffling walk to the door was the longest of Annie's life. She kept turning around, sure she would see the two men appear at any moment.

Once out in the cool evening air again, she grabbed Gloria's hand and pulled as hard as she dared. "We have to get clear of here as fast as we can."

"I'll run and get the car started, you bring along the little mother here." Annie grabbed her arm.

"No. Running would attract too much attention. We need to walk casually. Can you see behind us? Are they there?"

Sparkle was fumbling with the papers she had pulled from the filing cabinet, stuffing them into the already full envelope.

"No sign of 'em yet. Here Gloria, get this under you skirt and into the pocket."

"How am I supposed to do that? Everybody can see us here." The girl stopped then gasped as another pain hit.

"This is ridiculous, I'm going to get us some help." Annie turned to see who was around when she felt Gloria's fingers dig into her forearm.

"I'm fine, just hold on a minute." The girl puffed between each word. Then, just as quickly as the pain came, it subsided. "It's all right, let's keep going."

With some rustling and pushing, Gloria got the envelope into the pocket Sparkle had sewn in the generous material of the dress. The three kept up a slow but steady pace toward the front gate. Annie could feel the imminent presence of the union men behind them and grabbed Gloria's hand in hers, tugging.

"We need to move a little faster, they must be done searching the hall now. C'mon Gloria. Sparkle?"

"No, don't see anybody yet."

"All right, we're just about there." They'd chosen the side gate of the plant to exit, thinking it would be faster and the guards were generally less likely to spend time checking them.

One young man stood at the gate. As they approached, he stepped up and greeted them with mouth set in a hard line and body held rigidly straight.

"Pass ma'am." The words came out though his teeth. Annie had hoped for a jaded, weary guard, not one who was so new he took his job seriously. Swallowing, she stepped forward, sweat starting again beneath her shirt.

"Good afternoon. We were having a picnic lunch. It was such a perfect day being outside. The warm sun feels awfully good, don't you think? It's really lovely." Lines appeared on the young man's forehead as he tried to take in this spate of information.

Annie cleared her throat, finding her mouth so dry her tongue stuck to her teeth when she spoke. Touching the pass hanging on her shirtfront, she moved around the man, horribly conscious of the envelope of information stuffed in Gloria's dress. She looked back and saw that Gloria's face was red and little trickles of moisture glistened on her cheeks. She smiled a toothy grin at the young guard and he examined her visitor's pass and waved her through perfunctorily. Annie let out a sigh of relief when she saw why he'd been so preoccupied. Sparkle was striding forward, her bright pink outfit seeming to heat up the already warm atmosphere around them. She'd undone the top two buttons of her blouse and her knowing smile apparently stopped any further brain function on his part. Sparkle was ten feet past the gate when the guard finally found his voice.

"Ma'am." The words squeaked. "You'll have to come back here."

The color in Sparkle's face went from pink to white in a second and she looked at Annie with one eyebrow raised. Annie's stomach felt as if it were trying to rise and shoot out her mouth. She took a deep breath then made a motion with her hand for Sparkle to return to the gate. At the same time she pushed Gloria toward the car and followed Sparkle back. She scanned the route they had just taken from the union hall and saw Anderson and Waskom running down the steps. She walked as fast as she dared back to the entrance where Sparkle was turning on her most spectacular smile for the guard. She pushed her chest forward and walked in what could only be described as a strut. Annie wanted to yell at her to hurry but couldn't.

"What is it? Couldn't you see my badge?" The item in question hung over her left breast, strategically placed so the guard couldn't miss the badge or what was underneath it.

This time his voice squeaked as he spoke. "No ma'am, I need to look in your picnic basket."

Sparkle was pressing forward, her upper body hanging over the wicker suggestively. The guard's mouth was shut tight and his Adam's apple moved spasmodically. He finally pulled himself away from Sparkle's magnetic presence and rummaged through the picnic items.

"Okay ma'am, you can go." The young man attempted to look anywhere but at Sparkle's chest, without success. He appeared hypnotized.

"Thank you." Sparkle's voice trilled with soft warmth. The urge to laugh died when she turned to see their pursuers rushing toward the gate.

"Hurry. Let's go. They're coming." Their walk had taken them within feet of Cain's car. Gloria was trying to get herself into the back seat. Annie gently pushed her inside. As she closed the door, she heard a gasp and saw that Gloria's face was pinched tight and she had both arms wrapped around her mound of belly.

Sparkle started the car and yelled for Annie to get in. With another look at Gloria, she ran to get in the front seat. As she slammed the door, the blond pushed on the clutch, let out the gas pedal and they left in a flurry of dust. Sparkle let out a cheer and Annie had to join in.

Sparkle recovered first. "Are they following?"

"I can't see them. Sparkle, slow down a little. This road is too rough to go this fast." Annie could hear her words vibrate as they sped along. Sparkle had chosen a back way to the hospital, faster, but not paved and they kept hitting holes that threw them around in the car.

"Gotta lose those guys. You girls hang on. We'll get Little Missy here to the hospital. It won't be a place they'd be looking."

Annie grabbed the side and held on tight. She looked back at Gloria. Her face was frozen into a scream.

"Sparkle, slow down now! Gloria and the baby can't take this."

Her words finally got through to Sparkle and she let up on the gas only to hit another pothole which threw them sideways again. When the car slowed at last, a soul ripping wail of pain came from the back seat.

"What the hell is taking them so long?" Sparkle pressed her lips together and fought the tears that had threatened since they'd arrived at the hospital. She sat with her back firmly placed against the wooden rungs of a chair. Annie was pacing from the window to the door, then back again, her footsteps making hollow whomps on the striped linoleum floor of the waiting room. Birdie was sitting in a green upholstered chair, her feet not quite touching the floor. Light from a tall lamp made pools of pale yellow on the ceiling and the floor but gave scant illumination anywhere else. Sparkle had an awful urge to scream at them, make them stop acting as if it were normal to wait patiently to see if your friend and her baby would live or die.

They'd been sitting in the waiting room for three hours now and she was sure they'd been the three longest hours of her life. They'd called Birdie as soon as possible and she'd come over immediately, getting a ride with Joe Robletto.

When they'd arrived at the hospital, Sparkle had been enormously relieved. Now she just hoped her driving hadn't hurt either the mother or child. Getting her to the hospital alive had seemed like a miracle at the time, but as the minutes passed, she realized that it was only the first step. Now it was up to Gloria and all the people working on her to keep her that way. They had estimated that the baby was three weeks early. She wasn't sure if she should be happy or sad it was taking so long.

Now, all the could do was wait, something Sparkle was never good at. Twice she'd gone to the bathroom, expecting her lunch to come up, and twice she'd returned, feeling just as sick as when she'd left.

She stared at the door to the waiting room, her eyes blurring. With a start, she realized that a person was standing there. Someone dressed in white pants and top. The man was very young but his face was marked with tiny lines and his black hair was flat on one side and standing straight up on the other. Fatigue clung to his body like a strange aftershave. Sparkle knew without doubt that he had news of Gloria. This man was too young to have been at this very long. She wanted to ask him for his credentials. She realized that after all this anticipation, what she really wanted to do was to run from the room before he had a chance to speak.

"Excuse me, is one of you Annie?" Her tall friend had been pacing again, her back momentarily to the door. She turned and

Sparkle could feel the anxiety emanating from her, mirroring her own.

All three women approached the doctor and stood in a semicircle around him, hands and shoulders touching. Sparkle blinked furiously to clear her vision.

"Yes . . ." Annie's voice cracked, "I'm Annie. How is she?"

The doctor opened his mouth and Sparkle saw that one eye twitched. "It was a hell of a fight. The girl is going to be all right."

Birdie's voice was faint, breathless. "And the baby?"

For the first time the man's face lost the serious, brooding look and he smiled. "Now that's one feisty little bugger. He gave us a struggle getting him out but once we did he started hollering like mad. He's little but he's going to make it just fine."

The three women closed their circle and Sparkle felt warm relief flow through her.

"I knew she'd be fine." Birdie's voice was shaky.

Annie laughed. "Oh sure, that's why you've been over here praying for the past two hours."

"Figgered we could use all the help we could get."

Sparkle cleared her throat, wanting to say something smart, something caustic. Instead, when she opened her mouth all she could say was "thank you, thank you, thank you." Tears flooded her face. She wasn't even sure who she was thanking.

Twenty-four hours later, after leaving the new mother and her young son in the hospital, Annie sat in John Slattery's office wishing the whole mess done with so she could just go back to work.

Slattery's square form was pushed solidly into the oak chair and a cigar rested between his back teeth. "I'm sorry to keep you waiting. You said you had something for me?"

As usual, his smile was wide and his eyes thoughtful. He'd agreed to see her on short notice and she was grateful. They had risked so much to get the information about the rigged election that she did not want to hold it any longer than necessary.

Her throat was dry and she wished she had thought to grab a glass of water before leaving the Blue House. She ran her fingers through her hair and then leaned forward in her chair.

"You remember we talked outside the hall last week about it being a shame I hadn't won the election since it looked like I'd had a pretty good chance?"

The union boss nodded and the motion made the long stub of ash quiver dangerously. Annie had an urge to hold up the blue glass ashtray under the shaking object.

"My friends and I have come into some information that, well, it shows that . . . well, I don't quite know how to say it."

John Slattery sat forward, his eyes wide and eyebrows making a little teepee of concern in the middle of his face. "You take your time, Annie. What information did you get?"

Annie swallowed and tried to breath normally. "We found out that I did win the election and the information we have proves it. It looks like one of your men changed the tally sheets."

"You have them?" His jaw tightened. For just a moment, she was frightened. She realized that she was letting Sparkle's opinion of this man make her jumpy.

"Yes, I'm sorry sir. I wish I didn't have to tell you."

"Me too." One side of his mouth turned up, an echo of a real smile. "I won't ask you how you got them."

Annie let out a sigh, her legs beginning to relax. "I appreciate that sir. It was a risk."

He moved forward, resting his arms on the desk. "I suppose it was Waskom, as I'd suspected?"

She nodded.

"You understand I'll have to look at them, make sure that what you say is true. I can't just take your word for it."

"Of course." His question made her doubt what they had found and she began to chew on the inside of her lower lip. In the next moment, she realized there was no question he would be convinced when he saw the information.

"You didn't bring the papers with you?"

"Oh, I have them. They're safe. I can bring them here if you'd like. I just wasn't sure if Waskom would be here tonight. What will you do?"

Slattery pulled the cigar from his mouth, laying it carefully in the ashtray. He sighed and ran his hand through what little hair was left on his head. "That will take some thought. Obviously, we'll need to put you in as shop steward but it's going to look bad for the union. Let me think about this."

The boss drummed his fingers on the desk, then turned and stared out the window. Minutes stretched on. Finally he turned back to face her.

"You know, we might just be able to catch him red-handed. Would you be willing to help me in a little sting operation? Waskom has friends at the plant and in the union and we need to be careful that we get rid of him for good, not just a slap on the wrist and back tomorrow. Would you bring the papers to the old playhouse in White Center? You know the one that we hold the big meetings in sometimes?"

Annie stopped breathing for a second then let out a shaky laugh. "I guess I can do that. What time?"

"Seven o'clock. I'm not quite sure how I'll set this up. I think maybe I'll have one of the fellows I can trust tell him you're looking to sell those papers, make a little extra money. He'd believe that. He'd pay pretty big to get rid of them before somebody like me sees them. Do you think you could meet him like that? Pretend to be selling them?"

Annie nodded. This was becoming more complicated than she'd anticipated. He started speaking again and she swallowed hard, thinking how easy things were just days before. Now it was hard to think of anything but the tallies and Gloria's baby.

"I think what I'll do is have my boss, Joe Constantine, come along. If he hears Waskom making a deal to buy the papers back from you, he won't hesitate to get rid of him. Are you up for that? We can hide behind the stage curtains and hear everything you say. We'll be there if he decides to get rough."

Annie let out a breath. The whole thing seemed strange to her. "Why can't you just arrest him? This sounds pretty complicated and what if it doesn't work?"

He picked up the cigar and relit the end. Soon a thick cloud of smoke billowed out around him. She cleared her throat and waited until he looked at her again.

"The reason we need to do it this way is that Waskom is about the best connected union member we have. The tally sheets are just not enough, he might be able to explain the discrepancy. If we catch him in the act of trying to buy them back it's going to be obvious he had something to do with it." The large man exhaled slowly.

Annie swallowed and made the decision to tell all. Keeping secrets wasn't something she was good at. "There is one more thing. When we . . . when I picked up the papers, there were some other papers with them that were rather suspicious."

"How do you mean, suspicious?"

"Well, it looks like funds are being diverted."

"What funds?" He sat forward, his eyes cold.

Annie felt her face flush red with heat. After they'd returned, she and Sparkle had looked at the papers. Sparkle had insisted they showed the union was diverting money from operating and pension funds to somewhere else. She hadn't been convinced the pages were just fragments of longer total pages.

"Well, I don't know for sure. I'll just bring them along as well. You can sort it all out. Is that okay with you?"

"That would be fine."

Annie grabbed the arms of the chair and rose. She headed for the door before she even remembered she hadn't said goodbye. Turning, she found the union leader staring at her. She wondered if he were having second thoughts.

"I'll be there sir, it's the least I can do. Thank you for trusting me." He inclined his head and gave her the thumbs up sign. Her tension eased and she hoped she wouldn't let him down.

CHAPTER SIXTEEN

P retty good huh? We got 'em all."
Annie surveyed the stage and had to agree with Birdie. They did seem to have them all. For the rest of her life, Annie didn't think she'd forget the last hour they'd just spent in the theater. Slattery was still curled up in the fetal position, his vocalizing now bordering more on four letters than the earlier grunts. Anderson was wriggling ineffectively, trying to free himself from the gauze wrappings and hoop skirt. Waskom was silent, his shiny white face upturned and mouth open in the glow of the stage lights. Annie looked closer to make sure he was breathing, and was reassured to see his chest rise and fall.

Shock and disappointment nearly got her killed when Slattery demanded all the papers after a muffed attempt by Waskom to get them from her. Slattery's voice carried the length of the theater when he shouted to his two men that now he was going to have to dump her in Puget Sound, just when he was getting to like her. The brief scuffle after resulted in Annie being held down by Slattery. The hard upward thrust of her knee to the man's groin put the union boss out of action and then, just like in a movie, Sparkle and Birdie had come from behind the curtains to her rescue. Sparkle raced out and whacked Waskom over the head with a prop sword and Birdie threw a hoop skirt frame over Anderson. Then Sparkle wrapped them both with mummy gauze they'd found in the back room.

Sparkle stood near Annie and a grin split her face from ear to ear. "Not bad for three puny women, huh?"

"Not bad at all." Birdie bent over Waskom and touched his head. "I think you killed him. Why'd you have to crack him over the head so hard? I can't find any pulse. Oh wait, I got it." She held his arm by the wrist and a frown appeared on her forehead. "You'd better do a little rope magic on this guy too, Sparkle. I don't know how long he'll be out. Where'd you learn to tie somebody up like that?"

"There's lots of things I can do you wouldn't believe. I have many skills." Sparkle's mouth was pursed together with a look of disdain. She bent over the recumbent form, her hands moving quickly to strap gauze around the man's ankles and wrists.

Annie stared at her friend. "How did you ever think to wrap them and tie them up? I figured you would go for help."

Sparkle's laugh was deep and she pulled a cigarette from her trouser pocket. "We knew you were in trouble right off, we just couldn't figure out how many men were out here. We finally guessed there couldn't be more than three. We knew that you would take out at least one so all we had to handle were the other two. It was Birdie's idea to wrap them up, I wanted to use the gun we found but she said everybody would know it wasn't real and you can't do much damage with a stage pistol."

"Speaking of that, since we have the other two tied up, let's secure Slattery as well. It might be a while before we can get the police here." Sparkle's words were quiet and Annie felt the relief dribble away like dry sand.

She pictured the three of them trying to explain the situation to a bunch of policemen and sighed. It was too complicated. She wanted to bask a little longer in the knowledge that they had bested the three men, not worry about what to do next.

"All right. Sparkle, you were right. And since you're the expert, tie up our union boss' legs and hands. He's a lot trickier than I thought he was. Birdie, stay here and be sure nobody thinks that he can crawl away. There must be a phone in the office."

As she headed for the stairs leading off the stage, she turned back to her two friends. "Thanks you two. I don't know many

Marines who could have handled this. I really hated the thought of being fish bait."

The next day Annie found herself still smiling when she thought about the fight. She eased back and let her arm rest on the side of the plane, wishing this shift were over and she could go home. Her smiles were tempered with many sighs of exasperation. She'd been correct in her reluctance to call the police. Ten minutes after their arrival at the theater, they had been listening intently as a newly recovered John Slattery explained how the women had lured them in and then attacked with no provocation.

The only reason the police hadn't immediately let Slattery and his boys go was the damning evidence found in the papers. They had not been interested in the faked election results. The consensus seemed to be that it was their organization and they could run it as they pleased. No, the stopper for them had been the papers Sparkle had picked up, the ones detailing the diversion of union funds. Apparently the dollar amounts had been enough to make the police look twice, and put all three men in cells until they could investigate further.

The threat on her life had only raised eyebrows. Even with Sparkle and Birdie backing her up, the officer had been reluctant to do anything without hard evidence. A company official had made a phone call to the union boss in New York and a representative would be traveling to Seattle soon. She had no idea if he might be interested in the election results but she rather doubted it.

Annie yawned as she pulled the Cleco clip, then moved the rivet gun and automatically shot the rivet home. She'd only slept a couple hours before having to get up for work today and it definitely wasn't enough. The news had shot through the plant like electricity and she felt as though she'd been stopped a hundred times to explain what happened. Now she just wanted-ed to finish off this section of rivets and head home before she fell asleep where she stood. Craning her neck, she tried to see what time it was on the large clock on the shop wall. She was rewarded with a loud blast of the plant whistle. Janie Collins, the tired looking brunette who was bucking for her, poked her head around the side and yelled.

"How about we just finish this row, then call it a day? Swings should be able to finish it off now."

Annie nodded, then yanked Clecos and drilled the remaining ten rivets as quickly as she could. It had been a long day. Removing her apron, she saw several people heading her way, probably wanting to hear the story. With a quick thrust of her hand, she rolled up the apron and began to walk briskly toward the door. If possible, she'd like to not tell the story again for the rest of her life. She'd made it to the door and left the followers behind. All except one.

When she turned back to look, Otis was shuffling forward, trying to get her attention without yelling. With a sigh, she stopped. He was wearing a huge, quasi military jacket and pants that started below his armpits and stopped two inches above his shoes. His round face was red and tiny beads of sweat glistened on his brow.

"C'n I talk to you?" His voice was breathless and high pitched, almost as if the rolls of fat compressed his voice box.

"Sure but let's talk as we walk, I need to get home." She slowed, trying to match his rolling, awkward gait. "I need to thank you. Your help made it possible for us to put those men in jail."

They'd gone several paces and joined the main wave of people heading for the gate before he spoke again. "Is it true that Mr. John and Mr. Zachary are in jail?"

Understanding washed over Annie and she realized the dilemma Otis was having. He'd thought that he was doing some special work for the union boss. This was probably the only important thing he'd ever done. Their actions the night before would certainly spell the end of his 'special work' for the union. She leaned forward and spoke quietly.

"Yes, that's right. Both John and Zachary. They found some records showing they were sending dues money where they shouldn't have."

Lines appeared on his forehead. "Is it somethin' I did? Did I get them in trouble?"

"No. They got in trouble all by themselves. Don't worry, you didn't do anything wrong."

"Somebody tol' me they tried to hurt you."

Annie thought for a moment, trying to find the right words. "Well yes, they did try to hurt me but it's all right. Sparkle and Birdie were there and we managed to do a lot more damage to them than they did to us." Annie sighed. She was almost asleep on her feet. But the man had risked a great deal for her and she owed him.

"Otis, I can't thank you enough for your help. You did a brave thing and we all appreciate it. You don't have to worry, no one will know you got us the key. I'm not going to tell anyone." Annie stopped and a huge yawn caught her. "I'm sorry Otis, I guess I need some sleep. Give me a couple of days and we'll talk more, all right?"

The little wrinkle that had appeared on his forehead cleared and he seemed pleased. "That would be fine. You're my friend, Annie."

She walked away. He was indeed a friend.

She began the long walk to the front of the plant, her head now aching from the lack of sleep. She could almost feel the sheets against her skin when she stopped short. Cain had stepped in her path, his mouth set in a rigid line. The air left her lungs in a whoosh. She'd dreaded this meeting, had even gone out of her way not to have lunch in the usual place because she didn't want to talk with him yet. She knew he would be upset with her for not asking him to come along the night before. Now she realized he was more than upset.

"Hello Annie."

"Um . . . Cain"

He looked at her, eyes cool and jaw muscles working. When he didn't speak she swallowed hard and after a couple of false starts croaked out, "Well, how are you?" She could have kicked herself. What a dumb thing to say.

"I was fine until I heard about you three. How come I had to hear about it from somebody else?"

Annie scuffled her foot on the cement floor. No matter what she said, it wasn't going to sound good. "I'm sorry. I just didn't want any more people involved than already were. I didn't want to be responsible for people losing their jobs."

"How about next time you let me be the judge of that?" His words were slow and flat as if he were measuring them before delivery. "Annie, that's twice you didn't tell me when you were doing some pretty dangerous stuff. I thought we were friends. Hell, more than friends. Why don't you trust me?"

"Cain, it's not that. I do trust you. It's just that I can't stand anyone getting in trouble because of me. I feel responsible."

"You are not responsible for the world, girl. And you sure as heck are not responsible for me. You didn't seem to mind dragging Birdie and Sparkle into it."

She started to say that they were her friends but stopped. She could feel herself shrinking inside. When she looked up, he was staring at her, his face hard and uncompromising.

"I don't know what to say, Cain. I'm sorry, I guess."

The harsh lines around his mouth eased into sadness. "I don't know either, Annie."

With that he turned around and walked back into the plant. Annie watched him go.

As Sparkle rushed along the empty sidewalk, her foot slipped and she heard the snap of a heel. "Dammitall. Nothing's going right." Bending over, she yanked the shoe off her foot and examined the damage to the black pump. The thin heel was broken in half and there was no way of fixing it now. She laughed when she thought how the black lines she'd drawn up her legs would look without the shoes to conceal the fact that it wasn't silk stockings she was wearing. She could walk but not run. Two uneven steps later, she stopped and pulled the other shoe off, then hurried on bare feet toward the small drab building tucked between two warehouses in the quiet White Center area.

Cain's phone call had caught her off-guard. She had no idea why she was to meet him in this out-of-the-way area but he had said to hurry, that it was important. She hoped he appreciated the fact that it was hard to hurry with no shoes. He'd asked that Birdie come too but she was busy at the Blue House with dinner. Gloria was just home with the baby and everything was confused, Sparkle decided this was probably just more of the same.

Her musing brought her to the door of the weather-beaten building. A quick knock generated a movement inside, then the door opened and light from the doorway spilled out onto the damp earth and onto Sparkle, making her feel exposed. She paused when she entered to take note of the occupants of the small room. Annie had moved away from the door she'd just opened and rested against the side wall, her hands crossed in front like twin swords. When Sparkle looked at her questioningly, the tall woman gave the merest shake of her head.

Cain sat on a chair pulled away from the only table in the room, his shoulders hunched and head down between his hands. The taut stillness in the room made Sparkle think she had interrupted an argument. The third occupant was seated on another chair near the table and seemed to fill the corner with a solid presence similar to a quiet bear.

The stranger rose and she realized that he was not nearly as big as she'd first imagined, only two or three inches taller than she. His shoulders were enormous and forearms where his shirt was folded up revealed substantial muscles and a powerful chest. His thick neck led to a square, strong jawed face topped by sandy hair. Craggy brows hooded deep-set, black eyes.

Sparkle stopped in the middle of the room and looked around. No one spoke for several moments. She saw that the stranger was staring at her hands where the heels dangled from two fingers. She suddenly wished she were a bit more put together. There was a power to the man that made her want to be at her best.

"So what's so darn important that it couldn't wait until morning?" Her words seemed to question all three occupants of the room but her eyes were steady on the stranger.

Cain lifted his head from his hands and spoke quietly. " This is Joshua Reynolds, head of the IAM for the west coast. He's here to talk about our problem."

Reynolds looked down at a paper in his hands. "Henrietta Collins."

Sparkle felt her mouth contract into a grimace. "Sparkle, please."

Reynold's cleared his throat. "Annie asked me why Slattery had involved her in the first place. She told me that if he'd just told her that women couldn't run, you ladies would probably not have taken this any further."

Sparkle looked at him feeling startled, that question had never occurred to her. In fact, it seemed not much had made sense since Annie lost the election. "She's right. We would have just figured that was the way it was. Why did he?"

"I had the same question. The whole thing didn't make sense."

Joshua Reynolds stopped for a moment and put his hands, palm down on the table and Sparkle noticed that they were the hands of a workingman, hard and rough. She moved to the table and sat down, dropping the shoes to the floor with loud thud.

"John Slattery fancied himself a little bit better than the rest of us: tougher, smarter, quicker. I'll give him credit, he was pretty smart. It took a very clever arrangement to keep skimming off the money and not get caught. It's hard to tell but it looks like he'd been doing it for about the last six years, maybe longer. Apparently before the war he did the paperwork himself and stole better than double his salary each year. Not bad for an ex-mechanic.

"When the war started, he saw the opportunity to make more money. He brought in Anderson to do his paperwork and Waskom to handle any rough stuff. That way he thought he could blame them if any problems should arise. Waskom turned out to be more of a liability than he'd expected. He got tough with people for no reason other than he liked to."

Joshua stopped and looked at Sparkle. She felt her face flush. She was, for once in her life, unable to think of a thing to say. She'd never met anyone like this man.

"Apparently he had a run-in with some colored woman?"

Sparkle sank a bit in her chair, knowing exactly what he was referring to.

"You went after him with an open flame, didn't you?"

Sparkle nodded, wondering if he were considering firing her.

"You are a gutsy lady. I sure wouldn't want you mad at me."

She opened her mouth to say thank you but realized that wasn't right. She looked at Annie wondering what to say. Annie just shrugged. No help there.

She turned back to see Joshua smile, a tiny thing that just happened at the side of his mouth but Sparkle was shocked. Here she was, no makeup, broken shoes, nondescript skirt and blouse and the man was interested. And interested because of her actions, not just because of how she looked. She stifled an urge to run her fingers through her hair to straighten it out.

"Anyway, Slattery thought he could have it all. And one of the things he wanted was Annie."

"Annie? Our Annie?"

When he nodded, she turned back to face her friend. Annie's face was a caricature of a person in shock, mouth open, eyes wide, eyebrows elevated well above normal.

"Me?" The sound was a squeak.

"Yes, you. It seems that the more he was around you the better he liked you. He had some idea that if he got you involved, he could control you, maybe even make you a part of his group.

He wasn't happy with all the women working at the plant. He thought Annie was about the brightest and if he could get her on his side, he'd be set."

Annie's expression was still amazed. "Why in heaven's name would he think that? I never . . ."

"I know, it doesn't sound to me like he made a very good choice. You are intelligent and independent. When you ladies stole the tallies, he thought he had you right where he wanted you. That whole thing at the theatre was an elaborate set up. Slattery was going to act like some sort of magnanimous guy, saving Annie from being accused of wrong doing. Annie would be in debt to him. He thought she'd be grateful."

"That's crazy." This time Annie's voice was back to normal, even louder than usual.

"Well, he was a little crazy I guess. But look at what would have been the outcome if he'd succeeded. He'd know what was going on with both the brothers and the sisters. He thought he could do just about anything and get away with it. Some of the money he took was supposed to go for pensions and such. I don't know how we're going to put that right."

Sparkle shook her head. It was fantastic. The man must have been crazy to think he would ever get Annie to do something crooked. She was so honest it hurt.

"Well, that was his story. I'm inclined to believe it. He was really startled when Annie hung on to the paperwork and even fought to keep it. He underestimated you. All of you." This time both sides of his mouth turned up just a little. Sparkle wondered what it took to make him really smile.

"That was the easy part. This next part is what the three of us were talking about when Cain called you. I don't think there's much you can do. You see, although the charges against Slattery and Waskom look like they will stick, we still have a problem."

Sparkle decided what the man's voice sounded like was the slow rumbling of a distant train.

"Even though you women did expose the problem, you acted illegally by breaking into the office. We understand why you did what you did. But everyone knows now that you broke into the office. If we put Annie in as a shop steward, it will look like we're sanctioning that kind of behavior."

Sparkle wondered why Annie wasn't saying anything. "We didn't know who the heck to trust. Annie here trusted Slattery way too long."

Joshua cleared his throat and raised his head slightly. Sparkle noticed that his eyes weren't black but a very dark brown.

"It's more than that. Since this happened Cain and the rest of the stewards have been talking to the brothers and sisters. Everyone is up in arms about the whole thing. The brothers think we've gone too far and that letting women in is a huge mistake. The women think we aren't doing nearly enough. Both want something done now. We're talking about what can be done right away. This thing is getting out of hand. It looks bad to the rest of the members, probably like we can't control our managers."

Sparkle felt the chills replaced by prickling heat. "Well, it may look bad but that is exactly what it was." She glared at Annie only to find her staring at the floor.

Joshua broke her concentration. "There's a war on and we need to get back to work and get production up to where it has to be. Annie has volunteered to step out of the running, let the fellow who won the election stand as it was announced."

Sparkle jumped from the chair as if it had suddenly become hot. She turned to Annie. "You did what? You volunteered to step down? You should be pushing for them to put you in as steward."

For the first time Annie looked directly at Sparkle and for a moment the two women were alone in the small room. Sparkle swallowed hard when she recognized the stubborn look on her friend's face. Sparkle grabbed for the chair to steady herself.

"I think you should keep fighting Annie."

Annie's voice was low and flat. "No. This isn't a discussion, Sparkle. This is the way it's going to be. As far as I'm concerned, it's over."

Sparkle turned to Cain. "Can't you stop her? What kind of a friend are you, anyway?"

As she watched, Cain flinched and she could tell the question had hit home. She realized that she was taking out her anger on him and he didn't deserve it. He'd stood by them for the past year, even when that fool Annie kept insisting they were just friends. Right now he was looking at her tall friend with such sadness that Sparkle felt a part of it settle in her heart. If he had ever looked at her like that she would have followed him anywhere.

"I can't change her mind either."

"That's it then? You're giving up, just like that?"

Annie stepped forward and put her hand on Sparkle's shoulder. "They've agreed to drop all charges against everyone. Right now, that is the best outcome of this deal. We did break the law. There's no reason to argue. It's over."

Annie moved to the table, lifted the pen, signed on the bottom of page, and then handed it to Joshua. He seemed about to say something, then looked at the paper and folded it, making careful, slow creases in the document.

Annie walked to the door then turned to look at Cain. She lifted her hand slightly and Sparkle watched the pain on the man's face ease slightly only to be replaced by a shuttered, grim look as Annie shut the door quietly behind her. Sparkle knew her face probably mirrored the misery in Cain's.

Moments passed and no one spoke. Sparkle finally broke the silence with an explosive "Shit," then rushed to the door leaving the black shoes sitting beside the chair. Yanking the door open she searched the street for any sign of Annie only to find no movement marring the emptiness of the quiet lane.

CHAPTER SEVENTEEN

W arm June air slipped in through the front window of
the Blue House. Annie could hear crickets outside the
window and realized that summer was only a week away. She
eased back on the couch and smiled at Cain opposite her, his
long legs stretched out and stocking feet resting on the gray
ottoman. His eyes were half closed and she enjoyed this opportunity to just stare at him.

She thought back to the meeting with Joshua Reynolds and
shook her head. She was still trying to figure Slattery out. She
couldn't believe that he would think she would be part of his
scheme.

The only thing that might have been a clue was the fact that
whenever they were together, he seemed to be two people, one
watching and calculating and the other interested in her and
wanting to help. She remembered his eyes, kind one moment
and cold as ice the next. She wished she could read people better. This time it had almost killed her. The grandfather's clock
bonged twice and broke into her thoughts. She sat forward and
touched Cain's leg.

"I need to be going now. The meeting is in only half an hour.
Will you drive me?"

Cain cocked his head to one side. "I've told you before, you
ask a lot of a guy."

The easy, slow smile tugged at her heart. Sparkle and he had
been waiting for Annie after she'd walked home from the meeting with Reynolds the day before. By that time she had decided

that Cain wouldn't ever trust her again and she was feeling worse than when she'd heard about the election. When she'd seen his car in the drive, it was almost as if she'd been given a reprieve, another chance to make it right.

They'd talked for an hour. She'd found that he wasn't so much angry as he was disappointed. At the end, she'd promised to include him in any hare brained scheme she might come up with in the future. That seemed to satisfy him and she'd finally gone to bed, feeling better than she had in a week.

"How many women will be at the meeting?" He had taken his feet from the ottoman and was putting his shoes on.

"I suspect fifty or more. Sparkle told them it was a big surprise. It's just a shame it's not going to be the kind of surprise anyone enjoys that much."

"Have you decided what you are going to say?"

Annie hesitated. She'd started and stopped writing a couple of dozen times. Finally she'd thrown it all away. She would know when she stood up to speak. Nothing she'd put down was right and she didn't think it would help to worry about it any longer.

"No, but I guess I'll just tell them what I think. Let me them decide for themselves."

He stood and pulled his jacket on over his green plaid shirt. Annie thought that color made his eyes even a deeper blue than she remembered. He offered his arm. "Ready?"

Annie nodded and slipped her arm through his.

An hour later she looked out over the meeting room at the fifty or more women sitting and standing. The light breeze from the door touched her skin and she thought that it was almost too beautiful a day to have to do this. She finally took a deep breath and started.

"Thank you all for coming. I know it was short notice and I won't keep you long." She paused, thinking about the past six months and how much this group had taught her about people and how powerful they were working together. They had worked hard for a purpose and what she was about to tell them would end that. "Most of you have heard about the tally sheets and how they showed I won the election."

A couple of gasps from the audience indicated that not everyone had heard. "For those of you who didn't know, yes, we won. We put a woman shop steward in the union. And don't let anything I say now make you forget that. We can do anything if we try hard enough."

She saw Trudy sitting in the front row. Annie had spoken with her before the meeting, not wanting her to jump in and say exactly what she thought. This was hard enough without that. Now she saw that Trudy's lip was trembling. Annie looked away quickly, she wasn't sure she could make it through this without crying herself.

"Right now what we have is a problem. No one can concentrate on what's really important. Every minute we stop and talk about what the men are doing wrong, is one minute that we're not working on the planes. And every minute they stop and talk about how we're getting above ourselves is the same thing. We all have brothers or uncles or husbands fighting the war. And we all know women who are there with them."

She could see some people nodding, others shaking their heads. Some groups began to whisper, others voices could be heard up front. Finally, a woman at the back stood up.

"You know this is what they always say. It's never the right time. If we just wait a little longer. I don't think we should quit now. I think we should keep fighting. See what kind of product they can get out of here without us helping."

Annie could see that the group was torn. "Let me tell you what I see." She paused and the women settled back in their seats. They were listening to her again. "I see the war over. I see that we have homes and families and some of us have jobs. And I see that a few of us, and some of our daughters and more of their daughters will carry on with what we have started here. It won't end. But they'll do it when there isn't a war to win. They'll make our sacrifice mean something."

She took in a deep breath. Tears were very close. She swallowed and continued. "We can't be responsible for one man dying because we didn't get our jobs done. No slowdowns. No walkouts. I can't tell you how to think, I can only tell you how I see it. We are right, but the time is not right for this fight. I'm sorry I got this started." She took in shaky breath and stopped. She couldn't say any more.

Trudy stood in the front row and Annie winced. The woman cleared her throat, and then in the quietest tone Annie had ever heard her use, Trudy said. "I agree."

A low murmur filled the room. It was as if each person wanted to say something to the woman next to her. After five minutes, it was quiet again and a thin woman near the center of the room spoke.

"Thank you, Annie. We did the right thing to elect you to begin with. We think you're the right person for the job."

Annie stared at the women feeling proud to have been a part of their dream. She nodded, unable to speak. She was walking out of the room when she saw Birdie enter. With a wave of her hand, Birdie motioned for Annie to come outside. When they were outside, Birdie handed her a thin envelope. Annie turned it over and saw the Western Union insignia.

"Oh God, who?" Annie's hands shook as she tried to tear the envelope open. She felt Birdie's hand on her arm. When she finally got the paper out the words didn't make sense.

ANNIE STOP YOUR MOTHER PASSED AWAY LAST NIGHT STOP DOCTOR SAYS HEART ATTACK STOP WILL WRITE TONIGHT WITH DETAILS STOP IT WAS QUICK AND PAINLESS STOP I LOVE YOU STOP DAD

The words blurred as the tears she'd held back at the meeting slipped down her cheeks. She found she couldn't breath and pulled at the material of her jacket, trying to free herself of some obstinate pest. A noise like crashing water surrounded her.

Myrtle Tosh was not a woman who died. She was a woman of life who surrounded her family with bonds of love and hope so tightly that nothing could harm them. Her mother couldn't die, it was her father who had the bad heart. It was Annie who was in danger at the plant. And it was her brothers who were in danger overseas. She turned the page over and read her name and address, her eyes sliding across the words as if they were composed of poison. She saw wet drops land on the paper and made no effort to stop them.

She put her fingers on the typed words. And then she leaned against the building and tried to slow the spinning world.

Annie touched the honey-colored wood around the new kitchen window and ran her finger along the smooth surface. She wouldn't be around now to put the last finish on as she'd planned nor any of the other things they'd talked about. She'd risen before dawn, even before Birdie. Her plan had been to have everything packed and ready when Cain arrived to pick her up. But all she'd managed to do thus far was wander from room to room on the main floor of the boardinghouse. Each thing she'd touched and everything she'd seen reminded her of the year she'd been here.

There was the tiny B-17 she'd carved from the end of the two by four. It sat propped up on the cloudy glass that Birdie had saved from the sand pile they'd created building the new addition on the kitchen. A pile of Ben's little shirts rested on the red kitchen box. The lump in her throat seemed too large to swallow.

For the hundredth time she wondered if there wasn't another way. It had been four days since she'd received the telegram and she felt guilty she hadn't left yet, but tendering her resignation at the plant and clearing up loose ends had taken longer than she'd expected. She roamed back into the kitchen and sat on the hardback chair with the wobbly leg. She'd always meant to fix that. She leaned her elbows on the painted wood of the table and sighed. She had no idea leaving would be this hard. She rested her head in the soft pillow formed by her arms.

"What you doin' here, waiting for somebody else to start the coffee?"

Annie rubbed her eyes with the sleeve of her shirt then looked up. Birdie stood in the doorway, her paisley robe wrapped tight around and belted with a thick yellow cord. Her hair stood out in uneven rows of curls and fuzz. As she walked into the room, her slippers made shuffling sounds on the hardwood floor. When she got close enough to the table, she stopped.

Annie spoke before Birdie could say anything. "Yes, I'm waiting here for you to pour hot water over last night's grounds."

"Never." Pulling out another chair, Birdie eased down, her eyes never leaving Annie's face. "Yer down here trying to figure out how you're going to leave this place?"

Annie smiled weakly at her friend. "That's exactly what I'm doing. It's a lot harder than I thought it would be."

"A'hm afraid sometimes it seems like everything's jez harder than it should be."

Annie took a deep breath and began to speak when Gloria and Sparkle appeared at the kitchen door.

"My God, the sun isn't up and you two are out of bed. This must be a party." Birdie rose to start the water and the other two joined Annie at the table.

In deference to the boarders as well as the children, Sparkle had taken to wearing a red robe that wasn't sheer and was long enough to cover most of her. Or it would have if she'd remembered to pull it closed across the front. This morning the sides hung loose and revealed cleavage. Birdie stopped in her trip to the stove and pointed at the area of skin. Sparkle muttered something but pulled the material shut and tightened the belt. The familiar exchange without words further pierced Annie's already aching core. How could she leave these friends?

Birdie called to Gloria from the stove. "How long last night?"

The new mother's tone was proud. "From eleven to three. He's doing better all the time." No one had to ask what they were talking about. Little Ben was almost three weeks old and the length of each sleeping period was critical. Gloria put a hand over her mouth to conceal a yawn. As soon as that was over, she drew a band from her pocket and reaching up, pulled her hair back and secured it into a ponytail.

While the smell of coffee began to fill the room, Sparkle leaned back in her chair and stared at Annie. As she continued staring without saying a word, Annie felt like she was one big bruise, everything that happened hit her in the same place and hurt that much worse.

"So, you're going."

"Yes."

"I guess I understand. What did they say at the plant?"

Annie let out a snort, the first nearly funny thing that had happened in a week. "Well that's the easiest thing I ever did. I think they're glad I'm leaving."

Annie took the handkerchief from her pocket and blew her nose then stood up and stepped to the stove. She pulled four mugs from the cupboard and placed them gently on the counter she and Cain had made. Silence in the room was total save for the chirp of early morning birds outside. Taking a deep breath, she turned to face her friends.

"I have to get home to my dad. He's going to need me now."

Sparkle reached up and rubbed her head, causing tufts of hair to stick out. "I still think you should wait until he answers your letter."

Annie just sighed. "No matter what he says, this is something I have to do. He's going to be lost without my mother. I feel just awful that I couldn't get there in time for the funeral."

"When are you coming back?" Gloria's voice was quiet compared to others.

That was the one question she couldn't answer. "I don't know. I'm taking everything so if I don't come back, it won't be in your way."

"That's dumb. Of course you'll be coming back. Annie, this is your home now just as much as it is mine and Birdie's and Sparkle's." The new mother's voice broke at the end.

"That's enough Gloria. We don't want to make this harder than it has to be." Birdie frowned over her glasses, her eyebrows nearly coming together in the middle. "Annie's decided and that's enough for me. I'm not happy with her leavin' but it's her decision. We have to stand behind her." Birdie rose, took the pot off the stove, and poured the fragrant coffee into the mugs.

Sparkle ran a hand through her already wild hair. "What about Cain. What happens to him if you don't come back? That man has waited about as long as I think you can expect."

Annie felt a thud on the tender spot in her heart. "I know. That's something I'll have to figure out, I guess."

The room became quiet again and Annie and Birdie each picked up two cups and brought them to the table. The sound of a noisy robin came through the open window.

Annie stirred two sugars cubes into the hot liquid, then put her palms down flat on the table and looked directly at Sparkle. "I just don't know. And I'm going home today." Each time she said it, it became more real.

Sparkle's reached for the package of cigarettes in her pocket and pulled it out along with the matches. As she scratched a single stick against the rough surface, she started to speak, then stopped and lit the cigarette, inhaling deeply. After making two perfect smoke rings, she squinted her eyes and gazed at her friend through the cloud of white.

"I think you're giving up, just like you did with the union." She held up her hand when Birdie tried to interrupt. "But Birdie's right, I don't need to be making it harder on you. I won't say anything more. Just make sure that giving up doesn't become what you do about everything."

Annie gasped, feeling a stab of betrayal. She figured some people would feel that way but she hadn't realized it would be someone so close.

Annie and Cain loaded the trunk of the car with her things. As they pulled out of the driveway, she took one long look back then turned in her seat to face forward. The early morning sun had softened the blue paint peeling on the upper walls. She and Cain had thought they would paint the outside of the Blue House when they could get the material. At the time she'd groaned at the thought of the job, but now she yearned for summer evenings after work when they had planned to scrape the wood then apply the new blue color. She wondered if she would ever get numb to further stabs of hurt.

The first half of the car ride passed in silence. Finally, as they pulled on to West Spokane Street she had worked up the nerve to say something.

"I appreciate your doing this." She wanted to say more but felt herself pulling back, wanting to simply live through the next few minutes and get on the bus.

He didn't answer immediately, just stared at the light early morning traffic. "When I agreed to do this, I thought you'd planned on coming back. Sparkle tells me you are not sure. Why?"

Annie took in a deep breath. She wasn't sure she could answer why because she wasn't sure of the answer herself. She kept replaying Sparkle's remark about running away, then pushed it aside.

"I have to see how things look when I get home. You know my mom did a great deal around the house and even in the store. I just don't know how this will work now. Dad will need me."

"Annie, I need you. When are you going to live your life? You could have asked me to come with you but you didn't. I'm starting to feel that you will let everything in the world get in the way of our being together. I'm beginning to wonder if Howard was an excuse. Maybe you weren't all that interested even then." His voice was too calm. A thin wire of ice slid through her chest. This was what she'd most feared, that he would think all this confusion was because she didn't love him.

"I've always been interested. I can't imagine you could doubt that. My father needs me now. I don't know how long it will be." She realized she wasn't saying this right. In fact she wasn't sure she was doing anything correctly right now.

They'd stopped to wait for cars in front of them and Cain turned to her, his eyes sad. "Annie, I want you with me. I want to spend the rest of my life with you but I won't follow you and drag you back here, even though I think that's probably what it would take. And I'm not going to get some horrible disease or get hurt so badly you feel obligated to come back. You know where I am and you're going to have to make your own decision."

A horn sounded behind them. Cain put in the clutch and shifted to first gear. As they started forward Annie felt as if something were slipping away. Something important.

"I'll write you and let you know. I won't ask you to wait for me. I don't think I have the right." She waited for him to say that he would wait but the minutes stretched on and then they were at the bus station.

This appeared to be the most active place in Seattle this Sunday morning. People were laughing and jostling each other and running for buses. Small children screamed and ran around only to be caught by a parent and hustled off to a waiting area or a bus. Exhaust and dust settled around everything as the two of them pulled her cases from the back. A small boy raced by her and knocked over a suitcase. She bent over to pick it up and after she'd put it right, Cain stood only a few inches away, eyebrows drawn together and blue eyes looking down at her.

He pulled her close and kissed her, a kiss at once soft and yet demanding. When he stepped away, he murmured so low she almost didn't hear.

"Goodbye, Annie. I love you." With that he turned and got back in the car. The black coupe pulled easily out into traffic.

Annie held up a hand to wave but couldn't see if he'd looked in the mirror. As she watched him leave, she finally said what she should have said before. "I love you too, Cain."

CHAPTER EIGHTEEN

Birdie placed the pencil on the kitchen table and stretched her cramped hands. It was amazing to her that she could work all day at cooking or cleaning and not be tired or sore. But a half an hour of writing a letter and it felt like her hands were tied in knots. She caught a whiff of the sugar cookies in the oven and smiled. Rubbing her temples with her fingertips, she began to reread her words to Annie.

> *August 10, 1944*
> *We're sure happy that you are doing fine. We are fine too. Little Ben is growing like mad and pretty soon he'll be sleeping in that new crib Cain made. Lester came home a week ago and there's going to be a wedding.*

Birdie laughed when she read that part. It didn't even begin to tell of the excitement the night that the telegram had come. Gloria had first turned pale, then red then cried until they were worried that she would never stop. Two days later she was meeting the 11:10 train from Chicago. There had been great discussion about whether she should have told him about Ben before he got here. Gloria was worried what he would think of her. And that sure made Birdie laugh. Imagine thinking less of a woman because she bore your own child.

Gloria had decided that she would pick him up at the station and bring him home. Somewhere on the way she would tell him he was a father. She said that if he didn't want to come in and see Ben, than she would drive him right back to the station. Birdie and Sparkle had thought she was crazy but agreed since it was really her decision to make. Birdie didn't think she'd ever forget the look on Lester's face when he'd walked in the door and seen his son. He'd looked so proud and happy that he'd made them all cry. She picked up the letter again and continued to read.

> *Lester was hurt in Italy and is just now making it back. It doesn't look like he'll be going back in as his arm is pretty stiff. All I can say is thank God it's his shooting arm.*
>
> *You know, course, that Sparkle just got excited as the dickens about the wedding and is whipping up a dress for Gloria and one for me and one for herself. We all told her we didn't need anything like a big wedding but you know her. She got the minister from down the street and he's going to be here to do the marrying on August 25th. We sure wish you could make it but I know it's a long way to go just for a wedding. Maybe you could come back permanent like? Cain is hammering away at some sort of archway thing that they're supposed to stand under when they say 'I do'.*

She put the paper down and took a swallow of her chicory coffee, grimacing when she found it cold. She'd mentioned Cain on purpose. That boy was like a lost dog, hanging around the Blue House most of the time when he wasn't working at the plant. He seemed to like being around the children the most. As if that was one of the few things that still made him happy. But she knew she'd better not say that to Annie.

> *The Blue House is full most nights for dinner. I been serving really big Friday and Saturday night suppers for everybody and it was just like you said. I had to get the two Lowell sisters to help me along with*

Gloria and Letty. Seems like the more food I make, the more folks show up to eat it.

A high-pitched screech from outside brought her to her feet and looking out the kitchen window. William was pulling a wagon and his sister was trying to get in. He was threatening to hit her with a bent piece of wood but she could tell by the smile on little Hepsah's face that she was sure he wouldn't do anything but yell. That boy was so like his father, kind and gentle, that sometimes it made her cry.

William finally stopped, picked up his sister, placed her in the battered old red wagon, and tucked in the soft blanket he used to wrap up his pretty rocks.

Birdie sighed and sat carefully back on the wooden chair, hitching it forward to minimize the wobble. She looked at the clock on the wall and thought that she could sit another ten minutes or so before she started the potatoes for dinner. Picking up the letter one last time, she read the ending.

Tell your papa hello from all of us. It sounds like he's going to be all right. Think about coming to the wedding. We'd love to see you.
Love,
Birdie

There was nothing more she would write about that. She knew from what Annie didn't say in her letters that she was doing the same thing she'd always done, carrying through with what she thought was right. And it made Birdie want to hit her, even from this distance. She put the paper on the table and ran her fingers lightly over the penciled words, thinking about the redhead as she did. It seemed strange to her that of the four of them, Annie was the only one who had returned home.

Two months after she'd left Seattle, Annie felt as though she'd never left home. She helped her father with the store, rolled bandages with the women's auxiliary, helped in the food kitchen at the church for the needy and was thinking about joining the volunteer fire department. It was as if her life had come full circle. She'd stop and think sometimes about Seattle and her friends, particularly Cain, but shoved those thoughts away.

She stood at the window of her bedroom and caught the scent of roses, a fragrance that would always remind her of her mother. She was able, just in the last weeks, to think of her mother without the awful wrenching pain that nearly doubled her over. She could almost get through an hour or two now without thinking about the way Myrtle Tosh's face had shone when one of her children had done something especially well or the way her mouth tightened when she thought they weren't doing something right.

She wrapped her robe more tightly to ward off the early morning chill and walked to the kitchen, her robe making swishing sounds as she moved. The feel of the old house had changed, it seemed heavier, more ponderous since her mother was gone. She didn't know what she could do to change that.

When she got to the kitchen, she was surprised her father had already started the coffee and was cutting bread for toast. Crumbs were scattered around the cutting board and she saw that his hands trembled when he sliced through the loaf.

"You're up early, Dad. Couldn't you sleep?" The lines in his face were deeper and he appeared to have shrunk since her mother's death. It made her ache to watch him, each shake and misstep was another reminder that this once strong man would some day leave her too. She wanted to hug him tightly and infuse some of the strength of her own body into his failing one.

After he finished spreading jam on the bread he filled a cup for himself and one for Annie then eased himself into the worn seat of the painted chair.

"I've decided that sleep is overrated. I've managed to read my way through half the library in the last month. I've stacked all the newspapers and read them again in order. I still can't believe that Montgomery took off like a rocket from Lorraine to Brussels, then Antwerp. I lost that bet with Gladys. I always thought he was slow. And now that Ike has taken over control of the campaign in France, you can bet those Jerries are on the run. Since he took over the command of the European invasion forces, nobody has been able to stop us. He's about the best general this country has ever seen." His slapped his fist into his open palm. The slap was a weak thing, but at least he was pulling out the black pins and putting in the white ones as he'd done since the start of the war. For the first month, Annie didn't think she'd ever see that again.

"I see. Do you want some breakfast? I can whip up some eggs for you if you're hungry."

He looked at her over the top of his glasses and frowned. "How about we just have some oatmeal?"

Annie felt the sting of inadequacy. Since she'd been home her cooking skills had not improved. "You're just scared. I didn't burn them the last few times."

"True, but Annie I don't think you have the right kind of mind for it. I'd prefer that you fix the window in the pantry and I'll cook if it's all right with you."

She let out a breath, then settled back in the chair and nodded her head in agreement. "Okay, if you insist."

"I'm pretty sure I insist. And by the way, didn't you get a letter from your friends yesterday? What did they have to say?"

Warmth slipped through her and she grinned at her father. "They are fine. In fact, you remember Gloria, the girl from Portland who had little Ben?"

"Sure, you told me how that little tyke was nearly born in a closet."

Annie laughed. "That's right. Anyway, his daddy is home and he and Gloria are getting married. It's more than I could have hoped for. What a grand ending."

They sat in companionable silence for a few moments. Her father looked at her occasionally and then looked away.

"How is your ending going to come out, girl?"

Annie looked at him, her head cocked to one side. "What do you mean, my ending?"

"I mean how long are you going to be living in this house, cluttering up the place?"

Annie felt as if she'd been kicked. She half rose from the chair. "What do you mean, cluttering up the place? I'm here to help you. I'll stay as long as I need to."

"And how long is that going to be? You know that could be until they plant me too. What about getting on with your own life?"

She blinked and sat back in the chair. She wondered if he were saying this out of grief. She tried to keep her voice calm, reasonable like his. "What are you talking about? Who would help in the store? Who would help here?"

"That little Coolidge girl will be glad to come and give me a hand at work. She's a little crackerjack when it comes to getting things done. And if I need anything around here, all I have to do is snap my fingers and Gladys and her band of chattering women would be here in a second. Annie, I'm old and tired and mortally sad that your mother's dead. But she and I agreed before she died that you'd made a great decision when you went north. You started your own life and it was the best thing that ever happened to you.

"Now I appreciate you coming here and helping me through the worst of it but your heart isn't here anymore. Every time you talk about that man, Cain, I can see that you curl up from loneliness yourself. What if he doesn't wait forever for you?"

Annie looked at him, her mouth held tightly shut. "What about you?" Her voice wavered.

Her father reached over and put his hand on hers. "What about me? I've lived here all my life. My town and my neighbors are good people. God willing, your brothers will be home soon. I won't die because you're not here. Annie, I've told you about when your mother and I got married. She was sixteen and I was eighteen. She sneaked out of the house and met me beside the river. We took off in that old buggy of my dad's and never looked back. Tied that knot quick as we could so nobody from either side could split us up. Your grandparents on both sides just about had apoplexy."

"But what does that have to do with me?"

"You've got to stop worrying about everybody else and get going yourself. It's time, daughter. Lordy, it's past time. I don't know where you got the idea that you weren't doing it right if you weren't doing something for somebody else. I can't be there all the time giving you a kick to set you moving girl. You've got to go on your own. But do promise me one thing."

A breeze fluttered the curtains and seemed to linger around her. She took a deep breath of the clean, summer air and stared at her father and at his hand on hers. She wondered if he were telling the truth or only saying this to make her feel better. She finally took her hand from under his and went to look out the window. The wisteria vine covered most of the view with its twisting branches and leaves but if she stood just right, she could see the pine trees and overturned dingy at the corner of the yard. For a few moments she wondered at her own inability to see her life clearly.

"Dad, I . . .." She stopped then looked at him. He was sitting at the table, his coffee mug and uneaten toast still waiting for him. He appeared so frail but something in his eyes told her that the strong, young man of eighteen was still inside. And something in his words had begun to make sense. Anyway, it made sense to her now.

"Do promise me one thing, child."

"Anything, you know that, Dad."

"Promise me that if you can, you'll be married here at home. For your mother. She always wanted to have you married in the backyard. When your brothers are home and all the rest of the family can be here."

Her answer came out clear and strong. "I promise."

Cain pounded on the stake with a sledgehammer, careful not to break it as he drove it home. He certainly didn't want this archway falling on the happy couple just about the time the preacher said, "You may kiss the bride." He stepped back and looked at the structure and decided that it would certainly do. The neighbors had brought over some flowers to hang on it and it looked like a picture Sparkle had shown him from a magazine about weddings. After the ceremony, he thought he would move it back to the rear of the yard and maybe have someone plant a climbing rose near it.

He put the hammer down and stretched his arms, thinking that he had to get in the house and get his clothes changed pretty soon. Sparkle had talked him into wearing a borrowed jacket that was a little short in the arms but she said it made him look dressed up.

He wished Annie were here to stand back and take a look at the pretty thing with him. He shook his head. Wishing didn't make things happen. He sometimes thought he was going to be all right. Then, for no reason, the longing for her would sneak up and grab him. He started to pick his way through the chairs that had been set up around the archway and noticed a taxi parked in the drive. Squinting at the two people standing at the rear of the car, he wondered if this might be Gloria's mother and father. She had said she'd invited them and now couldn't decide if she wanted them to come or not.

As the lid of the trunk was slammed shut, Cain sucked in a huge breath. He'd know that red head anywhere. He'd certainly seen it in enough dreams since she'd been gone. She handed the one-armed driver some cash and the man got back into the cab.

By the time he had driven away, Cain was beside her, his heart slamming so hard in his chest he thought it might jump right out.

"You're here." He touched her shoulder. She turned to him and gave him a huge hug. After a moment she pushed him back and he fought the same devastated feeling he'd had in the woods that night.

"Yes, I'm here. And I'm going to stay here. And I love you. I'm sorry I was an idiot. And if you will still have me, I promise to quit being an idiot. Anyway, I think I will."

Her words made everything all right. He just looked at her and repeated, "I can't believe you're here."

She took one finger and poked him in the shoulder then smiled so wide it lit up her whole face. "See, I'm here. And you're here. Are we having a wedding today or not?"

She started to bend over and pick up a case but he stopped her and wrapped his arms around her and kissed her hard and long and deep because that was the only thing that seemed right.

Goodfellow Press Catalogue of Titles

The Quest by Pam Binder. Time cannot destroy the tapestry of a life woven with love and magic.
 ISBN 1-891761-10-2 $19.99/$23.99 Canada

The Dalari Accord by Matthew Lieber Buchman. Memory is the alien within.
ISBN 1-891761-04-8 $19.99/$23.99 Canada

A Slight Change of Plans by John Zobel. Sometimes the answer is right in front of you.
ISBN 1-891761-01-3 $12.99/$13.99 Canada

Matutu by Sally Ash. To find healing and love, an English violinist and an American writer must explore a Maori legend.
ISBN 0-9639882-9-8 $12.00/12.99 Canada

The Inscription by Pam Binder. An immortal warrior has conquered death. Now he must conquer living.
ISBN 0-9639882-7-1 $12.99/$13.99 Canada.

Cookbook from Hell by Matthew Lieber Buchman. One part creation. Two parts software. Season lightly with a pair of love stories and roast until done.
 ISBN 0-9639882-8-X $12.99/$13.99 Canada

Ivory Tower by May Taylor. Does the scent of lilacs herald a soft haunting?
ISBN 0-9639882-3-9 $12.99/$13.99 Canada

White Powder by Mary Sharon Plowman. It's hard to fall in love when bullets are flying.
ISBN 0-9639882-6-3 $9.99/$10.99 Canada

Bear Dance by Kay Zimmer. A man betrayed and a woman escaping painful memories struggle to overcome the barriers keeping them apart.
ISBN 0-9639882-4-7 $9.99/$10.99 Canada

Glass Ceiling by CJ Wyckoff. Facing career and emotional upheaval, Jane Walker makes a bold choice to explore east Africa with an unorthodox man.
ISBN 0-9639882-2-0 $9.99/$10.99 Canada

This Time by Mary Sharon Plowman. A man and a woman with differing expectations and lifestyles take a chance on love.
ISBN 0-9639882-1-2 $7.99/$8.99 Canada

Hedge of Thorns by Sally Ash. A gentle story unfolding like a modern fairy tale, of painful yesterdays and trust reborn.
ISBN 0-9639882-0-4 $7.99/$8.99 Canada.

AsYouLikeIt - A Goodfellow Imprint

Rozner's Constant by Jeffrey L. Waters. Now that you have inherited the secret of the universe, how do you stay alive?
ISBN 1-891761-11-0 $19.99/23.99 Canada

An Unobstructed View by Jenness Clark. Life's unobstructed views, while desirable, depend on where one is standing.
ISBN 1-891761-02-1 $12.99/$13.99 Canada

2001 RELEASES

Howl at the Moon by Polly Blankenship. A woman brings her son to the Texas home town she once abandoned to sample the vanishing joys of ranch life.
ISBN 1-891761-07-2 $22.00/$25.00 Canada

Diamond Lies by Johann Sorenson. Once you have found your true love, what do you do when the past shows up?
ISBN 1-891761-09-9 $22.00/$25.00 Canada

Altar Stone by Robert Hackman. Ancient spirits stalk the unsuspecting to live again in human form.
ISBN: 1-891761-14-5 $22.00/$25.00 Canada

Between Two Worlds by Suzi Prodan. As the new nation of Yugoslavia rises from the ashes of WWII, rebels learn the price of freedom.
ISBN 1-891761-12-9   Coming soon

2001 AsYouLikeIt RELEASES

Midnight Choir by Richard Clement. In 1907, a Seattle nurse witnesses a murder and becomes entangled with the detective she fears may be the killer.
ISBN: 1-891761-16-1   Coming soon

The Day the Music Died by Florine Gingerich. With the help of an unlikely ally, a young gypsy woman faces the horror of Nazi aggression.
ISBN: 1-891761-17-X   Coming soon

Yellow Finch by Ed Ratcliffe. Two sisters in Peru, struggle to keep loved ones together when their family is fragmented by a terrorist connection.
ISBN: 1-891761-19-6   Coming soon

Point of Departure by Doni Pahlow. Surprised by her ability to embrace change, a successful 42-year-old woman rediscovers Paris, and explores the secrets of her heart and soul.
ISBN: 1-891761-18-8   Coming soon

GOODFELLOW PRESS

Goodfellow Professional Services

206-782-2799
Fax 206-706-6352
info@goodfellowpress.com

Goodfellow Professional Services is dedicated to the education of writers and the promotion of the written word, not only as a vehicle for pleasure, but as a work of art. To this end the following services are available.

Editing Services

>Editing is done by Pamela Goodfellow, Editor-in-Chief of GP, or by an Associate Editor. All editing is done with two goals: supporting authors to reach their highest potential and aiding them in creating a work of fiction viable in the commercial market.

Weekend Workshops

>These two to five day workshops offer students complete immersion in the writing process. Sessions are led by Pamela Goodfellow, GP authors, and a variety of guest speakers. This forum provides both new and experienced authors with a motivational boost.

Ongoing and Private Classes

>Educational opportunities are available in several formats including: evening classes for groups of six or more, ongoing weekly critique sessions monitored by a GP author or editor, and weekend seminars by request for groups of twelve or more.

Speakers Bureau
> Authors, designers, and editors are available as speakers for classes, seminars, luncheons, and professional societies and conferences. Topics include all aspects of book creation, from writing to publishing.

For more information see our website at:

www.goodfellowpress.com

Goodfellow Press

8522 10th Ave NW
Seattle, Washington 98117
206-782-2799
206-706-6352 fax

GOODFELLOW PRESS 2001
EDITORIAL SERVICES RATE SHEET

<u>Editorial Services Rate</u>

1. Four-sentence exercise. $ 25.00
    This is great for pinpointing a problem area and
    working through it. Make up your own or we can
    assign one specifically for you.

2. One-page stand-alone scene (based on 300 words per
    page in 12 pt. type with 1" margins, double spaced).
    $ 50.00 (Each additional page is $ 25.)

3. One 5-page scene (1500 words) $ 125.00
    (Each additional page is $ 20.)

4. A short story of 10-13 pages (3000 - 4000 words)
    $ 300.00 (Each additional page after 13 is $ 35.)

5. A series of five 5-page scenes (each scene 1500
    words, total 7500).
    $ 500.00 (Each additional page is $20.)

6. Editorial Consultation (1-hr minimum):
    with an Associate Editor (face-to-face) $ 65.00
    with Pamela R. Goodfellow (face-to-face) $ 175.00

7. Editing of full manuscripts is done on a limited basis by individual review.
    Costs vary according to condition of manuscript.

Please specify what you want done and what you expect from us and send to:

For more information see our website at:

www.goodfellowpress.com

Goodfellow Press

8522 10th Ave NW
Seattle, Washington 98117
206-782-2799
206-706-2367 fax